PRAISE FOR *TERM LIMITS*

THE BLOCKBUSTER THRILLER THAT HAILED THE ARRIVAL OF A "MASTER STORYTELLER" (*BOOK REPORTER*)

"A page-turning read."

—Larry King, *USA Today*

"Ingenious. . . . . Outpaces anything recently published, including Baldacci and Clancy."

—*Florida Times-Union*

"A roller-coaster, edge-of-your-seat thriller with loads of insiders' low-down on D.C. politics."

—*Minneapolis Star-Tribune*

"A four-star, in-your-face, butt-kicking, bull's-eye of a political thriller, unlike anything I've ever read! Fast-paced and unforgettable."

—Richard Marcinko, *New York Times* bestselling author

"Nonstop excitement. Fans of political thrillers like those of Tom Clancy will love *Term Limits*. . . . The fast-paced story line is crisp and interesting."

—*Midwest Book Review*

"Adrenaline-charged . . . will keep you on the edge of your seat."

—*Newport News Press*

Novels by Vince Flynn

The Last Man
Kill Shot
American Assassin
Pursuit of Honor
Extreme Measures
Protect and Defend
Act of Treason
Consent to Kill
Memorial Day
Executive Power
Separation of Power
The Third Option
Transfer of Power
Term Limits

And by Kyle Mills

Enemy at the Gates
Total Power
Lethal Agent
Red War
Enemy of the State
Order to Kill
The Survivor

VINCE FLYNN

TERM LIMITS

EMILY BESTLER BOOKS
—
ATRIA

New York   London   Toronto   Sydney   New Delhi

EMILY
BESTLER
BOOKS

ATRIA

An Imprint of Simon & Schuster, Inc.
1230 Avenue of the Americas
New York, NY 10020

This Emily Bestler Books/Atria Paperback edition February 2022

EMILY BESTLER BOOKS / ATRIA PAPERBACKS and colophon are trademarks of Simon & Schuster, Inc.

For information about special discounts for bulk purchases, please contact Simon & Schuster Special Sales at 1-866-506-1949 or business@simonandschuster.com.

The Simon & Schuster Speakers Bureau can bring authors to your live event. For more information, or to book an event, contact the Simon & Schuster Speakers Bureau at 1-866-248-3049 or visit our website at www.simonspeakers.com.

Manufactured in the United States of America

5   7   9   10   8   6   4

ISBN 978-1-9821-8869-6
ISBN 978-0-7434-4923-6 (ebook)

To Tom Clancy, Robert Ludlum, Leon Uris,
J.R.R. Tolkien, and Ernest Hemingway,
for inspiring me to live my dreams

ACKNOWLEDGMENTS

WHEN I undertook the task of writing *Term Limits,* I had no idea how many people would eventually contribute their time and talents. I am grateful to all of you, but I am especially grateful to those who went that extra step in offering their skill, expertise, and friendship.

To Dan McQuillan, Paul Lukas, Liz Tracy, Mike McFadden, Kristin O'Gara, Judy O'Donnell, Matthew O'Toole, and Tom and Valerie Tracy, thank you for keeping me pointed in the right direction.

To Susie Moncur, for your advice and superb editorial skills. To Jeanne Neidenbach and my brother Kevin for keeping me supplied with fresh manuscripts. To my good friend Dave Warch for his humor and photographic talents. To Mike Andrews, Mike Dickson, Matt Michalski, and Dave, Don, and Mary at Stanton for all your enthusiasm and help. To Teresa McFarland and Maureen Cahill, you truly made the difference.

I also owe a great deal to all of the bookstores, media outlets, and readers in Minnesota who have supported me. Your positive comments have inspired me to raise the bar another notch for all of the books to come.

To the Secret Service agents, FBI special agents, and former Special Forces personnel who took the time to offer me insight into their dedicated lives—I couldn't have done it without you. A special thanks to Dick Marcinko, the former Navy SEAL and legend, for taking the time to give me a few pointers.

It is next to impossible for a writer to succeed in the highly competitive world of New York publishing without a top-notch agent and a great editor. I have been blessed with both. To my agent, Sloan Harris, and Nasoan Sheftel-Gomes from International Creative Management, you are the best. To Emily Bestler and everyone else at Pocket Books, you have made my dreams come true.

Last but not least, I would like to thank my mother and father. Your support, love, and encouragement have meant the world to me.

. . . Governments are instituted among Men, deriving their just Powers from the Consent of the Governed, that whenever any Form of Government becomes destructive of these Ends, it is the Right of the People to alter or to abolish it, and to institute new Government . . . it is their Right, it is their Duty, to throw off such Government, and to provide new Guards for their future Security.

—Thomas Jefferson,
The Declaration of Independence

CHAPTER 1

THE old wood cabin sat alone, surrounded by trees and darkness. The shades were drawn, and a dog lay motionless on the front porch. A thin stream of smoke flowed out of the chimney and headed west, across the rural Maryland countryside toward Washington, D.C. Inside, a man sat silently in front of the fireplace, shoving stacks of paper into the hot flames.

The papers were the product of months of tedious and meticulous work. Each sheet represented hour upon hour of surveillance notes, in-depth subject profiles, and maps of neighborhoods throughout the D.C. metropolitan area. He knew when the police patrolled, when the newspapers were delivered, who jogged and at what time, and most importantly, where his targets slept and what time they awoke.

He and his men had stalked them for months, watching and waiting, patiently discerning which part of their daily routine could be exploited—and when they would be most vulnerable. His strong hands reached for the fire and stopped short. Letting them hang near the flames, he flexed them straight, then pulled them into tight fists. The men he had been stalking had sent him to some of the most obscure places on the face of the planet to kill people who were deemed a threat to the national security of the United States of America.

He had lost track of the number of people he had killed in the service of his country. He had not intentionally blocked the tally from his mind, it was just something he had never bothered to calculate. Whatever the number was, he held no regrets for the men he had killed. They were honorless, evil psychopaths—killers of innocent civilians.

The solitary figure sitting in front of the fire was an assassin of assassins, an exporter of death, trained and funded by the United States government. His short blond hair glowed as he stared deeper and deeper into the flames, the crisp fire eventually turning into a hypnotic blur. Tomorrow he would kill for the first time on American soil. The times, places, and targets had all been chosen. In less than twenty-four hours the course of American politics would be changed forever.

The sun rose over Washington, D.C., marking the start of what would be a long and busy day. With the president's annual budget twenty-four hours away from a full House vote, the town was in a frenzy. Congressmen, senators, bureaucrats, and lobbyists were making a last-minute push to amend or strike certain elements of the budget. The count was too close to call, and the leaders of both parties were exerting great pressure on their members to vote along partisan lines.

No one was exerting more pressure than Stu Garret, the president's chief of staff. It was nearing 9 A.M., and Garret was ready to explode. He was standing in the Blue Room of the White House watching the president read "Humpty-Dumpty" to a group of kindergartners, and his anger was increasing by the second. Garret had told the president that the photo op with the kids was out of the question, but the White House press secretary, Ann Moncur, had convinced the president otherwise. It was rare for Garret to lose to anyone; even on the smallest point. But Moncur had sold the president on the idea that, in the throes of a cutthroat budget battle, it would be good PR for him to look as if he were above the dirty political horse-trading of Washington.

Garret had been working around the clock for the last month trying to get the votes needed to pass the budget. If the budget was defeated, their chances for reelection would be severely hampered. The count would be close, but there was a plan to make a last-minute charge. The only problem was that Garret needed the president back in his office making phone calls, not sitting in the Blue Room reading nursery rhymes.

As was typical of everything at the White House, the event had started late and was now running over its original half-hour slot. Garret looked down at his watch for the tenth time in the last five minutes and decided enough was enough. Looking to his left, he glared at Ann Moncur, who was standing several feet away. Garret slid between the wall and several other White House staffers and worked his way toward Moncur. When he reached her, he pulled her back and cupped his hand over her ear. "This is the dumbest stunt you've ever pulled. If the budget gets torpedoed tomorrow, you're history. This circus has gone fifteen minutes over schedule. I'm going to the Oval Office, and if he isn't there in five minutes, I'm going to come back in here and personally throw your ass out on the street."

Moncur strained to smile and look relaxed. She glanced around the room and noticed that some of the other staffers and several members of the press were watching. She nodded her head several times and was relieved when Garret stepped away and headed for the door. For obvious reasons, Moncur didn't care for the older, crass chief of staff. Simply put, he was a pain in the ass to work for.

Michael O'Rourke walked purposefully down the hallway of the Cannon House Office Building. It was just after 9 A.M., and the building was crowded with people. O'Rourke avoided making eye contact with anyone for fear of being stopped. He was not in a good mood. O'Rourke didn't like Washington; in fact, it was safe to say he hated Washington. Midway down the hall, he turned into an office and closed the door behind him.

Inside were five men wearing dark suits and drinking coffee. O'Rourke shot his secretary a quick glance, but before she could respond, all five men closed in on him.

"Congressman O'Rourke, could I please have a moment of your time? I just need five minutes," pleaded the man closest to the door.

A short, pudgy man pushed his way to the front. "Congressman, I would like to speak to you about how the farmers in your district will be affected if you don't vote for the president's budget."

The thirty-two-year-old freshman congressman held up his hands. "Gentlemen, you're wasting your time. I've already made up my mind, and I will not be voting for the president's budget. Now if you will kindly vacate my office, I have work to do." The group started to protest, but O'Rourke opened the door and waved them into the hallway. All five men stumbled to grab their briefcases and then headed off dejectedly, in search of another congressman to cajole.

The portly lobbyist hung back and tried to give it another shot. "Congressman, I've talked to my people in your district, and they've told me you have a lot of farmers waiting for the crop-failure money the president has in his budget." The lobbyist waited for a reaction from O'Rourke but got none. "If this budget doesn't pass, I wouldn't want to be in your shoes come next election."

O'Rourke looked at the man and pointed toward the door with his thumb. "I have work to do."

With the vote so close the lobbyist was not willing to give up easily. "Mr. O'Rourke, if you vote no on the president's budget, the American Farmers Association will be left with no other choice than to support your opponent next year."

O'Rourke shook his head and said, "Nice try, but I'm not running for a second term." Waving good-bye, the young congressman grabbed the door and closed it in the lobbyist's face. O'Rourke turned to face his secretary, Susan Chambers.

Susan smiled and said, "I'm sorry, Michael. I told them you had a full calendar, but they insisted on waiting around to see if you would fit them in."

"No apologies needed, Susan." Michael left the main reception area and walked into his office. He set his briefcase on the chair beside his desk and picked up a stack of pink messages. Yelling toward the door, he asked, "Has Tim come in yet?"

"No."

"Has he called?"

"Yes. He said that since there isn't a snowball's chance in hell of the president taking the funding for the Rural Electrification Administration out of the budget, he's going to get some errands done and be in around one." Tim O'Rourke was Michael's younger brother by two years and his chief of staff.

"I'm glad everyone is so positive around here."

Susan stood up from behind her desk and walked to the doorway of O'Rourke's office. "Michael, we're only being realists. I admire that you're trying to do what's right, but the problem is, guys like you don't win in Washington."

"Well, thank you for your vote of confidence, Susan."

Susan looked up into O'Rourke's bloodshot eyes. "Michael, were you out again last night?" O'Rourke nodded his head yes. "This bachelor life is going to kill you. Why don't you make an honest woman out of that adorable girlfriend of yours?"

O'Rourke had been hearing it from everyone lately, but he was in no position to get married. Maybe in another year . . . after he got out of Washington. He looked down and sighed, "Susan, I'm Irish, we tend to get married late in life. Besides, I'm not so sure she'll have me."

"That's a lie and you know it. She adores you. Take it from a woman: I've seen the way she looks at you with those big brown eyes. You're the one, so don't screw it up. There aren't too many like her out there." Chambers slapped him in the stomach. "I hope being crowned the most eligible bachelor in Washington hasn't gone to your head!"

O'Rourke frowned and shook his head. "Very funny, Susan."

Chambers turned and walked away, laughing.

"I'm glad you're getting such a kick out of this, Susan. Hold all of my calls. I have an appointment at noon, and until then I don't want to be disturbed."

"What if your grandfather or Liz calls?"

"No one, I don't want to be disturbed." O'Rourke shut the door and sat down behind his desk.

CHAPTER 2

WHEN the president entered his office, he found Garret and his budget director, Mark Dickson, sitting on a couch by the fireplace, poring over the prospective vote count, trying to figure out whom they could sway to their side. Stevens knew his chief of staff was in a bad mood, and he did not have the energy for an argument. So he decided to defuse the situation and take orders. As he walked over to them, he took off his jacket, threw it on the other couch, and clapped his hands together. "All right, Stu, I'm all yours for the rest of the day. Just tell me what you want me to do."

Garret looked up and motioned for his boss to take a seat. Garret and Dickson had been in the office since 6 A.M., putting together a final list of possible holdouts. With one day to go, they had secured 209 votes. The opposition had 216 votes, and ten congressmen were still undecided. Garret had a piece of paper in front of him with two headings: UNDECIDED and POSSIBLE DEFECTORS. Ten names were under the undecided heading, and six under the possible-defectors heading. Both columns had shrunk considerably in the past week as the vote approached.

"All right, here's the current situation, Jim." No one but Stu Garret ever called the president by his first name. "We need to put this thing to bed today. Basset and Koslowski are up on the Hill playing good cop–bad cop with the fence-sitters. We're going to try and start a stampede by noon." Tom Basset was the Speaker of the House, and Jack Koslowski was the chairman of the House Appropriations Committee.

"Are we in a position to do that?" the president asked.

Garret leaned back in his chair, placed his hands behind his neck, and smiled. "Tom Basset has a meeting with Congressman Moore at eleven, and when that meeting is over, Frank Moore is going to make an announcement that he's backing the budget."

"How much is it going to cost us?" asked Dickson.

"Only about ten million."

"You guys are going to bag Frank Moore for ten million? That's nothing more than pocket change to Frank." The president shook his head. "How are you going to get him to settle for so little?"

Garret's smile emanated confidence. "We recruited some outside help to get him to see things our way."

"What kind of help?"

Garret paused for a long moment and replied flatly, "Arthur Higgins arranged to have some photos taken of the congressman and a certain young woman."

Arthur Higgins. There was no more mysterious name in all of Washington. Stevens seriously wondered whether it was in his best interest to know any details. Arthur Higgins was an ominous and legendary figure in the power circles of Washington and many of the world's other capitals. For forty years Higgins had run the most secretive branch of the CIA. Officially he never existed nor did his department. Higgins had been the author and controller of the Agency's most delicate and dangerous covert operations since the height of the cold war. Several years earlier he had been forced out of the CIA in a heated power struggle. What he had been doing with his time and talents since was something that was whispered about behind closed doors.

Stevens looked up from the paper and said, "You're going to blackmail Frank Moore?"

Garret smiled and said, "Essentially."

"I don't want to know the details, do I?"

"No." Garret shook his head. "Just trust me when I say Moore will see no other choice than to vote our way."

Stevens nodded solemnly and replied, "Next time, I would prefer it if you would let me know about these things before they're set in motion."

"Understood." After a brief silence Garret turned their attention back to the task at hand. "Jim, I need to get you working on a couple of these possible defectors. Our staffers have been feeling these guys out, and I think that two of the six will give us their vote if you promise not to back their opponent in the next election. Out of the ten undecideds and the six possible defectors, we're going to have to get at least nine or the budget is dead, and if that happens, we may as well kiss next year's election good-bye."

"What about any possible defections from our side?" the president asked.

Garret leaned forward. "Don't worry about that. If one of those little pricks steps out of line, Koslowski will cut every penny of federal money from their district. We're not going to have any traitors." Besides being chairman of the House Appropriations Committee, Jack Koslowski was the party's chief neck-breaker on the Hill. He was known and feared by all as one of the roughest players in D.C. "What I need from you this morning are some real nice down-home phone calls to a couple of these rookie congressmen, telling them how much their vote would mean to you and the country. Maybe even invite them over here for lunch."

The request was met with a grimace by the president, but Garret continued, "Jim, I know you don't like mixing with the common folk, but if you don't get a couple of these boys to switch over to our side, you're going to have to do an awful lot of ass-kissing come election time." Garret paused, giving the president time to reflect on unpleasant memories of the campaign trail. "If everything goes well with Moore, which I'm sure it will, I want to schedule a press conference at noon to try and spook the rest of these guys into settling. At the press conference I want you to stand up and complain about congressional gridlock. Tell them that you can't start fixing this nation if they don't pass your budget. You know the routine. I wrote a speech for you last night, and when we're done with the phone calls, I want to run through it with you." Garret hadn't actually written the speech. One of his staffers had, but Garret was not one to give credit to others.

"How do you want him to respond if they start asking about us buying votes?" asked Dickson.

"Flat out deny it. Tell them that there are several congressmen who feel very strongly about getting certain kinds of economic relief to their districts, which are in dire need of help. Deny it, deny it, deny it! This thing will all be over in a couple of days, and then the press will move on to something else. If they start to lay into you about any frivolous parts of the bill, just squirm your way out of it, and then look at your watch and end the press conference. Tell them you have to meet some diplomats from one of the former Soviet republics." Garret quickly jotted down a note to himself. "By the time you go on, I'll have an excuse ready."

The president nodded his head in a positive manner. He was a professional politician, and Garret was one of the best handlers in the business. He trusted Garret completely when it came to manipulating public opinion.

Garret stabbed his index finger at the list of congressmen. "All right, let's stay focused on the game. I don't give a shit what the press thinks, just so long as we get this budget passed." Garret picked up a pen and circled three names under the possible-defectors heading. "Now, Jim, these three boys are as big hicks as they come. They're a couple of Mr. Smith Goes to Washington types. Just like Jimmy Stewart in the movie. All three are freshmen and are full of ideals. If you call them up and beat the commander-in-chief drum, I think we can get them to jump sides. Give them the old 'Rome wasn't built in a day, we can't save the nation overnight' speech." The president nodded his head, signaling a full understanding of the performance needed. "These next two guys are the ones I was telling you about. If we promise not to back their opponents in the next election, they'll give us their votes. All they want is a personal guarantee from you . . . they said they don't trust my word." Garret let out a loud laugh. "Can you imagine that?"

The president and Dickson joined in with smiles and a couple of chuckles. Garret pressed on. "Now this last rep is a real nut-bag, and I'm not so sure she'll play ball. Koslowski wanted her name on the list. She's from one of his neighboring districts in Chicago. She's a black freshman and she scares the shit out of me. She's a bona fide race-baiter. She'll call anyone a racist, and I mean anyone. She'd call the pope a racist if she had the chance. I think in exchange for her vote she's going to want to be invited to several high-profile events and be put on some of the more powerful committees. At which point she will stand up and call our biggest financial backers racists and embarrass the shit out of them. I would prefer to avoid having to deal with her if at all possible."

The president massaged his fingers. "Why is she on the list?"

"I told you, Jack put her on there just in case we need a vote at the last minute. We're not going to deal with her unless we absolutely have to. Now let's get started with the three rookies."

The first name at the top of the list was Michael O'Rourke. The president picked up his pen and stabbed the tip at O'Rourke's name. "Michael O'Rourke—where have I heard that name before?"

Garret looked over at his boss and shook his head. "I have no idea. He's a freshman independent from Minnesota." Garret glanced down at his notes. "He was on Senator Olson's staff before he was elected. He graduated from the University of Minnesota where he played hockey. After college he went into the Marine Corps and fought in the Gulf War. It says here he was leading a squad of Recon Marines behind enemy lines during the air war conducting target assessment when they saw a coalition pilot shot down. He and his men rushed to the pilot's aid and held off an entire company of Iraqi soldiers until the cavalry showed up. He was awarded the Silver Star."

The president continued to stare at the name and mumbled to himself, "I know I've heard that name before."

Mark Dickson interjected, "Sir, you may have read about him in the papers. He's recently been crowned the most eligible bachelor in Washington by the social columnists."

Stevens stabbed his pen down on the piece of paper several times. "You're right. That is where I've heard about him. I caught the secretaries swooning over his picture several weeks ago. Very handsome young man. We could probably use that to our advantage. What else do we know about him?"

Garret looked through some notes that an assistant had made for him. "He's thirty-two-years-old and from Grand Rapids. His family is big in the timber business." Garret raised his eyebrows when he looked at the estimated value of the O'Rourke Timber Company. "They've got some serious money. At any rate, he says he won't vote for your budget unless all of the funding for the Rural Electrification Administration is cut."

The president let out a loud laugh and asked, "That's the only thing he doesn't like about it?"

"No." Garret shook his head. "He says the whole thing sucks, but he's willing to sign on to it if, and only if, you cut the funding for the REA."

The president frowned at the word *sucks*. "That's ridiculous. We'd lose half the votes we already have, and we wouldn't gain more than a handful."

"Exactly."

"Well, let's call him and find out just how serious he is when he's got the president of the United States breathing down his neck." Stevens pressed a button on his phone console. "Betty, would you please get Congressman O'Rourke on the line for me?"

"Yes, sir."

Stevens looked up from the phone. "What else can you tell me about him?"

"Not much. He's an unknown. I'm banking on the fact that once he hears your voice, he'll be in such awe that he'll roll over like a good-old, small-town boy."

O'Rourke was deep in thought when Susan's voice came over the intercom. He finished the sentence he was working on and pressed the intercom button. "Yes, Susan, what is it?"

"Michael, the president is holding on line one."

"Very funny, Susan. I told you I didn't want to be bothered. Please, tell the president I'm a little busy at the moment. I'll try to get back to him after lunch."

"Michael, I'm not kidding. The president is holding on line one."

O'Rourke laughed to himself. "Susan, are you that bored?"

"I'm serious, he's on line one."

O'Rourke frowned at the blinking light and pressed it. "Hello, this is Congressman O'Rourke."

The president was sitting behind his desk, and Stu Garret and Mark Dickson were listening in on the call from separate phones on the other side of the room. Upon hearing O'Rourke's voice, the president enthusiastically said, "Hello, Congressman O'Rourke?"

Michael leaned forward in his chair when he heard the president's familiar voice and said, "Yes, this is he."

"This is the president. How are you doing this morning?"

"Just fine, sir, and how are you?" O'Rourke closed his eyes and wished Susan would have listened to him.

"Well, I would be doing a whole lot better if I could get some of you people over there to back me on this budget."

"Yes, I'd imagine you would, sir." O'Rourke's monotone response was followed by a brief silence.

"You know, Congressman, that's a beautiful part of the country you're from. One of my roommates at Dartmouth had a little cabin up near Grand Rapids. I spent a week there one summer and had a fantastic time. That is, with the exception of those darn mosquitoes. They could pick you up and carry you off during the middle of the night if you weren't careful."

"Yes, they're pretty bad at times." O'Rourke had yet to show an ounce of emotion in his voice.

The president pressed on, speaking as if he and O'Rourke had been friends for years. "Well, Michael, the reason I'm calling is to tell you that I really need your vote tomorrow. And before you tell me yes or no, I want to talk to you about a couple of things.

"I've been doing this for over twenty-five years now, and I remember when I was a freshman representative. I came here filled with piss and vinegar. I was going to change this place . . . I was going to make a difference. Well, I quickly realized that if I didn't learn to take the good with the bad, I was never going to get anything done. I've been there, Michael. I know what you're going through.

"I remember the first presidential budget I had to vote on. There were some things in that budget that made me want to vomit. I vowed to fight it, until some of the older guys pulled me aside and pointed out that there would never be a budget that I would completely agree with. I took another look at it, and then after a closer review, I realized that I agreed with about eighty percent of the stuff that was in there.

"Michael, there are four hundred and thirty-five members in the House of Representatives. There is no way I will ever be able to send a budget up there that everyone agrees with. Now, I know you want the REA disbanded, and to be honest, I've wanted to kill the damn program for the past twenty years, but we're in a goddamned war here, Michael. If I torpedo the REA, my budget will be sunk faster than the *Titanic*. I agree with you in theory. The REA has to go, but in the real world if I want to pass all the other things that will help make this country a better place to live, I have to make some compromises. And the REA is one of those ugly things I have to let slide, so we can achieve what is best for the country."

The president paused for effect, and O'Rourke offered no response.

"Michael, do you understand the position I'm in? I will never be able to present a budget that will make everybody happy. I need you to ask yourself if you're being realistic. . . . I'm up here taking the heat. I'm running the show, and if this budget doesn't get passed, I will be severely hampered in my ability to put this country back on its feet. I'm asking you for a big favor. . . . I was in your shoes once before. . . . I need you to ignore the twenty percent that you don't like and help me pass this budget. If you come on board, Michael, I can guarantee that you'll go a long way in politics." Stevens paused to give O'Rourke some time to think of the ways the president of the United States could help his career. "What do you say, Michael? Can I count on your vote tomorrow?"

There was a long, awkward silence as O'Rourke sat in his office and cursed himself for taking the call. He did not want to get into a debate with the president right now. So, true to his typical form, he cut straight to the heart of the matter. "Mr. President, there is very little that I like about your budget. My vote will be no tomorrow, and there is nothing that will change that. I'm sorry to have wasted your time by accepting this call." Without waiting for a response, O'Rourke hung up.

CHAPTER 3

THE president sat in disbelief behind his desk, staring at the phone. He looked over at Garret and asked, "Did he just hang up on me?"

"The guy must be an idiot. He's definitely not going to be around this town for long. Don't let it bother you. I'll have Koslowski take care of him." Garret rose and started to walk toward the door. "I'll be right back. I have to get something from my office. Mark, get him started on the calls to Dreyer and Hampton. Jim, all they want is a verbal guarantee from you that you won't back their opponents in next year's election. I'll be back in five minutes."

Garret walked down the hallway, ignoring all in his path. He entered his office, closed the door, and headed straight for his desk. Before grabbing the phone, he picked up a pack of Marlboro 100s and shoved one in his mouth. After lighting it, he took two deep drags and filled his lungs. The president wouldn't allow Garret to smoke in the Oval Office, so he tended to find an excuse about every hour to sneak away to his office. He picked up the handset of his phone and punched in the number for the direct line to Jack Koslowski's office.

A gruff voice answered the phone on the other end. "Yeah."

"Jack, Stu here. How are things going?"

"We're holding the line. No one is going to break ranks on this one. All we need is for you boys and Tom to come through."

"We both know Tom will have Moore delivered to us by noon, but we need some people to jump ship from the other side."

"Who do you have in mind?"

"For starters I need you to lean on this O'Rourke clown. The president just tried to give him the soft shoe and it went over like a lead balloon. Stevens gave him a five-minute speech and then O'Rourke hung up on him."

"You're shitting me. He hung up on Stevens?" Koslowski started to laugh.

Garret did not think it was funny. "Lean on him hard, and if there's anyone else you can think of, we need them by noon."

"I'll put my boys on the street and see what I can do. I'll let you know as soon as I find anything out." Both men hung up.

Congressman O'Rourke was sitting at his desk, reading over some documents and dictating notes, when the door to his office burst open. A slender, well-dressed man, who looked vaguely familiar, pushed his way past Susan and approached Michael's desk.

In an irritated voice Susan said, "I'm sorry, sir, but I told this man that you weren't taking visitors this morning."

The man stepped forward. "I apologize for the intrusion, Congressman O'Rourke, but I'm one of Chairman Koslowski's aides. He has a proposal he would like you to consider, and he needs an answer immediately."

Michael leaned back in his chair and realized where he'd seen the dark-haired man before. Michael's gaze turned from the aide to his secretary. "Thank you, Susan, I'll see the gentleman." Susan retreated from the office and closed the door. The chairman's aide stepped forward and extended his hand across the desk. O'Rourke remained seated and took the man's hand.

"Congressman O'Rourke, my name is Anthony Vanelli."

O'Rourke placed his Dictaphone on the desk behind several stacks of files and said, "Please take a seat, Mr. Vanelli." O'Rourke had heard several stories about the aide and doubted this would be a friendly visit.

Vanelli sat down in one of the chairs in front of O'Rourke's desk and crossed his legs. "Congressman O'Rourke, I've been sent here to find out if you're still going to vote against the president's budget, and if you are, what we can do to change your mind."

"Mr. Vanelli, I assume you know I spoke to the president this morning."

"I am fully aware of that, Congressman O'Rourke, but time is running short and we need to know who is standing with us and who is standing against us."

O'Rourke leaned forward and placed his elbows on the desk. "Well, Mr. Vanelli, I have made my position very clear from the start. I will vote no for the budget unless the president cuts all funding for the Rural Electrification Administration."

"All right, Congressman, let's cut to the chase. We live in the real world, and in the real world, the Rural Electrification Administration is going to continue to exist. It's just the way things operate around here. You have to try to get over the little things and concentrate on the big picture. You can't damn the whole budget just because you don't like one little part of it."

"Mr. Vanelli, I would hardly consider a half billion dollars little. The thing you people don't understand is that I consider most of the president's budget to be a waste. I am merely focusing on the Rural Electrification Administration because it's an easy target. You must agree with the simple logic that when an institution is founded to solve a problem, once that problem is solved, the institution should be closed. All of rural America has been electrified for over twenty years, but we continue to bleed the taxpayers for about five hundred million dollars a year, just so congressmen and senators can send pork back to their constituents. It's a crime that the president is predicting a one-hundred-billion-dollar budget deficit and garbage like this isn't being cut." O'Rourke looked down to make sure the Dictaphone was still running.

Vanelli stood from his chair and walked toward the other end of the office. "They told me you were a flake," he said over his shoulder.

O'Rourke smiled to himself as he looked at Vanelli's back and said, "Excuse me. What did you just say?"

Vanelli turned around and strutted back to the desk. "Enough of the bullshit, Mike. I'm not here to talk political theory with you, nor to discuss what is ethically correct. That's for people like you and your loser friends to waste time on."

"Mr. Vanelli, I don't remember giving you permission to call me by my first name."

"Listen, Mike, Mikey, or dickhead, I'll call you whatever I want. All you are is a naive little freshman congressman who thinks he has all the solutions. We're about the same age, but we're worlds apart. I'm a realist and you're an idealist. Do you know where idealists get in this town? Nowhere! They go absolutely nowhere! They sent me down here to give you one last chance. You either get on board with the president's budget or your career is over. The choice is simple. You help us out and Chairman Koslowski will make sure some extra money finds its way into your district. If you don't, you'll be out of a job next year."

O'Rourke looked up at the man standing over his desk and rose to meet the challenge. The six-foot-three, 210-pound O'Rourke smiled slightly and asked, "Mr. Vanelli, what exactly do you mean, my career will be over?"

Vanelli took a step backward and replied, "You either play ball with us or we'll ruin your career. Chairman Koslowski will make sure he cuts off every penny from getting to your district. We've got people right now who are digging through your past. If we find anything dirty, we'll spread it all over town, and if we don't, we'll make something up. We own enough people in the press. We could ruin you in a week. We're done playing nice guy." Vanelli shook his finger in O'Rourke's face. "I'm going to wait in your lobby for exactly five minutes. I want you to sit in here and think about having your career ruined over one stupid vote, and when you're done, I want an answer." Vanelli turned for the door.

O'Rourke reached forward and grabbed the Dictaphone with his left hand. He took his thumb and pressed the rewind button. The tiny machine started to squeak as the tape spun in reverse. Vanelli heard the familiar sound and turned to look. Michael held up the tiny machine and pressed play. Vanelli's voice emanated from the small box. "We've got people right now who are digging through your past. If we find anything dirty, we'll spread it all over town, and if we don't, we'll make something up. We own enough people in the press. We could ruin you in a week."

Vanelli stormed across the room and lunged for the Dictaphone. "Who the hell do you think you are?"

O'Rourke's right hand shot up and grabbed Vanelli's outstretched hand. O'Rourke had practiced the judo move thousands of times while he was in the Marines. In one quick motion he twisted Vanelli's hand until the bottom of the wrist faced the ceiling, then forced the hand back toward the elbow. Vanelli collapsed to his knees in pain. O'Rourke continued to exert enough force to keep him on the floor.

Vanelli looked up with a pained face and screeched, "Let go of my fucking wrist, and give me that goddamn tape." O'Rourke increased the pressure and Vanelli let out a squeal.

"Listen to me, Vanelli. Just because you're from Chicago and you have an Italian name doesn't mean you're tough. You're an aide to a congressman, not a hit man for the Mafia."

Vanelli picked up his right hand and reached for his bent wrist. Before he was halfway there, O'Rourke slammed the wrist back another inch and Vanelli's free hand shot back to the floor as he let out a scream.

"Listen to me, you little punk! I don't know who you think you are coming in here and threatening me, but if you or your scumbag boss ever bother me again, you'll have the FBI, *60 Minutes,* and every other major news organization in the country crawling up your ass. Do you understand?" Vanelli was slow to respond, so O'Rourke increased the pressure and repeated the question. "Do you understand?" Vanelli shook his head yes and started to whimper. O'Rourke set the tape recorder on his desk, dropped to one knee, and grabbed Vanelli by the chin. He stared into his eyes and in a firm, precise voice said, "If you ever screw with me again, I'll do a hell of a lot more than twist your wrist."

Garret came bursting into the Oval Office. He'd been running back and forth between his office and the president's all morning, sneaking puffs of cigarettes and screaming into his phone. He strutted across the room to where the president and Dickson were sitting. "I've got great news; Moore is on board." The president punched his fist into the air, and all three men let out a yell.

"Jim, I think we should postpone the press conference until one P.M."

"Stu, you know I hate postponing those things. It's just going to make us look like we're unorganized."

Garret grabbed a fresh piece of paper and leaned over the table. He wrote the number 209 in the upper left-hand corner and 216 in the upper right. "We were at two hundred and nine votes versus two hundred sixteen this morning. Since then we've picked up Moore, Reiling, and one of those hicks. They were all undecided, and we got Dreyer and Hampton to defect. That's minus two for them and plus five for us. That puts us at two hundred fourteen apiece." Garret stood up and screamed, "God, I love this tension. We're going to win this damn thing." The president and Dickson smiled.

"I see where you're headed with this, Stu," said the president. "You would like to turn this thing into a little victory announcement."

"Exactly. If we can wait until one, I think Jack and Tom can pick up enough votes to give us a little breathing room. Tom's office has already leaked that Moore settled. The rest of the gamblers will be making their deals as soon as possible."

The president looked up at Garret with a smile and conceded. "Stu, do what you have to do to move it from twelve to one o'clock, but try to be gentle with Ms. Moncur."

Garret nodded, then headed off to get the job done. He would be about as gentle with Ann Moncur as a five-year-old boy is with his three-year-old baby brother. He was in one of his zones. Victory was just around the corner, and he would do anything to win. He had no time for frail egos and overly sensitive, politically correct appointees. He was on the front line and they were nothing more than support people. It was always amazing to him that the people who complained the most were usually the ones who were trying to justify their jobs. The people in the trenches never complained. They just continued to produce results. Koslowski was like that. He didn't care if it looked pretty or not, he just made sure the job got done. Their new ally, Arthur Higgins, was a producer. No bullshit, no complaining, only results. He made a mental note to thank Mike Nance, the national security adviser, for setting that one up. God, did he do a nice job on Frank Moore. That could be the one that put them over the top.

CHAPTER 4

THE president and his entourage were standing in the ante-
room located behind the White House Press Room. They
could hear Ann Moncur explaining to the White House press corps
that the president had a busy afternoon and would not be able to
answer a lot of questions. Stevens was a little nervous. It had been
almost four months since his last press conference. The honeymoon
between him and the press had ended in the middle of his second
year of office. During the first year and a half he could do no wrong.
The press had backed him during the election, and he had in turn
given them unprecedented access. The honeymoon soured when
certain members of the press corps remembered that their job was
to report the facts and keep the public informed. Several potential
scandals were uncovered, but before they became full-blown stories, Stu Garret stepped in and put out the fires. Documents were
shredded, people were paid to keep quiet or lie, and everything was
emphatically denied and denounced as a ploy by the opposition to
smear the president. When the scandals finally died, Garret laid
out a new strategy for the president when it came to dealing with
the press: act hurt, betrayed, and keep your distance. The president
gladly complied with his chief of staff's plan, and the new strategy
had partially worked.

Some in the press were in awe of the president and yearned for the relationship they had had with him during his first year in office, but the hardened reporters saw right through the scam. Too many documents had miraculously disappeared, and too many sources had changed their story overnight. The old guard of the press corps had been around too long to be taken in by the feigned isolation of the president. They were cynical, and to them, professional politicians did nothing that wasn't calculated. If the president was isolating himself from the press, it wasn't because his feelings were hurt. It was because he had something to hide.

Garret had pulled the president away from the rest of the group and was reminding him which reporters he should steer clear of during the question-and-answer period. "Now, Jim, don't forget, no more than four questions, and whatever you do, don't recognize Ray Holtz from the *Post* and Shirley Thomas from the *Times*." The president nodded in agreement. Garret grabbed him by the shoulder and started to lead him toward the stage. "I'll be right there if anyone backs you into a corner, and remember, only four questions and then you have to go meet the new premier of Ukraine. If they whine about how short it is, just smile and tell them you're sorry, but you've got a full calendar and you're already running behind."

The president smiled at Garret. "Stu, relax, I've done this before."

Garret smiled back. "I know, that's what makes me nervous."

Ann Moncur was still addressing the gallery when she noticed the reporters look to her right. She glanced over and saw the president standing in the tiny doorway.

"Good afternoon, Mr. President. Are you ready to take over?"

The president bounded up the two small steps and walked toward the podium, extending his right hand. "Thank you, Ann." The two shook hands, and Moncur went to join Stu Garret and Mark Dickson, who were standing against the wall. While the president organized his notes, the photographers were busy snapping shots.

After a brief moment, he cleared his throat and looked up from the podium. With a slight smile he greeted the press corps, "Good afternoon."

The press responded in kind, and the president's slight smile turned into a big one. Like most politicians, Stevens knew how to work the crowd, and his most successful tool of all was his larger-than-life smile. What most of the people in the room didn't know was that the smile had been rehearsed. Few things in this administration happened by accident. Stu Garret made sure of that. The smile had its desired effect, and the majority of the people sitting in the gallery smiled back. The president placed his thin, well-manicured hands on the edges of the podium and cleared his throat again. "I have called this press conference to announce a victory for the American people. During the past week, this administration has battled partisan politics, disinformation, gridlock, and a thirty-two-vote deficit to secure the successful passage of my budget in the House of Representatives. As of noon today, we have obtained two hundred twenty votes, enough for a narrow margin of victory.

"I would be remiss if I did not take this opportunity to thank the esteemed Speaker of the House, Mr. Thomas Basset, for all of the hard work he has done to ensure passage of this budget. His hard work will help put us another step closer to getting this country back on the road to a speedy economic recovery." The president glanced down at his watch, then brought his gaze back to the reporters. "I'm sorry for being so brief, but I have an extremely busy calendar today, and I'm already running an hour behind. I have a couple of minutes to field a few brief questions."

Hands immediately shot up, and a dozen or so reporters started to shout questions.

The president turned to his right and looked for the familiar face of Jim Lester, the ABC White House correspondent. Lester was sitting on the edge of his chair, right hand raised, obediently waiting to be called on. Stevens pointed in his direction and called his name. The rest of the reporters fell silent as Lester rose from his chair.

"As of this morning, sir, it was reported that you had secured approximately two hundred ten votes. How did you pick up the remaining ten so quickly, and are any of those new votes coming from congressmen who were previously committed to voting against your budget?"

"Well . . . we picked up the ten so quickly because there are a lot of people up on the Hill who know, despite what the opposition has been saying, that this is a good budget. There are a lot of people in this country who need the relief this budget will provide, and there were several congressmen who, after taking a more serious look at the budget, realized it would be mean-spirited *not* to vote for it." The president turned his head away from Lester, and the hands shot up immediately. He rested his gaze and forefinger on another friendly face, Lisa Williamson, the White House correspondent for the Associated Press.

"Mr. President, are you worried that with such a narrow victory in the House, your budget will have a harder time getting through the Senate, where the opposition holds a much higher percentage of seats?"

Stevens wasted no time responding. The question was anticipated and the answer prepared. "Not really. The American people want this budget, and our senators know that. They will do what is right and they will pass the budget." Stevens started to turn to find another reporter before he finished answering the question.

More hands shot up, and this time the president turned to find Mick Turner from CNN.

"Mr. President, the successful passage of this budget through the House will be a political home run for your administration. How much do you think it will improve your position when negotiating with the Japanese during next month's trade talks?"

"Well, the Japanese have a history of walking away from these talks in a better position than when they entered them. This is somewhat ironic when one considers the fact that they have been running an ever-increasing trade surplus with us for the last fifteen years. The trade deficit that we run with them is hurting American labor. We are putting out high-quality products and the Japanese refuse to open their markets. This trade deficit is stifling our economy from reaching its full potential, and most importantly, it is costing us American jobs. There is no doubt that the passage of my budget will be a signal to the Japanese that we are finally ready to reverse a trend that previous administrations let get so out of control.

"I have time for one more question."

While Stevens was talking, his head swiveled to take in the whole press gallery. He noticed a stunning brunette sitting in the section usually reserved for foreign press. He decided that since voters cared little about foreign affairs, he would be safe calling on her. He pointed toward the back of the room. "The young lady in the back row." The president was expecting to hear a foreign accent and was somewhat shocked when she stood and spoke perfect English.

"Mr. President, Liz Scarlatti from the *Washington Reader.* Congressman Michael O'Rourke from Minnesota has said that even though he thinks your budget is, quote, 'stuffed with more pork than a Jimmy Dean sausage,' he would still be willing to vote for it if you shut down the Rural Electrification Administration, an agency that is estimated to cost the American taxpayer five hundred to seven hundred million dollars a year. This agency was founded in 1935 for the sole purpose of bringing electricity to rural America. . . . My question is this: Mr. President, I know that the leaders of our country are very busy, but have you or anyone else in Washington noticed that all of rural America has had electricity for over twenty years? And now that you've been informed, what are you going to do to shut down this wasteful program?"

Many of the reporters in the audience started to chuckle.

With a forced smile, the president pulled out his best, good-old-boy drawl. "Well, Ms. Scarlatti, first of all, this budget is one of the leanest budgets that any president in the last twenty years has sent to the Hill." Eyes started to roll in the audience. The cynical members of the press were getting sick of hearing the factless rhetoric of the president. It was cute for the first year, but they'd grown tired of it. "And second of all, I have been trying to shut down the REA ever since I took office, but the hard fact remains that if I killed the REA, my budget would never make it out of committee."

Before the president could continue, the fiery brunette shouted again from the back row. "Mr. President, don't you think it is a harsher fact of reality that your budget is forecasting a one-hundred-billion-dollar deficit and you are still funding federal agencies that are obsolete? Not to mention the fact that you have done nothing to control the growth of Social Security and Medicare!"

Stu Garret could see that the president was in trouble, so he stepped forward and touched his elbow. The president turned and Garret pointed to his watch. Stevens turned back to the press and said, "People, I'm running very late. Let me finish the young lady's question and then I'm going to have to leave. . . . This administration is very concerned about finding and getting rid of government waste. Vice President Dumont is heading up a task force right now that is vigorously searching for ways to cut government waste. This has been a major priority of my administration and will continue to be one. Thank you all very much for your time and have a good day." The president stepped back from the podium and waved good-bye. Reporters continued to shout questions as Stevens walked off the stage.

Once backstage, Stu Garret grabbed him by the arm and pulled him close. "What in the hell were you doing calling on someone you didn't know?"

"She was sitting in the foreign-press section. I called on her because I thought she would ask me a question on foreign affairs. Relax, Stu, I handled it fine."

Garret frowned deeply. "Foreign affairs, my ass. You were thinking of another type of affair. You know which reporters to call on if you want a question on foreign affairs. That was stupid. From now on, stick with the program!"

CHAPTER 5

THE blue van wound its way through the tiny Washington, D.C., neighborhood of Friendship Heights. Dark green letters strewn across the side of the van read, "Johnson Brothers' Plumbing, 24 Hour Emergency Service Available." Inside were two men, both in their late twenties, both extremely fit. They were wearing dark blue coveralls and matching baseball hats. The van slowed down and turned into a narrow, poorly lit alley. Ten yards into the alley the van rolled to a stop and the driver pulled the gear lever up and into reverse. Pulling back out into the street, the van stopped again and then headed back in the direction from which it had just come. To anyone who may have been watching, it looked as if the plumber's van was harmlessly searching for a house in need of its services.

Back in the alley, behind a row of garbage cans, the dark-haired former passenger of the van crouched silently and observed. After several minutes, he stood and slowly started down the alley, going from shadow to shadow, quietly walking on the balls of his feet. Six houses down, he stopped behind a garage on his right. It belonged to Mr. Harold J. Burmiester. He grabbed a plastic bag from inside his pocket, reached over the seven-foot fence, and dumped the bag's contents into the backyard. Huddling between the corner of the fence and the garage, he pressed the light on his digital watch. It was 10:44 P.M. He would have to wait another fifteen minutes to make sure the bait was taken.

Burmiester felt that high-tech security systems were a waste of money. His was the only house on the block that did not have one, and the only house on the block that had never been burglarized. This distinction was directly attributable to a rather large German shepherd named Fritz.

The unwelcomed observer waited quietly in the shadows, as he had done on dozens of previous nights, waiting and watching, recording times and taking notes—always reassured by the punctuality of the retired banker.

At 10:55, the backyard floodlight was turned on, and a silhouette of the fence was cast across the alley onto the neighbor's garage. A moment later, the door opened and the tags on Fritz's collar could be heard jingling as he bounded down the steps and across the yard. Every night at exactly 10:55, Burmiester would let Fritz out to go to the bathroom, then let him back in five minutes later, just in time for his owner to watch the nightly news.

The dog ran straight to the back fence, where his master had trained him to go to the bathroom. Fritz was urinating on the fence when he started to sniff frantically. Dropping his leg, he ran toward the corner where the meat had been deposited and immediately started to snap up the small pieces of beef. The motionless man listened intently as the dog feasted on the meat. After several minutes, the creaking noise of the back door opening broke the silence of the cool night air, and without being called, Fritz sprang away from the fence and ran into the house.

12:05 A.M., FRIDAY

Sen. Daniel Fitzgerald's limousine lumbered north along Massachusetts Avenue. It was just after midnight, and the senator was sitting in the backseat, drinking a glass of Scotch and reading the *Post*. He'd just left his third party of the evening and was on his way home. Fitzgerald was the chairman of the Senate Finance Committee and one of the most powerful men in Washington. He had a full head of gray hair and a red, bulbous nose that was a direct result of his heavy drinking. The senator had two vices—women and alcohol. He had already been married three times and was currently separated from his third wife. He'd been through approximately a half dozen treatment programs, none of which had worked. Several years earlier, he'd decided to stop fighting his addiction. He loved the booze, and that was that. During all of the personal turmoils of ruined marriages, bouts with depression, and six children that he didn't know, the senator had always clung to one thing—his job. It was all that was left in his life.

Fitzgerald had been in Washington for over forty years. After graduating from Yale Law School, he had gone to work for a prestigious law firm in Boston, and then, at the age of twenty-eight, he was elected to the United States House of Representatives. After serving as a congressman for three terms, one of the two Senate seats in his home state became available. At the urging and financial backing of his father, Fitzgerald launched the most expensive campaign New Hampshire had ever seen. The political machine his father had built ensured a victory, and Fitzgerald was elected to the United States Senate.

For the last thirty-four years, he'd survived scandal after scandal and hung on to that seat like a screaming child clutching his favorite toy. Fitzgerald had been a politician his entire adult life, and he knew nothing else. He'd grown numb to the day-to-day dealings of the nation's capital. The forty-plus years of lying, deceit, deal cutting, career trashing, and partisan politics had become so ingrained in Fitzgerald that he not only thought his behavior was acceptable, he truly believed it was the only way to do business.

Dan Fitzgerald had been pulled into the vacuum of Washington politics, and like so many before him, he'd checked his conscience and morals at the door. For Fitzgerald, such things as integrity, hard work, taking charge of one's own life, individual freedom, and the Constitution of the United States had little meaning. To him, being a leader of the country was not about doing the right thing. It was about holding on to power. Holding on no matter what it took. Fitzgerald was addicted to power no differently than a crack addict is addicted to the rock. He always needed more, and he could never get enough.

Fitzgerald lived only for the present and the future. He had never bothered to look back on his life until now. He was experiencing something that many of his predecessors had gone through late in their careers. He'd sold his soul and integrity to get to the top, and now that he was there, he was starting to realize it was a lonely place. With old age staring him straight in the face, he was, for the first time, forced to look back on his life with a critical eye. He had always known he was a failure as both a father and a husband. Everything he had, he'd put into his career.

Leaning his head against the window, he took a long pull off the fresh drink and closed his eyes. Senator Daniel Fitzgerald had never been interested in the truth, but now in his waning years, he could no longer escape it. He had never liked being alone. He had always needed others around to feel secure, and it had only gotten worse over the years. He had worked his whole life to get where he was, and now that he was there, he had no one to share it with. But, even worse was that deep down inside something was telling him he had wasted his life fighting for the wrong things. He finished off the glass of Dewar's and poured another.

The limousine turned off Massachusetts Avenue and wound through the narrow residential streets of Kalorama Heights. One block before its destination, the limousine passed a plain, white van. Inside were two men who had been waiting—waiting and preparing for this night for over a year.

The limo stopped in front of Fitzgerald's $1.2-million brown-stone, and the driver jumped out to open the door for his boss. By the time he got around to the rear of the car, Fitzgerald was out of the backseat and stumbling toward the house. Fitzgerald fancied himself too important a man to shut car doors, so as usual, he left it for the driver to take care of.

The driver shut the door and wished his employer a good night. Fitzgerald ignored the pleasantry and continued up the steps to his front door. The driver walked back around to the other side of the limo and watched Fitzgerald punch in his security code and unlock the door. When the door opened and the senator stumbled into the foyer, the driver got into the limo and drove away.

Fitzgerald set his keys down on a table to the left of the door and reached for the light switch. He flipped it up, but nothing happened. He tried it several more times, and the result was the same. Swearing to himself, he looked around the dark house. The front door was bordered on both sides by panes of glass six inches wide that ran from the top of the door to the floor. Through the two narrow windows, the streetlight provided a faint glow to the front hallway. From where Fitzgerald stood, he could barely make out the white tile floor of the kitchen, just thirty feet away, straight down the hallway.

As he started for the kitchen, he passed the dark entryway to the living room on his right and the stairs that led to the upper floors on his left. His heavy, expensive wing tips echoed throughout the house as they struck the hardwood floor with each step. The dim light shining through the windows cast a long shadow of him that stretched down the hallway toward the kitchen. With each step his round body blocked more and more of the light coming from the street. By the time he reached the kitchen, he was surrounded by darkness. He turned to his left and searched for the light switch. Before Fitzgerald could find it, a pair of gloved hands came out of the darkness and grabbed him from behind.

The blond-haired intruder yanked the older man off his feet and slammed him face first into the tiled floor. Dropping down on his target, the powerful man thrust his knee into the center of Fitzgerald's upper back and grabbed the senator's head with both hands. In one quick burst of strength the assassin brought all of his weight down on the back of Fitzgerald's head and yanked up on his chin. The noise that the senator's neck made as it snapped shot through the quiet house like a brittle tree limb broken over a knee. The crack was followed by silence, and then an eerie gurgling noise that emanated from Fitzgerald's throat. The dying senator's eyes opened wider and wider until they looked as if they were about to pop out. About thirty seconds later the gurgling noise subsided, and Fitzgerald's body lay lifeless on the cold, tile floor.

The assassin rose to his feet and exhaled a deep breath. He looked down at the dead body on the floor with a sense of great satisfaction. The killer standing over Fitzgerald had just avenged the deaths of eight of his closest friends—eight men who had died a senseless death in a desolate desert, thousands of miles away, all because men like Fitzgerald didn't know how to keep their mouths shut. The killing of Fitzgerald was personal, but the next two would be business. The thin arm of a microphone hung in front of the assassin's square jaw. He spoke with a precise voice, "Number one is in the bag, over." After a brief second, a confirmation came crackling through his earpiece, and he went back to work.

Grabbing the body by the ankles, he dragged it down into the basement and deposited it in a large storage closet. The assassin took one last tour through the house, collecting the electronic listening devices he had placed there the previous week. Before leaving, he zipped the collar on his coat up around his chin and pulled his baseball hat down tight over his short, blond hair. He stood at the back door momentarily, looking out the window into the small yard. The wind was picking up, and the trees were swaying back and forth. Once again he spoke softly into the mike, "I'm on my way, over." He locked the door and closed it behind him. Casually he walked across the yard, through the gate, and into the alley. When he reached the end of the alley, the white van stopped just long enough for him to climb in, then sped off down the street.

3:45 A.M., FRIDAY

The blue Johnson Brothers' Plumbing van was again driving through the streets of Friendship Heights. It pulled into the same alley it had stopped in five hours earlier. While the van was still moving, the passenger jumped down onto the pavement and walked beside it, crouching and holding on to the door. The dome light on the inside of the van had been removed. As the van stopped, the broad-shouldered, dark-haired man quietly closed the door and darted into the shadows. He waited while the van drove away. Slung over his shoulder was a large black canvas bag. After several minutes passed, he started to make his way down the alley. When he reached Burmiester's fence, he pulled a can of WD-40 out of his bag and sprayed the hinges of the gate. He waited for the oil to take effect, then carefully lifted the latch on the gate and opened it. Slipping into the backyard, he dropped down behind a row of bushes and looked up at the windows of Burmiester's house and the neighbors', waiting to see a face peering out or a light being turned on, announcing that someone had seen him. For almost five minutes he sat behind the bush, waiting and watching. There was time to be careful and that was the way he liked it, the way he'd been trained.

The man reached into the bag, this time retrieving a pair of wire cutters. Cautiously rising to his feet, he walked along the edge of the garage and then darted across the small open space to the back stoop, where he crouched down. Again, he used the can of WD-40, spraying the hinges of the screen door. While he waited for the oil to soak in, he grabbed the pair of wire cutters and cut the phone line running into the basement of the house. He put the wire cutters back in the bag and grabbed a glass cutter. Jumping up on the stoop he opened the screen door about two feet and slid in between it and the back door. The back door was wood with the top third split into four sections of glass. He placed the cup of the glass cutter in the middle of the bottom left pane and swung the cutting edge around the suction cup in a clockwise direction. After five revolutions, he took both hands and pressed in on the newly created circle. The freshly cut piece of glass popped free and stayed attached to the suction cup. Sticking his arm through the hole, he unlocked the door, opened it, and stepped into the kitchen, carefully closing the door behind him. He stood completely still and looked out the window, staring at the neighbors' houses, looking for anything that might have changed while his ears focused on the inside of the house. He heard the dog breathing and turned to see him lying on a piece of carpet in front of the kitchen table, completely relaxed and limp. Pulling the microphone down from under the brim of his baseball cap, he spoke in a soft whisper, "I'm in, over."

His partner was sitting in the blue van, six blocks away, around the corner from a small, twenty-four-hour convenience store. He was monitoring the local police scanner. Calmly, he spoke into the microphone hanging in front of his mouth, "Roger that, everything is clear on my end, over."

The man in the kitchen of Burmiester's house pushed the microphone back up under the brim of his hat and slowly removed the black bag from over his shoulder. Gently placing it on the floor, he retrieved a gas mask and a green tank with a clear rubber hose attached to the end. With the tank and mask in hand, he walked down the uncarpeted hallway toward the front door and the staircase that led to the second floor. When he reached the foot of the staircase, he stopped and leaned forward, placing his hands on the fourth step. Again he paused, not moving, just listening. After he was sure that Burmiester had not been awakened, he started to crawl up the steps, keeping his hands and feet away from the center of the stairs, leaning forward, trying to keep his weight as equally distributed as possible, not wanting the old stairs to creak and wake the owner.

When he reached the second floor, he stayed on his knees and continued to crawl slowly toward the master bedroom, about twenty feet away. Once again, he waited patiently and listened. Gently, he stuck the rubber tube under the door, put his gas mask on, and opened the valve on the tank. Sitting down with his back against the wall, he started the timer on his watch.

After fifteen minutes had elapsed, he turned off the valve and pulled the tube out from under the door. Slowly, he opened the door and peeked into the room. Burmiester was lying with his back to the door and showed no signs of movement. The intruder pushed the door the rest of the way open and walked over to the bed. Reaching down, he nudged Burmiester several times. The old man didn't move. He took the glove off his right hand, placed it on Burmiester's neck, and checked his pulse. After checking it twice more, he concluded with relief that the old man was fine. The intruder did not know the man he was standing over, and he did not wish to see him die. Harold Burmiester was not the man he was after tonight. He walked around the bed to the double window that looked out onto the street below and stared straight across at the house opposite Burmiester's. He lowered the mike and said, "I'm in position. Everything looks good, over."

The response came crackling back through his earpiece immediately. "Roger, everything is quiet on this end, over."

Five miles away on the other side of the Potomac River, the second team had moved into position. The nondescript white van was parked on a quiet side street. Inside, the blond-haired assassin was undergoing a change. He'd taken off his dark jeans, jacket, and

boots and had replaced them with a gray pair of sweatpants, a blue
sweatshirt, and a pair of Nike running shoes. He sat still while one
of the other men carefully applied black makeup to his face, neck,
and ears. The makeup was for camouflage, but not in the typical
military sense. It was meant to be noticed and to deceive, not to
conceal. After the makeup job was completed, a tight, black Afro
wig was placed over his blond hair, and a pair of brown contacts
were inserted over his blue eyes. Next, he put his headset back on
and pulled a University of Michigan baseball hat over his head.

5:55 A.M., FRIDAY

The screen covering Mr. Burmiester's bedroom window had been
taken off, and the owner of the house had been carefully moved
from the master bedroom down the hall to one of the guest rooms.
The intruder was sitting on a wooden chair, staring out the window at a pair of French doors located on the second floor of the
house across the street. Resting on his lap was a Remington M-24
military sniper rifle with a customized silencer attached to the end
of the barrel. A round was in the chamber but the rifle was still on
safety. The alarm on his watch had beeped five minutes earlier, and
he was trying to stay relaxed. The sky was just starting to brighten
and the birds were chirping. His target would be rising any minute,
and he was making a conscious effort to control his breathing and
keep his adrenaline level low.

A light was turned on across the street, and the drapes on the
other side of the French doors turned from gray to yellow. In one
fast motion he brought the rifle up into a firing position, pressing the stock between his shoulder and left cheek. His finger came
up and flipped off the safety, while he centered the crosshairs on
the middle of the French doors. He continued taking slow, controlled breaths. A blurred shadow moved from behind the curtains.
The shooter inhaled deeply, and just when his lungs were fully

expanded, the doors across the street opened. As they swung inward, they revealed the pudgy, pink-and-white body of Congressman Jack Koslowski. Wearing only a pair of baby blue boxers, he turned and started for the bathroom.

The center of the crosshairs were resting on the small of Koslowski's hairy back. The right hand of the assassin rose slightly, and the rifle followed. The crosshairs slid up the spinal column, past the shoulder blades, and rested just below the bald spot on the back of Koslowski's head. The upper body of the assassin twisted as the sight followed the target across the room. The left forefinger started its slow, even squeeze on the trigger. A second later it caught, and the hammer slammed forward. The hollow-point round spiraled its way down the barrel, through the silencer, and sliced its way into the still morning air.

The bullet slammed into the back of the congressman's head, the hollow point collapsing upon impact. Instead of continuing its clean, tight spiral, the now flattened tip was three times larger than its original size as it ripped through the brain, pushing everything in its path toward the front of the congressman's head. The round tore through the right eye socket, taking with it chunks of bone, brain, and flesh. The momentum of the impact propelled Koslowski forward and pinned him against the side of the bed, leaving his body bent backward and his legs and arms twitching. The assassin had already chambered another round and was maneuvering the crosshairs back into position. The next shot struck Koslowski at the base of his skull and immediately severed all neural communication between the brain and the rest of his body.

6:15 A.M., FRIDAY

Across the Potomac River, in McLean, Virginia, the other group sat and waited for their next target. They were parked across the street from Pimmit Bend Park, facing north on Balentrane Lane, which dead-ended into the park. The driver listened to the police scanner and chewed a piece of gum. Another man was in the back of the van looking out the rear windows at the park. From where they were positioned, he could see the formerly blond assassin leaning against a tree next to the jogging path. He was stretching his legs as he waited, trying to make himself look like just another runner. Several joggers and walkers had already passed by and had taken notice of what they thought was a black man getting ready to exercise in their lily-white park. As he let go of his right leg, the assassin grabbed his left leg and pulled it up behind him. He placed his left hand against a tree for balance and looked at his watch. Their next target was due any minute.

The target was Senator Robert Downs, the chairman of the Senate Banking Committee and the reigning "prince of pork" in the United States Senate. He lived less than three blocks away and walked his collie religiously every morning, between 6:00 and 6:20 A.M. It was almost a quarter after, and he was due any minute. As the assassin looked up from the tree, he saw the familiar brown English driving cap of Downs bobbing up and down just on the other side of the slight rise in the path. He was fifty yards away, walking at his usual, leisurely pace. When Downs reached the crest of the small hill, the assassin noticed a woman in a brightly colored tennis warm-up about thirty yards behind the senator. She was walking at a fast pace, flailing her arms and swinging her hips from side to side. As they approached his position, the woman was almost ready to pass the senator. The assassin noticed she was wearing a Walkman, and he breathed a slight sigh of relief. No innocent people were to die.

When Downs was about twenty yards away, the assassin turned his back to his target, leaned against the tree, pulled his right leg up, and started to stretch again. He could hear the dog panting and the nails of his paws as they struck the black asphalt path. He let go of his right leg and grabbed his left. In a low whisper he spoke into his mike, "How do I look, over?"

The man sitting in the back of the van looked to his right and left and then responded, "The only two people in sight are our target and the woman coming up behind him, over."

"That's a roger, over." The assassin turned his head to the right and looked over his shoulder. Downs was within striking distance and the woman was right on his heels. The assassin looked down at the base of the tree and concentrated on his peripheral vision. By the time the two walkers reached the tree, the woman had passed Downs and was steadily increasing the distance between herself and the senator.

The assassin stepped out onto the path and fell into line behind Downs. After about three strides his left hand slid underneath his baggy sweats and grabbed the waistband of his running tights. His right hand reached in and grabbed the handle of the 9mm Beretta. Picking up the pace, he closed in on the senator. Pulling the gun out, he extended his arm and placed the tip of the silencer inches from the back of his target's head. Two quick rounds were fired into the base of the skull, and Downs stumbled forward, landing face first on the pavement. The assassin turned and sprinted across the park to the waiting van. The female walker continued her trek without missing a stride as the old collie stood over her dying master and sniffed at the pool of blood that was forming next to his head.

CHAPTER 6

THE sun had risen in the fall morning sky and was fighting to stay out as the wind picked up and the clouds rolled in. A steady stream of gold and red leaves rustled past the black dress shoes of FBI special agent Skip McMahon. McMahon was the special agent in charge of the FBI's East Coast Quick Response Team. The Quick Response Team, or QRT as it was referred to within the Bureau, was composed of an elite group of agents. Their mission was straightforward: to arrive at the crime scene of a terrorist attack and start the immediate collection of evidence and pursuit of the perpetrators while the trail was still warm. The unit had planes, helicopters, and mobile crime labs on twenty-four-hour standby and could be at a crime scene anywhere from Chicago to Miami to New York within hours.

McMahon rested his large body against a police car and held a cup of coffee under his nose. An old football injury to his knee was giving him more trouble than usual this morning. He told himself it was the cold, damp morning air and not his age. The veteran agent watched without emotion as a black body bag containing Senator Fitzgerald was loaded into the back of an FBI van. This was the third crime scene he'd been to this morning, and the quiet intensity of the murders was setting in. It was a foregone conclusion that the murders were linked. They wouldn't tell the press that, but it didn't take a genius to figure out they had to be connected. He looked down at both ends of the street and shook his head at the crowd of media and curious onlookers who were gathered on the other side of the police barricades. Clasping the cup of coffee with both hands, he closed his eyes and blocked out the surrounding commotion. He tried to imagine exactly how Fitzgerald had been murdered.

McMahon was a strong believer in visualization. In an inexplicable way, he thought that a killer left an aura at the scene of a crime. It was not unusual for McMahon to go back to the places where people had been murdered months, even years, after the crimes had been committed and sit for hours playing scenario after scenario through his head, trying to gain the slightest insight into the mind of the murderer.

Putting himself in the shoes of the killer, he thought about the different ways Fitzgerald could have been murdered. After a while he started to look for similarities in the way Koslowski, Downs, and Fitzgerald had been killed. He was making a mental checklist of the questions that needed to be answered: How many killers? Why were they killed? Why these three politicians? Who would have the motive? McMahon was laying the foundation for his investigation. Everything he was thinking would be transferred onto a blackboard back in the tactical situation room for his team to review. His concentration was broken by a familiar voice calling his name. McMahon looked up and saw his boss, Brian Roach, walking toward him with his always present bodyguards.

"Skip, anything new to report?" Roach had been with the Bureau for twenty-six years and had served as its director for the last four. He had been a good agent in his day, but that was all history now. Running the FBI meant forgetting almost everything he'd learned about law enforcement and concentrating on politics and administration.

McMahon pushed himself away from the squad and stepped toward Roach. "The forensic teams are going over the crime scenes, and the pathologists should be starting the autopsies within the hour." McMahon extended his right hand.

Roach shook it and grabbed the larger McMahon by the arm, walking him several steps toward the sidewalk. Roach's bodyguards fanned out in a circle.

"It's all set. You're in charge of the investigation. There are going to be some people who aren't going to be too happy about that, but I don't care. The fact is you're the best investigative agent we've got, and I need someone I can trust running this thing." Roach put one hand in his pocket and straightened his tie with the other. "Skip, the pressure to solve this mess is going to be incredible. It's going to come from every direction, and most of it's going to be political. I'll do my best to screen you from it, but I'm not going to be able to block it all."

McMahon shrugged his shoulders. "Nothing we're not used to, right?"

"Yeah, but this is gonna be different. My head hurts when I think about all the political pressure that's going to be put on us to solve this thing. The other reason why I'm putting you in charge is because I know how much you hate dealing with the press and politicians. We can't have any leaks. Make sure your people know, their careers are over if they breathe a word to anyone outside the unit about the investigation."

"Understood."

Roach looked at his watch. "I need you to come to the White House with me and give a quick briefing. It's driving the president nuts that the only information he's getting is from the TV." Roach noticed the frown on McMahon's face and said, "All I need you to do is give them the basics on what you've found at the three crime scenes. Come on, let's go." Roach nodded toward his limo and they walked away from the crime scene with the bodyguards in tow.

McMahon and Roach had known each other for a long time. The two men had met when McMahon was a second-year agent and Roach was fresh out of the FBI's Academy. Over the last twenty-some years, they'd become good friends. Roach, from the start, wanted to rise to the top of the Bureau, and McMahon never wanted to be anything more than an agent. McMahon's lack of ambition was twofold. First and foremost, he was a realist. He knew himself well and understood that he would never be able to bury his pride and brownnose his way to the upper levels. The director had to be able to play the Washington game, something the elite investigator was not well suited for. McMahon didn't beat around the bush; if he thought you were wrong, he told you. It didn't matter who you were. This, of course, had not always gone over well. There'd been several politicians and at least one former director who had wanted his career with the FBI terminated.

Luckily for McMahon, he was very good at what he did. This was the second reason for his lack of ambition. He loved his job. Throughout the Bureau, McMahon was recognized as the best homicide investigator. He was not one to follow FBI procedure like a robot. Other agents from around the country consulted with him on their investigations. He had his own unique way of doing things. During his time at the Bureau he had watched some great investigators waste away after being promoted into cushy administrative jobs. Not Skip McMahon. He had told Roach four years earlier, when his friend became director, "The day you pull me out of the field is the day I retire."

Before climbing into the director's limo, McMahon yelled to Kathy Jennings, one of the agents who worked under his command. Jennings was talking to a group of agents, all of whom were wearing their standard crime-scene blue FBI windbreakers. She put her conversation on hold and approached her mentor. Her long auburn hair was pulled back into a tight ponytail. She greeted the director professionally and then turned to McMahon.

McMahon took a deep breath, told Jennings that he'd be back as soon as possible, and then started to rattle off a list of things for the young agent to check on. "Make sure every level of law enforcement within three hundred miles is notified to be on the lookout for multiple males traveling in generic American-model cars." McMahon began sticking the forefinger of his right hand into the palm of his left hand as he went down his list. "Remind them to arrest anyone who they think is the slightest bit suspicious and to hold them until one of our people arrives. Make sure they understand that last part clearly, and make sure the suspect profiles are faxed to all of their officers. When you're done with that, find out how the teams are doing with the surveillance tapes at Dulles and National, and if anything comes up, call me immediately."

Jennings nodded and watched her boss slip into the backseat of the long dark car.

As they drove down the street, McMahon filled Roach in on the specifics of Fitzgerald's death. The director had already been briefed via phone on the murders of Koslowski and Downs. The drive from Georgetown to the White House took less than ten minutes. As they pulled into the White House compound, Roach asked, "What are the chances we'll catch these guys before they get away?"

"We have checkpoints set up on all the roads heading out of town, every airport within three hundred miles is being watched, and the Navy and the Coast Guard are tracking every vessel that's headed out to sea."

"So, what are our chances?"

McMahon frowned and said, "My gut tells me we're wasting our time. Whoever did this was good . . . really good. They either left the country immediately or they're holing up somewhere waiting until things cool down."

"You're probably right. But we have to be really careful on this one. Otherwise, I'll be sitting in front of a joint committee next year getting second-guessed by a bunch of old men who want to show their voters back home that they know more than the director of the FBI." Roach paused for a moment. "Besides, don't forget those pros that set off the bomb in the World Trade Center. Who would have thought they would have been dumb enough to try and get the deposit back on that van? These criminals aren't always as smart as we think they are."

"Brian, it doesn't take a great criminal mind to park a van loaded with explosives in the underground parking garage of the World Trade Center. But there aren't many organizations out there who can kill three different people, in three different locations, in one evening, and leave no traces. It's not like blowing up a pipe bomb at the Olympics. Any idiot can leave a bomb in a park. It's far more complicated to get up close and personal when killing someone."

Roach pondered McMahon's comments as the limousine came to a stop. The director's bodyguards opened the doors, and Roach said, "Before we go in, let me warn you about a couple of things. Everyone will understand that you haven't had a lot of time to prepare for this briefing, so keep it simple and try not to editorialize too much. The president won't say a lot, but watch out for Garret."

"Don't worry, I won't embarrass you . . . at least not intentionally." McMahon smiled.

"One other thing. Don't stick your neck out too far. If they ask you for an opinion, and they will, just tell them it's too early to tell."

McMahon gave his boss another nod. "Brian, I *have* done this before."

"I know, Skip, but you haven't dealt with this administration before." Roach lowered his voice to a whisper. "Just trust me, and watch what you say."

The director stepped out of the car first. Roach's bodyguards walked them to the door and into a small foyer. A Secret Service agent approached and escorted them to the Cabinet Room. It was not the first time McMahon had been to the White House, but it was the first time he'd been in the Cabinet Room. His other meetings had taken place in either the Oval Office or the Situation Room in the basement.

As McMahon and Director Roach were getting ready to settle into their chairs, the president, Garret, and National Security Adviser Mike Nance entered the room with Garret in the lead. Garret clapped his hands together loudly. "Come on, gentlemen, let's get this meeting started."

The president took his seat in the middle of the long table. Garret sat immediately to his right and Nance to his left. Sitting across from the president were Skip McMahon, FBI director Roach, CIA director Thomas Stansfield, and the CIA's top terrorism expert, Dr. Irene Kennedy.

Roach and Stansfield introduced their subordinates, and then Garret started the meeting. "Well, Director Roach, I sure hope you have some answers for us."

Roach looked to the president and said, "Mr. President, with the help of the congressional switchboard and several local police departments, we've secured the whereabouts of the remaining five hundred and thirty-two senators and congressmen. All of the Supreme Court justices, cabinet members, and Joint Chiefs of Staff have also been accounted for. Right now it looks like the only individuals they were after were Senator Fitzgerald, Senator Downs, and Congressman Koslowski.

"I have a meeting scheduled for one P.M. with Director Tracy of the Secret Service to discuss the resources we have available to provide protection for the remaining members of the House and Senate. I have already dispatched agents to protect the most senior members of both parties. Until we know more about what is going on, I think we should play it safe." Roach turned to Nance. "Mike, before I leave, I would like a minute of your time to discuss what resources we may be able to borrow from the military, such as MPs or Marines that are trained for embassy duty." Nance nodded and

Roach continued, "I'm going to have Special Agent McMahon take over from here and fill you in on the specifics of what happened late yesterday evening and early this morning. When he's finished, I will bring you up to speed on the interdiction measures we're taking. Special Agent McMahon has been to all three crime scenes this morning." Roach turned to McMahon and nodded.

McMahon cleared his throat and said, "Let me start by saying that this investigation is only a few hours old, so we don't have a lot of specifics." McMahon looked from one end of the table to the other as he spoke. "The first of the three to be killed, and the last to be found, was Senator Fitzgerald. Fitzgerald's limousine driver—"

Garret interrupted, "Don't you have a brief prepared, so we can follow?"

McMahon looked at Roach, giving him a chance to respond, knowing his boss's reply would be more diplomatic than his own. Roach turned to the president, intentionally bypassing Garret. "Sir, we haven't had time to prepare a report. We will have one on your desk by two this afternoon."

"That's fine. Please continue," the president responded.

Garret shook his head sideways and wrote something down on his yellow notepad.

McMahon started again. "As I was saying, Fitzgerald's limousine driver reports dropping the senator off at his house in Kalorama Heights just after midnight. Our preliminary guess on Fitzgerald's time of death is sometime between midnight and one-thirty A.M. The cause of death appears to be a broken neck. We'll know more after the autopsy is completed." McMahon paused for a second. "The back door of Fitzgerald's house shows signs of being picked, and his security system was defeated on-site. Fitzgerald's body was found shoved into a closet in the basement. Our best guess right now is that the perpetrator, or perpetrators, were waiting inside the house when Fitzgerald got home, killed him, and then moved the body to the basement." In a bland tone McMahon added, "We are questioning the neighbors to see if they saw anything last night, and a forensics team is going over the house checking for evidence."

"Agent McMahon, you sound as if you don't expect to find anything," interrupted Garret again.

McMahon looked at Garret hard. "Whoever killed these men is very good. It is highly unlikely that they left any useful evidence behind." He continued to stare at Garret without saying anything until the president's chief of staff looked away.

"Congressman Koslowski was the next one to die. From what we know so far, Koslowski got out of bed around six A.M. and was shot in the back of the head twice. The shots were fired from a high-powered rifle and were taken from the house across the street. The house belongs to Harold Burmiester, a wealthy, retired banker. When we entered the house this morning, we found that the phone line had been cut and the back door was missing a pane of glass. Burmiester's German shepherd was unconscious and, we presume, drugged. Burmiester was found tied up in a bedroom on the second floor. The screen had been removed on the window directly across from Koslowski's bedroom, and there were powder burns found on the windowsill.

"After talking to Burmiester, we've pieced together the following details: Just before eleven P.M. last night, Burmiester let his dog out. At this point, we think the dog was probably drugged. Burmiester went to bed around midnight in the bedroom where the shots were fired from. Sometime between twelve-thirty A.M. and five-thirty A.M. the perpetrator or perpetrators broke into the house, rendered Burmiester unconscious, and moved him to a different bedroom. They waited, and when Koslowski opened the doors, they took their shot. We're having some blood tests done on Burmiester and his dog, and we should know whether or not they were drugged by early afternoon. The crime boys are going over both houses and the neighbors are being questioned."

"Where was Koslowski's wife during all of this?" asked Garret sarcastically.

"Mrs. Koslowski sleeps in another room." McMahon again attempted to ignore Garret's irritating manner.

The coolly detached Mike Nance was observing McMahon. Nance, a graduate of West Point and a former director of the National Security Agency, usually stayed quiet in meetings. He preferred to sit back and take everything in. Unlike Garret, he believed a person could learn more by watching and listening than by asking questions.

With his eyes still focused on his notepad, Garret shouted out another question. "Has anyone reported hearing shots?"

"No, the distance of the shot was only about one hundred feet. Short enough that a silencer could be used without affecting the accuracy of the shot." McMahon continued to speak without giving Garret a chance to ask more questions. "As I'm sure everyone has heard by now, Robert Downs was killed in a park by his house, over in McLean. Two nine-millimeter rounds were fired into the back of his head at point-blank range. We have a description of a possible suspect from a woman who walks in the park every morning. She says that she passed Downs on the walking path this morning at approximately the spot where his body was found. She, along with several other people, have reported seeing a black man dressed in sweats, standing by a tree about twenty yards from where Downs was killed. None of these people say they've seen the person in the park before. Their guess is that he was around thirty years old. Our agents are still interviewing these people, trying to get as much information as possible. I apologize, gentlemen, for the lack of details, but, as I said earlier, this investigation is only a few hours old."

"Thank you, Mr. McMahon," said the president. "I fully understand that we are still in the early stages of this investigation, but nonetheless, I would like to hear some opinions. Does anyone have any idea why these three men were killed, and by whom?"

As usual, Garret was the first, and in this situation the least qualified, to respond. "Until we know more, I think it's a pretty safe bet that it's a terrorist group. One that's probably not so happy about the peace that's spreading in the Middle East, or one of those wacky militia groups from out West."

The president turned to the director of the FBI. "Brian, what are your thoughts?"

"Sir, it's too early to give an informed answer. There just isn't enough data to make an intelligent assumption. Almost anything could be possible. It could be anyone."

The president looked to McMahon and asked, "Mr. McMahon, I know we don't have all the facts, but please speak your mind." The president stared at McMahon and waited for a response.

"Well, sir, we have three important politicians murdered at three different locations within a five-hour period. Whoever pulled off this operation had to have been planning it for a long time. They took the time to study their targets and carefully picked when and how to kill each one. They were probably well financed and had access to some very talented killers. Those killers could be terrorists, ex-military commandos, or hired assassins. Given the information we have right now, your guess is as good as mine."

The president nodded and looked at his chief of staff.

Garret took the cue and said, "Gentlemen, the president needs to address the nation and try to explain what's going on. Now is not the time to be shy with your opinions." There was a long silence, and then Garret looked to the head of the CIA. "Director Stansfield, what's your take on what happened?"

"I would caution against drawing any conclusions until Special Agent McMahon and his people have had time to investigate." Stansfield's response was again followed by an uncomfortable silence. Both Director Stansfield and Director Roach had seen how Garret and President Stevens liked to operate, and neither felt the need to commit to anything with so many questions still unanswered. Roach and Stansfield had both started at the very bottom of their respective agencies, and over the years, they'd seen presidents come and go, and with them, their political appointees who ran the CIA and FBI. Some of these directors were more loyal to the man who had appointed them than to the agency they were supposed to be running. Not Roach and Stansfield: to them the FBI and CIA came first. Political expediency and posturing were things they liked to avoid at all costs. Political solutions were often good for the short term, and for the people making them, but they were more often than not disastrous in the long run.

The president sat back in his chair and quietly cursed himself for not replacing Roach and Stansfield when he had taken over the White House. Garret had wanted both men replaced, and Stevens was sure he would be reminded of this as soon as the meeting was over. If we hadn't had such a hard time getting cabinet members confirmed, Stevens thought to himself, none of this would be a problem.

During the first six months of the Stevens administration, four consecutive cabinet nominees had been shot down. Three had had to bow out after intense scrutiny by the press revealed some minor misdoings in their past, and the fourth made it to an actual committee vote but was embarrassingly rejected. By the time the cabinet was filled, the administration had expended so much political clout and had received such a grilling from the press that they decided rather than risking another potentially embarrassing confirmation hearing, they would be better off leaving Stansfield in charge of the CIA until a more opportune time arose. The president was coming to the realization that he had waited too long.

Stevens looked at Kennedy, the CIA's terrorism expert. "Dr. Kennedy, what is your opinion?"

Kennedy had the highest IQ in the room by a significant margin. The thirty-eight-year-old mother of one had a Ph.D. in Arabic studies and a master's degree in military history. The doctor leaned forward and took her glasses off. Her sandy brown hair was pulled back in a ponytail, and she was wearing one of her trademark pantsuits. She placed her arms on the table and started to speak in a confident tone. "I would have to concur with Special Agent McMahon. The men who conducted this operation are either terrorists, hired assassins, or military commandos. My assumption is that it was the latter of the three."

Garret blurted out, "What makes you so sure about that?"

"I think they were military commandos because Mr. Burmiester is still alive."

Garret's face squeezed into an irritated frown. "Mr. Who?"

"Mr. Burmiester, the man who lives across the street from Congressman Koslowski. If the people who ran this operation were terrorists, Mr. Burmiester would be dead. Terrorists do not go to the effort to anesthetize people who are in their way. They kill them. If terrorists did this, Mr. Burmiester would be dead as well as the woman who was walking in the park. These murders were committed by military-trained commandos.

"Terrorist and military commandos go through very complex training, and on the surface most of it is similar, such as hand-to-hand combat, demolition training, firearms training, et cetera. However, they are trained very differently in objective and operational planning. Terrorists do not care about human life. They operate by a different set of rules. Terrorists are trained to take out their target in a way that is usually very violent. The more violent the better. When they kill, they try to strike terror into the minds of the public. Hence the label *terrorist*. They use car bombs or they machine-gun people down with absolutely no concern for innocent lives.

"Commandos and assassins, who are almost always ex-commandos, are trained to kill only whom they need to, and to do it as quietly and quickly as possible. Commandos operate within certain moral parameters. There have been occasions, during times of war or national emergency, when those parameters were bent, and military commandos have killed an innocent bystander. This, however, is the exception to the rule, whereas with terrorists, killing innocent bystanders is the operational norm.

"When we look at conducting an operation like this, we choose our targets and then decide what is the best way to kill the least amount of people and get our assets out safely."

Garret was irritated by Kennedy's confident tone. "You seem awfully sure of yourself, Dr. Kennedy. Are you ruling out the possibility that these murders were committed by a terrorist group?"

"I do not think they were committed by a fundamentalist terrorist group. A group that, as you said earlier, would be unhappy with the peace that is being made in the Middle East. As far as the murders being committed by a group of domestic terrorists, such as one of your antigovernment, Aryan Nation types . . . I highly doubt they would have the trained personnel it would take to pull something like this off. Besides, why would they kill someone like Senator Downs? He's pro-NRA and pro-military. He's one of the few politicians those militia members like."

Garret gestured toward Kennedy. "Well, I'm glad to know that after hearing a ten-minute briefing, you've solved the case for us." Garret chuckled mockingly at Kennedy. "How can you say that so emphatically, with such little information?"

McMahon stared at Garret and thought to himself, God, this guy's an ass. Director Roach saw the look on McMahon's face and placed his hand on his friend's arm. McMahon pulled away and leaned back in his chair, continuing to stare at Garret.

Kennedy was used to men challenging her intellect and continued to defend her opinion in a professional tone. "It is my job to know how these groups kill, Mr. Garret. If a group, such as Abu Nidal, had committed these murders, they would have simply gone down to one of the more popular dining spots in town, planted a bomb, and exploded it during lunch yesterday. They would have easily killed a dozen senators and congressmen, and probably a few cabinet members."

"Why couldn't it have been a domestic right-wing paramilitary group?"

"It's possible, but as I said earlier, I don't think those groups have the resources to conduct an operation like this."

In a loud voice Garret half shouted, "If you're so sure that it wasn't terrorists, then who did it?"

McMahon leaned forward in his chair and placed both fore-arms on the table. At six foot three, 240 pounds, he looked like a bear ready to attack. Before Roach could react, McMahon was speaking. "Mr Garret, we are all professionals here. There is no rea-son to get emotional and raise our voices. You asked for our opin-ions and Dr. Kennedy has respectfully done so. She has given us some very intelligent insight into a case where it is greatly needed. She is not trying to tell us exactly who did it, she is merely helping us narrow our search." McMahon continued to stare at Garret as the chief of staff flushed angrily.

Mike Nance could not believe what he was witnessing. He had seen Stu Garret act like this in countless meetings during the last three years. It was a rarity to see anyone put him in his place, let alone an underling from the FBI. The tension in the room contin-ued to build as McMahon refused to back down. Director Roach was sitting back in his chair, hand over brow, dreading what might happen next.

The president ended the confrontation. "Everybody calm down. . . . We are all under a lot of pressure, and I'm sure it's only going to get worse. Let's relax and discuss Dr. Kennedy's theory."

While the meeting continued, Bridgett Ryan sat in her cubicle across town at NBC's Washington bureau and tried to look busy. Bridgett was a senior journalism major at Catholic University and was in the middle of a one-year internship with NBC. Her boss was Mark Stein, the network's D.C. bureau chief.

Bridgett's work schedule varied depending on her daily class load. This morning she had rolled out of bed at 9 A.M., found out about the murders, and instead of going to class, went straight to the studio. She'd been there for over an hour and a half and had done little more than pour coffee and scribble notes for Stein. She was sitting at her little desk outside of Stein's office when the mailman came by and dropped a bundle of letters on her desk.

One of her daily tasks was to open and sort her boss's mail. She pulled the rubber band off the stack and grabbed a large manila envelope from the bottom. It was addressed to Stein but contained no return address. She grabbed her letter opener, sliced through the top of the envelope, and pulled out the sheets of paper. After reading the first paragraph, her heart began to race. She started to read again from the top, and this time her hands began to tremble. She took a deep breath and read on. After finishing, she jumped up and threw open the door to Stein's office. Ryan yelled his name and held the sheets of paper up in the air. "Mark!"

Stein, who was on the phone, looked up and waved her away. He swiveled in his chair and turned his back to her. He was talking to his boss in New York. "Carol, I need more video crews, damn it! I need more reporters. How in the hell do you expect me to get all this footage for you? It's a goddamned zoo down here. We're falling all over each other trying to get the story. It's too big, we need more people!" Bridgett walked around his desk and waved the envelope in his face. Stein pulled the phone away from his head and placed his free hand over the receiver. "Bridgett, I'm busy! Not now!" Stein started to bring the phone back to his head, but Ryan was not to be deterred.

"Mark, this is really important!" She thrust the papers and envelope forward. "We just got this in the mail. It's addressed to you and I think it's from the terrorists!"

Stein grabbed the sheets of paper and started reading quickly. His boss could be heard in the background asking what in the hell was going on. When Stein was finished, he yelled into the receiver, "Carol, go to your fax, this is big!"

• • •

Garret had calmed down and was noticeably quieter. McMahon and Kennedy were discussing the latter's theory when the door to the Cabinet Room opened and Jack Warch entered. He was the special agent in charge of the president's Secret Service detail. "Excuse me, gentlemen, NBC is announcing that they have a letter from a group claiming responsibility for the murders."

Warch proceeded to the wall behind the president and opened a large cabinet containing a bank of six television sets. He turned on the four to the left, which were pretuned to the major networks and CNN. The top right TV was carrying the NBC signal. He turned up the volume and stepped away. The familiar face of George Blake, the NBC news anchor, appeared on the screen.

"I would like to caution you one more time that this letter is from a group that is claiming responsibility for the murders of Senator Fitzgerald, Senator Downs, and Congressman Koslowski. We have no proof that they are actually the group that committed the murders. The letter was received by mail at our Washington, D.C., studio just moments ago. It states the following." Blake looked down and read from the fax paper:

"'In 1776 the founders of the United States of America sent a Declaration of Independence to the King of England. In that Declaration, Thomas Jefferson wrote "that whenever any Form of Government becomes destructive . . . it is the Right of the People to alter or to abolish it, and to institute new Government." We are invoking this right to rise up and alter the course of our government. You have had your chance to correct America's course, and you have failed.

"'Senator Fitzgerald, Congressman Koslowski, and Senator Downs were killed as a warning to the president and the remaining members of the House and Senate. Your days of deficit spending and partisan politics are over. During the last twenty-five years, you have spent money we do not have on federal programs we do not need. Every year you have promised the American people that your number one priority is to cut spending and balance the budget. Despite these promises the federal budget has continued to grow.

"'You have had the time and the opportunity to bring spending under control and you have done nothing. You have shown that your own personal greed and the goals of your political parties are more important to you than the economic security and future of America. As a result of your selfish and incompetent leadership, we are now burdened with a national debt that is more than five trillion dollars. A national debt that is growing at a rate of more than a billion dollars a day and is projected to reach ten trillion dollars by the end of the century. If the national debt is not confronted, it will plunge our country into economic chaos.

"'The time to act is now. We are directing the president to withdraw his budget that is before the House, and with the help of the Office of Management and Budget and the General Accounting Office, to construct a balanced budget using zero-based budgeting. This budget will contain no new or raised taxes and will cut all unneeded federal programs. It will introduce means testing to control the growth of Social Security and Medicare and will adopt the military cuts as proposed by the Joint Chiefs without political interference. After this budget is passed, the president will submit a national crime bill that will focus on keeping violent criminals off the streets and in jail. The president, the House, and the Senate shall also implement a two percent national sales tax to be used solely for the reduction of the national debt.

"'If you are incapable of restoring the limited form of government that the framers of the Constitution intended, quit and go home. We will be watching your actions closely. This is the only warning we will give. If you do not respond to these demands, you will be killed. None of you are out of our reach—not even the president.'"

CHAPTER 7

A S the news anchor spoke the words "None of you are out of our reach, not even the president," all eyes in the room turned from the TV to President Stevens . . . all eyes except those of Special Agent McMahon. McMahon had turned away from the group and was clutching his digital phone, waiting for someone to answer on the other end.

"Special Agent Jennings."

"Kathy, this is Skip. Get someone down to NBC's studio on the double. Call ahead and tell them we're coming to seize that letter as evidence, and until we get there, I don't want anyone touching it. I'm sure half their damn newsroom has already put their finger-prints all over it."

"I've already got Phillips and Reynolds on their way over, and Troy is on the phone trying to get ahold of whoever is in charge."

"Good." McMahon paused for a second. "Listen, let's gamble on the chance that they sent more than one of these. Call the post office and find out when the other networks and major papers get their mail delivered. Send some people over to CBS, ABC, and CNN. Hopefully we can get our hands on one of these before it's been opened."

"Anything else?"

"No, call me if you find anything out. I'm on my way back to the office." McMahon hit the end button on the phone, placed it in his pocket, and spun back around.

"What was that all about?" asked the president.

"Just trying to see if we can get ahold of one of these letters before it has a dozen different sets of fingerprints on it."

"Can we take this seriously? I mean, isn't it quite possible that someone sent this trying to take responsibility for the murders even though they didn't commit them? Doesn't that type of thing happen all the time in these cases?" The president was visibly shaken by the letter and more precisely the mention of his office.

"Yes, sir, it's quite common to get letters and phone calls from groups who did not perpetrate the crime, but not this early. It usually starts days or weeks later. These murders were committed less than eight hours ago."

Garret, trying to reassert himself after being embarrassed by McMahon earlier, jumped to his boss's side. "That doesn't mean that someone couldn't have written that letter and dropped it off this morning, after hearing about the killings. I mean, Mr. Mc-Mahon, we have to keep our minds open about this."

McMahon desperately wanted to get up and leave. He needed to be back at the Hoover Building running this investigation. "Mr. Garret, anything is possible at this point." McMahon turned to the president to ask permission to leave, but before he could do so, Garret blurted out another question.

"How do we know it's not meant to confuse us? Maybe someone killed them for a different reason, like wanting to scuttle the president's budget or wanting to damage this presidency. Maybe they sent this letter to make us look in the wrong places."

McMahon glared at Garret for a brief moment and told himself to keep his temper in check. "Mr. Garret, we know very little so far. That is why we need to investigate. I will take all of your theories under advisement and keep an open mind." McMahon turned from Garret to the president. "Sir, if you don't mind, I really need to be out in the field coordinating this investigation."

"Why . . . yes . . . of course."

McMahon leaned over, whispered in Roach's ear, then rose and left the room.

The small conference room in Congressman O'Rourke's office contained the same furniture it had when O'Rourke had taken over the previous year. O'Rourke saw no sense in following the age-old Washington tradition of getting rid of perfectly good furniture and buying new stuff at the taxpayers' expense. O'Rourke, his brother Tim, Susan, and several staffers were sitting around the color TV watching George Blake continue to read the letter sent by the group claiming responsibility for the murders of Koslowski, Fitzgerald, and Downs.

O'Rourke sat without movement or emotion, staring at the TV, while the others shouted comments back and forth. His hands were pressed together in front of his face, forming a triangle. After Blake read the letter for the fourth time, Nick Swenson, one of O'Rourke's young staffers, turned to his boss. "Well, Michael, you don't have to worry about them killing you. It sounds like they're right up your alley."

O'Rourke glanced over at the blond-haired Swenson with a neutral expression. Inside, however, O'Rourke was far from emotionless.

Tim O'Rourke looked at his brother from across the table. "Michael, what do you think about all of this?"

O'Rourke slowly brought his hands down. "I don't think our country will miss the likes of Fitzgerald, Downs, and Koslowski."

Tim frowned and said, "Michael, that may well be true, but please don't say that in public. They were senators and congressmen, and no matter what you think of their politics, you can't go around saying they deserved to die."

"I didn't say they deserved to die. I only said they won't be missed."

"The press won't bother to make that distinction. They'll put on the front page of every newspaper, 'Congressman O'Rourke Says Koslowski, Downs, and Fitzgerald Deserved to Die!'" Tim held his hand up and punctuated every word.

"I don't care what the press does."

"I know you don't care what they do, Michael, but there are other people in this office who care about their careers and their future in politics."

Michael leaned in a little closer to his brother and in a lower voice said, "I'm not entirely comfortable with assassins running around our capital, but if it takes killing a couple of corrupt dinosaurs like Koslowski, Fitzgerald, and Downs to bring about some change, I'm all for it."

Tim O'Rourke sat back and frowned at his older brother. The source of Michael's severe dislike for the political hierarchy of Washington was deeply rooted. Ten years earlier, when Michael was a senior at the University of Minnesota, his life couldn't have been better. He was captain of the nationally ranked hockey team, he had a great group of friends, a wonderful girlfriend, and he was on schedule to complete his history major. There wasn't a gray cloud in Michael O'Rourke's life.

Michael was about to learn, not for the first time, just how quickly life could change. On a cold winter night, after one of his hockey games, his parents loaded two of Michael's three brothers and his little sister into the family Suburban and started their two-hour drive back to the O'Rourkes' hometown of Grand Rapids in northern Minnesota. About forty minutes from Grand Rapids, the large Suburban was hit head-on by a drunk driver who couldn't keep his car on the other side of the yellow line. Michael's sister, Katie, and his brothers Tommy and little Seamus survived the accident, but his parents didn't. The loving parents of five children were dead—killed by a thirty-four-year-old man with six previous drunk-driving convictions.

The deaths of his parents shattered O'Rourke's life. After graduating in the spring he joined the Marine Corps as his father and grandfather had done before him. After returning from the Gulf, he blew his knee out on a low-altitude nighttime training jump with his recon platoon. Several of the lines on his main chute fouled, and with no time to pop the backup, O'Rourke thudded to the ground at twice the normal speed. The same knee he had injured in college buckled under the impact and crunched like an aluminum can. The young lieutenant underwent a complete reconstruction of his knee, and his career as a United States Marine was effectively ended. O'Rourke left the service and joined Senator Olson's staff in Washington. Senator Erik Olson was a close friend of Michael's deceased parents. Michael looked at Washington through idealistic eyes and saw the new job as an opportunity to do something that would make a difference. Over the next five years Michael became one of the senator's most effective aides. He worked hard and fought not to fall into the trap of Washington apathy, but as time progressed, the behind-the-back dealings of the nation's power brokers wore him down. Washington politics was a disgusting game that only a certain breed could play. Anyone with honor and integrity was worn down and spit out by the political machine of party politics.

Right about the time Michael was ready to quit and head back to Minnesota the congressional seat in his home district opened. Senator Olson encouraged him to run, telling him if the system really bothered him so much, he should try to do something about it. Michael took on the challenge, and with the backing of his grandfather and Senator Olson, the young O'Rourke won the barely contested seat easily.

That winter, before Michael had taken office, tragedy struck again. The death of another person close to him had forced O'Rourke to look at Washington in a different light, and any joy he

felt over his recent victory vanished. His two-year term as a freshman congressman became a two-year sentence in a town he de-
spised more and more every day.

The phone started to ring, and Susan got up to get it. A moment
later she poked her head back in the room. "Michael, your grandfather is on line one."

"I'll take it in my office." Michael walked back to his office and
grabbed the phone. "Hello, Seamus."

Seamus O'Rourke was the president and sole owner of the
O'Rourke Timber Company. Seamus's father had started the company as a small lumberyard in 1918. When Seamus returned from
fighting in World War II, he took over the company and turned the
small mill into one of the largest timber companies in the Midwest.

Seamus was calling from the deck of the O'Rourkes' home in
Grand Rapids. It was located on Lake Pokegama, a beautiful island-
dotted lake almost ten miles long. The home was a gorgeous, modern log cabin set on the tip of a point that overlooked the largest
bay on the lake. The seventy-two-year-old grandfather clutched the
phone and took in the panoramic view of the sky blue lake and the
bright fall colors. "Is everything all right, Michael?"

"Yes, everything's fine."

Seamus leaned on the railing of the deck. Grandpa O'Rourke
didn't look a day over sixty. He walked three miles every morning with his band of dogs, which included two Labs, a husky, and
several others of mixed origin. The early-morning walks with his
dogs weren't the only thing that kept him looking young. Ten years
earlier, the unfortunate death of his son and daughter-in-law had
turned him into the de facto father of a twelve-year-old girl, two
sixteen-year-old twin boys, and Michael and Tim, who were in college at the time.

Seamus took a drink of coffee and asked, "What do you think
of the assassinations?"

Michael tapped a pencil on his desk calendar while he struggled to phrase his answer properly. "I'm torn. Part of me thinks it's exactly what we need, and part of me is very uneasy about it."

"I think that's understandable," replied Seamus in his deep voice. "What did you think of the men that were killed?"

"I don't think the founders of democracy would be sad to see them relinquish their seats of power."

Seamus laughed slightly. "That's for certain."

Michael spun his chair around and looked out the window. He could see the Washington Monument jutting upward in the distance. "Seamus," Michael said uncomfortably. "There is something I need to talk to you about. Are you still planning on coming to town this weekend?"

"Yes." Seamus detected something. "What's wrong?"

"I'm not sure. It might have something to do with what happened last night." Michael hesitated briefly. "I think it would be best if we talked about it in person."

Seamus got the point instantly. In Washington it was best to assume that anything said over the phone was potentially being recorded by God only knew whom. "Can you give me a hint as to what it's about?"

Michael rocked back and forth in his chair. "It involves a mutual friend of ours."

Back in Minnesota Seamus squinted at a fishing boat that was cutting across the entrance to the bay. The old man knew immediately whom Michael was talking about. "I see. Keep it under your hat until I get into town."

"All right."

"I'll see you in a couple days."

"Are you flying your plane?"

"Yes."

"Call me and let me know when you'll be landing."

"I will. Say hello to Tim and Liz for me."

"Will do." Michael hung up the phone and thought about the

individual he and Seamus had just alluded to. He definitely has the motive, Michael thought to himself. The motive and the ability.

News of the letter swept across the country. The real-life drama that was unfolding in the nation's capital had seized the attention of every American. The president sat in his high-backed leather chair, staring out the windows behind his desk in the Oval Office. He had been sitting in this position for the last ten minutes and had not moved a muscle. He was pondering the isolation of his office . . . thinking about the hard fact that he, the president of the United States, knew no more about what was going on than anyone else in the country. He thought of how short his budget victory had been. Today was supposed to be a day of celebration, a day when he could bask in front of the cameras and take another crucial step toward a second term. Instead, the unthinkable had occurred. His budget would never be passed without Jack Koslowski, and whoever was responsible for the killings was threatening his life as well. He thought about the possibility of these murderers getting near him and came to the comforting conclusion that they could not—not with all the Secret Service agents and modern technology that surrounded him.

He knew he would have to address the nation, but had no idea what to say. It was almost two in the afternoon, and Stevens had yet to stop and think about the deaths of his former colleagues or the loved ones they had left behind. He was immersed in himself and how the events of the day would affect his career, his place in history.

In the hallway outside the Oval Office, Ann Moncur was waiting to get in and see the president. If you wanted to have a meeting with the president, you had to go through his chief of staff, and Moncur was sick of going through Garret. The media was all over her, wanting a response from the White House on the killings. Everyone assumed the president would be addressing the nation, and she needed to let the press know when.

Stu Garret came rumbling around the corner with Mike Nance and the White House communications director, Ted Hopkinson. Hopkinson's unofficial title was *spin doctor*. With the help of Garret, he'd taken over most of Moncur's responsibilities. Garret had to keep the feminists happy and let them think Moncur was important. So he gave Moncur the title and let her brief the media on the day-to-day events at the White House, but that was as far as it went. All the strategy planning, intentional leaks to the media, opinion-poll analysis, and one-on-ones with the president were handled by Hopkinson.

Moncur stepped in front of Garret and blocked his entrance to the Oval Office. She had brooded all night about the way he'd treated her the day before and decided she wasn't going to take it anymore. In a firm voice she said, "Stu, I need to see him."

"Not now, Ann, we're really busy." Garret went to step around her and she moved in front of him.

"Stu, I've got the media all over my case. They want to know when he's going to address the nation."

"I will let you know as soon we decide," snapped Garret.

"Is that what you guys are going to talk about in there . . . his speech, the media strategy? I should be included." Moncur paused and Garret looked away, shaking his head no. "I'm sick of you cutting me out of the loop, Stu. I'm the White House press secretary, not him." Moncur pointed her finger at Hopkinson. "I should be involved in this."

Garret grabbed her arm and pushed her to the side, sticking his face directly in front of her. "Ann, I don't need this shit right now. We've got a crisis on our hands. Go to your office, and I'll let you know what time he will be addressing the nation as soon as we get out of this meeting. Now get the hell out of my way." Garret turned and entered the office with Nance and Hopkinson behind him.

The president heard the door open and spun around in his chair. Garret threw his arms up in the air. "How could this day get any worse? We've been busting our asses trying to get that budget passed, and just when we're in the clear, we get the rug pulled out from under us." Garret pointed toward the door. "And now I've got every clown and his brother trying to pick a fight with me. This morning it was that idiot from the FBI, and now it's that joke we call a press secretary."

The president stood from behind his desk and walked over to join the others in front of the fireplace. He sat in a chair with its back to the fireplace, and Garret sat by himself on the couch to Stevens's left, while Nance and Hopkinson sat on the other couch to the right.

"Gentlemen, what have you decided?" asked the president.

"Well, we've picked a time. We're going to have you address the nation at eight this evening. That way we'll get maximum exposure." Garret paused for a moment and looked at Nance and Hopkinson. "And it will give us some time to try and catch our breath and figure out what in the hell is going on. Right now, my gut reaction is that we come out hard and denounce these assassinations as a direct threat to the national security of the United States of America and label whoever sent the letter as terrorists.

"We have to start spinning this thing and get control of it. The media is all over the board right now." Garret looked down at his yellow notepad. "Ted has had people watching the broadcasts all morning, and the media is referring to the people that sent this letter as everything from assassins to terrorists to revolutionaries to murderers to perpetrators. We have to figure out if there's a way we can use this to our advantage and then lead the media on the story. We have to grab ahold of this thing and squash any public support there may be for this list of demands. We can't have these guys being seen as revolutionaries."

Garret paused for a moment and shook his head in frustration. "The nut-bags on talk radio are calling in and saying it's about time someone got serious about running this country and got rid of scumbags like Fitzgerald. I think we've got to nail this thing down while we still can, and your speech to the nation will be our first chance." Garret leaned forward. "Jim, if you can come out looking good and strong tonight, it would be a big bonus in light of the set-backs we're going to suffer over the loss of Koslowski. Every single person in this country will be watching you tonight, looking for guidance."

Garret leaned back. "Now, Mike and Ted differ with me a little. Ted, as usual, wants to wait until we get some polls back to decide exactly how firm we should be on this, and Mike also wants to move cautiously."

The president turned away from Garret and looked at Nance. *Cautious* was a word that was very appealing to him right now. "What did you have in mind, Mike?"

"Well, sir, I think it would be prudent to wait until we receive a little more information from our intelligence assets before we take a hard line. At this point, we have three dead politicians who seem to have been killed by a group that wants to pressure you and Congress into making some radical reforms. This whole thing could be that simple, or it could be a hundred times more complicated. We don't know if this letter is for real. The people behind it may want it to look like a simple revolution, but in reality they may have different motives."

Nance leaned forward in his chair and closer to the president. "Don't you think the timing on this is a little strange? Today was supposed to be the day your budget was to pass through the House. Everyone knew if you succeeded, your chances for reelection would be greatly improved. What if someone didn't want you reelected, or someone wanted to be president and decided the first thing they had to do was scuttle your chances for reelection?"

Nance was trying to accomplish two things by intentionally

confusing the president. First, he honestly did not like rushing into a complicated situation and taking a hard line without knowing all the facts. Too many times in his career he had had to clean up a mess after people had taken an uninformed stance on an issue, only to find out later they had chosen the wrong side. The other reason Nance wanted to keep Stevens unsure was because as long as the president was confused, he would continue to seek counsel from his national security adviser.

"Mr. President, it is an unnecessary risk to come out and commit to a stance immediately. Do you remember when the USS *Vincennes* shot down the Iranian Airbus? President Reagan got on national television and told the world that the *Vincennes* was under attack by Iranian gunboats when it fired on the Airbus. He took a firm position that it was the Iranians' fault. He painted himself into a corner and spent months trying to defend the wrong side of the argument. Our side screwed up and killed three hundred innocent people. We ended up looking like fools. Now, obviously, this situation is different, but all I'm asking is that we wait until the FBI provides us with some reliable information." Nance continued to speak in his even, nonconfrontational tone. "Then we can formulate a coherent plan of action. . . . Besides, thinking we can quash this thing right now is like thinking we can turn back a tidal wave. The public's distrust of politicians is at an all-time high. The demands listed in that letter are exactly what voters have been screaming for. If we're going to come out winners on this, we're going to have to be a little more crafty."

Hopkinson was shaking his head in agreement, but instead of addressing the president, he looked at Garret. "I agree. I would also like to wait until we get some of the results from these public opinion polls. It makes no sense to rush into this until we know exactly where we stand. Besides, I think Mike is right. This thing is like a tidal wave coming towards shore, and the smart thing to do is to get the hell out of the way and sit the storm out."

Garret leaned back and tapped his fingers on the side table next to the couch as his crossed leg bounced up and down. The president, Nance, and Hopkinson were used to Garret's mulling over an idea.

After a full minute of silence, the president became impatient and asked, "Stu, what do you think?"

Garret chattered his teeth several times and responded, "All right, you guys win. For tonight's address we'll play it safe. We'll go with somber and mournful." Garret jotted down a note to himself on his yellow notepad. "You can talk about the grief you feel over the loss of these good friends. We'll make it seem real personal. You can list some of their achievements and talk them up as real heroes of democracy."

"Let's not build them up too much," Nance said cautiously. "One of our deceased friends has quite a few skeletons in his closet that could come back to haunt us. Let the press make the first move on that one. . . . Let's just state the obvious and say these assassinations are a threat to our national security, and then you can make some comments about how these men gave their entire lives to the service of their country. Most importantly, we should keep it short."

Garret shook his head in agreement. "You're right. These guys are dead now. We don't owe them any more favors. If the press wants to turn them into martyrs, we can wait and jump on that bandwagon during the funerals next week."

Everyone nodded his head in agreement while Garret continued writing himself a note. When he was finished, he looked up at Hopkinson. "Ted, why don't you go tell Moncur what time we will be addressing the nation and get the speechwriters focused on the issues we've discussed. When I'm finished, I'll stop by your office to work on the details." Hopkinson stood and started for the door.

As soon as he was gone, Garret leaned forward and spoke in a low tone. "I am really pissed off with the way that meeting went this morning, and not just because that no-name agent got in my face. I'm pissed because here we are in the middle of a crisis and we can't even trust the very people we are dependent on to give us information. Now, I don't want to go back and rehash why Roach and Stansfield weren't replaced when we took office. We all know why they weren't, and we were all in agreement at the time. In light of our difficulties in getting the cabinet confirmed, the right thing to do was leave them in charge of the FBI and the CIA." Garret's balding, skinny head shook and his cheeks tensed. "Now, here we are in the middle of a major crisis, and I don't trust either one of them as far as I can throw them. What are we going to do about it?"

The president considered the question and answered, "Well, neither of them is willing to resign, and considering the crisis we're confronted with, I think trying to force them out would be unwise."

Nance sat still while both men looked to him for his opinion. He was the professional spook of the group, having spent most of his early years working for Army intelligence and then moving on to the National Security Agency. He had a sharp mind and was good at putting things in motion. The idea for blackmailing Congressman Moore had been his.

"If you're serious about getting rid of them," Nance finally responded, "you'll have to do it through public pressure and pressure from the Hill. They have to be embarrassed into leaving their jobs." He paused for a moment, his mind calculating the next move. "The pressure to solve these murders will rest solely on the shoulders of the FBI. If Roach doesn't make progress on the case, it will be very easy to turn the dogs loose on him." Nance held a finger up in the air. "And I have some ideas on how we may be able to speed up the process."

CHAPTER 8

THE sun was dropping over the western horizon, and dropping with it was the temperature. O'Rourke walked down the street with his hands in his pockets. He was wearing a pair of jeans, a flannel shirt, and a dark brown leather jacket. His left hand was wrapped around the handle of a .45-caliber Combatmaster made by Detonics. The palm-sized pistol packed a huge punch. As a congressman, O'Rourke had obtained a special permit to carry the weapon. He wasn't carrying the gun just because of the recent assassinations. He had started carrying it several years ago to protect himself against the roving packs of gang-bangers that roamed the streets of D.C. O'Rourke had been a bone-crushing defenseman for the University of Minnesota hockey team. With his size and speed, few people toyed with him on or off the ice, but the muggers of D.C. cared little about size. The second most traumatic event in O'Rourke's life had proved that.

The thought of his friend's mugging caused Michael to tighten his grip around the handle of the gun. One year earlier, Michael's best friend had been shot and killed just two blocks from the Capitol. Mark Coleman and O'Rourke worked on Senator Olson's staff and were roommates. One night Coleman was on his way home from work when he was stopped by a twenty-two-year-old crack addict. A witness saw the shaky young man walk up to Coleman and, without saying a word, shoot him in the chest, grab his wallet, and run. The police caught the man the next day. The murderer had already been convicted of armed robbery twice but was paroled early because of a lack of space in the D.C. jails.

O'Rourke hadn't been concerned that his roommate didn't come home that night. Coleman was engaged and spent most of his evenings at his fiancée's apartment. O'Rourke went into the office late the next morning. He had just won his congressional seat the previous week and was coming in to go over some transition notes with Senator Olson. Michael entered the office with no idea that his friend had been killed. The office personnel were gathered in the reception area hugging each other and crying when Michael walked through the door. O'Rourke stood in shock while one of the secretaries told him the news. Michael looked around the room at all of the people trying to comfort one another and instinctively withdrew. He backed out of the office and left the building.

When he got outside, he headed for the Mall and walked westward, passing the Smithsonian and the Washington Monument. Walking slowly, his mind flooded with memories of his friend and his parents. After passing the Reflecting Pool, he reached the Lincoln Memorial and stopped. He stood and stared back at the Capitol for a long time.

O'Rourke stared at the large rotunda and tried to grasp how a person could be shot and killed so close to the heart of the government of the United States of America. He sat on the steps of the Lincoln Memorial staring at the Capitol, trying to make sense of a senseless death, trying to understand what was happening to America, trying to understand why someone like Mark Coleman, who had worked so hard, who lived honestly, whose whole life was ahead of him, could be snuffed out by a worthless crack addict.

O'Rourke thought of all the meetings he'd sat in where fat-cat senators and congressmen threw around billions of tax dollars as if it were a Monopoly game—the money always going to support some special-interest group whose endorsement would be needed in the next election. When the subject of crime came up, it was talked about with enthusiasm and vigor, especially when the press was around, but behind the closed doors of committee meetings the politicians were always more willing to spend money on farm subsidies or defense spending than crime.

The reality of life had smacked O'Rourke harshly in the face that day. He looked at Washington and knew there was no way he could make a difference. The corruption of the system had become too entrenched, and even if there were thirty other congressmen just like him, they couldn't make a dent. The old boys controlled the committees and with that the legislative agenda and the purse strings.

O'Rourke had decided at that moment, one year earlier, as he looked at the large dome of the Capitol, that he was done with Washington. If he couldn't make a difference, he didn't want to be a witness and accessory to the corruption of Washington politics. The hell if he was going to stay in this town and turn into one of them. Washington was built on a swamp, and as far as Michael was concerned, it was still a swamp.

As O'Rourke turned onto Wisconsin Avenue, his mind returned to the present. He noted for the first time since taking office that real change might be possible. The shocking assassination of three of Washington's most prominent political animals was sure to force reform to the forefront.

O'Rourke walked across the street to Blacky's Bar and entered. Glancing over the crowd, he looked for a full head of black hair, and after two sweeps he found her. She was sitting at the far end of the bar surrounded by a group of men still in suits. The sight of her brought a smile to his face.

An attractive woman walked up and grabbed O'Rourke's arm. "Michael, you're late. You'd better get over there and save her. The vultures are closing in."

O'Rourke continued to stare across the bar. "Yes, I see that." He looked down and kissed the woman on the cheek. "Hello, Meredith, is she ready to kill me?"

"Michael, you could show up at midnight and she wouldn't be mad. May I take your coat?"

O'Rourke remembered he was carrying his gun and politely said, "No, thank you."

"Were things pretty tense on the Hill today?"

"Yeah, there was a lot of extra security."

"Well, you be careful." The owner squeezed his arm. "Get over there and save her. I've got a booth ready for you, whenever you're ready."

O'Rourke weaved his way through the crowd and stood behind the pack of cruisers salivating over his girlfriend. He took a deep breath and watched for a moment. O'Rourke placed his hands on the shoulders of the two men closest to him. "Excuse me, gentlemen."

The two men turned around and made some room. Liz was wearing a white blouse, short black skirt, black nylons, and black suede heels. A smile spread across O'Rourke's face, and he stepped forward to kiss her on the lips. Then brushing his nose along her cheek, he whispered, "You look great."

She smiled, wrapped her arms around his waist, and pulled him closer for another kiss. After several moments, O'Rourke grabbed her by the hand and said, "Meredith has our table ready. Let's go be alone."

The couple walked over to the open booth and sat down across from each other. O'Rourke grabbed her hands and stared at her. He loved her eyes. He loved everything about her . . . her thick, black hair, her olive skin, her sharp mind, her great sense of humor, but he especially loved her eyes. Despite his bad attitude toward Washington she had managed to work her way into his heart. Liz was bright, she was aggressive, she was caring, she loved kids. She was everything he wanted. Liz Scarlatti had entered his life a year ago, and even though the last thing he wanted was a relationship, he couldn't resist her.

They had met at a small blues bar in Georgetown. It was a busy weekend night and they happened to be standing next to each other when the band struck up a sultry version of "Sweet Melissa" by the Allman Brothers. The female lead of the band sang it in a slow, seductive way that brought the entire crowd into a rhythmic sway. Standing by the edge of the dance floor, O'Rourke bumped a little too hard into whomever he was standing next to, and when he turned to apologize, there was Liz.

The apology never got out of his mouth. He stared in awe at what he had no doubt was the most beautiful woman he had ever laid eyes on. His face was frozen, eyes open wide, lips parted slightly. Liz looked up at him with her big brown eyes, and that was it. O'Rourke felt his heart sink into his stomach, and he couldn't move. Luckily for him Liz didn't freeze. She slowly took the beer out of Michael's hand, set it on a ledge, and then grabbing him by the hand, she led him onto the dance floor. The rest was history.

Over the next year their attraction grew into a serious love affair with marriage on the horizon. There was only one problem at present—Michael wanted out of D.C. and Liz wasn't sure yet. She liked her job less and less every week, but hadn't grown to hate it yet. She had worked hard to get where she was and wasn't quite sure she was ready to give it up and move to Minnesota.

Scarlatti smiled at O'Rourke and asked, "So, did you see me on TV yesterday?"

The smile disappeared from O'Rourke's mouth. "What was that all about? You know how much I hate publicity." O'Rourke changed his voice and started to mimic her, "'Mr. President, Congressman O'Rourke says your budget is stuffed with more pork than a Jimmy Dean sausage.' Come on, Liz, I had reporters calling my office all afternoon." O'Rourke had been mad as hell yesterday when he saw her get up at the press conference and quote him, but now, sitting in front of her, all that anger was gone.

"Well, I'm sorry, Michael, you're a public figure, and what you say is news."

"First of all, I'm not eligible, and I have no control over what some flighty gossip columnist writes. With you, that's a different story. All I'm asking is that in the future we keep our relationship a little more private. What is said when we're in bed together stays between you and me."

Scarlatti leaned forward. "If that's what you really want, I will respect it, but I'll never understand your aversion to the press. You're the only politician I know who consciously tries to stay out of the limelight."

"Liz, we've been over this before. Let's not go over it again." Michael gave her a forced smile and then said, "By the way, congratulations! You looked very good yesterday. You were the only one who challenged him. The rest of those pansies rolled over and gave him nice, easy questions."

"That's why they get called on. Those press conferences are the biggest scams. The president calls on the same people every time because he knows they'll toss him a nice big fat one."

The president was sitting behind his desk in the Oval Office wearing a dark suit, striped tie, and white shirt. Pieces of Kleenex were stuffed between his collar and neck as a woman stood over him and applied makeup to his face. Stu Garret loomed over the other shoulder and read off a list of last-minute reminders. Ted Hopkinson was in the midst of a final check to see that everything was in place. In five minutes they would be live in front of the nation.

Garret waved away the woman who was doing the makeup. "That's enough. He looks fine! . . . Now, Jim, remember, start out looking somber. We want to show them that you're in pain. Stay kind of slouched over during the first part, like you did during the

last rehearsal. When we get to the last part, about democracy and
the founders of this country, I want you to become more stiff and
rigid. Sit up straight, but don't pound your fist on the desk like you
did during the last rehearsal. It comes off a little too strong. Just
stick with your old standby. Pull that arm in tight and shake your
fist at the camera. Not too fast. Shake it slow and deliberately, like
you're emphasizing every word." Garret mimicked the move.

Hopkinson approached and pulled the Kleenex out from under
the president's collar. "Sir, you know the routine. Please don't touch
your face, your shirt, or your tie. The makeup will smear and we're
going to be live in minutes."

Scarlatti and O'Rourke were glancing at their menus, and discussing the assassinations, when the subdued roar of the Friday-night
crowd dropped to a hushed silence. When they looked up, the
president's face was on every TV in the bar. Several people made
sarcastic remarks and were shouted down by the other patrons. The
president started to speak.

"Good evening. I will be very brief and to the point tonight. It
is with deep sorrow that I come to you, to discuss a great loss to our
nation . . . the tragic deaths of Congressman Koslowski, Senator
Fitzgerald, and Senator Downs. . . . These three great statesmen have
given over eighty years of service to the people of America. During that time, they fought with passion for the things they believed
in: freedom, democracy, and the welfare of every man, woman,
and child in America. Their careers were long and illustrious. Between them, they authored hundreds of bills that have helped make
America a better place to live and work. Their leadership, guidance,
and wisdom will be greatly missed in the hallowed halls of Congress, and I will greatly miss their friendship." The president looked
down for a moment and paused. "I would ask all of you, my fellow
Americans, to keep Congressman Koslowski, Senator Fitzgerald,
Senator Downs, and their families in your prayers. They were not

perfect; none of us are. Yet they overcame their imperfections and gave everything they had to their country and their fellow countrymen. For this, we will always be indebted to them." The president paused again, his face drawn, staring into the camera.

"We, in the nation's capital, are in shock over the senseless, violent murders that were committed this morning. We are a very close group. Many of us have worked beside each other for decades. I, myself, have known Congressman Koslowski, Senator Fitzgerald, and Senator Downs for over thirty years. I have met their wives and children. I have watched their children grow up, get married, and have children of their own. It is extremely painful for us to see three men, who have given so much, struck down in one senseless flurry of violence." Again, the president looked down and paused for a moment. When he looked back up, he picked up a piece of paper and held it up to the camera.

"Many of you are aware of this letter that was received by the media today. The FBI has informed me there is a very good chance this letter is from the group that committed the murders of Congressman Koslowski, Senator Fitzgerald, and Senator Downs. The FBI also believes there is a very good chance this letter was sent as a piece of disinformation, sent to lead the investigation in the wrong direction. Due to the investigation taking place, I cannot expand on this any further. All I can say for now is that FBI director Roach has assured me that the terrorists who killed these defenseless men will be caught and brought to justice."

The president waved the letter in the air and sat more upright. "The people who committed this crime represent the antithesis of democracy. They represent tyranny. What happened this morning was not just the murder of three important politicians. It was an attack on the United States of America. It was an assault on the ideals of democracy. Our country was founded by men and women who fled the tyranny of monarchies and dictatorships from all over the world. They made America a place where everyone could have a say in how the country was run: a government for the people, by the people, and of the people. Over the years, we have fought in countless wars defending freedom and democracy. Millions of American men and women have died so that we could continue to live free, to have a say in how our government works, so that democracy could flourish!" The president became more animated.

"The cruel and inhumane murders that were perpetrated this morning represent what those millions of Americans died fighting against. They were acts of tyranny, the harsh, violent, and forceful rule of the few over the many. Democracy and diversity have made America great. We are great because everyone has had a say, not because a militant few have shoved their beliefs and ideals down the throats of the rest of the country. Even if the demands of this letter were genuine, which we do not think they are, I could not accept them. If you, the American people, want to make changes in the way your government is run, those changes must take place in a peaceful and democratic way. They must take place within our current legislative and legal system. You have chosen me to be your president, and I have taken an oath to uphold the laws of this land and to protect the national security of America.

"The people who committed these crimes are terrorists and cowards. I will continue the policy of my predecessors. I will not deal with terrorists. The FBI, along with the cooperation of our other law enforcement and intelligence agencies, will hunt these animals down and put them behind bars. Many Americans have died fighting for democracy. Congressman Koslowski, Senator Fitzgerald, and Senator Downs are three more names that will be added to that long and noble list. They were patriots who not only believed in democracy and freedom, who not only lived and enjoyed the fruits of democracy and freedom, they were men who fought for democracy and freedom so the rest of us could enjoy it.

"The deaths of these three great Americans are a tragedy and loss to our entire nation, but America is a country that has suffered many losses in her long and glorious battle to sustain freedom. Throughout our history we have been faced with great trials and tribulations. We have, as a nation, always risen above these obstacles and emerged stronger! Next week, we will, as a nation, bury these three honorable men. We will mourn their deaths as a country, and then we will do as they would have wished." The president picked his right hand off the desk and clenched his fist. Continuing to speak, he slowly thrust it forward, toward the camera. "America and democracy are too big and good to be brought down by tyranny. We will push on, we will persevere, we will overcome!" There was a long pause as he continued to stare into the camera and let the words he'd spoken hang, and then in closing he said, "Good night, and may God bless each of you."

CHAPTER 9

THE president continued to stare into the camera until Hopkinson stepped in and pulled him out of his chair. "Sir, all of these mikes are still live, and the camera is sending out a feed."

The president nodded, knowing what his communications director was implying. The previous year Stevens had told several off-color jokes following his Saturday-afternoon radio address. He thought the microphones had been turned off, but they weren't. The press had jumped all over him, but since the jokes were actually funny, the damage was minor. Hopkinson and Garret were always on the alert to prevent a similar mistake.

Garret walked over and said, "Come on, gentlemen, let's go to my office." He shook his head toward the door, and the president and Hopkinson followed.

When they entered Garret's office, the president turned to Hopkinson and asked, "How did I look?"

"You looked fine, sir."

"Did it look genuine and heartfelt?"

"I thought so, but we'll know more in about an hour. I've got a polling group calling five hundred homes right now to try and get an early read on what the public thinks."

Stu Garret sat down behind his desk, shoved a cigarette in his mouth, and turned on the little brown smoke-eater next to his ash-tray. After taking a deep drag, he pulled the cigarette away from his lips and started to speak, his lungs still filled with smoke. "You did a nice job, Jim. If we handle this thing right, I think we're going to see a big jump in your approval ratings." Smoke started to seep out of Garret's nose, and he tilted his head back, exhaling a deep gray cloud toward the ceiling. "There's nothing like the exposure you get from a crisis."

Back in Blacky's, the roar of conversation had returned as the patrons discussed the events of the day and the president's speech. O'Rourke was intentionally keeping his mouth shut as Scarlatti stared at him. He looked over the top of his menu at her big brown eyes.

"Michael, you know I'm dying to hear what you have to say about this whole thing."

"About what?"

Scarlatti pulled the menu out of his hands. "Don't play coy with me, Michael, I'm serious. I really want to know what you think about this. I mean, it isn't every day two senators and a congressman get assassinated."

Michael thought about sugarcoating his comment and then opted for the direct approach. "In a nutshell, Liz, I think Koslowski, Downs, and Fitzgerald were the scum of the earth. They represented the core of what is wrong with this town."

"Come now, Michael, how do you really feel about them?" asked Scarlatti sarcastically.

"Listen, I'm not crazy about our political leadership getting gunned down under the cover of darkness, but considering where we're headed, I'm not so sure these assassins aren't doing all of us a huge favor."

Scarlatti looked down and said, "I'm afraid there are a lot of people out there who would agree with you. Doesn't it worry you at all ... as a congressman ... that these terrorists may turn the gun on you eventually?"

"No." Michael shook his head. "There are bigger fish to fry than me. And besides, I'm not so sure they're terrorists."

"You don't think they're terrorists?" asked Liz with a quizzical expression.

"No. It's an overused cliché, but one man's terrorist is another man's freedom fighter. These guys haven't killed any civilians." O'Rourke paused for a second. In a voice just above a whisper he continued, "If no one else dies, and this group can bring about the changes they stated in their demands, this will be one of the best things that has happened in this country since the civil rights movement."

"Well, from what the president just said, there's reason to believe that letter is a fake."

"Come on, Liz." O'Rourke frowned. "You're a reporter. Do you really believe a word that comes out of Stevens's mouth? The White House is already trying to spin this thing and they don't even know what's going on. Those guys are sitting over there right now shitting in their pants." O'Rourke picked up his fork and tapped it lightly on the place mat. "Today was supposed to be a big day for them. The president was going to pass his budget, but instead he wakes up and finds out that two senators and his point man in Congress have been assassinated. Then he receives a letter telling him it's time to get his act together, or he's next. Liz, this is their worst fear, and not just the president, all of them. They've played their little game of party politics for years. Every election they say they're going to cut all the wasteful spending, give a tax break to the middle class, and balance the budget. They say anything to get elected, and then, once they're back in office, it's the same old crap: more spending, no tax breaks, and more deficits."

Scarlatti shook her head and smiled.

O'Rourke looked at her and asked, "What?"

"I guess I'm just a little shocked. I would have thought that you, of all people, Mr. Law and Order, would have been denouncing what happened today. I mean, I'm the liberal. I'm supposed to be supporting anarchy, not you."

"This isn't anarchy, Liz. It may be a revolt, but it's not anarchy." Smiling, he said, "Besides, you're a member of the press. You're supposed to be neutral . . . remember?"

Special Agent McMahon was sitting at the head of the table in a large conference room down the hall from his office. The room was quickly becoming the command center for the investigation. He was staring at the TV in disbelief. The president had just finished his address to the nation, and McMahon did not like what he had heard. He grabbed the phone next to him and dialed the direct line to Roach's office.

After several rings, the director answered, "Hello."

"What in the hell was that all about?"

"I have no idea," Roach responded flatly.

"Has anyone from the Bureau told them we believe the letter is a piece of disinformation?"

"No," sighed Roach.

"You didn't actually promise him that we would catch these guys, did you?"

"Skip, you know better than that."

"What in the hell is going on? I don't understand why in the hell he would say something like that."

"I think I might. Why don't you meet me in my office tomorrow morning at eight? The president wants to see us at noon. That should give us time to go over some things."

"I'll be there at eight."

"How are things going on your end?"

"So far the preliminary reports on the autopsies haven't turned anything up, and the letters we intercepted were negative for prints. They may find out more after they pick them apart, but I doubt it."

"Have any of those people from the park come in to try to give us a composite of the guy they saw?"

"Yeah, we've got three who think they saw the perp. Right now they're in separate rooms giving their descriptions to different artists. When they're done, we'll bring them together and compare."

"Good. I assume we're taking extra precautions to make sure their names aren't leaked?"

"As far as the press knows, there are no witnesses to any of the killings."

"Have we made arrangements to provide protection for them?"

"It's already been taken care of."

"All right, stay in touch. I'll be here until about ten."

McMahon hung up the phone and buried his face in his hands. He didn't move for almost five minutes. He was trying to think of a reason why the president would say the letter was a decoy. He stood and looked at the two agents sitting to his left. "Kathy and Dan, come with me."

McMahon walked out of the room and down the hall to his office. Special Agents Kathy Jennings and Dan Wardwell followed. When Jennings and Wardwell entered the room, he shut the door and motioned to the couch. The two agents sat down. McMahon paced for a moment and then stopped.

"I think we all agree that the letter mailed to NBC was sent by the same group that killed Koslowski, Downs, and Fitzgerald. It's a no-brainer. The letter was mailed before the murders took place and it names the men who were killed. Are we all in agreement?"

Jennings and Wardwell nodded yes.

McMahon held up a copy of the letter. "I would like to hear your opinions on whether you think this letter is what it appears to be or if you think it is, as the president said, 'a piece of disinformation.'"

The two agents looked at each other for support, neither quite sure of the answer their boss was searching for. Wardwell spoke first. "Who, at the Bureau, told the president they thought the letter was a piece of disinformation?"

"No one did, as far as we know, but that is not what I'm concerned about. I don't want any of that to seep into your train of thought. What I want to know is, based on the evidence you've seen, do you think this letter is a piece of disinformation?" McMahon leaned against the edge of his desk and waited for an answer.

"Based on what we know, no, I don't think this letter is a piece of disinformation," Wardwell said.

"Why do you think it's genuine?" McMahon asked.

"You tell me why I should think otherwise."

"That's not the way I want you to go about this." McMahon started to shake his head and wave his hands. "Let's try this. Dan, I want you to assume that whoever murdered these guys had an ulterior motive. Kathy, I want you to argue that they didn't have an ulterior motive. Now, Dan, if the motive for killing those three guys wasn't to scare the politicians into doing what that letter says, then what was it?"

There was a long silence while Wardwell pondered the question. All of a sudden he slapped his thighs with both hands. "Oh, my God. I didn't even think about it. The president's budget was supposed to be passed today. You take those guys out, and the budget is dead."

"If the motive was to derail the budget, then why kill all three of them? Koslowski was in charge of the Appropriations Committee. All they had to do was kill him and the budget would have been dead. Why kill the two senators?" McMahon prodded.

"Well . . . if they wanted to cover their tracks and not make it look like they were trying to stop the budget, they would have killed more than just Koslowski."

"Fair enough." McMahon paused and tapped his finger on his

chin. "Assuming you're right, why would someone take such a big risk just to stop the budget?"

"There could be a million different reasons . . . probably, all of them having to do with money. Maybe there was a new piece of legislation in there that was going to cost someone a whole lot of money, or maybe they had just cut funding for a program, and the people who have been receiving that money weren't very happy about it. The budget is a huge piece of legislation. There could be over a thousand new entries in there that could drastically affect someone or some group's finances," Wardwell said.

There was a short silence while they thought about Wardwell's comments, and then Jennings spoke up. "Yeah, or it could just be a group of Americans pissed off at the way these jerk-offs run the country."

McMahon turned to Jennings. "All right, hotshot, it's your turn."

Jennings sat forward on the couch. Her gun hung loosely in a shoulder holster under her left arm. "There are a lot of Americans out there who are sick and tired of the way these guys are running the country. Our own Counterterrorism Department has reported an alarming rise in threats against politicians over the last eighteen months. If I were an individual who was worried about losing money because of a new piece of legislation, Fitzgerald, Koslowski, and Downs would be the last three I would kill. They were the biggest spenders on the Hill. . . . Unless the president has some hard evidence that there's an ulterior motive behind these killings, I think they're just spewing political rhetoric."

"Don't you think the timing is a little strange?" McMahon asked.

"What timing? That they were killed right before the budget was supposed to be voted on?" Jennings shook her head sideways. "No, I don't. This afternoon you told me what that Kennedy woman from the CIA had to say about these murders being committed by military-trained commandos. Well, I thought about that for a while and then called my old firearms instructor from the FBI Academy. His name is Gus Mitchell. Have either of you ever met him?"

"Sure, I know him real well," McMahon answered. Wardwell shook his head no.

"Well, Gus is an old Delta Force commando, so I called him and ran Kennedy's theory by him. We could only talk for a couple of minutes because he had to go teach a class, but in that short time he said something that didn't really sink in until you brought this budget thing up. Gus said one of the most difficult things about planning an operation like this would be to pick a time where you were guaranteed that all of your targets would be where you wanted them. When you look at these assassinations from the killers' standpoint, the morning before the budget is supposed to go to a vote is the perfect time. All of the congressmen have to be in town to vote, and all of the senators stay in town to try to influence the outcome. Any other day, and these guys are flying in and out of town with little or no notice."

McMahon nodded his head up and down while he thought about Jennings's new angle. It might be worth his time to go give Gus Mitchell a little visit.

O'Rourke and Scarlatti were walking down the sidewalk. Scarlatti had both arms wrapped around O'Rourke's waist, and he had his arm around her shoulder. The cold night air felt good on their faces. Liz reached up and kissed him on the chin. O'Rourke smiled and noted it was the first time he had done so in days. Everything had been so tense, so serious, over the last several weeks. It felt good holding on to Liz, but something told him things in Washington were going to get worse before they got better.

When they reached O'Rourke's house, they walked up the steps to the front door. The first level of the brownstone was a two-car garage. Parked on the same side of the street and down about three houses was a black BMW with dark-tinted windows and diplomatic license plates. The man behind the steering wheel watched as the handsome couple entered the house. He looked up and down the street to see if anyone had followed.

As Michael and Liz entered the house, O'Rourke's yellow Lab, Duke, jumped up from his spot on the kitchen floor and ran down the hallway. Liz let go of Michael to greet the excited dog.

"Hello, Duke. How are you? I've missed you." Scarlatti patted him on the side and scratched his neck, while the eighty-pound Lab wagged his tail. O'Rourke said hello to his roommate of seven years and patted him on the head. Scarlatti stood up. "Where's your ball, Duke? Where's your ball? Go get your ball." Duke frantically tapped his paws on the hardwood floor and then bolted down the hallway in search of his ball.

O'Rourke took Scarlatti's jacket, hung it up, and said, "Hey, don't get him too excited. I've got more important things for us to do than play fetch."

"Come on, Michael, he's been inside all day. He needs to blow off a little steam."

"Tim came by during lunch and took him for a jog, and believe me, I need to blow off a lot more steam than Duke does." O'Rourke smiled and wrapped both arms around her waist.

"Easy, big boy. You'll get yours soon enough."

"I'm going to hold you to that promise."

"Don't worry, you won't have to." Scarlatti stood on her toes and kissed him. A second later Duke returned and dropped his blue ball at their feet. They ignored him for a while and continued to kiss until Duke let out a loud bark. Scarlatti let go of O'Rourke and grabbed the ball. She waved it in front of Duke's mouth several times, then threw it down the hallway.

O'Rourke patted her on the butt and started up the stairs. "I'm going to go fill the bathtub. When you're finished with Duke, why don't you grab a bottle of wine and come on up." Scarlatti smiled and nodded her head.

When O'Rourke reached the second floor, he walked down the short hallway to his den. Standing in front of his selection of CDs, he ran his eyes over the thin plastic cases turned on their side. He stopped at one of Liz's favorites. O'Rourke grabbed the Shawn Colvin CD, put it in, and hit play. The light by the window was on, and the shade was open. He walked over, turned off the light, and stood for a moment looking down at the dark street below. The young congressman reflected back to a hunting trip he had taken almost a year ago. A trip where he had divulged a dark and damaging secret involving Senator Fitzgerald. For the first time since the murders, Michael allowed himself to wonder if the person he had told that secret to was capable of taking the lives of Fitzgerald, Koslowski, and Downs. O'Rourke did not have to search deep—the answer was a resounding yes.

The assassin looked up at the shadow standing in the window on the second floor. The windows of the car were cracked slightly so he could hear what was going on outside the car. For several minutes, he continued to scan the street, checking to see if there were any new people or cars he hadn't seen on previous nights. He did so with minimal movement. Only his eyes darted back and forth, using the mirrors to look behind. After several minutes, he started the car and drove off. He had seen what he needed.

CHAPTER 10

ROACH and McMahon were sitting in the Oval Office waiting for the president, Garret, and whoever else would be attending the meeting. It was almost twelve-fifteen, and no one had entered the room since a Secret Service agent had let them in at noon. The two FBI men were sitting in front of the fireplace, one on each couch. Neither had said a word since arriving. The president and Garret were up to something, and Roach wasn't quite sure what it was, but until he figured it out, he would move with caution.

At that same moment, the president, Garret, Hopkinson, Speaker Basset, Senator Lloyd Hellerman, and a half dozen secretaries and aides were crowded around the large conference table in the Cabinet Room. They were scrambling to put together a media strategy that would help make the best of a dire situation. Most of the men in the room were aware of the nation's overall distrust of politicians, but none of them had imagined how bad it had gotten. Hopkinson was starting to get polling information back, and it was shocking. A poll conducted by *USA Today* showed that almost 40 percent of those questioned believed the country would be better off without Fitzgerald, Koslowski, and Downs.

When Garret heard the news earlier, he had snickered, "Let's see where those numbers are on Monday." The reason he was so confident was because his phone had been ringing off the hook since the president's speech. Americans loved a conspiracy. They would eat up the idea that the letter was sent to confuse the FBI, and that the murders were committed in connection with a dark plot. The seeds had been planted, and the notorious rumor mill of D.C. and the media would take care of the rest. Speaker Basset and Senator Hellerman had even taken the bait. They had both arrived early this morning and stopped by Garret's office to ask him if anything further had been learned about the dubious authenticity of the letter. Garret told them that even he was being kept in the dark—that the agency that had provided them with the information was taking careful steps to research the lead. Garret assured them that as soon as he found anything out, they would be the first to know.

One of the secretaries came down to the end of the table where the president and Garret were sitting and reminded them, for the third time, that Director Roach was waiting in the Oval Office. The president looked at his watch. It was 12:20 P.M. "Stu, twenty minutes is long enough for them to wait."

Garret nodded his head. "Yeah, I suppose you're right." Garret told the others they would be back and to continue without them. He and the president left and stopped by Mike Nance's office before heading on to the Oval Office.

The president entered his office first, followed by Garret and then Nance. Roach and McMahon rose to meet the commander in chief. The president walked over to both men and shook their hands. "Gentlemen, I apologize for being late, but things have been extremely hectic around here. Please be seated." All five men sat down, and the president continued, "Well, has the FBI found anything out since yesterday?"

"We have the preliminary autopsy reports on all three bodies," Roach said. "Agent McMahon has brought copies and is prepared to go over them with you, if you wish."

Garret leaned back and crossed his legs. "That's all right, just leave them here and we can look them over later." Garret looked over at McMahon and stuck out his hand, expecting McMahon to personally deliver the documents.

McMahon glanced at him and then handed all three briefs to Mike Nance, who was sitting next to him on the couch. Nance kept one and passed the other two on to the president. The president kept one and gave Garret the last copy. Garret snatched it from his boss's hand and placed it in his folder. Without looking at either Roach or McMahon, Garret asked, "What else do you have for us?"

Director Roach nodded to McMahon, and McMahon handed Nance three more briefs. Roach noted, "We have three witnesses that saw the man who we think killed Senator Downs in the park. If you turn to the third page, you'll find a sketch of the perpetrator. As you can see, it's pretty generic. None of the witnesses got a straight shot of the man, and he was wearing a baseball hat."

"What are you planning to do with this sketch?" the president asked.

"Well, in light of Dr. Kennedy's theory, I would like to start checking the personnel files of our Special Forces."

The usually stoic Nance sat forward and cleared his throat. "I think that, for now, Dr. Kennedy's theory should be kept very quiet. It is completely unsubstantiated, and the press would have a field day if they found out the FBI suspected United States military personnel. Besides, there are some national security issues involved with rifling through top secret personnel files."

"You're not actually taking her theory seriously, are you?" Garret asked.

"At this stage of the investigation, we are taking every lead seriously. I also understand the possible ramifications of Dr. Kennedy's theory being leaked to the press." Roach looked over at Nance. "And I also do not expect the military to hand over top secret files.

I was thinking more along the lines of having them pull photos of retired Special Forces personnel only. We would promise them that Special Agent McMahon and the three witnesses would be the only ones to see them."

Nance's look of discomfort lessened but did not vanish.

"They wouldn't have to provide us with anything other than photographs. The witnesses wouldn't even need to know where the photos came from."

"We might be able to arrange something along those lines, but I don't think the brass will like it," Nance responded.

"Hold on a minute," interrupted Garret. "Before we go running off on wild-goose chases, I think we should have a little more evidence than a theory from some little bookworm."

McMahon stared at Garret and would not look away. He'd promised Roach that he would keep his cool and his mouth shut during the meeting. McMahon kept thinking to himself, How does a guy like this get to be the chief of staff for the president of the United States?

Roach cleared his throat and took center stage. "Well, since you've broached the subject of leads, could you tell me what information you have that would lead you to believe the letter is a piece of disinformation?"

Before the president could answer, Nance spoke. "Right now, we are not at liberty to discuss that information. The lead is still being investigated."

Instead of responding, Roach stared at the president and thought to himself, What are these guys up to?

Nance continued, "The information will be passed on to you as soon as it can be verified. The people who are looking into this want to be very careful that they don't compromise any assets by moving too quickly."

Roach thought to himself, You bet your ass you'll pass it on to me, or you'll find a subpoena sitting on your desk. The director shifted his gaze away from the president and back to Nance. "Who is investigating it?"

"I can't say anything just yet. It's a strange situation that I really can't go into."

Roach looked over at McMahon and they both thought the same thing. You can tell the entire nation on TV, but you can't discuss it with the director of the FBI.

Garret sensed they weren't buying Nance's excuse, so he jumped into the fray. "Director Roach, you seem as if you doubt us. Don't you think the fact that these men were murdered on the eve of the passage of the president's budget is more than just a mere coincidence?"

"I think the timing of the murders is directly related to the president's budget," answered Roach, the concession catching Garret off-balance.

"So you do think there's a good chance this letter is meant to mislead us?" Garret asked.

"I think anything is possible at this point. Agent McMahon is investigating several leads that involve the timing of the murders."

Garret leaned forward and looked at McMahon. "What type of leads are you pursuing?"

"I am not at liberty to discuss them at this point. We are still in the early stages of running them down."

Garret sat back and quietly cursed himself for being suckered into the trap.

"Special Agent McMahon, I understand that whatever leads you have may not be very solid right now, but I would still like to hear them," the president said as he watched McMahon look to Roach.

"Come now, gentlemen. Whatever is said in this office will stay in this office," the president continued.

McMahon almost laughed out loud but suppressed the desire. "Mr. President, if you'd please pardon my candor, you appeared on

national television last night and told the entire country you had reason to believe that the letter is a piece of disinformation. Now, I can
only assume that for you to say something like that, you must have
some pretty solid facts regarding the authenticity of that letter . . .
facts that you are not willing to pass on to us, the people who are in
charge of investigating these murders. For now, we have agreed to
respect your decision to not share that information. I would hope
that you would also understand our position and give us some time
to run these leads down before we pass our information on to you."

Everyone was silent while the two sides thought about the
hand McMahon had just played. Garret was furious. Who in the
fuck did this no-name agent think he was, coming into the Oval
Office and denying the president information?

Nance, on the other hand, admired the move. In light of the
position he had just taken, they had no choice but to accept Mc-
Mahon's excuse.

The maneuver had been planned by Roach and McMahon before they left the Hoover Building, and now it was the director's
turn. "Mr. President, I realize things were very tense and confusing last night, but during your speech you said the Bureau told you
there was a good chance the letter was a piece of disinformation."

"I'll take the blame for that," Garret blurted out. "I was in
charge of editing the speech and I missed it. Sorry." Garret's apology smacked of blatant insincerity.

Roach looked at Garret for a moment and then back to the
president. "You also quoted me as saying that I guaranteed the perpetrators would be caught and brought to justice."

Again, Garret fielded the question. "That was my fault also. I
should have caught it. We meant it to sound more general, but it
came out sounding like a direct quote. I apologize."

Roach nodded his head in a feigned acknowledgment of Garret's apology. He knew they would lie. He just wanted to see how
they would do it. Roach looked away from Garret. It was time to

get down to important matters. "Sir, my main concern right now is not the authenticity of the letter; it is the security of the remaining five hundred and thirty-two senators and congressmen. The letter clearly states that if these reforms are not acted on, this group will kill more politicians. They have even made a direct threat to you, sir. For now, we have to assume the letter is real and that they will strike again. We have to arrange for protection." The president, Nance, and Garret nodded their heads in agreement. "I have spoken with Director Tracy of the Secret Service, and most of the chiefs of the metro-area police departments. We are meeting this afternoon to discuss additional security measures. The tab for this protection, sir, is going to be rather large. I am going to need you to authorize special funding."

"Don't worry about the money. Whatever it costs will be taken care of." The president waved his hand in the air emphasizing that money was the least of their concerns. "How are you planning on handling the security?"

"Well, Director Tracy and I have agreed that initially we should concentrate on giving the best security to the senior-ranking members of both the House and the Senate. He and I are working on pulling agents out of the field so they can provide personal protection for the ranking members. The presidential security detail will not be weakened. If anything, Director Tracy is thinking about adding more agents. This afternoon, we will determine how many of the ranking members we can protect with just the agents from the FBI and Secret Service. When we run out of agents, we will have to start using local police officers for the protection of the less senior members. We are also looking at using federal marshals, Treasury agents, and various military units. Director Tracy has also recommended that we shut down Lafayette Park and the streets surrounding the Capitol and the House and Senate office buildings. The White House is very secure, but the same cannot be said of the Capitol and the House and Senate office buildings. To bolster the security in and around the Capitol we are considering moving in a light armored division from the Army."

Garret scoffed and shook his head vigorously. "A light armored division? Are you talking just personnel or are you talking equipment also?"

"Equipment and personnel," Roach responded in an even tone.

"You mean to tell me you're going to surround the Capitol with tanks?"

"No, with Humvees, armored personnel carriers, and Bradley fighting vehicles."

"Like I said, you're going to surround the Capitol with tanks."

"No, light armored divisions don't have tanks. That would be an armored division."

"I know the difference," Garret said in a mocking tone. "But the average American doesn't." Garret looked to the president and said, "I think we're going a little overboard here. We can't have tanks driving down the streets of Washington, D.C. We'll look like the fucking Chinese, for Christ's sake."

The president paused while he digested Garret's comments. "I agree with Stu. For now let's try to keep things as normal looking as possible. I don't want the press and the American people to think we're panicking. Besides, these killers would have to be suicidal to try something at the Capitol."

Roach nodded his head in compliance and then went on. The meeting lasted for another ten minutes while Roach continued to give them a broad overview of the extra security measures. When he was done, the president walked them to the door and thanked them for coming.

Roach and McMahon did not say a word until they climbed into the limo. Once the doors closed, Roach immediately started to shake his head in disapproval. He did not swear but wanted to. Roach liked to stay on a nice, even keel, while McMahon was just the opposite.

"What a bunch of assholes."

"I take it you didn't believe a word of their story," Roach said.

"Are you kidding me? He gets on national TV and announces to the country that he believes the letter is phony, but he won't tell the director of the FBI or the agent running the investigation where he got the information. It's a crock of shit."

"Why would he make it up if it's obviously a lie? If he has any information, he will have to come forward with it."

"You're damn right he will. If he doesn't, we'll hit him with a subpoena and an obstruction of justice charge. This is our baby, not the NSA's or the CIA's. This is domestic and it's our jurisdiction," McMahon said.

"Yeah, that's what worries me. They know they have to hand over what they've got." Roach paused and looked out the window. "So, what are they up to?"

"I have no idea. Politics is your department, but if they're still proclaiming this letter is fake two days from now and they haven't handed anything over to us, I'd get the Justice Department involved."

CHAPTER 11

AFTER leaving his meeting at the White House, McMahon drove out to the CIA's headquarters in Langley, Virginia, and picked up Dr. Kennedy. McMahon had asked her the previous evening to accompany him for the interview with Gus Mitchell, the former Delta Force commando. For the early part of the drive down to the FBI Academy, the conversation centered on the investigation and Kennedy's theory of who the killers were. As Kennedy continued to articulate her points, McMahon couldn't help but wonder where this woman had come from. What had possessed her to join one of the most exclusive communities in government? It was obvious that with her brains, understated savvy, and the way she carried herself, she could have entered any profession and been extremely successful.

McMahon waited for a pause in the conversation. "I hope you don't mind me asking, but how did you end up in the employment of the CIA?"

Kennedy looked out the window of the government-issue Ford and said, "My father used to work for the State Department. Throughout most of his career he was stationed in the Middle East. He married my mother, who was Jordanian, and I grew up in a bilingual household." Kennedy looked over at McMahon. "There aren't a lot of Americans who are fluent in Arabic and who understand the customs and history of the area."

McMahon nodded his understanding. "You must have been a very highly sought after commodity."

"I suppose you could say that."

McMahon checked his side mirror and changed lanes. "You said your father used to work for the State Department. Is he retired?"

"No, he passed away."

"I'm sorry to hear that."

Kennedy clutched her purse with both hands. "Thank you." She looked at McMahon. "It was a long time ago, almost twenty years." Her eyes squinted while she thought about how long it had been. "It doesn't seem like it happened that long ago."

"He must have been pretty young. How did he die? If you don't mind me asking."

Kennedy shook her head. "He was stationed at our embassy in Beirut and was killed by a car bomb."

McMahon cringed. What a shitty way to go. "That must have been hard. You had to have been in your teens."

"Yeah, it wasn't the best time of my life, but I have a lot to be thankful for. My mother and I are very close. I have a great brother and four-year-old son whom I absolutely adore." Kennedy gave McMahon the smile of a proud parent.

McMahon smiled back while the pieces fell into place. The motivation of losing a parent to terrorism was more than enough of a reason to devote one's life to the fight against it. "What's your little boy's name?"

"Tommy." Kennedy fished a picture out of her purse and showed it to McMahon.

"He's a good-looking little fella. I assume he looks like his father."

"Unfortunately, yes."

"Sore subject?"

"The divorce was finalized about seven months ago. How about you, any wife or children?"

"None that I know of," McMahon said with a grin. "I was married once. It was a mistake. I was too young, I drank too much, and I was married to my job."

"The Bureau?" asked Kennedy. McMahon nodded. "Never found the time to remarry?"

"Not with this job. I can barely take care of myself."

"I read your file. It looks like you've been pretty busy over the years."

McMahon gave the young doctor a sideways glance. "You read my file?"

Kennedy shrugged her shoulders. "I read a lot of files."

"So do I. I'll have to make it a point to read yours when I have the chance."

Kennedy smiled. "Don't waste your time. It's pretty boring stuff."

"I'll bet," replied a grinning McMahon.

A short while later they pulled up to the guard post at the FBI Academy. McMahon and Kennedy showed their identification and were admitted. McMahon drove the car through the large campus and parked in front of a small office building by the firearms range.

Mitchell's office was located on the first floor. When they arrived, Mitchell was sitting with his feet up on the desk, reading a magazine. He was wearing black combat boots and dark blue coveralls. Over the left breast of the coveralls, *Instructor* was embroidered in yellow, and across the back in large letters were the initials *FBI*.

Mitchell jumped to his feet and said, "Skip, it's great to see you. You don't get down here enough, now that you're a big shot."

McMahon shook Mitchell's hand but ignored the friendly

needling. He turned to Kennedy and said, "Gus, meet Dr. Irene Kennedy."

"It's nice to meet you, Dr. Kennedy. You work at Langley, correct?"

"Yes." Kennedy smiled. "Please call me Irene."

"Irene it is." Mitchell motioned for his guests to follow him. "There's a small conference room down the hall. Let's use that instead. My office is a little cramped for the three of us. Can I get either of you some coffee?" Mitchell looked to Kennedy first, as his early years as a Southern gentleman had taught him.

"Please." Kennedy brushed a strand of hair back behind her ear.

"Skip?"

"Sure."

Mitchell disappeared and Kennedy raised one of her eyebrows. McMahon noticed the expression and asked, "What?"

"They are a unique breed, aren't they?"

"Who?"

"Commandos," replied Kennedy. "You can spot them a mile away. It's in their eyes."

"Really? I've never noticed."

"When we recruit them to be agents, we have to teach them how to mask their alertness."

McMahon was thinking about the doctor's comment when Mitchell returned with three cups of coffee. The three settled into chairs and McMahon asked Mitchell, "How much do you know about what happened yesterday?"

"Just what I've read in the papers and Irene's theory."

"What did you think of it?"

"Well, before I get into that, I'd like you to fill me in on the details. I usually don't believe what I read in the papers."

"Neither do I." McMahon set his coffee down. "It all started with Senator Fitzgerald. His neck was broken by someone using their bare hands. There were no signs of a struggle, no bruises on his neck or anywhere else. Our pathologist tells me it was done from behind with a jerking motion from left to right. We think whoever did it was waiting in the house, and when the senator arrived home, he jumped him. The body was found in a storage closet in the basement." McMahon paused as Mitchell made several notes. "The lock on the back door was picked, and the approximate time of death was twelve-fifteen A.M. The next one was a real piece of work. The perps broke into the house across the street from Congressman Koslowski's and waited. Koslowski got out of bed, opened the shades, and they shot him twice in the back of the head. Approximate time of death was six oh five A.M. When we showed up at the house across the street, we found a sedated German shepherd and a groggy owner. We did blood tests on both the dog and the owner and found heavy traces of sedatives. When we pumped the dog's stomach, we also found half-digested pieces of meat with traces of drugs. The owner had no needle marks, so we're assuming he was chloroformed."

"Does this guy let his dog out before he goes to bed every night?" Mitchell asked.

"Yes, every night before the local news," McMahon responded.

Mitchell nodded his head as if he already knew the answer before it was relayed.

"The next murder was committed at approximately six twenty-five A.M. in a park by Senator Downs's house. We have several witnesses who have reported seeing a man loitering in the area just prior to the death of the senator. He was shot in the back of the head with two nine-millimeter rounds at point-blank range."

Mitchell glanced over his notes for a moment and then stood and grabbed a green marker. In the upper left corner of the white board, he wrote the number 1 and 12:15 A.M. next to it. Next to that, he wrote the number 2 and 6:05 A.M. Then the number 3 and 6:25 A.M. When he was finished, he stepped back and looked at the board for a minute.

"We have three assassinations in about six hours." Mitchell put the cap back on the marker and tapped it on the board. "The key to any covert operation is stealth and surprise. In the perfect operation you get in and out before anyone knows you were there, which these men obviously accomplished. When you're planning something like this, the first thing you have to do is select your targets. After selecting them, you move into a surveillance mode. You follow these guys around and try to find a pattern. One guy walks his dog every morning at a certain time, another gets out of bed every morning at a certain time. When I was with the Delta Force, we took out a guy one time . . . I can't say where or who, but our intelligence boys told us the target had this habit. He would get out of bed every morning and the first thing he would do was open the shades of his bedroom window. People, especially successful people, are habitual creatures. They're organized. This makes them more productive. I would be willing to bet you that this Koslowski character opened those shades every morning. I'd also bet Downs walked his dog in the park every morning."

"They did," answered McMahon.

"After you find the targets, the most difficult thing to do is to pick a window of opportunity to take them out. Now, when you're looking at three big hitters, like these guys, that would be tough. As politicians, they travel on short notice and are always going in a million different directions. Downs may walk his dog every day, but only when he's in town. Koslowski may open those shades every morning, but only when he's in town. Fitzgerald may sleep in that house, but only when he's in town. As the assassin you have to pick a time when you know all of your targets will be where you want them to be, and you have to do it in advance. The day the president's budget was to go to the House for a vote would be the perfect time. None of them are traveling. They all stay right here in town so they can influence the outcome."

McMahon nodded. It made sense. How else could you be sure these guys would be where you wanted them?

Mitchell took the cap off the marker and circled the times of the deaths. "If I were running this operation, this is how I'd do it. The local news is at eleven P.M., right . . . well, at around ten P.M., I'd put one team into action and they'd drop the drugged-up meat into the backyard for the dog. Either before then, or shortly after, I would send one or two guys into Fitzgerald's house and wait for him to come home. I've got another team playing backup nearby. They're probably sitting in a car a couple of blocks away, monitoring the local police scanner. Fitzgerald comes home and my guys take him out. They slide out of the house and are picked up by their backup. They hold their breath and wait to see if anyone saw them and called the cops. If all goes well and the cops don't show up at Fitzgerald's, I proceed with phase two. Some time between one A.M. and four A.M., another team breaks into the house across the street from Koslowski's. They take care of the old man, but don't kill him or the dog. This definitely offers some valuable insight into the minds of the assassins. Let me finish and we'll go over it later. They set up the shot and wait. Now, these guys could be the same guys who took out Fitzgerald, but I doubt it. If I'm short on assets, I would have the first team take care of Fitzgerald and then have them get set up for Downs. I would use the second team only for Koslowski.

"This is where timing is crucial. These guys know that once Koslowski is killed, they only have twenty to forty minutes before the news spreads all over town. Team Two kills Koslowski and clears the area. Team Three or Team One, depending on how many assets you have, is now risking exposure. They wait for Downs, knowing that the clock is ticking. The assassin may be the guy these people saw loitering around the park. He waits for Downs while his backup is nearby. Downs shows up and the assassin pumps two rounds into the back of his head. The assassin clears the area, and all the assets are undercover before anyone knows what's going on. It's a very smooth job. The only thing I would have done differently is use a sniper shot on Downs. It makes no sense to expose one of your men like that. Did any of those witnesses get a good look at him?"

"No, not really, their descriptions were pretty vague. Black male, between five feet nine and six feet tall and between one hundred and sixty-five and two hundred pounds. Approximate age thirty. No one got a real clear look at his face."

"Well, whoever planned it seemed to do everything else right, so I have to assume he had a reason for killing Downs the way he did. Anyway, what you've got here is a minimum of four people and a maximum of maybe ten to fourteen depending on how many backup assets he had available."

"So you think these guys are commandos?" McMahon asked.

"Well, you can never be sure, but my instincts tell me they are. If they were terrorists, they would have killed that old man, and besides, why would terrorists send a letter stating that we need to start reforming our government or the killing will continue? I mean, who's to say who's a terrorist and who's a commando? These labels can get real sticky. The IRA for years was considered, and by some people still is considered, a paramilitary group. They achieved that status by attacking only military and government targets. Well, as soon as they started setting off bombs and killing innocent civilians, they became terrorists.

"These people haven't killed any civilians. They've killed three politicians. They even took extra steps not to kill that old man by drugging him. In my book, they're commandos. They didn't kill any civilians. One thing is for sure, they're not terrorists in the Middle Eastern or European sense. Irene is right. When those nuts go after a target, they do it very violently and with no concern for noncombatants."

"Then who do you think did it, an American paramilitary group?"

"You mean like those white-supremacist idiots that live out West?" Mitchell shook his head. "Those clowns don't have the skill to run an operation like this. They could have killed one or maybe two of these guys with a rifle shot, but they don't have the kind of talent to break a man's neck bare-handed. Do you have any idea how hard it is to do that with your bare hands? It's not like it is in the movies."

McMahon and Kennedy shook their heads. "Let me tell you a little story." Mitchell smiled. "I really shouldn't be laughing about this, but it's kind of funny. When they train you to be a Delta, they teach you a lot of different things, and one of them, of course, is hand-to-hand combat. Well, most of the shit they teach you, you can't practice it all the way through, like breaking a guy's neck for instance. I mean, how in the hell do you practice breaking a neck? Anyway, I'm on one of my first missions and my job is to take out a sentry who's walking patrol. I'm sitting there with my partner. We'd crawled over a hundred yards to get to this one bush, and we're waiting for the guard. When the guy passes by, I jump out and grab him. I execute the move just like my instructors taught me, but nothing happens. Luckily, my partner was right there to finish him off with a knife before he could make any noise. The point of the story is that I was the elite of the elite. I was a Delta Force commando, and I couldn't pull it off. Don't get me wrong, I know several guys who have managed to perfect the move, but they are few and far between. It's just too difficult to learn. Your typical hit man or assassin would have slit Fitzgerald's throat or put a bullet in the back of his head."

Kennedy pondered Mitchell's comments and then asked, "Based on what you've heard, who do you think did it?"

There was a long pause while Mitchell thought about the question. "My gut reaction . . ." Mitchell stopped and looked out the window. "My gut reaction is that this operation was pulled off by United States Special Forces commandos."

McMahon took a deep breath and said, "Please elaborate."

"I was in the Special Forces for almost fifteen years . . . I've worked with Navy SEALs, Green Berets, Rangers, Marine Recons, I've met them all. Do you know what the one thing is they all have in common?"

"No."

"They all hate politicians. The two professions couldn't be more fundamentally different. Commandos live by a warrior's code, honor and integrity above everything. Do what you say and mean what you do. Politicians just say whatever will keep them in office. Now, where you run into the problem is when you have the unprincipled, honorless politician telling the principled, honorable warrior what to do. The way the relationship works, with the politicians in the position of authority, they're destined to foster disgust and animosity among the troops.

"I don't know of a single Special Forces soldier who thinks Washington isn't run by a bunch of idiots. We've had operations exposed because those damn fools don't know how to keep their mouths shut. We've worked for months planning missions, and then had the plug pulled at the last minute because some politician didn't have the guts to authorize it. You have to understand the mentality of a commando. They've given everything they have to this country, and in return they see those whores selling America down the drain. I don't mean all of them. There are some good, honest politicians, but they are a rarity. Most of those guys are lying, misdirected egomaniacs. They think it's just a game." Mitchell paused briefly. "There's a lot of hate and distrust between the military and Washington. There always has been, and it's even worse when you start talking about Special Forces personnel."

"So, you think the letter is for real?"

"Who knows?" Mitchell paused again and looked out the window. "If I had to put money on it, I'd bet it's for real. Shit, turn on the radio, go to your local bar, people are sick of the way this country is run. . . . These murders weren't committed as part of a plot to derail the Stevens administration. They were committed the morning of the vote because the vote assured the assassins that all of their targets would be where they wanted them to be. My bet is that these guys are ex–United States Special Forces commandos and they mean everything they said in that letter. Which of course means that unless these idiots start taking their demands seriously, you're going to have more dead politicians on your hands."

CHAPTER 12

DIRECTOR Roach stood in the kitchen of his suburban Maryland home. Sunday-morning mass was at eleven-thirty, and they would be leaving shortly, but first he wanted to scan the morning press shows and see what type of lines the administration would be floating. Speaker Basset was the featured guest on *Inside Washington,* a weekly political talk show. Roach was leaning against the counter, looking at the small color TV next to the sink. His youngest child walked into the room and opened the refrigerator door. Roach bent over and kissed the top of her head. "Good morning, Katie."

"Hi, Dad." Katie Roach was twelve years old and had not been a planned pregnancy. Her next closest sibling was eight years her elder. Patty Roach had given birth to the youngest of the four Roach kids at the age of forty. Two of Katie's brothers were in college, and the oldest boy had already graduated. Roach often caught himself smiling at Katie and thinking how much his and his wife's lives had been blessed by this wonderful little girl.

The youngest of the Roach clan stood motionless in front of the open refrigerator door, her eyes scanning the shelves, searching for nothing in particular. "Dad, can I have a can of Coke?"

"*May* I have a can of Coke," Roach corrected her, and patted her on the head. "Yes, you may have a can of Coke." Katie snatched the can from the door and scampered out of the kitchen.

A moment later Patty Roach came around the corner. "Brian, I don't want her drinking a can of soda before mass."

Without taking his eyes off the TV, Roach replied, "Honey, she's twelve years old, a little sugar isn't going to kill her."

"I'll try to remember that when she's bouncing all over the pew in twenty minutes. Come on, turn off that TV. I don't want to be late."

"Hold on, I want to watch this for a minute."

"Brian, I don't want to be late again this week."

"Honey, take Katie and get in the car. Tell the guys to get saddled up, and I'll be out in a minute." The "guys" Roach was referring to were his personal protection detail, more commonly known as his bodyguards. Patty left the room and Roach turned his attention back to the TV.

The panel on the show consisted of three reporters, one of whom acted as the host. This morning's special guest, House Speaker Thomas Basset, and the three reporters sat in a semicircle, around a horseshoe news desk. Roach stepped across the room and turned up the volume.

"Speaker Basset, this week was an extremely difficult one for many of us here in the nation's capital . . . probably more so for you than most. You were very close to these three men. You have worked with them for . . . most of your adult life . . . not always agreeing, but more often than not finding a common ground. How have the events of the last several days affected you?"

Basset shifted in his chair. "They have been, to put it lightly, very difficult. . . . What most people don't understand is just how tight of a community we are here in Washington. Our wives all know each other, many of our children went to school together, we see each other at the local churches on Sunday, we're a very tight group. The last three days have been extremely painful." Basset shook his head and looked away from the camera.

"How have you, personally, taken the deaths of your colleagues?"

"I'm grieving right now . . . there's a lot of pain. You go to bed one night and wake up the next morning only to find out that three men who you have worked with for over thirty years have all been brutally murdered. It's shocking. It's very painful."

"I know this week is going to be hard for you, but what are your plans for bringing the House back into legislative session?"

"I will take my time to grieve and remember these great statesmen appropriately, and then we will turn to the president for guidance. President Stevens is a very strong leader, and with his help we will move forward and get back to the business of governing this country."

"Mr. Speaker, everyone is very aware of the letter that was sent to the media by the group claiming responsibility for the murders. There have been some rumors circulating around town regarding the authenticity of this letter. The president even hinted at it in his speech the other night. Can you shed some light on any of these rumors?"

"To the best of our knowledge, the letter was sent by the group that committed the murders. The letter was postmarked the day before the killings and names all three of the deceased. What is in question right now is the actual reason why these murders were committed."

The host leaned forward. "Do you mean to imply that the murders were not committed for the reasons stated in the letter?"

"That is what we are exploring."

"What leads you to believe the letter is not what it appears to be?"

"Well, the FBI is very suspicious of the timing of these murders."

"Why?"

Basset hesitated for a moment. "They are uncertain that the murders were committed solely for the reasons stated in the letter."

The host became visibly excited as he asked his next question. "What facts have they discovered to back this up?"

"The FBI is being very tight-lipped about this, as I'm sure you can understand. All I know right now is that they have received some information that has led them to believe the murders were committed for reasons other than those stated in the letter."

Roach looked at the TV and shook his head. "What in the hell are these guys up to?"

The host continued, "What type of information?"

Basset frowned. "I can't go into it right now."

One of the other reporters jumped in. "If you can't tell us what the FBI has learned, can you tell us what they are speculating the real motive to be?"

Basset shifted uneasily in his seat. Garret and the president had briefed him on the plan. He found the possibility of the murders being committed for the purpose of toppling the Stevens administration and the party to be plausible. At this point, in this town, anything could be possible. What he felt uncomfortable doing was intentionally lying about what the FBI believed to be the reason for the murders. But Basset had learned long ago not to probe too deep. It was easier on his conscience to ponder his actions lightly.

With no visible guilt or awkwardness Basset uttered his pre-planned response. "The FBI thinks the murders were committed to try and stop the president's budget from being passed."

Roach tried to stay calm as he pinched the bridge of his nose tighter and tighter. The program broke away for a commercial and he turned off the TV. As he walked to the door, he asked himself once again, "What in the hell are they up to?"

Eleven miles away, Michael O'Rourke sat in his living room with Liz and Seamus. Seamus had arrived earlier that morning. Michael and Seamus watched the broadcast with irritation while Liz was busy pecking notes into her laptop. She had a column that was supposed to be on her editor's desk by 5 P.M.

The program came back on the air, and the one woman on the panel started to ask questions. "Mr. Speaker, I know this must be a very difficult time for you and your colleagues, and I would not for a moment want you to think that I am condoning these murders, but the assassinations have thrust into the spotlight some reforms that the American people have endorsed for quite some time. The idea of term limits has an approval rating of almost ninety percent, and a balanced-budget amendment has an approval rating of close to eighty percent. Everyone agrees the national debt needs to be reduced, and this letter brings up a point that no one in Washington is willing to address, and that is, cuts in Social Security and Medicare. It is a horrible tragedy that three of our country's elder statesmen have been assassinated, but maybe some good can come of it, if it forces you and the rest of your colleagues to make some overdue and needed reforms."

Basset took a deep breath. They had anticipated a question along these lines, and Garret had helped prepare an answer. Basset paused for a moment and stared at the reporter. "I would like you to try and tell the wives, children, and grandchildren of those three men what good could possibly come from this." Basset shook his head in a disgusted manner.

"Mr. Speaker, I am not saying that this isn't a horrible tragedy for the families of these men. What I am asking is, what is it going to take for the leaders of this country to implement the reforms that the American people want? I mean, if these horrible murders are not going to move you to action, what will?"

"We do not even know if these demands are sincere. As I have told you, the FBI believes the intent of that letter to be bogus . . . and besides, I resent the fact that we have not even had time to bury these honorable men, and you are talking about kowtowing to the demands of their murderers."

"Mr. Speaker, I am not talking about kowtowing to anyone. I am only asking if you plan to implement certain reforms that the American people want."

"I can answer absolutely and emphatically, no! The government of the United States of America has never, and will never, negotiate with terrorists."

"No one is asking you to negotiate with terrorists, Mr. Speaker. We are talking about making several simple, long-overdue reforms."

Basset started to shake his head back and forth. "The key word in that sentence was *simple*. Running this country is a very complex and difficult task. A couple of 'simple reforms' as you phrased it will not even solve some of the minor problems our country has." Basset turned to the host. "And I would like to add, things are not as dire as some would lead us to think. The president has been doing a fine job. The economy is strong, and we have been reporting smaller budget deficits than the previous administration."

The reporter was not to be deterred by simple political rhetoric. "So you plan on doing nothing, Mr. Speaker?"

"No. I plan on bringing the House back into session as soon as we are done paying respect to our fallen colleagues, and then we will pass the president's budget. A budget that, I might add, the American people want."

O'Rourke got off the couch and tossed the remote control on Liz's lap. "What's it going to take for these guys to learn? Seamus, do you want to go for a walk?" Michael's grandfather nodded and got out of his chair. Michael left the room and appeared in the doorway a moment later with two coats and Duke's leash. He handed one of the coats to Seamus and bent down to snap the leash onto Duke's collar. He stood and looked over at Liz, who was focused on the TV. "Honey, we'll be back in an hour or so."

Without looking up, she replied, "I'll be here. You two have a nice time."

Michael watched her diligently type away while she stayed focused on the program. Walking behind the couch, he bent over and kissed her on the cheek. "Don't pull any punches, honey."

Scarlatti smiled and said, "I never do."

"That's why you're my favorite journalist."

"I hope that's not the only reason."

Seamus grinned at Michael, and the two of them, along with Duke, left the house. When they reached the sidewalk, Seamus said, "You two seem very happy."

"We are. If it wasn't for our jobs, I would have probably asked her to marry me by now."

The stoic Seamus said, "Well, you have my approval." As an afterthought he added, "If it matters."

Michael wrapped an arm around his grandfather and with a big grin said, "You're damn right it does."

Duke began sniffing everything in their path, zigzagging back and forth across the sidewalk. Michael looked over his shoulder and said, "There's something we really need to talk about."

"Does it have anything to do with what you mentioned on the phone the other day?"

"Yes. Remember the hunting trip we went on last year with—"

Seamus raised his hand and cut Michael off. "Don't mention any names." Seamus looked up and down the street. Washington gave him the creeps. "With all of these damn embassies around here, the FBI, the CIA, the NSA, and all of the defense intelligence agencies, it's a wonder any conversation takes place in this town without being recorded."

Michael nodded. "Well, you know who I'm talking about." The younger of the two O'Rourkes lowered his voice. "On that trip I gave him some highly sensitive information about a senator who cost the lives of half the men in his unit."

"I remember."

Michael paused and said, "I think that he might be involved in these assassinations."

"And?" Seamus shrugged his shoulders with indifference.

"You don't think it's a big deal?"

Seamus retrieved his pipe from his jacket. "Yes, I think it's a big deal." He packed some tobacco in the bowl and sucked a flame down into it. Exhaling a cloud of smoke, he said, "Michael, partisan politics has always existed in this country and it always will. In a way it's healthy. The parties act as another check and balance. They pulled the same crap when I was your age; the only difference was, when push came to shove, they were responsible enough to balance the budget. The problem today is that men like Koslowski, Fitzgerald, and Downs . . . the old guard . . . they control the system. All of this shit went down on their watch, and they did nothing to prevent it. In fact they resisted commonsense change at every turn. They are the reason we are five trillion dollars in debt, and I couldn't be happier that they are dead."

Michael gave Duke's leash a slight yank to get him to slow down. "I'm not sad they're dead either. I've seen up close and personal the way they do business, and I couldn't be happier that they're gone. My problem is that I'm not entirely comfortable with the idea that I may have set this whole thing in motion by relaying a highly classified piece of information that I wasn't even supposed to know."

Seamus waited for another walker to pass before he gave his answer. "We went over this before you told him. You commanded a recon unit when you were in the Corps. If some little silver-spoon millionaire politician compromised a mission that you and your men were on because he had had one too many martinis . . . and his loose lips led to the deaths of half of your unit, would you want to know?"

Michael sighed deeply and said, "Yes."

"That's all the farther you need to look, Michael." Seamus took several more puffs off his pipe while they walked. "Have you talked to anyone else about this?"

"No."

"Not even Liz?"

"No."

"Good. Keep it under your hat. If our boy is behind this, we're fortunate. This is the first chance we've had for real change in thirty years."

"I agree. It's just that something like this could spin out of control real fast, and I don't want to see him get taken down."

"Don't worry. He isn't going to get caught. He's been doing this for years, in places a hell of a lot more dangerous than the United States."

Director Thomas Stansfield sat in his office with only his desk lamp on. Outside the window of his corner office, powerful floodlights illuminated the formidable compound of the Central Intelligence Agency. Three years ago he would never have been found in the office on a Sunday night. He would have been sitting at home with his wife. Stansfield's demanding job required him to work some long and strange hours, but Sunday evenings had been the one night of the week, barring an international crisis, when he would drop everything to be at home. He and his wife would typically watch *60 Minutes* while making dinner, maybe relax in front of a fire, watch a movie, and then call the girls out on the West Coast. They had two daughters, both married, one living in Sacramento and the other in San Diego.

This calm, comforting, and loving part of Thomas Stansfield's existence had vanished with little notice. Sara Stansfield had left his life too quickly. During a routine physical, a tumor had been discovered. When the doctors went in to take it out, they found that the cancer had already spread to several glands. Two months later, Sara was dead. It had been the most painful two months of Stansfield's life. That he worked in a profession where emotions were looked on as a liability—a profession where tough-minded and emotionally neutral people played a serious game—did not help things. When Sara died, Stansfield had been the Agency's director for just over a year. Just when he'd reached the top of his profession, he'd lost the most important person in his life.

Those who were close to him offered their private condolences, and they were appreciated. Some offered to help with the workload until he was up to it, but Stansfield had kindly refused. After Sara's funeral, he spent several days with his daughters and three grandchildren, reminiscing about his beautiful wife and their loving mother and grandmother. The sons-in-law respected the feelings of a very private man and kept their distance. When the weekend was over, he put his loved ones on a plane and went back to work. Even three years later, Sara was often on his mind. The pain was gone and had been replaced by fond memories, hard work, and trips to see his daughters and grandchildren.

Stansfield was a first in the history of CIA directors. He had no military experience, he was not a lawyer or a politician, and he was not Ivy League educated. Stansfield had entered the Agency during the midfifties, after graduating from the University of South Dakota. He had something the Agency was searching for desperately—he was fluent in three languages: English, German, and Russian. Being raised on a farm in rural South Dakota during the pretelevision days gave his German-immigrant father and his Russian-immigrant mother plenty of time to teach their children the languages, customs, and folklore of their native lands. Stansfield had been one of the CIA's most productive agents during the fifties and sixties. In the seventies he became a case officer, in the early eighties he was the Agency's station chief in Moscow, and then in the late eighties he became the deputy director of operations. At the time, he thought he'd reached the end of the ladder.

That was until the previous president did something that surprised everyone. The CIA, at the time of the collapse of the Soviet Union, had grown to rely heavily on nonhuman data. They were spending most of their resources spying the high-tech way, with satellites and other electronic devices. The electronic information that the Agency collected was valuable, but nowhere near as valuable as a well-placed agent. During that president's second year, he was confronted with his first national-security crisis and was forced to face the harsh reality that his intelligence agencies could not give him the information he needed. All of those billion-dollar satellites and million-dollar spy planes could not tell him what he needed to know. What he needed was someone on the ground, someone on the inside. A spy.

Following that incident, the president put together a task force and asked them to come up with a strategy for correcting this shortcoming. Stansfield was placed on the task force, which he thought was nothing more than a waste of time and energy. After months of late meetings and lengthy debates, the task force briefed the president on its findings. They told him that America needed to increase its human intelligence-gathering apparatus on a global scale. They told him it would take a long-term commitment, and that it could be a minimum of six to ten years before they started to see any tangible results from their efforts. To Stansfield's amazement the president not only agreed, but decided that since the current director of the CIA was retiring shortly, it would make sense to have someone who understood the human side of the business running the Agency.

Some people were upset that they had been passed over for the position, but most of them had no choice but to respect the decision. Stansfield was an icon, a real-life spook. He had earned his spurs running around behind the Iron Curtain risking his life. He had risen through the ranks and put in his time.

The phone on Stansfield's desk started to ring, and he looked over the top of his spectacles to see which line it was. The light blinking on the far right told him it was his private line. He grabbed the phone and said hello.

"Tom, Brian Roach here. Sorry to bother you on a Sunday

night, but I need to run a couple of things by you." It wasn't unusual for Roach to be calling his counterpart at the CIA, but tonight he felt a little uncomfortable.

"No problem at all, Brian. I'm just trying to get a head start on the week. What can I help you with?"

After a prolonged pause, Roach said, "Tom, I need to ask you a couple of questions, and if you don't want to answer them, please just tell me."

"Go right ahead."

"Tom, do you or does anyone at the Agency possess any information that would lead you to believe the murders were committed for reasons other than those stated in that letter?"

Stansfield's eyebrows frowned at the question. "Not that I know of."

"No one at the Agency has told the White House that they have discovered some information that suggests the motives of the killings were something other than those stated in that letter?" Roach asked again, more firmly.

"No, I thought you guys were the ones that came up with that theory."

Roach breathed a long, frustrated sigh. "No, we haven't told the White House anything."

"Then why are the president and all of his people running around town saying that you have?"

"That's what I would like to find out."

"It sounds like they're up to something." Stansfield leaned back in his chair and turned to look at a map of the world on his wall.

"Yeah, I've been getting the same feeling." Roach paused and took another deep breath. "Any advice?"

Stansfield thought about the question. He was normally careful about giving his opinion, but he and Roach were of the same cloth. He had a lot of empathy for his counterpart at the FBI. It might be

Roach whom they were doing a job on this week, but it could easily be him next time.

"I think it may be a good idea to drop a little hint to the media that you have no idea what the White House is talking about."

Roach pondered the advice for a moment. He liked the direct approach. "Thanks, Tom, I appreciate the advice. If you hear of anything, please let me know."

"Will do." Stansfield set the phone back in its cradle and closed his eyes. Mike Nance and his associates made him nervous. Nance was the real brains over at the White House, the man with the connections.

Garret was sitting in his office with his feet up on the desk and an array of newspapers before him. It was just after six on Monday morning, and his plan was coming along nicely. With a cigarette dangling from his lips he snickered at how easy it was to manipulate the media. The front page of the *Washington Post* read, "Murky Conspiracy Rumored to Be Behind Murders." The front page of the *New York Times* read, "FBI Thinks Murders Were Committed to Stop President's Budget." The *Washington Reader* read, "FBI Thinks Letter Is Bogus." Garret laughed out loud. It had been so easy. It made no difference if it was made up or not, the damage had been done. The American people would read the headlines and believe what they saw. Public support would rally back to the president, and they would ride it into a second term. Garret shook his head and grinned as he thought of the power he wielded.

Garret's plan was simple. All he had to do was continue to portray the president as a victim and hope those idiots over at the FBI could catch these people. He smiled at how easy it was to play the power game against principled men like Roach. While they took the time to decide if a course of action was right or wrong, Garret worried only about being caught. He had no time for petty little laws and technicalities, and he definitely had no time for someone else's morals. He was there to get things done, and to play the game by his own rules.

Director Roach's limousine pulled up in front of the Hyatt hotel at 6:55 A.M. He was there to give a brief speech to the National Convention of Police Chiefs. Because of the assassinations, he had considered having one of his deputies handle the speech, but after talking to Stansfield, he decided to give it himself. He'd just finished scanning a *Washington Reader* article stating that the FBI thought there was a conspiracy behind the murders. As his bodyguards opened the door of the limo, a small mob of about eight reporters and cameramen closed in. Roach stepped out of the limo and said hello to the group. A tall, blond-haired woman got to him first. "Director Roach, could you please tell us what information the FBI has discovered that would lead you to believe the letter sent to the media after the killings is a cover for the real reason Senator Downs, Senator Fitzgerald, and Congressman Koslowski were killed?"

To the surprise of Roach's bodyguards, their boss stopped to answer the question. The reporters jostled each other to get their mikes in Roach's face.

"As of right now, we believe that letter to be sincere and are very concerned about the possibility of further assassinations."

A tall male reporter blurted out the next question. "Director Roach, do you think the murders were committed in an attempt to derail President Stevens's budget?"

"No, I do not. We think the assassinations took place on the eve of the budget vote because it guaranteed the assassins that Congressman Koslowski, Senator Downs, and Senator Fitzgerald would be in town."

"I don't understand. The White House has been reporting that the FBI believes the murders were committed to derail the president's budget," said a somewhat confused reporter.

"Those reports are incorrect." Before another question could be asked, Roach turned and entered the hotel. Within minutes, his comments were being played as the lead story on every morning network news show.

Without knocking, Garret opened the door to Nance's office and barged in. Nance glanced up from his TV, which was showing the taped interview of Roach.

"What in the hell is he doing?" asked Garret as he pointed at the TV.

Nance turned his head away from the TV. "Relax, Stu, this was expected. You didn't really think he would sit there and let us use him, did you?"

"Hell no, but I at least thought he'd come to us, not go to the press," Garret said, glaring at the TV.

"Calm down, we already got what we wanted. The polls have swung ten points in our favor. The people think there's some big conspiracy to ruin the president. The press loves the story and will run with it, regardless of what Roach says. We'll have Moncur release a statement saying it was improperly implied that the FBI had discovered the information when it was in fact another government agency. They'll all assume it's the CIA, and it'll make the story that much better. Besides, we can use this 'Roach thing' to our advantage. He fired the first shot. With a few leaks to the right people, the press will be printing stories saying there's bad blood between Roach and the White House, and if he doesn't make some progress in solving these murders, things will get very uncomfortable for him. Combine that with the fact that our friends in the media will be more than willing to do a butcher job on a saint like Roach, and we'll have his letter of resignation in our hands by next month." In a rare moment of emotion, Nance smiled at Garret, and the gesture was returned.

CHAPTER 13

THE Bell Atlantic van was parked on New Hampshire Avenue, a half block from Dupont Circle. The two men in the back checked their makeup and equipment one last time. On top of their Afro wigs they were wearing yellow plastic hard hats. They were also wearing blue coveralls with a Bell Atlantic patch over the left pocket. They nodded to the driver, grabbed their bags, and climbed out of the van. Casually, they walked down the stairs leading to the Dupont Circle platform of the D.C. metro. Upon reaching the platform, they climbed on board the metro and took the red line to Union Station. They arrived about five minutes later and got off. Threading their way through the other subway riders, they walked to the end of the platform and stepped out onto the small ledge running along the side of the tunnel. After about fifty feet they reached a doorway and stopped. The shorter man handed a bag to his accomplice and went to work on the lock. Twenty seconds later they were in.

They stepped through the vault door that led to one of the underground tunnel systems that ran beneath Washington, D.C. The system they had just entered housed mostly phone lines and various utility pipes. The sewers carrying the city's waste and water runoff were located in another system that was buried even deeper.

As they walked through the squared cement tunnel, the taller of the two men had to tilt his head to one side to avoid hitting the lights that were spaced about every fifty feet overhead. They took a series of turns, and after about three minutes they were standing in front of another door. Again, the shorter of the two went to work on the lock. When he was finished picking it, he opened the door and placed a piece of duct tape over the lock. The two men stepped into the subbasement of a twelve-story office building and let the door close behind them.

The shorter of the two headed for the staircase and disappeared. The second man weaved through the mass of pipes and structural supports until he found what he was looking for. He pried open the steel access panel to the main duct of the building's ventilation system and placed it on the ground.

The other man had just finished climbing to the sixth floor of the multitenant office building. They had scouted the building months in advance. The top five floors were leased by a law firm, and the rest of the floors were half filled with lobbying firms, smaller offices, and various other businesses. Vacant suites were interspersed on all of the floors except the top five. He opened the staircase door and looked down the hallway. With no one in sight, he casually walked down the hall and stopped at the third door on his right. Setting his bag down, he started to pick the lock. Speed was not crucial; acting relaxed and nonchalant was. He wasn't worried about one of the office workers seeing him. If they did, they wouldn't be surprised by someone from the phone company going into an empty office suite.

Finishing with the lock, he entered the room and walked over to the tinted window. Dropping to one knee, he set his bag down and emptied the contents, laying them out on the floor in a precise manner. In under a minute he assembled the rifle and placed the nitroglycerin-tipped round in the chamber. Twenty seconds later the rifle was affixed to the top of a tripod. The assassin eased his left eye in behind the scope and stared down at the front door of the building directly across the street. He then turned on the laser sight, and a small red dot appeared on the tinted window. Twisting the screws on the tripod, he locked the rifle into place, and then, reaching into his bag, he grabbed a glass cutter and placed the suction cup in the middle of the red dot. Slowly, he swung the cutting piece in a clockwise motion with his right hand. Instead of popping the newly cut piece free, he tied one end of string around the glass cutter and the other end around one of the tripod's legs.

Pulling the microphone arm down from under the short brim of his hard hat, he said, "Chuck, this is Sam, come in, over."

Despite the whine of the machinery in the basement, the second man heard his partner loud and clear. "This is Chuck, over."

"Everything is set on my end, over."

"Roger, everything is set down here, over."

Secret Service agent Harry Dorle had been pulled out of the field and directed to head the personal protection detail for Congressman Thomas Basset. Since Basset was the Speaker of the House, he was deemed a high-profile target by the FBI and the Secret Service. Dorle had been the special agent in charge for the presidential detail of the previous administration. When his boss lost his reelection bid to Stevens, it was the end of Dorle's assignment. Like most of the presidents before him, Stevens wanted a changing of the guard. The Secret Service did not object to this tradition because they knew it was good for their agents to be rotated. It helped prevent complacency and boredom.

Dorle sat in the lobby of Speaker Basset's Capitol office and waited for the Speaker to give the word that he was ready to leave. The tall, middle-aged agent looked calm on the outside, but inside he was a wreck. He had read the report on the Koslowski, Fitzgerald, and Downs assassinations, and it scared him. The assassins were professionals. Three hits, all in one night. One a

bare-handed kill, the second a rifle shot, and the third a point-blank hit. These guys were not your run-of-the-mill Aryan Nation types. They were pros, and with the way Basset liked to gallivant around town, he would be an easy target.

Because there were so many congressmen and senators to protect, the Secret Service had not been able to give Dorle the number of agents he wanted. They had given him only five men and women, and the Speaker's normal Capitol Police detail had been increased to eight officers around the clock. Dorle made a cursory effort to ask Basset to cancel all public appearances until things cooled down, and as Dorle had expected, Basset declined. This, of course, made Dorle's job extremely difficult. He knew the only way to really protect Basset was to keep him locked up in his house, his office, or his armor-plated limo. As soon as Basset left either of the three, Dorle's ability to protect him was reduced significantly.

They were minutes away from leaving for Basset's taped interview with CNN. Dorle told his new boss that he thought it was a bad idea, and Basset had politely told him he wasn't going to cancel. CNN had been advertising the appearance of the Speaker since late Sunday afternoon, and although it would be tape-delayed, it wouldn't take a genius to figure out when the taping would take place. Dorle could not remember being more worried about an assignment. Whoever these killers were, they'd had months to plan what they were doing. They'd stalked and studied their targets, and if that letter was for real, they would strike again.

Dorle was gambling with his assets. He just didn't have enough men to do a complete job. He had sent four of his Secret Service agents and two of the uniformed officers ahead to do an advance check of the CNN building. They were to do a quick check of the street, the exits, and the rooftop. He would put four of the uniformed cops on body detail. They would surround Basset as he got out of the limo and walked into the studio. Dorle had contemplated using his Secret Service agents for the body detail; they were trained to do it, but they were more valuable to him doing other things.

Speaker Basset and his aide, Matthew Schwab, appeared in the lobby, and Dorle rose to his feet. "Are you ready to go, sir?"

"Yes," Basset answered.

Dorle brought his left hand up to his mouth and spoke into a tiny microphone. "Art, this is Harry, over."

The Secret Service agent just outside the office door responded, "This is Art, over."

"Bobcat is ready to roll, over." Bobcat was the code name that had been given to Basset.

The agent looked up and down the hall and nodded to the police officer holding the elevator. "The hallway is secure, over."

"Roger, let the boys downstairs know we're on our way, over." Dorle turned to Basset and motioned for the door. "Whenever you're ready, sir." Dorle opened the door and Basset and Schwab stepped into the hallway. The entourage of Basset, Schwab, Dorle, the other Secret Service agent, and two cops started for the elevator. Dorle took up the rear, while the other three men surrounded Basset and Schwab. The entourage stepped into the elevator for the short ride to the garage level.

When the door opened, another police officer was waiting for them, and the group moved out for the underground parking garage. Dorle wasn't nervous about anything happening in the Capitol. The assassins would have to be suicidal to try something with all the military personnel and police in the building.

When they reached the garage, the limo was waiting with one police squad parked in front and another behind. Schwab and Basset were quickly ushered into the backseat. Dorle brought the Capitol Police officers together for a quick reminder of how things would go when they arrived at their destination. When he was finished, the police got into their squad cars, Agent Art Jones climbed behind the wheel of the large, black Cadillac, and Dorle got into the backseat with the Speaker and Schwab. Before giving the order to pull out, Dorle brought his mike up to his mouth and said, "Advance team Bravo, this is Alpha, do you read? Over."

The leader of the advance team at the CNN studios heard the call through his earpiece and had to cut off one of the building's private security guards in midsentence. "This is Bravo, over."

"We are en route with Bobcat. What is your sit report? Over."

"About as secure as we could get things on such short notice, Harry, over."

"Roger, our ETA is two minutes. If anything changes, let me know immediately, over." Dorle looked at his agent behind the wheel. "Let's move out, Art." Jones flashed the limo's brights at the lead police car, and the motorcade sped out of the parking garage.

The assassin looked out of the window and down at the two police officers in front of the CNN building. They'd just stepped off the curb and were standing on the street, waving by cars and cabs that wanted to stop in front of the building. He spoke into the mike hanging in front of his mouth. "Chuck, stay loose. They should be arriving any minute, over."

The response came back immediately. "Roger, everything is set down here." The man standing in front of the ventilation shaft took off his hard hat, placed it in his bag, and pulled out a gas mask. Reaching back into the bag, he grabbed two gray canisters and set them on top of the ventilation unit.

The motorcade pulled up in front of the building and stopped. Dorle immediately noticed that, despite telling the drivers of both squads to give the limo at least thirty feet on either end, they had forgotten and the limo was boxed in. "Art, call the guys in the squads and tell them to move their cars farther away from the limo." Dorle turned to Basset. "Sir, please stay in the car for a minute while I check things out." Dorle exited the limo and met his agent in charge of the Bravo team on the sidewalk. "How are we doing?" he asked the junior man.

"Fine. The exits are secured, the elevator is being held, and Alan is on the roof keeping an eye on things."

The assassin looked down at the two men on the street and guessed that they were either Secret Service or FBI. It had been expected. He spoke into his mike, "Chuck, get ready to pull the pin."

The man in the basement pulled the gas mask down over his face and grabbed one of the canisters. Back on the sixth floor, the assassin watched as the man who had stepped out of the limo waved several police officers over and started to organize them around the door of the limo. None of these men would do any good. The assassin had chosen the sixth floor so the angle of the shot would be such that four seven-foot-tall officers would make no difference. They didn't want to kill anyone other than Basset. That was also the reason the nitro-tipped bullet was being used. Unlike most rifle bullets, this one would explode on impact and not exit the target. A typical rifle bullet would spiral through the target and exit with enough velocity to inflict damage, and even death, to anyone unfortunate enough to be standing on the other side.

The assassin saw the man who had gotten out of the limo a moment earlier stick his head into the open door and then step back as he helped Basset out of the backseat. The assassin clutched the butt of the rifle a little tighter, placed his right hand on the string, and spoke into the small mike hanging in front of his mouth, "Chuck, drop the smoke."

The man in the basement pulled the pin from the first canister, tossed it into the open vent, and quickly grabbed the second canister and did the same. He then grabbed the metal access panel and covered the opening. The smoke from the two canisters immediately shot upward through the ventilation system, pushed by the warm air leaving the furnace. The man then walked briskly to the wall and waited.

The assassin on the sixth floor concentrated on taking slow, deep breaths. When he saw the head of Basset pop out of the limo, his right hand yanked the string attached to the glass cutter, and the newly created circle of glass dropped to the floor. Basset was ushered into the middle of the four police officers, and the group started to move toward the door. The assassin spoke into his mike, "Pull the alarm." In the basement, his accomplice yanked on the fire alarm. The loud buzzing of the alarm reverberated throughout the building and spilled out onto the street.

Dorle and his agents were sweeping the street and looking at everyone but Basset. When the alarm went off, the police officers surrounding Basset did what their instincts told them to do. They stopped and looked to see where the noise was coming from. At the same time the police officers' instincts kicked in, so did Dorle's. He lunged forward and screamed, "Keep moving!" As he reached the back of the first officer, he heard what he instantly knew was the loud crack of a rifle shot. He continued to push the group as he yelled, "Move! Move!" He took two steps, and then the officer in front of him stumbled and fell, landing on the fatally wounded Basset. Dorle placed his hand on the back of the officer to prevent himself from falling and looked down to see if Basset had been hit.

The answer was immediately obvious. There was blood everywhere. The nitro-tipped bullet had ripped apart the back of Basset's head, and the white shirts of the Capitol Police officers were covered with blood and a good portion of the Speaker's brain. Dorle kneeled over the pile and brought his mike to his mouth. "Bobcat's been hit! I repeat, Bobcat has been hit!" Two of the Secret Service agents were now standing between the street and the pile of bodies on the ground, their Uzis drawn, and their eyes searching the buildings across the street.

• • •

The assassin quickly disassembled the rifle and put everything back in the bag. Smoke was filling the room and he yanked his gas mask over his face. Grabbing the bag, he ran down the hallway toward the stairwell. Once in the stairwell, he pushed his way past the scared office workers who thought the building was on fire.

Dorle looked down at what was left of Basset's head and knew the Speaker was dead. Just then, the voice of the Secret Service agent on the roof of the CNN building came barking over Dorle's earpiece. "I think the shot came from the building directly across the street!"

Dorle jumped to his feet and started shouting orders. "Art, call for backup, let's secure that building!" Turning to one of the cops, he yelled, "Take two of your men and head around the back! I don't want anyone leaving the area! And be careful!" Grabbing the two agents who had their Uzis drawn, he ran across the street for the front of the building. They darted between the cars that had stopped to see what was happening. They made it to the other side of the street, and just as they reached the front of the building, an onslaught of frantic office workers met them coming the other way. They were blocked from getting inside. Three blocks away at Union Station, the blond-haired assassin was wearing loose jeans, a large sweatshirt, and a baseball hat. He walked over to a row of pay phones. Union Station, like most large train and subway stations, had hundreds of pay phones. It was an easy place for a person to come and go unnoticed. The man reached into his left pocket and pulled out a quarter. The dirty-blond hair that came out from under the cap and down to his shoulders was not natural. Neither was his posture. Instead of standing erect and looking like an athletic, six-foot-tall man, he was slouching. To the casual observer he looked like a slightly overweight man who was no taller than five ten. He punched the seven digits into the phone and pulled a small recorder out of his pocket. A female voice answered on the other end, "Good afternoon, American Broadcasting Corporation. How may I direct your call?"

The man pressed the play button on the recorder, and a computerized voice emanated from the small speaker. "Do not hang up. This message is from the group that is responsible for the killings of Senator Fitzgerald, Senator Downs, Congressman Koslowski, and Speaker Basset."

The twenty-three-year-old receptionist felt her heart jolt. She panicked for a moment and then remembered that all calls coming into the main switchboard were recorded.

After a short pause the recording continued. "Speaker Basset was killed because he and the rest of his colleagues have failed to take our demands seriously. We are not terrorists. We have killed no innocent civilians; in fact, we have gone to great lengths to avoid doing so. We are not, as the White House has led the media to believe, part of a conspiracy to topple the Stevens presidency. We are a group of Americans who are fed up with the corruption and complete lack of professionalism that exists in Washington, D.C.

"We gave you a chance to implement in a peaceful, democratic way the reforms you have been promising. You have failed to do so, so we have intervened. Do not test us again or we will be forced to impose more term limits. We have the resources and the resolve to kill any congressman, any senator, and even the president.

"We will grant a cease-fire and give you the remainder of the week to bury Koslowski, Downs, Fitzgerald, and Basset. After they have been laid to rest, we expect immediate action on the reforms we have proposed."

CHAPTER 14

IT was still light out as Harry Dorle passed through the Secret Service checkpoint and parked his car outside the staff entrance to the West Wing of the White House. Getting out of the car, he asked himself for the hundredth time since the shooting how the assassin had gotten away. The police had sealed off the entire block within minutes of the attack. All of the people who had evacuated the smoke-filled building had been roped off and were being questioned for the third and fourth time by the FBI and the Secret Service. So far, every one of them had checked out as a legitimate office worker. The building had been searched with dogs and was empty. What a mess, he thought to himself. I've had twenty-three good years and now this.

As he reached the entrance, Jack Warch opened the door. "Harry, I'm sorry . . . I'm really sorry." Warch had replaced Dorle as the special agent in charge of the presidential security detail. The two men had known each other for most of their professional careers.

Dorle nodded his head in acknowledgment, but kept his eyes averted. They walked to the main floor, Warch leading and Dorle following, neither saying a word. When they reached the door to the Roosevelt Room, Dorle stopped and asked, "Jack, is the president in there?"

"No, he's over on the residential side talking to Mrs. Basset."

Dorle looked down at the ground and shook his head. Warch put his hand on his friend's shoulder. "Harry, it wasn't your fault."

Dorle looked up. "Yeah, yeah, I know."

When they entered the room, Stu Garret was pacing back and forth talking to Alex Tracy, the director of the Secret Service. Mike Nance was at the far end of the table, sitting by himself and observing the conversation between Garret and Tracy. Garret turned and stopped speaking as Warch and Dorle entered. The room fell silent and no one spoke for a moment.

Director Tracy finally broke the silence. "Gentlemen, please sit down." Everyone sat with the exception of Garret. Director Tracy looked at Dorle. "Harry, are you all right?" Dorle nodded his head yes, but said nothing. Tracy stared at him a while longer and went on, "Harry, have you met Stu Garret and Mike Nance before?"

"No."

There was another awkward silence while Dorle waited for Nance or Garret to say something, but neither made the effort. Then Garret stepped toward the table. "Agent Dorle, we have been receiving reports all afternoon and we know the basic facts about what happened. What we don't know, and what I would really like to know, is, *how* did it happen?" Garret said in one of his more confrontational tones.

"What do you mean 'how'?" asked Dorle.

"I'll tell you what I mean by *how*. I want to know *how* in the hell the Speaker of the House, the third most powerful man in this country, was killed in broad daylight while he was surrounded by a dozen Secret Service agents and police officers." Garret leaned over, placed both hands on the table, and stared at Dorle as he impatiently waited for a response.

Dorle looked at Garret and realized how this meeting was going to go. He'd heard all about Garret and his style, so he sat up a little straighter and prepared himself for the confrontation. It had been a long day and Dorle was not in the mood to be dumped on. His face tensed slightly as he spoke. "Speaker Basset was killed because he refused to cancel a public appearance. He was warned that we could not guarantee his safety, and he chose to ignore our advice."

"That's bullshit, Dorle. He was killed because you and your men didn't do your jobs. It's as simple as that." Garret banged his fist on the table.

Dorle rose out of his chair to meet Garret eye to eye. "Oh, no, you're not." Pointing his finger at Garret, he said, "I'm not going to sit here and let you hang the blame for this on me."

Garret interrupted Dorle and shouted, "Agent Dorle, you are in the White House, and I run the show around here. You will sit your ass back down right now and keep your mouth shut!"

"I don't give a flying fuck if you're the king of Siam! I told him it wasn't a good idea to go out in public, and he ignored me. I did my job, and if Basset would have listened to me, he'd still be alive!"

Garret looked over at Director Tracy and screamed, "I want this man fired right now!" Without waiting for Tracy to respond, Garret snapped his head around to Warch and pointed at Dorle. "Get him out of here now! I want his ass thrown out on the street!"

Dorle went to step toward Garret, and Warch rose out of his seat, blocking him. "Harry, it's not worth it."

"Bullshit, I don't need this crap. I've been around too long to take shit from this little Hitler."

Garret looked back at Director Tracy. "I want him fired right now! I want his badge before he leaves this building."

Warch pushed Dorle out the door and closed it behind him.

Dorle was shaking and his face was red from yelling. "Jack, I'm not going to take the blame for what happened to Basset."

"I know, Harry. I know, just relax."

Dorle took a couple of deep breaths. "I haven't lost my temper like that in years."

"You've had a long day, and Garret doesn't usually bring out the best in people."

"I can't believe that guy. Does the president actually listen to him?"

"I'm afraid so."

Back in the Roosevelt Room, Mike Nance stood and gestured for Garret to follow him. He opened a door at the opposite end of the room and walked across the hall to the Oval Office. Garret walked around the large table and through the door. When he entered the Oval Office, Nance closed the door behind Garret and stood staring at him for a full thirty seconds while he waited for Garret to calm down.

In a steady voice Nance said, "Stu, you've got to learn to control yourself."

"Mike, this whole damn thing is falling apart. We've lost Koslowski and Basset. Do you know what our odds are for getting him reelected with those two dead?" Garret held up his hand and formed a zero. "They're zip, Mike. You and I are going to be out of a job next year. This whole thing is falling apart, and it's because idiots like that Dorle can't do their job."

Nance looked at Garret and wondered momentarily if he really was nuts. "Stu, you have to get ahold of yourself. A lot of things could happen between now and election time. Losing your temper doesn't do us a bit of good. We have a lot of work to do tonight, so calm down. The important thing right now is to get the public behind us. We have to find a way to turn this thing around. It's not going to be easy, but we have to keep our heads."

Garret nodded in agreement and Nance said, "Let's go back in there and keep our cool."

Speaker Basset had left the Capitol's underground parking garage in a black limousine less than twenty-four hours earlier. He was now being returned in a black hearse. As the vehicle rolled to a stop, the back door was opened, and a special detail of six military personnel in dress uniform lifted the flag-draped casket out of the hearse and onto a gurney.

After consulting with Speaker Basset's family, President Stevens had given the order to make arrangements for Basset to be included in the already planned ceremony for Senator Fitzgerald, Congressman Koslowski, and Senator Downs. All four of the deceased had stated in their wills that they were to be buried in their home states. With the obvious security issues arising from the string of assassinations, it was decided that it would be best to have Basset join his three fallen comrades rather than have a separate ceremony in two days.

After a short elevator ride to the main level of the Capitol, the gurney was discarded and the special detail carried the coffin down the hallway, across the cold, stone floor, and laid it on the rectangular, black catafalque. The four flag-draped coffins sat underneath the center of the Capitol's large dome, each one pointing outward, marking the four major points of the compass. It was almost 10 A.M., and with the exception of a military color guard, the rotunda was void of all people.

One by one, the families were given a private moment alone, to mourn over the coffin of their deceased relative. Each family took about half an hour, and at noon the media was let in and allowed to start coverage of the event. The cameras started to roll, and the senators and congressmen filed in to pay their last respects. Just after 2 P.M., the legislators were shuffled off into secure areas of the Capitol, and the doors were opened to the public. A steady stream of people filed by the coffins until just after midnight, when the crowd started to thin.

Senator Erik Olson was sitting in his study trying to decide if he should go against the wishes of the president, the FBI, the Secret

Service, and his wife. It was almost 1 A.M., and he couldn't sleep. Too much was on his mind. He knew that the right and honorable thing to do would be to walk behind the caissons as the procession of coffins were moved from the Capitol to the White House. The daring daylight assassination of Basset had made every congressman and senator realize just how vulnerable they all were. Basset had been given more protection than any of his colleagues, and they'd still gotten to him. Not only did they get to him, but they got away without a trace.

The FBI and the Secret Service were not taking any more chances, and the politicians who were still alive had become extremely agreeable in the wake of the recent events. Earlier in the day, when the final security arrangements were being made for the funeral procession, it had been decided by the Secret Service and the FBI that no one, not even family members, would walk in the open, behind the caissons. None of the senior senators and congressmen had argued. They were not eager to join the ranks of the fallen four.

But for a variety of reasons, Olson felt that he should walk behind the caskets. First of all, it was a tradition that should be kept and honored, and secondly, he felt that someone needed to show that the government of the United States was not afraid. Someone needed desperately to look like a leader. Every politician in the country was cowering behind locked doors and bodyguards. Olson couldn't blame them, especially the ones who had been unscrupulous during their time in Washington. The senator from Minnesota had gotten along with all four of the dead men, but he held no false illusions about their character. They were four of the most unethical politicians in Washington.

Olson was a historian by training and was more worried about the broad implications these murders would have on the future of American politics. History was the great teacher, he had always told his students. History repeated itself for many reasons. Mostly because people really hadn't changed all that much over the course of modern civilization, and more so because history set precedents and gave people ideas. Olson did not want what was happening in his country to become a precedent. The events that had started the previous Friday needed to be stopped and dealt with in a swift and just manner. There was no room in a democracy for terrorism. Someone needed to stand up; someone needed to act like a leader. Someone needed to walk behind those caissons tomorrow and show that he was not afraid.

The silver-haired Swede pictured himself walking alone on the slow, one-mile journey and wondered if any of his colleagues would have the courage to join him. He started to mentally scroll through a list of names, searching for someone who would be bold enough to accompany him. After a brief moment, a name popped into his head and he went no further. Reaching for his phone, he dialed the number.

Michael patted Duke on the head and dropped his keys on the kitchen counter. As he picked up a stack of mail, he was relieved to see Liz's purse sitting by the phone. O'Rourke quickly thumbed through the mail and then set the entire stack back on the counter. He yanked his tie off and started to unbutton his shirt as he headed for the stairs. Duke followed, and Michael stopped in the front entryway and said good-night to his canine buddy.

It was late, he was tired, and he needed to talk to Liz. Guilt was starting to weigh heavily on his shoulders. The young congressman plodded up the stairs and into his bedroom. Liz was sitting on her side of the bed reading a book and wearing one of his gray University of Minnesota T-shirts. Michael smiled at her and sat down on the edge. Liz set her book down and took off her glasses. "You look like crap, honey."

"Thanks," O'Rourke grimly responded. He dropped his face into his hands and groaned.

Rubbing his back, Liz asked, "What's on your mind?"

Without raising his head he said, "I'd like to tell you about it but I don't think I can."

Liz threw off the covers and swung her bare legs off the bed. As Liz pulled him upright and took his hands away from his face, Michael was cursing himself for the way he had phrased his last comment. The worst thing you can say to a reporter is that you know something but you can't talk about it.

"What is bothering you?" asked Liz.

Michael turned and kissed her on the lips. She returned his kiss for a second, then grabbed him by the chin and pushed him back. With her most serious look she repeated, "What is bothering you?"

Deep down inside, Michael wanted to tell her, but he had to be careful. This would have to be handled in stages. "What would you say if I told you I think I know who the assassins are?"

Liz opened her eyes wide. "You're not serious?" Michael nodded yes. Tucking one of her legs up on the bed, she moved back a foot. "You are serious." Michael nodded his head again.

"Who are they?"

"I don't think I should tell you."

"Why?" asked an incredulous Scarlatti.

"Because knowing who they are might drag you into this, and right now there is no telling where it's going."

"Are you going to talk to the FBI?"

Michael looked down at the floor. "No."

Liz got down on her knees and looked up at him. "You can't be serious."

"I am."

"You have to go to the FBI, Michael! You're a congressman!"

"Darling, I'm not going to the FBI . . . at least not for now. And I don't want you talking to anyone about this." Scarlatti frowned and Michael said, "Liz, I confided in you because I trust you. Don't mention a word of this to anyone."

Reluctantly Liz said, "All right, all right . . . I won't say anything." Liz reached up and ran her fingers through his hair. With a frown she asked, "Who are they?"

Michael looked into her brown eyes and said, "For your own good I'm not going to tell you."

Liz began to protest but the moment was broken by the ringing of the phone. Michael looked for the cordless phone and realized it must be on the charger in the den. If someone was calling this late, it must be important. O'Rourke dashed down the hall and grabbed the phone. "Hello."

"Michael, I'm sorry to bother you so late. I hope I didn't wake you." It was Michael's former boss, Senator Olson.

"No . . . no, I was awake. What's up?"

After an uncomfortable pause, Olson asked, "Michael, I need to ask you a big favor."

"What can I help you with?"

"I've decided to walk in the procession from the Capitol to the White House tomorrow . . . and I was wondering . . . if you would walk with me?"

"I thought they weren't going to let anyone walk." O'Rourke had been given a memo at the office that described the agenda for the day's events and stated that no congressmen or senators would be allowed to accompany the horse-drawn caissons to the White House.

"Michael, I am a United States senator. No one is going to tell me I can't walk in that procession. I've thought about it long and hard. I worked with those men for over thirty years, and although I didn't particularly care for all of them, I still feel it is my duty to stand by them one last time. Someone in this town needs to show a little courage."

"Why would you risk your life trying to honor four of the most dishonorable men who have ever been elected to public office? They were a disgrace! I can't believe you're even considering it!"

Olson almost lost his temper. "I'm sorry you feel that way, Michael. If I had known you disliked them so much, I would not have asked you to join me." Without saying good-bye the senator slammed the phone down.

The line went dead and O'Rourke looked at the receiver, debating if he should call Olson back. He decided against it and set the phone down. He was torn between his loyalty to Olson and his disgust for what men like Koslowski had done to America and its political system. The thought of honoring them in any way made him tense with anger. The decision would be easy if it weren't for the fact that Michael felt more indebted to Erik Olson than any other person in the world. Erik and Alice Olson had been best friends of O'Rourke's parents. After Michael's parents died, the Olsons had stepped in to help fill the void for Michael and his younger brothers and sister. O'Rourke glanced over at a picture on the wall. It was of his graduation from college, and he was flanked by the Olsons. O'Rourke continued to look at the other pictures and noticed that the Olsons were in many of them. They had been there a lot over the last ten years—all of the birthdays and holidays where Erik and Alice Olson had made the effort to act as parents for the parentless O'Rourke family.

He drifted to another photo. A large, framed black-and-white his mother had taken just before her death. It was of the lake and woods in front of their family cabin in northern Minnesota. A fresh blanket of snow covered the frozen lake and hung heavy on the thick, green pine trees, weighing the branches down. Taken after a snowstorm, the beautiful photo always reminded him of that sad time in his life. In the early years after his parents' death, he had been tempted to take it down on many occasions because of the emotions it evoked, but he had kept it up out of respect for his parents and a belief that it was better to confront the pain and fear than run from it.

As he stared at the photo on the wall, he thought about the

funeral of his parents. He remembered standing in the cold ceme-tery, covered with snow, a crisp, cold wind coming out of the north and a dark, gray sky overhead. He stood over the graves while everyone else waited in the cars so he could say a last good-bye, alone. He couldn't remember how long he stood there, only that it was cold and that his vision was blurred by the steady stream of tears that had filled his eyes.

The memories flooded to the surface, and Michael remem-bered it was Erik Olson who had come to his side that cold day and led him away from the graves—back to his brothers and sister. Michael turned and saw Liz in the doorway. He held out his arms and they met halfway. Grabbing her tightly, he kissed her cheek and then whispered, "I don't ever want to lose you."

CHAPTER 15

ROM 10:30 A.M. to almost 11:30 A.M. Senator Olson was besieged by everyone from his secretary to the president, all trying vigorously to dissuade him from walking in the procession. He stood his ground and refused to change his mind. The president called again just before the procession was to start, and after he failed to talk Olson out of it, the decision was made to let him have his way.

At 11:55 A.M. four caissons, each pulled by three pairs of white horses, arrived at the foot of the Capitol steps. Senator Olson stood off to the side and admired the precision of the young military men as they lifted each coffin off its catafalque and marched toward the door. As Olson moved to follow the last coffin out the door, a warm hand was placed on his shoulder. The thin, small senator turned to see the smiling and apologetic face of Michael O'Rourke.

"I'm sorry about last night, Erik."

Olson reached up and patted O'Rourke's hand. "Thank you for coming, Michael. This means a lot to me." The two men turned, walked out the door, and descended the Capitol steps.

One by one each coffin was carried by its special detail and placed on top of the black, two-wheeled carriages. As the last coffin was placed on its caisson, the order was given and a lone drummer started to beat out the cadence. Following military tradition, each caisson was followed by a horse and a soldier walking beside it. O'Rourke, Olson, and four of the senator's bodyguards fell in behind the last riderless horse. Another command was given and the procession moved out to the beat of the drum.

The street was lined with a large crowd of onlookers and media as the procession traveled down Pennsylvania Avenue toward the White House at a somber, dignified pace. The commentators covering the event for the networks commented at length that Senator Olson was the only one of the remaining 531 congressmen and senators who had elected to walk behind the procession. O'Rourke was dismissed by all as one of Olson's bodyguards.

The large, red-brick colonial was located on a secluded four acres of rolling Maryland countryside that overlooked the Chesapeake Bay. There were estates just like it up and down the coast of the Chesapeake, some smaller and some bigger. None of them, however, were as secure. Several years earlier, the owner had paid close to a million dollars to convert the turn-of-the-century house into a fortress. The bulk of the perimeter security system was composed of night-vision cameras, underground motion sensors, and laser-beam trip wires. The next line of security was in the actual construction of the house. All the windows were double-paned, bulletproof Plexiglas, and all the exterior doors were triple-hinged, two-inch-thick steel, covered with wood veneer and anchored into reinforced-steel frames. Four bodyguards were present at all times.

The owner was Arthur Higgins. To those who knew him or had heard of him, he was known simply as Arthur. He had unofficially worked for the CIA since its inception, and over the last forty-some years he had done most of the Agency's dirty work. When Director Stansfield took over, Arthur was ordered to cease all association with the Central Intelligence Agency and all other United States government agencies. He had blatantly ignored the order.

In the large library of the house, Arthur sat at his desk and watched the TV coverage of the funeral procession. He knew each

of the men who had been killed, several of them well. He felt no
sorrow over their deaths, and that didn't surprise him. Arthur
prided himself on being emotionless. He believed emotions were
something that clouded one's judgment. But when the face of Senator Olson came on the screen, Arthur's eyes squinted tight, as he
fought to suppress the anger rising up from within. Not many
people in the world could elicit an instantaneous physical response
from Arthur, but Senator Olson was one of them.

Just before the procession reached the White House, one of the
commentators for CBS realized that the man standing next to
Senator Olson was not wearing a tan trench coat and sunglasses
like the other four bodyguards. He was wearing an expensive black
dress coat and a nice silk tie. After informing his producer of this
obvious fact, the producer put his assistants to work trying to find
out who this unknown man was. Minutes later, as the procession
was arriving at the gates of the White House, CBS announced that
Senator Olson was walking with Congressman Michael O'Rourke,
who was also from Minnesota. The cameras were naturally drawn
to O'Rourke's good looks, and the producers at every network
scrambled to find out more about the unknown congressman.

The procession stopped in front of the White House, and the
four coffins were taken by their special details and placed on four
black catafalques in the East Room. The room was packed with
leaders of foreign nations, ambassadors, U.S. Supreme Court justices, and a select group of U.S. senators and congressmen, with the
families of the deceased politicians sitting in the first several rows
of chairs. When Olson and O'Rourke entered the room, no chairs
were left, so they stood in back with the other people who could not
find a seat. After the last special detail had left, the congressional
chaplain stood and read a long prayer for the repose of the souls
of the four men. President Stevens then stood and gave a surpris-
ingly short, somber, and nonpolitical eulogy. He spoke only of the

tragedy of death before its time, the importance of prayer, and helping the loved ones who were left behind heal properly. He was followed by several senators and congressmen, who mentioned some touching personal moments, but who also stayed away from saying anything controversial.

All of the politicians who rose and spoke avoided the subject that was in the forefront of everyone's mind, the subject that they were all afraid to broach, for fear of falling in the footsteps of the four dead men who lay before them. Senator Olson was the last to speak, and he directed all of his comments to the families of his deceased colleagues.

Once again, the flag-draped coffins were carried, one by one, out of the East Room, and this time were loaded into four black hearses that would deliver them to Andrews Air Force Base. From there, they would each be loaded onto a C-141B Starlifter for the flight back to their home states.

President Stevens was now taking the time to offer each family member his condolences as they stood to leave. The crowd was starting to filter out into the hallway, and Olson turned to O'Rourke. "Michael, I need to talk to the president for a minute. Would you like to meet him?"

O'Rourke looked down at his friend and then across the room at the president. "No, I'll wait here."

Olson looked at the young O'Rourke, as he'd done many times before, and asked himself why Michael had decided to get into politics. "Have you ever met him before?"

"No."

"Well, then come on." Olson stepped away and waved his hand toward the president.

"I have no desire to meet him. I'll wait for you in the hallway."

Olson knew by the look in the stubborn O'Rourke's eyes that it was worthless to ask a third time. The senator nodded his head and turned to make his way toward the president.

CHAPTER 16

IT was dark out when O'Rourke parked his dark green Chevy Tahoe in front of Scarlatti's apartment building. He was thirty minutes late. Looking forward to spending some time with her, he bounded up the steps. He could always put everything else out of his mind and relax when he was with Liz. O'Rourke knocked on the door, and a moment later it opened. Instead of greeting him with the usual kiss, Scarlatti turned and walked back into the apartment. O'Rourke picked up on the angry signal and tried to figure out what he might have done to upset her. He was almost always late, so it couldn't be that. He followed her down the hallway and into the kitchen.

"Liz, are you all right?"

Scarlatti did not respond. She stirred the pot of noodles boiling on the stove.

Michael grabbed her by the shoulders and turned her around. O'Rourke saw the tears in her eyes and tried to put his arms around her, but she backed away.

"What's wrong?"

"You have no idea, do you?" Scarlatti asked with a voice that was far from steady.

O'Rourke looked at her and shook his head.

"I can't believe you don't know." She started to shake her head back and forth, wiping the tears from her cheeks. "I'll tell you what's wrong, Michael. You're a congressman, and if you haven't noticed lately, there's a group of people that are going around killing politicians and you happen to know who they are." She shook her head at him and took a deep breath. "Well, despite knowing there are people out there who would like to kill you, you decide to walk right down the center of Pennsylvania Avenue in front of thousands of people. Not only did you do that, but you didn't even have the courtesy to call and tell me." Liz paused again and stared at O'Rourke.

O'Rourke looked down at her big, brown eyes and thought to himself, *God, I don't need this right now.* The only thing that kept him from verbalizing it was that he knew she was right.

"I was sitting in the newsroom, and someone ran up to my desk and told me you were on TV. The next thing I knew, the commentator is saying that no one else would walk in the procession because the FBI thought it was too dangerous. I sat there for twenty minutes of hell." Scarlatti stared at him as she tried to stop crying. O'Rourke went to step forward, but she put out her hand. "No, I'm not finished yet. I sat there praying that nothing would happen to you. Pictures of Basset getting his head blown off kept flashing across my mind. All I could think of was that I was going to lose you." She broke down and began to sob into her hands.

O'Rourke stepped forward and tried to wrap his arms around her. She pushed him away and walked to the other side of the kitchen, trying to gain some composure. "Michael, you have no idea how much I love you." She looked up at the ceiling and paused. "Just last night you told me you never wanted to lose me. Well, how in the hell do you think I feel? Do you think I want to lose you? Did it ever occur to you to pick up the phone and let me know what was going on? Did you ever stop and think about me today . . . about how I was feeling, wondering if someone was going to shoot you? How would you feel if it was me? How would you feel if I died? That

would be it, Michael. Our future together would be gone and none
of our dreams would be realized. We would never have the chance
to have children and raise them, nothing. Damn it, Michael, this is
my life, too!"

O'Rourke moved across the room and grabbed her. She tried to
move away again, but he held on and pulled her into his chest. He
whispered into her ear, "Honey, I'm sorry. I should have called, but
I was never in danger."

"How can you say you were never in danger. It's been open sea-
son on politicians for the last week. They could have easily—"

Michael put his finger over her lips. "I know who they are,
Liz . . . they would never do anything to harm me."

The sun had risen again, and down in the subbasement of the
White House a Secret Service agent opened an obscure door for
Stu Garret. The president's chief of staff walked in and sat down
next to another Secret Service agent. Garret grabbed a pair of headphones and put them on as he looked up at the bank of monitors.
President Stevens was standing in front of the fireplace in the Oval
Office waiting for his breakfast appointment. A moment later, the
door opened and Senator Olson entered the room. The president
walked over and shook his guest's hand. "Good morning, Erik."
Garret could hear them talk as if he were standing right next to the
two men.

President Stevens led Olson over to a small table that had been set for
breakfast, and the two men sat down. A steward entered the room
and started to serve the meal. Senator Olson received a bowl of oatmeal with a side of brown sugar and a halved grapefruit, while the
president received his usual bowl of Post Toasties with skim milk and
a cup of fruit.

The steward poured both men a cup of coffee and left the room.
The president dabbed the corner of his mouth with a napkin and

said, "Erik, I would like you to know that I'm happy you've made the effort to come see me, especially in light of the current situation and the poor working relationship between our two parties."

Olson nodded his head, signaling a frustrated understanding. "I'm glad you've agreed to see me, sir. I know these are hectic times for you."

"They're hectic for all of us."

"Yes, I suppose you're right," Olson sighed. "That is why I'm here this morning. The situation we are confronted with is bigger than partisan politics." Olson stopped as if he were searching for the right words to use. "I am very concerned about what might happen if certain members of my party propose that we implement some of the things this group is asking for."

The president raised an eyebrow at the comment. "Considering the philosophical tenets of your party, and the stress that we are all under, I can see where that might become a possibility, one that I would not welcome."

"Neither would I, sir." Olson glanced down at his oatmeal and then at the president.

The president nodded, implying to Olson that he should continue.

"Last Friday we started a new chapter in our country's history, one that is potentially very dangerous. The idea that one small group can dictate, through violence, the policies of this country runs completely against all of the democratic principles upon which our nation was founded. These acts of terrorism absolutely and emphatically cannot be tolerated if we want to leave a civilized and democratic nation for future generations of Americans."

The senator paused for a second, then continued, "As you said earlier, the relations between our parties have been very strained as of late. Much of that has to do with the recent fight over your budget. It is my feeling that we must put those differences aside and move forward with a unified front. There will be some compromises that will have to be reached, but the important thing is that we cannot, for a minute, entertain the idea of appeasing these terrorists."

President Stevens leaned back in his chair. "I agree. Appeasement is out of the question. That has been my official position from the outset. It does, however, worry me that you think certain members of your party may be willing to exploit this situation for personal and political gain. What do you propose our course of action to be?"

"I think we need to bring the leaders of both parties together and discuss what needs to be changed in your budget to guarantee a swift and resounding passage through both the House and the Senate." Olson placed both elbows on the table and waited for the response.

"Erik, I had enough votes to get my budget passed before this whole debacle started. I'm not so sure I need to change it at all."

Olson looked straight into the president's eyes. "Sir, if your budget was put to a vote today, it wouldn't stand a chance of getting out of the House. Koslowski and Basset are gone, and these assassinations have scared the hell out of the remaining congressmen. I've heard rumors that a few of them are contemplating quitting." Olson paused to let his comments sink in. "The only thing that will get your budget passed is a strong, unified front from both parties, and that means some deals will have to be struck. I'm not saying that drastic changes need to be made, only that you will have to meet us halfway."

The president nodded his head positively. The proposal was beginning to make more sense. The two statesmen continued to discuss the formation of their new alliance, while several floors beneath the meeting the wheels were spinning in Garret's head. This might be the perfect way out, he thought to himself. Show a unified front with the president standing in the middle, holding both parties together. The public would eat it up. Stevens would look stronger than ever. His approval rating would go through the roof, and no one from either party would be able to challenge him for a second term. And that meant Garret could have any position—secretary of state, secretary of defense, whatever he wanted.

McMahon entered Director Roach's office ten minutes late for their seven-thirty meeting. "Sorry, Brian, I got tied up trying to untangle a dispute, a dispute that I don't have the time, energy, or political clout to deal with."

Roach was sitting at the conference table in his office. He had stacks of files laid out in an orderly manner in front of him. He preferred the large work surface of the conference table to his desk. McMahon plopped down in a chair at Roach's end of the table.

Roach had a feeling that whatever was bothering McMahon was about to be dumped in his lap. "What's the problem, Skip?"

"The problem is that no one from the president to Nance to the secretary of defense to the chairman of the Joint Chiefs, no one, and I mean no one, is cooperating in letting us take a look at the Special Forces personnel files."

"Why?"

"In short, Brian . . . they're in the business of trusting no one." McMahon shook his head several times. "I suppose they think we're going to walk in the front door of the Pentagon with a hundred agents and start rifling through their top-secret files. Whatever their reasons are, I don't care. I need to start looking at those files, whether the brass is paranoid or not. I'll work in conjunction with them, and I'll try to step on as few toes as possible, but we have to be given access."

Roach nodded. "I'll look into it this morning and hopefully have an answer to you by this afternoon. What else do you have for me?"

McMahon handed his boss two files. "These are the ballistics and autopsy reports for Basset. I received them late last night."

"Anything unexpected?"

"One interesting point. The guys down in the lab are pretty sure the bullet was loaded with nitroglycerin."

The director's eyes opened wider. "Really?"

"Yep, it's a pretty sure way to make sure one shot does the job, I suppose."

"How does a person go about getting their hands on a nitro-tipped bullet?"

"We're looking into that right now. I've got our ballistics people talking to the people over at ATF, and they're trying to put together a list of people who dabble in stuff like this. They're obviously illegal in the U.S., but some of the guys in the lab seem to think there might be some small manufacturers abroad who do work like this."

Roach closed the ballistics report and placed it on top of a pile of files for later reading. "Interesting; you may want to bring the CIA in on this. They've got a much better handle on the international side of this stuff than the ATF does."

"I've already set the wheels in motion, which brings me to my next question." McMahon paused while he shifted in his chair. "I would like to borrow Irene Kennedy from the CIA for a while."

"You mean Stansfield's expert on terrorism?"

"Exactly."

Roach wrote himself a note. "I'll call Stansfield as soon as we're done. I don't think it'll be a problem."

"Good."

It was almost noon when Garret left the Oval Office to retrieve something from his office. The morning had been productive, and with the help of Olson, the coalition was coming together faster than expected. All politicians, regardless of party affiliation, were scared, and the idea of strength in numbers was appealing. Garret entered his office and started sucking on a cigarette. Several minutes and another cigarette later, Mike Nance entered and closed the door behind him.

Nance saw the smile on Garret's face and asked, "What are you so excited about?"

"I'll tell you in a minute. What did you want to see me about?"

"I received a phone call last night from a friend . . . a friend who says he would like to sit down with us and discuss our options."

"Who would that friend be?"

"Arthur," responded Nance in a lowered tone.

Garret thought about it for a minute. "Did he say what it was about?"

"He doesn't usually like to talk about things over the phone. He only said that he would like us to meet him at his estate tonight for dinner."

Garret shook his head. He wanted to meet Arthur, but tonight was out of the question. "Can't do it, and neither can you. The president is going to read a prepared statement along with Senator Olson and several of both parties' bigwigs tonight at eight." Garret stopped to see if the news would elicit any emotion from his calm friend. To Garret's slight frustration, Nance's expression didn't change.

"The president is going to announce that he's holding a closed-door summit at Camp David this weekend. He's inviting the leadership from both parties. Senator Olson offered the olive branch this morning and we jumped all over it. They're going to back the president in a show of unity against these terrorists and work together to pass his budget through the House and Senate."

"What are they asking for in return?"

"They're going to ask for a few changes in the budget, but the bottom line is we're going to come out of this deal looking like the great unifiers. Stevens's approval rating will go through the roof."

"That's assuming you can keep all of these egos satisfied."

"Yeah, yeah, I know, it's not going to be easy, but considering where we were twenty-four hours ago, this is a godsend." Garret looked hard at Nance. "Don't ruin this for me yet, I need the energy to get through the day. It's going to be a long one."

Nance cracked a thin smile. "What would you like me to tell our friend?"

Garret thought about the response. "Tell him we'll try to set it up for Saturday night. There's a remote chance we might be able to sneak away from Camp David, but we can't count on it."

Ann Moncur had announced to the press, just after 1 P.M., that the president would be addressing the nation along with the majority and minority leaders of the House and the Senate at 8 P.M. Instead of holding the meeting in the drab White House pressroom, Hopkinson had convinced Garret and the president to hold it in the ornate and stately East Room. They would stand where the coffins had been just one day earlier. Hopkinson had told them the symbolism would not be missed by the press, especially after he spoonfed it to several reporters who owed him favors.

The president would be compared to the Phoenix, the legendary bird that rose out of the fiery ashes, stronger and more pure. The parallel would be drawn that the president, despite the trials and tribulations suffered over the past week, was rebounding as a stronger and better leader.

Hopkinson snickered to himself as he felt the rush and excitement that he got from manipulating public opinion. The media was already present and impatiently waiting for the new coalition to be unveiled. Copies of the president's speech had already been distributed, and most of the reporters were reading it over. Hopkinson stood in the doorway of the side entrance to the room, and at exactly 8 P.M., he signaled the producers to go live. A moment later, the president entered the room with the ranking members of both parties following closely behind. The president took his place behind the podium, and the party leaders fell in behind, providing the intended backdrop.

With the look of a general about to go into battle, Stevens started his speech. "Good evening, my fellow Americans. This past week has been a difficult one for our country. Our nation has lost some of its finest leaders. We have lost four men who gave everything they had to their country . . . our country. I would ask you, once again, to please keep these men and their families in your prayers." The president paused and bowed his head briefly.

Hopkinson was standing off to the side, looking more like a stage director for a play than the White House communications director. Hopkinson nodded his approval that the president had remembered the preplanned gesture of bowing his head as if in prayer. Stevens had practiced the speech nine times. Each time, Hopkinson had meticulously analyzed every gesture and movement until he felt he had the desired performance. Now he stood and anticipated every preplanned head nod, hand motion, facial expression, and change of inflection in the president's voice.

Stevens looked back up and stared into the TelePrompTer to his left. "During our history as a nation we have been confronted with some very trying times. We have always survived because of our strength and diversity. We have survived because the leaders of our country have had the courage to put personal beliefs aside, come together, and do what is right for America. That is why we are here tonight." The president turned and motioned to the men behind him. "The group that stands with me tonight represents the two parties that have helped shape America and make it great. During normal times it would be very difficult to get us to agree on almost anything, but when the very fabric that our democracy was woven from is threatened, we agree without a single deviance. That is why we have come together tonight. We have come together to announce that we are putting our differences aside and are going to move forward as a unified group.

"We will not cower to the demands of terrorists. The survival of this country's democratic principles is far more important than our individual beliefs. Tomorrow afternoon, I will fly to Camp David with the leaders of both the House and the Senate. We will spend the weekend going over my budget and putting together a bipartisan agenda for the following year. We are the people who have been elected to run this government"—Stevens again turned and motioned to the men and women standing behind him—"and we will not be blackmailed by terrorists!"

As the president continued to speak, the blond-haired assassin looked at the TV and began to form a mental checklist of the things he would have to do before the sun rose. He got off the couch and went to the basement of the apartment building. He stopped at his storage closet and checked to make sure the wax seal on the bottom door hinge had not been broken. After being satisfied that no one had entered his locker, he walked past four more doors and stopped in front of another closet, which was assigned to an elderly gentleman on the first floor. Again, he checked the wax seal on the bottom hinge, then picked the lock.

Entering the ten-by-ten-foot closet, he walked to the back wall and moved several stacks of boxes, uncovering a stainless-steel trunk. It weighed almost fifty pounds, but the assassin carried it up to his apartment without breaking a sweat. Setting the case down on the floor of his bedroom, he unlocked and opened it, retrieving a red Gore-Tex ski jacket, a Chicago Cubs baseball hat, a pair of work boots, a brown shoulder-length wig, a pair of nonprescription glasses, a large video camera, a small red toolbox, and a large black backpack.

The man placed a pair of running shoes, tights, dark blue sweatpants, a sweatshirt, and a plain, dark baseball hat in the bottom of the backpack, then packed the rest of the equipment. When he was finished, he pulled a strand of hair from his head and placed it next to a book on the coffee table. Looking around the apartment, he took note of where everything was, then grabbed the trunk and backpack. Locking the door behind him, he walked down to the basement and put the trunk back in the old man's locker. Reaching into his pocket, he pulled out a black candle and lit it. When a small amount of wax had pooled around the flame, the assassin bent over and let a single drop run down the bottom hinge of the door. He checked to make sure the wax had properly dried, then headed up one flight of stairs, through the small lobby, and out onto the sidewalk.

He was not a smoker, but he pulled a pack of Marlboros out of his pocket and lit one. Standing casually, he puffed on the cigarette but did not inhale it. His eyes narrowed as he methodically studied every window of the three apartment buildings across the street, looking for anyone standing in the shadows behind a curtain or the black, circular shape of a camera lens peering back at him. If the FBI was onto him, that was where they would be. He didn't think they were, but he reminded himself that the whole idea behind surveillance was not to be seen.

After finishing the sweep of the buildings, he tossed the cigarette butt into the street and walked away. He walked for almost eight blocks, turning at random to make sure no one was following. After he felt safe, he turned into a narrow alley and ducked behind two Dumpsters. Quickly, he put on the wig, hat, red jacket, and glasses.

He emerged from the other end of the alley a different man. His stride was longer but slower, more gangly, less precise and athletic than before. Three blocks later, he stopped at a pay phone and punched in a series of numbers. The phone rang once and he hung up, waited thirty seconds, and dialed the number again. This time he let the phone ring five times before hanging up. Two blocks later, he climbed behind the wheel of a beige Ford Taurus and drove off.

• • •

The two men were leaning on their pool cues and drinking a pitcher of Coors Light in the back room of Al's Bar in Annapolis. Neither of them preferred the taste of Coors Light, but they did like that it had such a low alcohol content. The larger of the two was lining up a combo when the digital phone on his hip rang once and stopped. Both men looked at their watches and counted the seconds. Thirty seconds later, they counted five more rings. Instead of leaving right away, they finished their game and switched to coffee. It was going to be a long night.

Ted Hopkinson strutted into the Oval Office as if he were floating on clouds. The president was being attended to by one of Hopkinson's assistants, who was wiping makeup off his face. "Sir, you did a wonderful job. I haven't seen the press this together on an issue in a long time. They bought the whole speech, hook, line, and sinker."

Stevens showed a slight grin. "Yes, it looks like it was a winner." The president nodded toward the four TVs that were turned on. Only the sound on the one tuned to ABC was up. The White House correspondents for the three networks and CNN were all standing in different areas around the White House, giving their summation of the president's speech. When they were finished, the anchors took over for their take on the event, and then the special analysts came on to give their two cents. The media loved it. The story just kept getting better and better, and with it, so did their ratings. The public's desire to watch this real-life drama was insatiable.

When all the makeup was removed from the president's face, he buttoned the top button of his shirt and slipped his tie back into a tight knot. Hopkinson turned his attention away from the TVs and back to the president. "Sir, I really think we're going to see a big jump in your approval ratings tomorrow."

Garret and Nance entered the room. Garret slapped Hopkinson on the back and congratulated him on a job well done. Garret then nodded at the door, and the communications director grabbed his assistant and quietly retreated. Garret turned to Stevens and grinned from ear to ear. "Nice job, Jim."

Stevens looked up and smiled. "Thank you."

"I can't believe the way this thing is coming together. The press is eating it up. If we can pass a budget, we won't even have to hold an election next year." Garret could barely contain his excitement. The thought of locking up a second term this early was appealing. Not having to crisscross the country for three months campaigning was even more appealing. Sure, they would have to work a little, but not like last time. Instead of three states a day, and a speech every two hours for the last month, they could relax and run a TV campaign out of the White House. It would be so nice not to have to go out and press flesh with every Tom, Dick, and Harry, Garret thought to himself.

Nance was standing off to the side, watching the president and Garret. Nance let them continue to speculate about a second term for a minute and then stepped in. "I hate to ruin your little celebration here, but the elections are a long way off, and a lot could happen between now and then." The comment got both Garret's and the president's attention, and both men became more serious. "You've done a great job solidifying this coalition on such short notice, and hopefully, if things go well, we'll pull it off. . . . But, we need to understand that this new alliance could fall apart, as fast or faster than it was put together." Nance paused for effect. "The *New York Times* printed a poll today that said over thirty-seven percent of the people they surveyed thought the country had not suffered by losing Basset, Koslowski, Fitzgerald, and Downs. I'm getting a sense that the common person is empathizing with these assassins. The people are fed up with politics as usual, and if we're not careful, we're going to turn these assassins into dragon slayers. We can't ignore them. They are not just going to go away." Nance walked over to the fireplace, his hand on his chin and his forefinger tapping his lips. "They will strike again, and they will continue to strike until we give in or they get caught." Nance turned around and looked at the president and Garret. "We'd better hope they slip up, because if they don't, that alliance will crumble. None of those men have the guts to put their lives on the line if this thing gets any hotter."

The assassin sat in his car across the street from the local ABC studio. It was not the first time he'd waited for the news van to return from the White House, but it would be the last. Just after midnight, the van that was assigned to the White House returned and drove into the underground parking garage. The assassin waited for another twenty minutes, then got out of the car, grabbing the video camera and backpack. As he walked across the street, he put the camera up on his right shoulder and tilted his head down. The brim of his hat and the camera screened his face. On his way through the front door, he passed a female reporter and cameraman on their way out. They were both wearing red, Gore-Tex ski jackets with the ABC logo over their left breast.

The assassin kept his head down and headed straight for the stairs leading to the underground parking garage. When he reached the garage, he waved to the security guard, who was sitting in a room with a large glass window. The man had his feet up on the desk and was watching TV. He casually looked up and, upon seeing the red jacket and camera, turned his attention back to the TV. The assassin walked through the row of vans and cars and stopped when he reached the one with the right license plate. It took him less than thirty seconds to pick the lock. Casually, he slid the door open and climbed in, closing it behind him. Setting the camera down, he grabbed an electric screwdriver out of his backpack and went to work. A minute later, he popped the cover off the control board and started searching for the right wires. After finding them, he spliced several wires and carefully attached a transponder. When he was done, he tested the transponder several times, then put the cover back on the control board. Packing up his gear, he stepped out of the van and locked the door. Once again, he walked by the window on his way to the stairs, his face covered by the brim of his hat and the camera.

Outside, the assassin climbed behind the wheel of the Ford Taurus and drove west on K Street through downtown. It was almost 1 A.M. and the traffic was light. Several miles later, he turned onto Wisconsin Avenue and headed north. The pedestrian traffic was quite a bit busier in Georgetown, as the young professionals and college kids tried to get a head start on the weekend. Almost a mile later, he pulled into the Safeway on Wisconsin and Thirty-fourth Street. Even at this hour, the parking lot was half-full. That was what he wanted. If a cop drove by, he wouldn't think twice about a man sitting alone in the parking lot of a twenty-four-hour grocery store. He would assume he was waiting for his wife, but if he was seen parked alone on a side street, that would be a different story.

He pulled the car into a spot up front and tilted the steering wheel all the way up. He took the wig, hat, and glasses off, placing them in a large, green trash bag. Next came the jacket, camera, and small toolbox. Then he quickly took off the boots, followed by his pants and underwear. He was naked from the waist down and put on the running tights and sweatpants. Taking off the flannel shirt, he replaced it with the dark sweatshirt, put on the worn running shoes, and checked to make sure everything was in the trash bag, including the backpack.

Backing out of the spot, he drove through the lot and pulled back onto Wisconsin Avenue. The trash bag could have been thrown away in one of the grocery store's Dumpsters, but the homeless people would find it, and homeless people talked to cops. The assassin had a small office building picked out about two miles away where the garbage was picked up on Friday mornings. Almost five minutes later, he pulled into the alley behind the small, brick building and stopped. Jumping out, he lifted the lid of the Dumpster, shifted several bags to the side, and placed his bag inside, covering it up with the others. He gently let the lid of the Dumpster close, not wanting to make any loud noises, and got back in the car. Within seconds he was back on Wisconsin and headed south.

Several minutes later, he was winding through the small neighborhood of Potomac Palisades. When he reached the corner of Potomac Avenue and Manning Place Lane, he parked the car and got out, closing the door gently behind him. The temperature had dropped to around forty degrees, and a slight breeze was rustling the dry, fall leaves. The forecast called for fog in the morning, but there was no sign of it where he was, high on the bluffs above the Potomac. On the other side of the street was a small boulevard of grass and then thick woods that led down a steep hill to the Potomac Parkway and then just beyond that to Palisades Park and the Potomac River.

He crossed the street and entered the tree line. Finding a small footpath that he had used before, he zigzagged his way down the steep, forested hillside. Stopping just short of the road, he checked for the headlights of any approaching cars, then darted across the two-lane highway and down into a small ravine. Settling in behind a large tree and some bushes, he looked up at the underside of the Chain Bridge, which ran from D.C. into Virginia. The lights from the bridge cast a faint yellow glow that reached the tops of the trees above him and then faded before hitting the forested floor. Palisades Park was not your typical metropolitan park. There were no softball diamonds or football fields. It was heavily wooded with a few jogging trails and some large patches of marshland.

The assassin pressed the light button on his digital watch and checked the time. It was nearing 2 A.M. and his accomplices would be arriving shortly. Looking in the direction of the river, he could see a thin layer of fog spreading out across the floor of the forest. The noise of car tires on gravel caught his attention, and he looked up over the edge of the ravine. A blue-and-white *Washington Post* newspaper van came to a stop, and a man dressed in blue coveralls quickly got out of the passenger side and slid open the door of the cargo area. Reaching inside, he grabbed two large, black duffel bags and ran to the tree line, setting the bags down about fifteen feet from where the blond-haired assassin was waiting. The man let out three curt whistles and waited for a confirmation. The assassin did the same, and the man walked away and climbed back in the van.

Picking up the two large bags, the assassin placed the shoulder straps around his neck and let the bags rest on his hips. Next, he threaded through the woods and crossed under the Chain Bridge. The Potomac River was not navigable by anything other than a canoe or a raft at this point, and the river only ran under the far western end of the bridge. As the assassin worked his way toward the river, the trees became smaller and more sparse. By the time he reached the middle of the bridge, the fog was up to his waist. Turning south, he walked about thirty yards and found a small clearing.

He set both bags down and opened the one on his right. The fog and darkness made his task more difficult, but he was used to working under strange conditions. Inside one of the bags was a small gray radar dish mounted on a square, metal box, a car battery, some power cables, and camouflage netting. The assassin hooked the car battery up to the radar unit and tested the power. When he was satisfied, he covered it with the camouflage netting and opened the second bag, pulling out a wooden board about three feet long. Attached to the flat side of the board in an upright position were six plastic tubes about an inch in diameter and twenty-four inches long. Each tube was painted dull green and was loaded with a phosphorus flare. He pulled some small bushes out of the ground and placed them around the tubes so the open ends were pointed straight up into the sky. To the base of the makeshift launcher, he attached a nine-volt battery, and a small transponder. The assassin checked everything over, making sure the transponders were operating properly, then grabbed the empty bags and started to weave his way back toward the eastern end of the bridge.

CHAPTER 17

THE morning sun rising above the eastern horizon was invisible because of the thick fog that blanketed the nation's capital. Although the streets were quiet, there were signs that the morning rush of people heading to work was near. The blue-and-white *Washington Post* newspaper van pulled up to the corner of Maryland and Massachusetts at the east end of Stanton Park. Both men got out of the van. The driver opened the back doors, and his partner walked over to the *Washington Post* newspaper box that was chained to the streetlight. He got down on one knee and picked the padlock. A moment later it sprang open, and the chain dropped to the ground. He grabbed the box and carried it to the back of the van. While he loaded it, his partner took an identical box and placed it where the other one had been. He checked several times to make sure the door wouldn't open. After being satisfied, he pulled a remote control out of his pocket and punched in several numbers. A red light at the top told him the small radar unit placed inside the empty box was receiving the signal. He nodded to his partner and they got back in the van.

They were thankful for the cover that the fog provided, but were getting anxious. They would have liked to have started this part of the operation earlier, but were forced to wait until the real

Washington Post vans had delivered Friday morning's edition. With one more drop left, they drove around the south end of Stanton Park and turned onto Maryland Avenue. A block later, they turned onto Constitution Avenue and headed west. As they neared the White House, both men could feel their hearts start to beat a little faster.

The Secret Service paid close attention to the streets around the White House, and with the current heightened state of security, there was little doubt that they would be on their toes. If it weren't for the fog, they wouldn't risk dropping one of the boxes so close to the White House. The driver pulled up to the southeast corner of Fourteenth Street and Constitution Avenue and put the van in park. The White House was less than two blocks away. Both men pulled their baseball hats down a little tighter and got out to repeat the drill for the last time. This was the fifth and final radar unit. The first two were placed on the other side of the Potomac River in Arlington, Virginia, one to the south and west of the White House and the other directly west. The third radar unit was placed to the north of the White House at the intersection of Rhode Island and Massachusetts. With the final two units in place to the south and east, the trap was completed.

Quantico Marine Air Station is located approximately thirty miles southwest of Washington, D.C. The air station is divided into two parts: the green side and the white side. The green side supports the base's normal Marine aviation squadrons, and the white side supports the special Marine HMX-1 Squadron. The HMX-1 Squadron's primary function is to provide helicopter transportation for the president and other high-ranking executive-office officials. The squadron's main bird is the VH-3 helicopter. The VH-3s at HMX-1 are not painted your typical drab green like most military helicopters. They are painted glossy green on the bottom half and glossy white on top. The presidential seal adorns both sides of the aircraft, and inside the cabin are a wet bar, state-of-the-art communications equipment, and plush flight chairs. These are the large helicopters that land on the South Lawn of the White House and transport the president to such places as Andrews Air Force Base and Camp David. The helicopter is typically referred to as Marine One in the same way the president's 747 is referred to as Air Force One.

At first glance HMX-1 would seem like a cushy assignment for a Marine helicopter pilot—nothing more than an airborne limousine driver. In reality, it is the opposite. They are some of the best pilots the Marine Corps has to offer, and they are trained and tested constantly in evasive maneuvers, close-formation flying, and zero-visibility flying. If there is an emergency and the president needs to get somewhere, it doesn't matter if there's a blizzard or a torrential downpour. HMX-1 flies under any weather conditions.

The squadron consists of twelve identical VH-3s. Two of the twelve birds and their flight crews are on twenty-four-hour standby at the Anacostia Naval Air Station, just two miles south of the White House. This precaution is a holdover from the cold war. Standard operating procedure dictates that in the event of an imminent or actual nuclear attack, the president is to be flown on board Marine One, from the White House to Andrews Air Force Base. From there, he is to board Air Force One and take off. As far as the public is concerned, no president has had to take this apocalyptic journey for reasons other than training. Despite the fall of the Iron Curtain, the drill is still practiced frequently by the Marine Corps and Air Force pilots.

All ten of the VH-3s at HMX-1 were to be used in today's flight operations, and their flight crews were busy checking every inch of the choppers, prepping them for flight. The two helicopters at Anacostia would stay on standby and be used if any of the ten developed mechanical difficulties. It was just after 8 A.M., and the rising sun had burned off most of the fog. Small pockets were left, but only in low-lying areas. The visibility had improved enough that the control tower decided to commence the transfer of the

CH-53 Super Stallion helicopters from the New River Air Station to Quantico. A total of forty of the dull green monsters were flying up from Jacksonville, North Carolina—four for each of the VH-3s that would be ferrying the president and his guests from the White House to Camp David.

The doors to the hangar were open, and the roar of helicopters could be heard in the distance. Several of the mechanics walked out of the hangar to look at the approaching beasts. It was a sight they never got tired of. The Super Stallion was a tough-looking chopper. It had the rare combination of being both powerful and sleek and was one of the most versatile helicopters in the world.

The CH-53s rumbled in over the tops of the pine trees in a single-line formation at about 120 knots. The choppers were spaced in three-hundred-foot intervals, and the column stretched for over two miles. Their large turbine engines were thunderously loud in the cool morning air. One by one they descended onto the tarmac and were met by Marines wearing green fatigues, bright yellow vests, and ear protectors. The ground-crew personnel waved their fluorescent orange sticks and directed each bird into the proper spot. As each chopper was parked, the engines were cut and flight crews scampered under the large frames to secure yellow blocks around the wheels.

The traffic between Georgetown and the Capitol was never good, but in the morning it was almost unbearable. O'Rourke limped along in his Chevy Tahoe, thankful that the height of the truck allowed him to feel a little less claustrophobic.

Senator Olson's recent attempts to form a coalition with the president had Michael worried. O'Rourke desperately wanted to talk to his old boss before he left for Camp David. Grabbing his digital phone, the young congressman punched in the numbers for Erik Olson's direct line, and a second later the senator answered.

"Hello."

"Erik, it's Michael. Are we still on for lunch Monday?"

"Yes, I've got you down for eleven forty-five."

"Good." O'Rourke took a deep breath. "Erik, I'm a little troubled by this alliance that you're helping to form. What exactly do you hope to accomplish this weekend?"

"What do you mean?"

"Are you guys going to make any effort to cut the budget, or are you all going to scratch each other's back and put the country another half trillion dollars in debt?"

Olson was caught off guard by the blunt comment. "Michael, things are very complicated right now . . . and considering our current national security crisis, a balanced budget is the least of my concerns."

"Erik, the most serious problem facing our country today is the national debt, not the fact that a couple of corrupt and self serving egomaniacs were killed."

Olson paused before answering. He did not want to be drawn into a fight with O'Rourke. "Michael, I understand your concern, but the important thing for America right now is to stop these terrorists, and the first step to doing that is to show a unified front. We cannot be threatened into reforms. This is a democracy."

"So you're not going to suggest any budget cuts." O'Rourke made no attempt to hide the disgust in his voice.

"Michael, there are more important things for us to worry about right now than a balanced budget."

"That's bullshit, Erik. You know it, and I know it. Look at the damn numbers. Now is our chance to do something about it!"

"Michael, right now the national debt is of secondary concern. The important thing is to not appease terrorism."

"Erik, why are you so dead set on calling these people terrorists? They haven't killed any civilians. They killed four corrupt politicians who have abused and manipulated the powers of their office—four politicians who have mortgaged the entire future of this country so they could keep their special-interest groups happy and get reelected."

"Michael, I won't listen to you talk about those men that way!" Olson's voice became shaky.

"It's the truth, Erik. Don't turn these guys into something they weren't, just because they were assassinated."

Olson paused for a moment. "Michael, let me tell you something. I love you like a son, but you have a lot to learn. I've been in this town for over thirty years, and things aren't always as simple as you make them out to be."

It was O'Rourke's turn to raise his voice. "Do you want to hear simple, Erik? I'll give you simple. Over the last twenty years, you and all of your colleagues have spent our country into a five-trillion-dollar black hole. During that time we weren't confronted with a serious economic crisis or a major war. You had no valid reason to spend that kind of money. . . . I know you weren't a willing participant, but the harsh reality is that you were there and you didn't stop it. You have run up a five-trillion-dollar tab, and you're all going to retire and stick us with the bill. That is the legacy that you will leave for your children." O'Rourke paused for a second. "Shit, even now, with someone threatening your life, you aren't willing to do the right thing. This is your last chance to do something about the mess you've created. Don't let it slip away!" O'Rourke hit the end button on his phone and swore as he slammed on his brakes to avoid hitting a bicycle messenger who had cut in front of him. The truck came to an abrupt halt as its driver gripped the steering wheel tightly with both hands. Through clenched teeth O'Rourke asked himself out loud, "What is it going to take for these guys to do their jobs?"

Olson stared at the receiver and then gently placed it in its cradle. Why were the Irish so damn emotional, he thought to himself. He knew O'Rourke was right about the debt, but violence was not the answer. The system needed time to correct itself. It did not need to be jump-started by terrorism and threats. Law and order needed to be maintained.

After about ten seconds, he opened his bottom desk drawer and pulled out a file marked "National Debt." One of his staffers gave him monthly updates on the debt and the projections for the future. Olson opened it and looked over the summary page. The official numbers provided by the Stevens administration put the national debt at around $5.2 trillion. Olson knew this number did not represent the total national debt. Money had also been borrowed from the Social Security fund, and knowing the government's track record on underestimating the cost of programs, he figured the debt was probably closer to $6 trillion. He quickly glanced over some estimates of what the debt would do over the next five, ten, fifteen, and twenty years. The numbers were truly horrifying. O'Rourke was right. If it wasn't confronted, it would eventually bring the country to its knees. A bankrupt America was not the legacy he wanted to leave for his grandchildren, but neither was an America that tolerated terrorism.

Jack Warch climbed up the last flight of stairs and onto the roof of the White House. Special Agents Sally Manly and Joe Stiener followed as Warch surveyed the rooftop scene. He was pleased to see that the six countersniper agents already on the roof were at their posts and watching their area of responsibility. Warch was under a lot of stress and was trying his best to look calm. Joe Stiener went into the small guardhouse and filled up three cups of coffee, handing one to his boss, one to Manly, and keeping the other for himself.

Warch walked over to the south edge of the roof and looked up at the gray sky. Stiener and Manly stood several steps behind their boss and said nothing. After the sun had burned off the early-morning fog, it had looked as if it would be a bright day, but then, just before ten, a thick blanket of high, gray clouds moved in. A slight wind was coming from the southwest at about five to ten knots. Warch's gaze shifted from the sky to the treetops, and he couldn't help but notice the bright fall colors of the changing leaves. While sipping his coffee, he thought about how little he'd slept the past week. He was nearing the end of his rope and was looking forward to handing the president off to the Camp David team and getting some much needed sleep. But before he could do that, he had to get the president to Camp David in one piece.

Late the previous evening, they had met to discuss security arrangements, and Warch had recommended to the president that the meetings be held at the White House instead of Camp David. Garret had shot the idea down before the president had a chance to think it over. Garret had said, "Jim, the public needs to see that you're not confined to the White House. They need to see you get on board Marine One and fly off to Camp David for the weekend. It will make you look like a leader, and besides, Camp David is more secure than the White House."

It was debatable whether Camp David or the White House was more secure, but that wasn't the issue. The real security threat came in flying the president from the White House to Camp David.

Warch had been briefed by McMahon on the assassinations and was mystified that, whoever these people were, they had been able to kill four high-ranking politicians and not leave a single clue worth beans. He was impressed with the skill and professionalism of the killers and afraid that the president would be their next target. These assassins had shown their ability to think and plan ahead, and it worried Warch that, as usual, the president's itinerary was public information. The assassins would know approximately when the president was leaving the White House and when he would be arriving at Camp David.

In Warch's line of work he had to assume the worst. For that reason, he was taking extra precautions today. Warch looked down at the reporters and photographers who were staking out positions on the west side of the South Lawn. Warch shook his head in frustration. He hated the press. If he had it his way, he'd ban them from the White House compound. They did nothing but make his job more difficult.

It was 10:48 A.M. and the president's weekend guests were starting to arrive for the 11 A.M. lunch and photo op. A large black limousine pulled into the White House compound and drove up the executive drive. Warch watched his agents perform their duties with their usual precision. He glanced around the roof to make sure his other agents were staying focused on their area of responsibility and not looking at the new arrivals. The back door of the limo opened and Sen. Lloyd Hellerman stepped out. Four of Warch's tallest agents surrounded the senator and ushered him toward the White House. The media stayed where they were supposed to, but shouted questions as Hellerman was rushed toward the door. The senator looked toward the media and slowed for a second. The two agents on the left and right grabbed Hellerman by the biceps and kept him moving through the doorway and into the White House. Warch had given his people specific instructions: "I don't want anyone standing around outside. As they arrive, get them from the limos into the building as quickly as possible." The South Lawn of the White House was secure, but Warch wasn't going to take any unnecessary chances. He turned to one of his two assistants. "Joe, how are things going down at Quantico?"

The Secret Service agent put his hand over his earpiece. "They're going through their preflight briefing right now."

Warch nodded his head and asked Sally for her binoculars. He started to scan the rooftops of the buildings to the east. "How are our sniper teams doing?"

"They're in position," answered Agent Stiener.

Warch turned to the north and continued to look at the rooftops. "What about the ground teams?"

"They're ready to move out whenever you want."

Warch lowered the binoculars and thought about it for a minute. "Move them into position at eleven-fifteen. Remind them, if they see anyone carrying anything larger than a briefcase, I want them searched. And don't forget to remind them not to look at the choppers as they fly in and out. I need them looking at the street." Warch stopped and looked down at the gate as another limo pulled up. The photographers started snapping photos and the reporters started to speak into the cameras. Warch looked at the news vans that were parked off to the side and pointed at them. "Joe, remind Kathy and Jack to do a lockdown on those vans and take them off their live feeds before the first chopper lands. That's before, not during." Warch turned to Agent Manly. "Sally, what's the situation with the advance team at Camp David?"

"So far so good. The six Marine recon units out of Quantico were inserted by helicopter about two hours ago. They've got the hilltops along the approach route secured, and they're scouting the valleys for any potential hostiles."

Warch nodded his head. "Nice work so far. Let's stay sharp."

HMX-1 did not have a briefing room large enough to accommodate all one hundred pilots involved in today's flight operations, so folding chairs were set up in the corner of the hangar and the maintenance crews were asked to stop all work on the choppers while the briefing took place. The first several minutes of the briefing were handled by the ODO, or operations duty officer, who briefed the pilots on the weather conditions. The pilots sipped coffee and listened respectfully—some took notes on their knee boards while others memorized the details.

With the advent of shoulder-launched, surface-to-air missiles such as the American Stinger, the Secret Service had been forced to find a safer way to transport the president on board Marine One. In times of heightened security they implemented what the Marine pilots referred to as "the shell game." This was a tactic developed by

HMX-1 during the early years of the Reagan administration. Multiple Marine Ones would land, one at a time, at the White House or wherever the president was, and then take off, every helicopter heading in a different direction. The intended result was to confuse any would-be terrorist or assassin about which helicopter the president was on. This tactic was used often with only two or three VH-3s.

When the president's itinerary was known in advance, and there was a heightened terrorist alert, HMX-1 called in the CH-53s for escort duty. Escort was a kind description of the Super Stallions' job. The pilots of the drab green helicopters knew their real job was to shield the president's helicopter from a missile. This was accomplished by flying in a tight formation with Marine One in the middle surrounded by four Super Stallions. Tight-formation flying with choppers as big as the VH-3 and the CH-53 was not an easy thing. Because of this, the Marine Corps saw to it that their pilots were drilled frequently in today's exercise. The last thing the illustrious group of warriors wanted to be remembered for was killing the president in a midair collision.

After the weather briefing was finished, the squadron commander, a Marine colonel, took over. He handed out the flight assignments and got down to the nuts and bolts of the briefing. Ten VH-3s were flying today, and they were designated by their order of takeoff as Marine One, Marine Two, Marine Three, and so on. For training purposes the CH-53s were already split into groups of four. The first four that landed this morning were to escort Marine One, the second four were to escort Marine Two, and so on. The batting order was announced, and each division, which consisted of one VH-3 and four CH-53s, was given its bearing on which it was to leave the White House. Because it would take almost twenty minutes from the time the first VH-3 took off from the South Lawn to the time the last one did, the divisions were given different flight paths from the White House to Camp David. If all ten divisions left the White House and flew along the same flight path, it would give a terrorist time to move into position and take a shot at one of the later groups.

The blond-haired assassin was wearing contact lenses that made his blue eyes look brown. Once again his face, neck, and hands were covered with brown makeup, and a short, Afro wig was covering his hair. He exited George Washington Memorial Parkway and pulled the maroon van into the Glebe Nature Center. Finding a space close to the edge of the riverbank, he parked the van by a small, stone wall. About a mile to his south was the Key Bridge, and below him and just to the north was the Chain Bridge. Climbing into the back of the van, he turned on the control board and monitors. The van had been purchased with cash from a bankrupt TV station in Cleveland four months earlier. The small satellite dish on the roof pulled in the broadcast signals from the three networks and CNN. He was only concerned with CNN's and ABC's broadcasts. He put those two on the top monitors. CNN was giving a live update from the South Lawn, while ABC was still showing its regularly scheduled program. Reaching to his right, he dialed ABC's live-feed frequency into the receiver. The signal was fuzzy at first, but after some fine-tuning the picture became clear.

The White House correspondent for CNN was speaking from the South Lawn, so the assassin turned up the volume and listened. "The president's guests have been arriving now for the last fifteen minutes or so." The reporter looked over her shoulder and gestured at another limousine pulling up. "Security is very tight and tensions seem to be running high. The president is scheduled to sit down for a light lunch with the leaders of both parties shortly. After lunch, probably sometime around noon, they will be boarding helicopters and flying to Camp David for the weekend." The anchor in Atlanta thanked the reporter for the story and broke away for a commercial. The assassin checked his watch and leaned against the small back of the control chair. It would be another hour before the action started.

The president and the leaders from both parties were sitting around the large conference table in the Roosevelt Room, while Navy stewards served lunch and photographers from the press pool snapped pictures. They sat in a prearranged order, Republican next to Democrat, adversary next to adversary. This was done to give the impression of genuine unity within the group. Several reporters stood in the corner and shouted questions that were ignored. The event was a photo op, not a press conference, but as was always the case, the reporters who handled the White House beat asked questions regardless of what they were told to do. The constant flurry of questions and the politicians' refusal to answer them made for an awkward situation as the cameras continued to flash away.

The political leaders sat at the table and smiled at one another, trying to look good for the cameras. As each question was half shouted at the group, the participants looked to the president to see if it would be answered. Etiquette dictated that no one answer anything unless the president answered first or gave the approval for someone else to speak. One of the photographers broke away from the pack and walked around to the other side of the table so she could get photos of the men sitting across from the president. Stevens noticed this and became uncomfortable. During the last several years, the small bald patch on the back of his head had grown significantly. Stevens had become increasingly insecure about this simple fact of aging and as a result made a conscious effort not to be photographed from behind.

Before the photographer could move into position, the president looked up at Moncur and said, "Ann, I think that's enough." Moncur stepped in front of the cameras and reporters and escorted them to the door. When the door was closed, everyone looked around the room to make sure none of the reporters had stayed behind. Once they were sure they were alone, the mood changed immediately. The fake smiles vanished and the conversation picked up. There were a lot of deals to be made before the weekend was over.

About twenty minutes later, Jack Warch entered the room and asked for the president's permission to address the group. Everyone stopped talking while Agents Manly and Stiener walked around the table and handed each person a piece of paper. "Ladies and gentlemen, this sheet lists which helicopter you will be flying on and who you will be flying with. If you'll notice, the president is not on this list, and there is no one listed as flying on the last helicopter. For security reasons we will not announce which helicopter the president will be on until the last minute. If we decide to put him on the first helicopter, all of you will be bumped to the next chopper, and if we decide to put him on the fifth helicopter, those flying on helicopters five, six, seven, eight, and nine will be bumped to the next flight." Warch quickly glanced around the room to make sure everyone was with him. "The helicopters will be coming in at quick intervals, so I would ask that you be ready to go when your helicopter lands. When your helicopter lands, Secret Service agents will escort you to the chopper and a Marine will help you get situated and buckled in. . . . Do any of you have any questions?" Warch again looked around the room and noticed with satisfaction that the mood had become more serious. He turned to the president. "Sir, that's all I have for now."

The president thanked Warch, and the agents left the room.

Warch was walking down the hallway, telling Manly and Stiener several more things that he wanted checked, when Stu Garret approached from the opposite direction and stopped them. "Have you decided which helicopter the president is flying on?"

"No, I haven't."

Garret looked at his watch. "We're supposed to start this whole show in thirty minutes and you haven't made up your mind?"

"No, I haven't decided yet, Stu, and if you'd please excuse me,

I have a lot of things to take care of." The increasingly impatient Warch stepped around Garret and continued down the hallway. Warch had decided after witnessing Garret's unwarranted and childish temper tantrum two evenings earlier that it was time to be more firm with the temperamental chief of staff.

The elderly-looking gentleman parked his rental car by the front gate of Arlington National Cemetery and got out. He was wearing a tan trench coat, an English driving cap, and using a cane that he didn't need. On the lapel of his trench coat was a veteran's pin and an American flag. He smiled and nodded to the guard at the main gate as he entered the cemetery and started the climb up the hill to the Kennedy Memorial and Robert E. Lee's house.

He looked at the rows of tombstones as he walked up the slope and said a quick prayer for his fallen comrades as he went. This national shrine, this place of honor, had an unearthly feel to it. He did not see his friends die all those years ago so America could be destroyed by a bunch of self-serving politicians.

When he reached the front yard of Lee's house, he turned and looked to the east. Beneath him, across the river and beyond the Lincoln Memorial, he could see the White House. He situated himself beneath a large oak tree and leaned against its trunk.

A short while later, he heard a rumble in the distance and turned to the south. Beyond Washington National Airport, he saw the first formation of helicopters moving up the Potomac. The four large, dull green helicopters surrounded the single shiny, green-and-white presidential helicopter. As they reached the Potomac Railroad Bridge, the formation gained some altitude, passed over the Jefferson Memorial, and came to a stop over the Tidal Basin, which sat between the Jefferson Memorial and the Mall. The old man looked back and forth between the five helicopters and the White House. He saw more movement to the south and turned again.

Two more formations were working their way up the Potomac,

and the first of these two stopped just on the south side of the Potomac Railroad Bridge. A third appeared farther down the river, and then a fourth and a fifth just where the river started to bend back to the west and out of view. All five of the formations were holding their positions with about two hundred feet of separation. The noise of their large twin turbine engines and the thumping of their rotor blades echoed throughout the Potomac River Valley.

From his perch on the roof of the White House, Warch could see and hear the helicopters just to his south. The Tidal Basin, in front of the Jefferson Memorial, was approximately a half mile away, and the five helicopters held their position directly over it, waiting for the order to proceed to the White House. In the distance Warch could see the second group of choppers hovering. He looked toward the Mall and focused his binoculars on a group of Park Police officers who were in charge of securing the area from the Capitol to the Lincoln Memorial. Most of them were staring at the loud choppers hovering over the Tidal Basin. Turning to Manly, he said, "Sally, get on the radio and remind the people on the street that they are to pay attention to what is going on around them and to ignore the choppers." Agent Stiener was scanning the surrounding rooftops with his binoculars, and Warch tapped him on the shoulder. "Joe, tell Kathy and Jack to take the networks off their live feed." Stiener lowered his binoculars and spoke into his mike.

Special Agents Kathy Lageski and Steve Hampson were standing by the news vans talking to each other when they received the order from Stiener. Out of habit, both agents brought their hands up and pressed down on their earpieces as Stiener gave them instructions. Without pause, Lageski and Hampson turned and went to work. Lageski started with the CNN van and approached the producer who was sitting at the control board. "Tony, we have to take you off the air."

The producer nodded to Lageski and then spoke into his headset, "Ann, they're taking me off the air. I'm going to tape." The producer waited another couple seconds and then started to flip switches. Before shutting down the live feed, he put in a fresh tape and checked to see if it was recording properly. Lageski watched over him as he turned off the power on the transmitter that sent out the live signal. After the producer was finished, he stepped out of the van and Lageski shut the door.

"Tony, if you need to get back in there, ask me first." The producer nodded and Lageski moved on.

Stiener informed Warch that the networks were off their live feed, and the special agent in charge looked down at the news vans and then up at the first group of helicopters hovering less than a mile away. "Are our guests ready to go?"

Stiener raised his mike to his mouth and relayed the question to one of the agents downstairs. A moment later he looked up at his boss. "They're all set downstairs."

"Good, send in the first group, Sally."

Agent Manly gave the order and then asked Warch, "Which bird do you want to put Tiger on?" Tiger was the code name that the Secret Service used for the president.

Warch thought for a moment. "Let's go with number three. Don't let anyone know until number two lands."

The old man leaned against a tree and looked intently at the five helicopters hovering by the Jefferson Memorial. He hoped that the pilots flying those things were as good as he'd been told. He did not want to see any Marines die. The choppers started to move north toward the White House, and the old man pulled a digital phone out of his pocket, punched in a phone number, and hit the send button. He let the phone ring four times and hung up.

• • •

The assassin looked at the digital phone sitting on the control board and counted the rings. When it stopped after the fourth one, he dialed in a frequency code on the control board and pressed the send button. The signal was received less than a second later, and the transponder that was planted in the ABC van the previous evening kicked in. The power to the transmitter was restored, and the live feed was back on line. A couple of seconds later, the bottom left monitor went from a fuzzy, gray picture back to a clear picture of the South Lawn.

Warch watched the choppers as they flew across the Mall toward the White House. As they approached, the rotor wash became intense. Warch's tie started to flap up into his face, and he reached down, tucking it into his shirt. The lead Super Stallion hovered directly over Warch's head as the shiny green-and-white VH-3 in the middle descended and landed gently. The four ominous, loud Super Stallions held their positions hovering about two hundred feet above the ground, waiting for the VH-3 to ascend back into the formation.

Warch looked down and watched eight Secret Service agents escort the first two passengers to the foot of the VH-3. A Marine helped the two VIPs into the helicopter and then pulled up the steps and closed the door. Even over the loud roar of the Super Stallions, Warch could hear the VH-3 increase the power of its engines. The executive helicopter gracefully lifted off the ground and stopped at an altitude even with her escorts. She hovered for a brief moment, then all five helicopters simultaneously banked to the right and headed northeast. As the choppers increased power and passed over the White House, Warch and the other agents widened their stances to steady themselves against the intense rotor wash.

The next group of helicopters was already passing the Washington Monument and moving toward the White House. There was a brief moment of relative silence as the rumble of the first group lessened in the distance and the roar of the approaching group grew. Manly turned to Warch and Stiener. "God, those damn escorts are loud."

Warch and Stiener nodded their heads in agreement. The next formation swooped in over the South Lawn a little faster than the first, and the VH-3 wasted no time dropping rapidly and performing a quick, controlled landing. Once again the passengers were escorted by Secret Service agents to the chopper and loaded on board. The VH-3 lifted back into formation, and without pausing, all five helicopters banked to the left and continued to bank as they came back around to a southwesterly course, passing over the Reflection Pool. The next formation was moving toward the White House and Warch looked at Manly. "Is Tiger ready?"

Manly nodded her head yes.

President Stevens strode across the South Lawn wearing a dark wool suit with a faint gray pinstripe, a blue pinpoint oxford, and a deep red tie. Surrounding him were six Secret Service agents, the one just behind him carrying a bulletproof tan trench coat, ready to throw it over the president at the slightest sign of trouble. Garret walked on the left side of the president so as to avoid getting between his boss and the cameras. Stevens smiled broadly and waved to the cameras and reporters. He and Garret had debated whether he should give the press his serious and determined look or his happy and excited look before getting on board Marine One. Garret suggested a combination of the two—a happy and determined look. The president, being the consummate actor, understood completely the subtle difference between happy and excited and happy and determined. As they reached the helicopter, Stevens stopped and snapped off a sharp salute to the Marine in dress blues standing at the foot of the steps.

The crew chief, a Marine corporal wearing an in-flight headset, tan, long-sleeve shirt, and blue pants with a red stripe, met

Stevens at the top of the steps and helped him through the small doorway. Garret, the Secret Service agent carrying the tan trench coat, and another agent came through this door, and the other four came on board through a second door that was located just behind the port-side wheel flange. Normally only one agent would fly with the president and the rest of the detail would follow in the next chopper, but times were far from normal. The two doors, with steps built into them, were pulled up quickly and secured. Everyone took his seat while the crew chief made a quick pass to make sure everyone was strapped in. Before taking his own seat, he spoke to the pilots over the in-flight headset, telling them they were buttoned up and ready to go.

The helicopter leapt into the air and rose up into the middle slot of the formation. Stevens looked out his small, starboard window and was surprised at how close the large, green helicopters were. Unlike most military helicopters, the inside of Marine One was soundproofed against the noise of the large engines and the rotors, so conversation could take place without having to shout. The president looked to Garret and pointed out the window. "Stu, did you see how close this thing is?"

Garret shrugged his shoulders. "You know how these flyboys are. They're probably just trying to show off."

The digital phone started to ring in the old man's pocket. He made no attempt to answer it. Staring at the four dull green helicopters that were hovering above the White House, he counted the rings. The call was a signal telling him that the president was on board the helicopter that was about to rise back into the formation. After the third ring he opened the left side of his trench coat. Taped upside down to the inside of his jacket was a small, black box. The face of it contained a number pad, an enter button, and a power switch. The old man reached inside with his right hand and flipped the power switch to the on position. He glanced around to see if anyone was watching, then returned his attention to the helicopters hovering over the White House. He saw the green-and-white VH-3 rise into the air and punched two numbers into the remote, but did not hit the enter button. He had to wait until the formation started to move, otherwise the president's helicopter would drop straight back down into the relative cover of the White House compound. The noses of the helicopters dipped slightly and the group began to move. The old man hit the enter button and said a quick prayer.

The signal was received a second later by the tiny surface-to-air radar unit that had been placed in the *Washington Post* newspaper box two blocks to the south of the White House. The unit immediately started to sweep its wide-band search radar over the formation of helicopters. The band narrowed in less than two seconds from acquisition, to track, to fire control.

Simultaneously, inside the cockpits of all five helicopters, missile warning lights began flashing, and the onboard threat sensors came screeching to life. The loud wailing of the threat sensor told them that they were being illuminated by fire-control radar. There was no time to think, only time to react as their training had taught them. Heart rates quickened and heads snapped around to see if a missile was already in the air. Their threat sensors informed them that they were being illuminated from behind, and within seconds all five helicopters simultaneously increased power and moved forward, dropping to as low an altitude as possible. As they screamed over the roof of the White House, the copilots hit their flare-dispenser buttons, hoping to confuse an approaching heat-seeking missile.

Jack Warch felt his heart climb into his throat as he saw the flares come shooting out of the tails of the helicopters. The huge choppers moved just above his head, straining to gain speed, their bright red flares streaming down and pelting the roof of the White House. Without hesitation, his hand mike snapped up to his mouth. Trying to scream above the deafening roar of the helicopters, he yelled, "Sniper teams, look for a missile launch!"

He watched the choppers gain speed as they tore across Lafayette Park, skimming the tops of the trees, and willed them to go faster. The seconds seemed like minutes as he watched and waited to see a red streak and then an explosion. Several flares landed by his feet, and he ran to the north side of the roof, following the choppers. About a half a mile away from the White House the formation banked hard to the left and Warch lost sight of it.

Atop the hill at Arlington the old man tracked the formation of helicopters as they scrambled for safety. Quickly, he punched in the codes for the radar units that had been placed to the east and north of the White House.

Seconds later the helicopters picked up the azimuth of the new threats and banked hard to the left. Heading due west, they raced over the rooftops of downtown, gaining speed quickly and continuing to drop flares. The old man punched in the codes for the last two radar units. They immediately started sweeping the horizon from the west and southwest with their search radar—the trap was complete.

As the pilots reached the Potomac River, they did exactly what their instincts and training had taught them. They skimmed over the top of the Key Bridge and dove almost two hundred feet to the deck. The formation pulled up dangerously close to the blue-gray waters of the Potomac and raced northward, below the tree line and underneath the coverage of the radars that had been harassing them. The warning lights on their dashboards subsided, and the shrill of the threat sensors ceased.

The engine of the van was running and the assassin was standing next to the stone wall waiting for the helicopters. He heard them coming before he could see them. When they appeared, he was immediately impressed by how low they were flying and how tight they'd kept the formation. That wouldn't last much longer, he thought to himself. Pressing in the code for the flare launchers and radar unit, he placed his thumb over the enter button and waited. As they passed underneath his position, he looked at the blur of rotors spinning below and said, "Now just keep your cool and don't run into each other. I don't want any dead Marines on my hands."

The Chain Bridge, unlike the Key Bridge, was only about fifty feet high and was slung low across the Potomac. The assassin waited for just a moment longer, and when the lead Super Stallion was about two hundred yards from the bridge, he hit the button. The radar powered up and the helicopters were so close that the radar immediately narrowed its search to fire control.

Again the threat sensors on board the choppers came howling to life. Seconds later all six of the bright red phosphorus flares snaked their way out of the tubes and into the sky leaving a trail of smoke behind them. The combination of the visual threat of the red streaks and the fact that the pilots thought they were locked onto by a surface-to-air missile caused the lead pilot to do what came naturally. He'd been trained for almost fifty hours in close-formation escort duty, but he'd also been trained for well over two hundred hours in missile-evasion tactics. All this plus the fact that there was nothing more unnatural for a pilot to do than fly a straight and steady course when being tracked by fire control radar caused him to jerk his stick to the left.

Upon seeing and hearing the danger that was ahead, the other three Super Stallion pilots had already started to loosen the formation, and when the lead escort broke left, the other three scattered, as much out of the fear of a midair collision as their desire to evade what they thought was an approaching missile. The helicopters in the three and six o'clock slots broke to the right and stayed low, because it was better to pass through a hot zone quickly than to gain altitude and lose speed. The helicopter in the nine slot was forced to pull up to avoid hitting the lead escort, who had cut her off.

All of this left Marine One alone, in the middle of the river, a sitting duck. There was no time or room to react. Marine One passed through the smoke trails of the flares while the helicopter's threat sensors continued to flash and warn of imminent death. Gripping the controls tightly, the pilots of Marine One braced themselves for impact and cursed their escorts for abandoning them.

CHAPTER 18

THE old man was back behind the wheel of his rental car and driving across the Arlington Memorial Bridge. When he reached the east side, he got onto the Potomac Parkway and headed north. Exiting off the Parkway, he entered the Foggy Bottom neighborhood of Washington, D.C., less than a mile from the White House. Parking in a ramp where there would be cameras and attendants would not be wise, so he circled and waited for a space on the street. It was just past twelve-thirty and the streets and sidewalks were crowded with people coming and going to lunch. After finding a spot, he got out and left the unneeded cane in the passenger seat. Two short blocks later he found the preselected pay phone, inserted a quarter, and punched in a phone number.

After several rings, a deep voice answered on the other end. "Hello, you've reached Special Agent Skip McMahon. If you'd like to leave a message, please do so at the beep. If you need to speak to one of my assistants, press zero."

The old man pulled a Dictaphone out of his pocket, placed the speaker up to the phone, and pressed the play button. "Special Agent McMahon, we know you have been placed in charge of investigating the assassinations of Senator Fitzgerald, Congressman Koslowski, Senator Downs, and Speaker Basset. We are sending you this message because we do not want to fight our battle in the media. We suggest the president and his people follow suit. We are in possession of several Stinger missiles and could have easily blown Marine One out of the sky this afternoon. You can tell the president that the only reason he is still alive is because we did not want to kill the Marines and Secret Service agents on board.

"If you continue to ignore our demands and manipulate public opinion through the media, we will have no choice but to escalate our war. So far we have assassinated only elected officials, but we are adding the names of Stu Garret and Ted Hopkinson to our list of targets. We are very well informed about what goes on inside the Stevens administration and know that these two men are responsible for most of the lies that have been spoon-fed to the media over the last week. If you continue to label us as terrorists and the president as the noble defender of the Constitution, you will die. This is our last warning. No matter what they tell you, Mr. President, the Secret Service cannot protect you from us. They can make our job more difficult, but they cannot stop us from ending your life. This is your last warning."

Marine One landed on the helicopter pad at Camp David, and a pale-faced President Stevens was draped in his bulletproof trench coat and rushed into a waiting Suburban. The president sat in the backseat in between two Secret Service agents. No one spoke as the tan truck sped up the narrow, tree-lined path. The Suburban stopped in front of the cabin, and again Stevens was rushed inside. Two of the agents went inside with him, and the other four took up posts outside.

The president stood in the main room and looked at the most senior agent. "Where is Mr. Garret?"

"He's being brought in another truck."

There was more awkward silence as the agents averted their eyes from the president's. Again Stevens looked to the senior agent and asked, "How did they know which helicopter I was on?"

"We don't know, sir."

Stevens said nothing; he gave no look or expression of emotion. He continued to stand in the midst of his protectors for another minute, then without saying a word he walked in between them and down the hallway. The agents followed. Stevens entered his bedroom and turned to close the door behind him. The two Secret Service agents came to an abrupt halt.

The president held up his hand. "I want to be alone."

The agents nodded respectfully and Stevens closed the door. Walking across the room, he took off his jacket and threw it on the bed. With several yanks back and forth, his tie came loose and dropped to the floor. He stood leaning over the dresser staring into the large mirror on the wall. The reality of what had almost happened was starting to sink in. He felt a cold chill shoot up his spine, and his entire body shuddered. Standing up straight, he quickly walked over to the wet bar, grabbed a thick glass tumbler, loaded it with ice, and filled it to the brim with vodka. After taking a large gulp of the cold, clear liquid, he walked over to the fireplace and noticed that it was stocked with wood and kindling. Stevens set his drink down on the mantel and picked up a box of long matches sitting in a basket next to the hearth. Grabbing one of the twelve-inch matchsticks, he struck it across the coarse strip on the side of the box. The matchstick broke in half, and Stevens tried again, this time holding the match closer to the tip. The red tip sparked and then burst into flames. Stevens waited until the wood stem caught fire, then stuck the long match under the logs, lighting the dry pieces of kindling.

The fire caught quickly and he pulled up a chair to watch the flames spread. Sliding off his loafers, he placed his feet on the hearth and took a deep breath. The warmth of the fire helped him relax and momentarily forget about the afternoon's life-threatening events. He stared into the fire and watched it burst into a full blaze as the white bark on the birch logs crackled and curled from the flames. The images of the helicopter ride began to surface again, and he took another gulp from his drink. But still he saw the flares shooting out of the helicopter next to them, the violent jerking of the craft as it banked and then dropped like a rock, pulling up just short of the river's water, Stu Garret screaming and demanding to know what was going on, the escorts scattering and the red streaks shooting up in front of them.

Stevens became unsteady again, and he started to shake. He grabbed his drink with both hands to keep it from spilling, his body trembling as he pulled the glass to his lips with both hands wrapped tightly around it. He took four large gulps, finishing the rest of the vodka, and stood to pour another. As he walked to the bar, the murders of Basset and the others flashed sharply across his mind, and he realized for the first time just how vulnerable he was. The crystal tumbler with the presidential seal engraved on the side slipped from his hand and shattered on the stone floor. Stevens continued to the bar and started to pour another drink, the glass neck of the vodka bottle clanging off the rim of the tumbler as his hands continued to shake uncontrollably.

Garret arrived at the main cabin just minutes after the president and went straight to the conference room. He grabbed the nearest phone and punched in the number for Ted Hopkinson's office. After several rings Hopkinson's secretary answered and Garret barked, "Get me Ted!"

As each second passed, Garret became more and more irritated. With sweat forming on his forehead, he gripped the phone tighter and tighter. According to Garret's watch, which he looked at about every five seconds, he had been on hold for two minutes and thirteen seconds when Hopkinson finally came on the line.

"Where in the hell have you been?" Garret spat into the phone.

"Stu, it's a zoo around here! The press is crawling all over the place. They want to know what the hell is going on. A couple of them just asked me if the president is dead!"

"Shit!"

"Stu, we've got to get control of this thing!"

"Yeah, I know, just shut up for a minute while I think of the best way to handle it." There was a moment of silence while Garret scrambled to come up with a plan of action. "We're going to have to put him on TV. Grab a cameraman and a reporter from the press pool and get your ass up here."

"I can't. The Secret Service has shut the compound down. They're not letting anyone come or go."

Garret screamed into the phone, "Screw the damn Secret Service. Thanks to those idiots I almost got my ass blown out of the sky twenty minutes ago. You find Warch and tell him I said if he wants to keep his job to get a chopper for you pronto. If he gives you any shit, find Mike Nance and have him get one from the Pentagon. Get moving!"

"What are we going to have him say to the press?"

"Goddamn it, Ted, do I have to do everything around here! You're the damn communications director! You're paid to figure out what he says to the press! Get moving!" Garret slammed the phone down and headed for the door. On his way through the main living room he ran into Special Agent Terry Andrews. Andrews was the Secret Service agent who had been carrying the president's bulletproof trench coat when they boarded Marine One. Garret approached him and said, "Andrews, I don't want any crap, just straight talk. What in the hell happened while we were airborne, and how did they know which bird we were on?"

The tall ex-Marine looked down at Garret and replied, "We don't know how they knew which helicopter we were on, sir."

"What about missiles? Were there any missiles launched?"

"We're not sure at this point, sir."

"What do you mean, you're not sure? You get ahold of your boss and tell him I want some answers, and I want them quick!" Without waiting for a response, Garret turned and left.

CHAPTER 19

THE scene at the Chain Bridge was intense, to say the least. The media, the Metro Police, the Virginia State Police, and the FBI had all descended on the scene within minutes of each other. McMahon arrived shortly thereafter with an FBI special-response team and ordered that the media be moved back with whatever force necessary, short of shooting them. The Virginia State Police closed off the west end of the bridge, and the D.C. Metropolitan Police were manning the east end. Traffic was being diverted, and the FBI had taken over the crime scene. Two Park Police helicopters were busy warding off the media helicopters that came swooping in like vultures, trying to get live footage of whatever was so interesting to the FBI.

Skip McMahon stood looking over the south edge of the Chain Bridge, watching Kathy Jennings and two other agents carefully inspect the devices they'd found. McMahon had decided to send only Jennings and two other agents down until the special evidence team arrived with their equipment. The fewer agents the better for now. Until they knew exactly what they were dealing with, there was the chance of contaminating evidence. Jennings was pointing at the ground and one of the agents was taking photos, while the other one stuck small yellow flags into the ground.

McMahon heard the sound of an approaching helicopter and looked up to see one of the shiny green-and-white presidential VH-3s approaching. The large helicopter swung in over the bridge and descended, its churning rotors blowing sand into the air. McMahon turned away, shielding his face from the flying debris. When the bird touched down, the pilots cut the engines and the swooping sound of the blades lessened. The swirl of sand started to subside and McMahon turned to see Jack Warch approaching. McMahon extended his hand and greeted the younger man. "I'll bet you've had better days, Jack."

Warch shook his head and frowned. "This ranks with the worst of them."

McMahon grabbed Warch by the shoulder. "Come on, let me show you what we've found." McMahon led Warch over to the side of the bridge and pointed down at Jennings and the other two agents. "My agents found a small, gray metal box with a dish attached to the top and a piece of wood with some vertical tubes. Both have batteries and transponders attached, so it would appear that they were activated by remote control. Which of course means the people we're after are long gone."

"Can I take a look at the stuff?" asked Warch.

"Not yet. I have a special evidence team and a mobile crime lab on the way. I want to keep the area as sterile as possible until they get here." Warch nodded and McMahon changed gears. "Jack, how did they know which helicopter he was on?"

"I have absolutely no idea. We didn't even know until just minutes before he took off."

"How did they know which route he would take to Camp David? Don't you guys send all the choppers along different flight paths?"

"Yeah, they all fly in different directions, but this was not the route they were supposed to take."

McMahon had a confused look on his face. "Well, how did they end up down here?"

"Right now we think they were forced to fly into the river valley."

"How?"

"Do you have a map of D.C.?"

McMahon said yes and the two walked over to the car. Skip retrieved a map from the glove box and spread it out on the trunk, using his gun, handcuffs, and digital phone to weigh down three of the four corners.

Warch pointed to the White House and said, "The squadron commander tells me that when the group left the White House, they were lit up by fire-control radar from the south. About ten minutes ago my people found a small, gray box with a radar dish. It was concealed inside a *Washington Post* newspaper box on the corner of Fourteenth and Constitution." Warch tapped his finger on the spot just a block to the south of the White House. "The group took evasive maneuvers and fled to the north. About ten seconds after they were lit up by radar to the south, they were lit up again by radar to the north and east. The helicopters headed west away from the threat, and as they approached the Potomac, they were lit up again from the west. The squadron commander tells me his boys are trained to head for the weeds when something like this happens, and that a river valley offers the perfect protection because they can dive below the radar and an approaching missile. So when these guys reached the Potomac, they went for cover and headed in the only direction that they hadn't been threatened from . . . to the northwest." Warch took his hands and set them on the map forming a *V,* the base located at the White House and the open end at the Chain Bridge. "They created a trap and drove the helicopters into it."

"So what happened when they got here? Did they fire a missile?"

"Supposedly the pilots thought they were in the clear. They have threat sensors that tell them when a missile is locked onto them, and I guess they make this screeching noise. Well, when they dove into the river valley, these things stopped screeching and they thought they'd avoided the threat, and then all of the sudden these red streaks pop up in front of them and the threat sensors start screaming again. The lead escort thought they were missiles and he broke formation." Warch shook his head in frustration. "Which he's not supposed to do. The whole idea behind this strategy is that the escorts are supposed to protect the president's bird, and if need be, take the hit."

McMahon put his hands up in the air, palms out. "Hold on a minute. I've got a bunch of people telling me they saw a missile, and I've got some other people telling me that they were flares. I'm inclined to believe the second group because no one reports hearing an explosion, and my agents found several warm but burned-out flares. Now, what do your pilots tell you? Were there missiles launched or not?"

"The other pilots don't think so. They say they were flares."

Perplexed, McMahon shook his head.

Warch said, "I don't get it either. The pilots that were flying Marine One said they were dead meat. . . . They said that when the lead escort broke formation, they thought they were going to be blown out of the sky. We're either very lucky or these terrorists screwed up somewhere."

McMahon stared at the horizon and rubbed his forefinger across his lips as he sifted through the new information. A short while later he announced, "We're missing something. . . . Something doesn't fit here. Why go to all of that effort and not take a shot?" Both of them pondered McMahon's question, and then McMahon shook the dazed look out of his eyes and said, "We'll have time for this later. How's the president?"

"My people tell me he's pretty shook up. I guess the ride was rough." Warch stopped and his jaw tensed. "They also tell me that damn Stu Garret is on one of his rampages, yelling at everyone and demanding answers. . . . This whole stupid thing was his idea from the start."

"What do you mean?"

"I told them I didn't think having the meeting at Camp David and moving the president was worth the risk." Warch brought his hand up to his eyes and said, "I've had it up to here with Garret."

"Jack, let me give you a little piece of advice. There's only one way to deal with a jerk like Garret. You meet him head-on, and you don't take any crap. Half the reason why he's the way he is, is because people let him get away with it."

"Believe me, I've thought about punching his ticket more than once, but I like my job too much."

McMahon was about to add another editorial comment on the behavior of Garret when he heard Kathy Jennings yell from below. McMahon and Warch looked over the edge of the bridge.

Jennings craned her neck upward and held a digital phone in her outstretched hand. "Hey, Skip, I just got off the phone with some Air Force people over at the Pentagon. I read them the serial numbers off this thing and they say it's one of ours. It's an older-model radar unit that they used to put in the nose cones of fighters like the F-4 Phantom."

Warch and McMahon traded glances, and McMahon yelled back down, "Did you ask them how someone would go about getting their hands on one of them?"

"Yeah, they said there's thousands of them available on the surplus-military-hardware market."

"I assume they keep records of what they do with all this stuff."

"Yep, they told me they'll start tracing it for us."

"Great," responded McMahon, and then he continued in a sarcastic voice, "By the way, you didn't happen to find any unused missiles down there, did you?"

"Not yet."

"All right, good work." McMahon turned back to Warch. "Well, at least it's a start."

"Yeah, listen, I've got to get out to Camp David and brief the president on what happened. Give me a call if you find anything out, otherwise let's plan on talking later."

"Will do."

During Warch's short flight to Camp David, he'd prepared himself for what he knew was an assured confrontation with Garret. He thought about the way the chief of staff had treated Dorle after the Basset assassination and knew he was in for the same treatment. What McMahon said was right, he'd put up with Garret's reckless and unprofessional abuse for almost three years, and now was the time to put an end to it. He knew exactly how to handle it. It would be kept between him and Garret, no one else needed to know.

Special Agent Terry Andrews was waiting for Warch on the porch of the main cabin when the Suburban pulled up. Warch walked up the steps, and Andrews led him over to a more secluded area of the porch.

Andrews spoke in a low voice. "What have you found out?"

Warch relayed the discussion he'd had with McMahon and then asked, "How's the president?"

"He's trying to get some rest."

"Where is Garret?"

"He's in the conference room with Hopkinson trying to figure out how they're going to spin this story to the media. I was in there just before you landed, and they were debating whether or not they should hold a big ceremony and pin some medals on those Marine pilots. I tell ya, Jack, it takes all the strength I have to not crack that damn idiot across the head. He's been screaming his head off for the last hour demanding to know what's going on. He told me the Secret Service is going to pay for this fuckup."

"We'll see."

The two men walked into the cabin and down the hall to the conference room. Warch opened the door and entered first. Garret was standing over Hopkinson's shoulder telling him what to write.

He looked up at Warch and pronounced, "It's about time you got here. You'd better have some answers for me."

Warch ignored Garret and looked at Hopkinson. "Ted, would you please excuse us?"

Hopkinson did nothing for a moment and then started to stand. Garret put a hand on his shoulder and pushed him back into his seat. "Anything you have to say to me, Ted can hear."

Warch glared unwaveringly into Garret's eyes and said, "Not this, this is for your ears only." The lean Warch took off his jacket, laid it over the back of a chair, and pointed at the door with his thumb. "Ted, please excuse us, this will only take a minute. Terry, you too."

Hopkinson got out of his chair, and he and Andrews headed for the door. As they were doing so, Garret snapped, "This had better be good."

Warch continued to stare at Garret and said, "Terry, please close the door." Andrews closed the heavy wood door behind him, leaving Warch and Garret alone.

Garret stayed on his side of the table and started in. "You'd better have some answers for me. First you guys screw up and get Basset killed, and then you almost get my ass and the president's blown out of the sky."

Garret continued to bark while Warch walked around the table. Warch was just a little shorter than Garret and weighed slightly less. Because of his slight size advantage and position of authority, Garret incorrectly thought there was no reason to physically fear Warch. Instead of backing away, Garret took a step forward and pointed his finger at Warch.

"Heads are going to roll over this one, Warch, and yours is at the top of the—"

Before Garret could finish his sentence, Warch grabbed his Adam's apple and slammed him backward into the wall. Garret stood pinned against the wall, his eyes wide open, and both hands wrapped around Warch's wrist.

Warch brought his face to within inches of Garret's and in a tense, quiet voice said, "Stu, I think it's about time you and I had a man-to-man talk. I'm finished taking your shit, and my people are done taking your shit! We're sick and tired of your emotional outbursts! Today's little ride up to Camp David was your idea! I told you it was an unnecessary risk, but you went ahead and for your own stupid reasons convinced the president that he should have the meeting up here. It was your idea, Stu, so I don't want to hear you say another word about it, or I'm going to start airing some of your dirty laundry in the press.

"No heads are going to roll. You are not going to ruin my career or any of my people's. In fact, you're gonna start treating them with respect, because if you don't, I'm gonna leak the story of how you and Mike Nance blackmailed Congressman Moore."

Garret's eyes opened wide, and Warch smiled. "That's right, Stu, I know all about the little arrangement you and Nance had with Arthur Higgins." Warch paused to let Garret sweat a little more. "I'll make a deal with you, Stu. From now on you start listening to me when it comes to security issues. What I say goes, and I don't want to see any more juvenile tirades. You start treating me and my people with the respect they deserve, and we'll get along fine. But I'm warning you, Stu, don't piss me off again, or I'll turn everything I have over to the FBI. And believe me, there are plenty of people at the Bureau who would love to take a bite out of your ass!"

CHAPTER 20

MICHAEL was parked in front of a brick apartment building in the Adams Morgan neighborhood of D.C. He sat behind the wheel and sipped a cup of piping hot Colombian coffee he had just picked up at the Starbucks two blocks away. He looked down at his digital phone and then up at the Ford Explorer that was parked three cars ahead of him. It belonged to the man he wanted to talk to. O'Rourke had already called up to the apartment twice and had got the answering machine both times.

O'Rourke was growing impatient. He desperately wanted to talk to the man who lived in the building. He tapped his hand on the steering wheel and guessed that his friend was out for a jog. O'Rourke knew he was in town because he had called his office and checked. Five minutes and half a cup of coffee later, he saw a man with a dark blue baseball cap and a large backpack thrown over his shoulder round the corner.

Michael set his coffee in the center console and got out of his truck. Straightening his tie, he walked up onto the curb and locked eyes with the man. "You're awfully hard to get ahold of."

The lean individual gave Michael a surprised look. "I'm sorry. I've been on the run."

"Don't you get your messages? I've called a dozen times in the last three days." Michael stuck out his hand, and his friend grabbed it.

"Sorry, I've been awfully busy." The man, who was six years Michael's elder, adjusted the backpack on his shoulder and glanced up and down the street with his alert eyes.

Michael looked around. "Am I keeping you from something?"

"I have a lot to do today, but I can always spare a few minutes for my little brother's best friend."

O'Rourke was warmed by the comment. The man standing before him was Scott Coleman, the older brother of Mark Coleman, O'Rourke's best friend who was killed a year earlier. Scott Coleman was the former commander of SEAL Team Six, America's premier counterterrorism unit. He also happened to be the person Michael had been worrying about since last Friday.

Coleman had left the SEALs almost a year ago after a highly decorated sixteen-year stint. Despite his illustrious career, he did not leave on a happy note. He had lost half of his SEAL team in a mission over northern Libya the previous year.

Upon returning from the mission Coleman was informed that their assault on a terrorist training camp had been compromised because a high-profile politician had leaked the mission. When his superiors refused to reveal the identity of the politician, Coleman resigned in disgust. O'Rourke had found out through Senator Olson, who was the chairman of the Joint Intelligence Committee, that Senator Fitzgerald was the person in question.

Michael had labored as to whether he should tell Coleman. They had grown closer since the death of Mark Coleman, and while on a hunting trip the previous fall Michael finally decided to confide in the warrior. Seamus was right: if they were his men, he would want and deserve to know. Coleman had taken the news about Fitzgerald in silence, and that was the only time he and Michael had discussed the issue. But when Senator Fitzgerald turned up dead a week ago, Michael could only wonder.

O'Rourke put his hands in his pockets and shifted uneasily. "That was quite a deal with the president's helicopter this afternoon. You wouldn't by chance know anything about who might do such a thing, would you?"

"Nope." Coleman stared unflinchingly at Michael with his bright blue eyes.

"Do you remember that hunting trip we went on last year?"

"Of course."

"Do you remember that bit of information I passed on to you?"

"Yep."

Michael returned Coleman's stare and nodded. After several moments of silence Michael decided to change his approach. "So what do you think about the assassinations?"

Coleman's face stayed expressionless. "I'm not doing a lot of mourning, if that's what you're asking."

"No." O'Rourke shook his head. "I didn't think you would be. Any idea who might be behind them?"

Coleman cocked his head to the side. "No, do you?"

"I might." Michael rocked back and forth on his heels. "Are you alone?"

"Yes."

"You haven't by chance talked to anyone at the FBI lately?"

O'Rourke shook his head.

"Good. Are you planning on talking to anyone at the FBI?"

"No. I think you and I can handle this one-on-one."

Coleman raised one of his eyebrows and shot Michael a questioning look.

"Hypothetically," asked O'Rourke, "if you knew who the assassins were, do you think you could give them a message from me?"

"Hypothetically?" Coleman folded his arms across his chest. "I suppose almost anything is possible."

"Tell them"—Michael leaned in close—"that there has been enough killing. Tell them to give us some time to implement their reforms before this thing gets any uglier."

"That sounds like a good idea, but I'm not so sure the president and his people have gotten the hint. And now our friend Senator Olson is trying to screw things up." Coleman shook his head. "I don't think these guys are done killing. At least not until the president and the others come around."

"So you think there will be more assassinations?"

"I wouldn't know."

Michael rolled his eyes. "Hypothetically."

"Hypothetically speaking . . . who knows?"

Both men stared each other down for a while, both refusing to blink. Finally Coleman looked at his watch and said, "I'm running late. I should really get going. Let's get together for lunch next week."

Michael reached out and grabbed Coleman's arm. "Scott, I understand why you're doing what you're doing. If Fitzgerald had compromised the security of me and my men during the Gulf and gotten even one of my men killed, I would have come home and gutted him like a pig. I'm not going to pass judgment on you, but I think it's time to let the politicians finish what's been started."

"Like they did in Iraq." Coleman shook his head. "I think these boys are going all the way to Baghdad. No half-assed jobs this time. You politicians, present company excluded, have a history of screwing things up when the clear objective is within reach."

Michael couldn't argue with the historical comparison. "Let it rest" was the only answer he could muster.

Coleman nodded and turned toward his apartment. As he reached the first step, he turned to Michael and said, "There is one thing you can do. Do you still keep in touch with Senator Olson?"

"Yes."

"It might be a good idea to tell him now is not a good time to get into bed with the president."

Michael felt the hair on the back of his neck rise. "Keep Erik out of this, Scott."

"I'm sure Erik will be fine. I'm just saying hypothetically it would be a good idea to warn him." Coleman gave Michael a half salute and entered the building.

McMahon walked down the executive hallway at a quicker than normal pace. The day had been one of nonstop commotion. The media was everywhere, sticking a microphone or a camera in McMahon's face at every turn. The events surrounding the president's unusual flight to Camp David were coming together like a jigsaw puzzle, and a crucial piece of the puzzle had just been discovered. McMahon hadn't had the chance to check his voice mail until just minutes before. The message left by the assassins had sat untouched for over five hours. McMahon nodded to Director Roach's secretary and continued through the door, closing it behind him.

Roach was on the phone and looked up at McMahon. McMahon towered over the edge of Roach's desk, waving his finger in a circular motion, signaling his boss to wrap up the conversation, that there was something more important to talk about. Roach nodded and told the person on the other end that he needed to go. Hanging up the phone, Roach asked, "What's up?"

"We got a message from our friends and it's been sitting under my nose all day."

"What do you mean 'friends'?" Roach asked with a quizzical look on his face.

"The assassins." McMahon walked around the edge of Roach's desk and punched his voice mail number into the phone. When it was ready to go, he pushed the speaker button. "Listen to this."

The computerized voice played from the small speaker. Roach sat transfixed, listening intently as light was shed on the afternoon's events. When the message was over, Roach asked McMahon to play it again. After it was played for the second time, McMahon saved it and looked to his boss for a reaction.

"Who in the hell are these guys?" Roach asked with a deeply puzzled look.

"They're not terrorists, Brian. Let's come to an agreement on that right now, and they're not some fringe white-supremacist group. If they were, they would have blown the president out of the sky. Terrorists don't give a shit about killing Secret Service agents or Marines. These guys are exactly who Kennedy said they were from day one. They're former commandos."

"I think you're right, and besides, terrorists wouldn't send this to us, they'd send it to the media. The more exposure, the better. . . . Can we be sure this is from the group responsible for the previous attacks?"

"I'm ninety-nine percent sure. The message was left about fifteen minutes after Marine One took off from the White House, and the computerized voice sounds the same as the one that was left with ABC after Basset's assassination. I'm having our lab analyze the sound signature right now."

"How long will it take them to verify?"

"They told me within the hour. When are you going to tell the president?"

"I'm flying out to Camp David in about thirty minutes to brief him. I'll wait and do it in person." Roach stared off at nothing for a moment while he thought about the tape. "You don't have to come if you don't want to. I'm sure you've got plenty to keep you busy around here. Besides, I know how much you hate these briefings."

"Are you crazy? I wouldn't miss seeing the expression on Garret's face when he hears that these guys are onto him."

Roach nodded his head in agreement and looked at his watch. "Be back up here in thirty minutes. I've got a chopper picking us up on the roof."

"One more thing, the boys over at the Secret Service have been getting beat up all day. If it's all right with you, I'd like to let Jack Warch take the lead on telling the president about the radar units and the flare launcher. I'll back him up on what we're doing to investigate the new evidence, and I'll let you handle the message from the assassins if you want."

"No, that's all right, you can handle it, and go ahead and let Warch take the lead."

McMahon left Roach's office and headed back to his.

The chopper ride from the Hoover Building to Camp David took about twenty-five minutes. Roach, McMahon, and two of the director's bodyguards sat in back. Roach utilized the time by having McMahon bring him up to speed on every aspect of the investigation. After landing, they were driven to the main cabin and escorted to the conference room.

It was just after 7 P.M. when the president and Garret entered the room, taking their spots at the head of the table. Mike Nance was seated at the far end of the table so he could observe everyone, while Stansfield, Roach, and McMahon were seated on the one side, with Warch and Director Tracy on the other.

Garret looked at Roach and in a tired voice asked, "Director Roach, do you have any new developments to report since we talked earlier?"

"Yes, as a matter of fact, we have received a message from the assassins. I'll let Special Agent McMahon fill you in." Roach turned to McMahon and nodded.

Each spot at the large conference table had a phone in front of it. McMahon pulled the one in front of him closer and punched in his voice mail number. "Just before we left this evening, we discovered a message left by the assassins. If you'll bear with me for a moment, I'll retrieve it." McMahon finished accessing the message, hit the speaker button, and slid his chair back. The message started to play:

"Special Agent McMahon, we know you have been placed in charge of investigating the assassinations of Senator Fitzgerald, Congressman Koslowski, Senator Downs, and Speaker Basset. We are sending you this message because we do not want to fight our battle in the media." Both the president and Garret looked up at McMahon upon hearing his name.

The message continued while everyone listened intently. When the tape ended with, "Mr. President, the Secret Service cannot protect you from us. They can make our job more difficult, but they cannot stop us from ending your life. This is your last warning," the pale president looked to Jack Warch and Director Tracy for reassurance but only got straight faces and silence in return. Garret leaned back in his chair and placed both hands under his armpits to keep them from shaking. The silence was only making him more uncomfortable, so he looked at McMahon and snapped, "How do we even know if this thing is real?"

McMahon responded in an even tone, "Some of our lab technicians analyzed it just before I left. They say it has the same voice signature of the recording we received after Speaker Basset was shot."

Garret started to grind his teeth. He didn't like surprises, and he had no doubt that McMahon and Roach had intentionally withheld the tape from him until just now. Through clenched teeth he asked, "How long have you known about this tape?"

"I checked my voice mail for the first time since this morning at about six this evening."

"When did the assassins leave it?"

"At about twelve-thirty this afternoon."

Garret sprang to the edge of the table. "You've had this since twelve-thirty and you haven't told us about it?"

"The assassins left it on my voice mail at twelve-thirty, but I did not discover it until six. Considering the fact that we were coming out here to brief you at seven, Director Roach and I decided that we would play the recording for you when we got here."

"Hold on, back up a minute. Don't you usually check your voice mail more than once a day?"

"On a normal day, yes, but I was a little busy today."

Garret pointed his finger at McMahon and raising his voice said, "The next time you get something this important, you let us know immediately! There is absolutely no excuse other than incompetency for not informing us of this recording as soon as you found it!"

McMahon was enjoying himself too much to let what Garret was saying upset him. Leaning back in his chair, McMahon folded his arms and smiled.

Jack Warch, who was sitting next to Garret, leaned forward and caught the chief of staff's eye. Warch gave Garret a hard stare. The message was clear. Garret looked down at his notepad and mumbled something to himself.

No one spoke for a while, and then a nervous President Stevens attempted to speak. The words didn't come out right the first time, so he started over. "Could they have shot down Marine One today?"

Without pausing for a second, Warch answered, "Yes."

In the most polite tone he could muster, Garret cleared his throat and said, "Jack, let's not be so presumptuous. We shouldn't jump to any conclusions until we get more information." Garret didn't like anyone getting the president frazzled unless it was him.

Warch shrugged his shoulders and said, "I am basing my opinion on nothing more than the facts. These assassins have shown an incredible propensity to plan ahead. They not only discovered which helicopter the president was on, but they forced Marine One and her escorts to fly a course they were not supposed to. I spoke with the pilots, and they said there is no doubt in their minds that Marine One could have been blown out of the sky this afternoon."

The president closed his eyes and shook his head. Several seconds later he looked at Warch and asked, "Can you protect me or not?"

"If you continue to ignore my advice, no."

"What do you mean ignore your advice?" asked the president in a pleading tone. He looked to Warch's boss this time for an answer, but didn't get one.

Warch had convinced his boss to stay out of it and let him put the fear of God into the president. Warch leaned forward and got the president's attention. "Sir, when you and Mr. Garret informed me that you wanted to hold your budget summit at Camp David, I told you it was a bad idea and that it should be held at the White House. Because you ignored that advice, you were almost killed today." Warch paused briefly, his voice taking on a more authoritative tone. "Special Agent Dorle told Speaker Basset that he should cancel all public appearances. The Speaker ignored his advice and now he's dead. . . . I have been telling you for two and a half years that security around the White House is lax, that the press is given too much freedom to come and go as they please. Well, it all came home to roost today. I found out how the assassins knew which helicopter you were on."

Warch again paused and looked at the president, letting the tension mount. He was going to play this hand for everything it was worth. "My agents tore apart everything that was within sight of the South Lawn. One of them found a transponder attached to the live-signal feed underneath the control panel of the ABC News van. While arranging security for this trip, I suggested that the media be banned from the South Lawn while the helicopters were coming and going. I thought this precaution was appropriate considering the fact that four politicians have been assassinated in the last week. This request was ignored because it was deemed too important of a news event to have a media blackout, so the media was allowed to tape the entire event. Several members of your staff even wanted to let the media carry the event live. I told them that was out of the question, and we reached a compromise that allowed the media to tape your departure and then show it later.

"Just before the first helicopter landed, my agents shut down the live feeds on all the news vans and made them go to tape. At some point after that, the assassins activated a transponder that they'd planted underneath the ABC News van's control board. Once this was turned on, they were able to watch everything that happened on the South Lawn in real time. These assassins know where our weaknesses are, and they know that our ability to protect you is directly related to your desire to be protected. They obviously understand the relationship between a politician and the media, and if you continue to make yourself accessible to the media and the public, we will not be able to protect you."

The president looked at his chief protector and said, "Jack, do whatever you need to make things more secure, and I'll listen to you."

Roach, noticing that the president was in an unusually decisive and agreeable mood, decided to make his move. "Mr. President, our investigation has hit a wall. We believe these assassins are former United States commandos. Special Agent McMahon and his people have received very little cooperation from the Special Forces people at the Pentagon. They are stonewalling us at every turn."

The president's head jerked from Roach to Nance. "Mike, what's the problem?"

"Well, sir, there are certain national security issues involved here. Most of these personnel files are either top secret or contain top secret information about covert missions."

The president cut Nance off for the first time in their professional relationship. "I don't want to hear about problems. I want to see some results." Stevens turned his head away from Nance and back to Roach. "I will have an executive order ready by tomorrow morning giving Special Agent McMahon permission to review any personnel file he wishes. We are done dragging our feet on this. I want these people caught!"

Nance looked at the president from the other end of the table and bit his lip. Stevens was too emotional right now, he would have to wait until later to discuss this issue. There was no way in the world someone without top secret clearance was going to get carte blanche on those files. Especially someone from the FBI.

While Nance tried to think of a way around this new problem, Warch briefed the participants on the evidence they'd found under the bridge—such as the radar dishes, and what efforts were being made to track the serial numbers. As the briefing continued, it dawned on Nance that Garret was unusually quiet. Nance attributed it to the threat the assassins had made on his life. Nance's mind moved from Garret to Stansfield. Why was Director Stansfield so quiet during the discussion of Special Forces personnel files? Surely it was in the CIA's best interest to keep those files away from the eyes of the FBI.

The meeting ended just after 8 P.M., and everyone left the conference room except Garret and Nance. When the door closed, Garret dropped his head into his hands and rubbed his eyes. "What a fucking mess."

Nance shifted in his chair and crossed his legs. He watched Garret and tried to guess what he was thinking. Nance tilted his head back and asked, "Stu, you were awfully quiet during the briefing. Did that tape get to you?"

Garret let his hands fall to the table and looked up with bloodshot eyes. "No . . . maybe a little . . . I don't know." Garret reached into his shirt pocket. "God, I need a cigarette." He shoved one in his mouth and lit it. After taking a deep drag he said, "They can't kill me if I don't give them the chance. I won't leave the White House for a month. I'll take one of the guest bedrooms and move in." Garret took several more deep drags and frowned. "I'm not scared of these terrorists. I'm worried about something else. We've got another problem, and it's not good. Warch knows about the job we did on Frank Moore. He told me he knows who was involved, and if I don't back off and listen to him, he'll tell the FBI." Garret stood up and started pacing. "When it rains, it pours. It's not like we don't already have enough problems, and now we've got this to deal with."

Nance watched Garret intently and kept his outward composure. "Did he mention my name?"

Without looking at Nance, Garret paused and said, "Yes."

"Did he mention any other names?"

"Yes."

"Whose?"

Garret looked at Nance briefly and then looked at a painting on the wall. "He mentioned Arthur's."

Nance felt a sharp pain shoot through his temples. "He mentioned Arthur?"

Garret reluctantly nodded his head. "I have no idea how he found out. I didn't talk to anyone about it."

Nance's demeanor remained placid, but inside he was boiling. Without having to think very hard he knew exactly how Warch had found out. He or one of his people must have overheard Stu talking to God-knows-who about their little blackmail operation.

"Arthur will not be happy about this. I'm sure he will want to talk to you at length. Clear your schedule for tomorrow evening. He wants to talk to us about something else, and it can't wait. I'll arrange for some discreet transportation."

CHAPTER 21

THE moon was showing only a sliver of white as it sat suspended above the tall pines. The four-door Crown Victoria approached the main gate of Camp David, and the two occupants in the backseat ducked down. The electric gate slid open, and the sedan accelerated past a mob of reporters kept at bay by a squad of Marines with M16s cradled across their chests.

The pack of reporters and cameramen pushed each other to try and get a glimpse of who was in the car. The sedan continued down the road and around the first turn, where it slowed. Two identical Crown Victorias pulled off the shoulder and took up positions in front of and behind the car carrying the national security adviser and the president's chief of staff.

Saturday's budget summit at Camp David had been a mixed success. Garret had come up with some accounting gimmicks that would make the budget deficit look smaller than it really was. This would enable the political leadership to say they had cut some spending, without actually making the tough choices. Their hope was that it would pacify the assassins and give the FBI some time to catch the killers.

Mike Nance's doubts regarding the stability of the new coalition were already proving true. Senator Olson had balked on the deal, telling the president he would have no part in misleading the American people. Olson argued that real cuts had to be made, or he was out. The silver-haired senator from Minnesota told the president he would stay quiet for one week, and if Garret was still playing his accounting games, he would expose the new budget cuts for what they were—a sham.

Nance and Garret spent most of the fifty-minute drive talking in hushed whispers. The Maryland country roads they traveled on were dark, and traffic was light. When they reached Arthur's estate, the lead and trailing sedans pulled off to the side, and the one carrying Nance and Garret approached the large wrought-iron gate. Two powerful floodlights illuminated the entrance to the estate. A large man dressed in a tactical jumpsuit and carrying an Uzi stepped out of the guardhouse and approached the sedan. A flashlight was taped to the underside of the machine gun's barrel, and the guard turned it on. He pointed it toward the back window and shone the light on Nance and Garret. After identifying both men, he told the driver to pop the trunk. Walking to the rear of the car, he checked the trunk and then walked back to the guardhouse.

Arthur was sitting behind the desk in his study watching the scene at the front gate. Embedded in the wall to the left of his desk were four security monitors and two large color TVs. Arthur watched the guard go back into the small booth, and a moment later the gate opened. The gate closed as soon as the car passed through. Looking at another monitor, Arthur watched the car snake its way up the drive and stop in front of the house, where it was met by two more guards, one of whom had a German shepherd at his side. Garret and Nance stepped out of the car and stood still while the dog sniffed them and a handheld metal detector was waved over their bodies. Finally, the door was opened from the inside, and a third guard led them down the hall to Arthur's study.

Arthur pressed a button on the underside of his desk, and an old framed map of the world slid down and covered the monitors. Rising from behind the desk, he walked over to the fireplace and placed one hand on the mantel. Even though Arthur was over seventy, he still had a rigid and upright frame. His silver hair was neatly combed straight back and stopped an inch above the white collar of his dress shirt. His fingernails were well manicured, and his expensive, worsted-wool suit hung perfectly from his slender frame.

The door opened and Nance and Garret entered. Arthur kept his arm on the mantel and waited for his guests to approach. Mike Nance stopped about ten feet away and in a formal tone said, "Stu Garret, I would like to introduce you to Arthur."

Garret stepped forward and extended his damp, clammy hand. "It's great to finally meet you. I've been looking forward to this for a while."

Arthur nodded his head slightly. "The pleasure is all mine." Then, motioning toward several chairs, he said, "Please, let's sit. Would either of you like anything?"

Nance eased his way over to Arthur's side. "Before we get started, I would like to go over a couple of things with you in private."

Arthur grasped the point and turned to his other guest. "Mr. Garret, do you like to smoke cigars?"

Garret was caught off guard for a moment. "Ah . . . ah . . . yes, I do."

Walking over to the coffee table, Arthur picked up a cherry-wood humidor and lifted the lid. Garret grabbed one of the cigars and smelled it. Arthur handed him a cigar guillotine, and Garret snipped off the end. "I'll show you to the door." Arthur led Garret across the room toward a pair of French doors. "The view of the Chesapeake is beautiful from the veranda. I think you will enjoy it." Arthur opened one of the doors. "We'll be out to join you in a minute." Closing the door behind his guest, Arthur turned and walked back to Nance. "What is the problem?"

"It seems that our involvement in the blackmailing of Congressman Moore is known by someone outside the original group."

"And who would that be?"

"Jack Warch, he's the special agent in—"

"I know who he is. How did he find out?"

Nance glanced toward the veranda and then told Arthur about the confrontation between Garret and Warch. When he was done, Arthur asked, "And how do you think Mr. Warch found out?"

"I think that Mr. Garret wasn't as careful as he should have been."

"I would concur."

Arthur was not an animated person, but Nance had expected him to display some type of reaction. Instead he got nothing. "What do you want to do about Warch?" asked Nance.

Arthur paused for a minute and pondered the question. "For now, nothing. I read his personality profile about four years ago; he's not the type to go to the press. Besides, the Secret Service is not in the business of embarrassing the president. In the meantime, tell Mr. Garret to back off, and I'll prepare a contingency plan to deal with Mr. Warch if he presses the point."

"I've already told Garret to back off, and he's obliged."

"Have you told him anything about my proposition?"

"No, I only said that you wanted to talk to us. As far as he knows, I'm in the dark."

"Good."

"Are you still going to tell him?"

"Yes."

"I'm not sure that's a good idea. You've always told me not to trust amateurs."

"I've always told you to trust no one." Turning and walking across the room, Arthur looked up at the stacks of books that covered an entire wall of the study and sighed. Nance obediently followed him, saying nothing, just walking quietly two steps behind his mentor.

"Mr. Garret has his faults, but he is a highly driven man who will do anything to succeed. He was loose-lipped about the Congressman Moore thing because he didn't see the risks inherent in not keeping his mouth shut. Thanks to Mr. Warch, he has learned his lesson. Besides, with someone like Mr. Garret, his ability to keep a secret is directly related to the seriousness of the issue. The more he stands to lose, the more apt he will be to stay quiet. If we up the ante, Mr. Garret will stay quiet."

"I see your line of logic, but are you sure we need him?"

"Yes, there are some concessions I'm going to want for helping him."

Nance nodded his head. "As you wish."

"Let's join our friend." Before going outside, Arthur picked up the humidor and offered a cigar to Nance and then took one for himself. The two then walked toward the French doors and out into the dark fall night.

Garret was standing at the edge of the veranda nervously waiting to be called back inside. He knew Nance was telling Arthur about the problem with Warch, and he was worried about how Arthur would react. He had heard some scary stories regarding the former black-operations director for the CIA.

Arthur Higgins had directed some of the Agency's most secret operations for almost thirty years before being forced out. The official reason given for his departure was his age and the fall of the Iron Curtain. But the whispers in the intelligence community were that he couldn't be controlled—that he had decided one too many times to run his own operation, independent of executive and congressional approval.

Garret turned when he heard the dress shoes of Nance and Arthur on the brick patio.

"How do you like the view?" asked Arthur.

During the five minutes that Garret had been outside, he hadn't even noticed the great dark expanse of the Chesapeake that was before him. He glanced over his shoulder to look at it and said, "It sure is a lot bigger than I thought."

Arthur smiled inwardly, knowing that Garret was not the type to appreciate the majesty of nature. He was such a simple, uncomplicated man. Not dumb, just one-dimensional and focused. He was easy to predict, which suited Arthur's needs perfectly. Arthur looked at Garret with his calm and confident face and in his smooth voice said, "Mr. Garret, I think I may be able to help you."

CHAPTER 22

McMAHON thought that, after the meeting with the president on Friday night, he would be spending all weekend with a team of agents poring over Special Forces personnel files. The president's promise of complete cooperation was shortlived. Saturday and Sunday had passed without a single file being reviewed. Someone had managed to change the president's mind, and McMahon had a good idea who it was. Late Sunday, McMahon received word through the Joint Chiefs that he was to show up at the Pentagon on Monday morning at 7 A.M. sharp. He was told he could bring two people to assist him in the reviewing of a select group of files. Just how select these files were, McMahon could only wonder. One thing was certain though, his patience was running thin.

As McMahon walked down a long, stark hall, located somewhere in the basement of the Pentagon, he wondered if this would be a waste of his time or if they were finally done jerking him around. He had decided to bring Kennedy and Jennings with him, and the three of them obediently followed the Army lieutenant who was escorting them to the Pentagon's offices for the Joint Special Operations Command, or JSOC, pronounced "jaysock." The actual field headquarters was located at Pope Air Force Base in North Carolina.

They had already passed through three security checkpoints by the time they reached their destination. At the door to JSOC they were asked for their identification by a Marine sitting behind bulletproof Plexiglas. After verifying their IDs, the Marine pressed a button and the outer door opened. The Army lieutenant led the three visitors into a comfortable and functional reception area, where he told them to take a seat.

Several minutes later a one-star general emerged with a cup of coffee in his left hand. The man had short, bristly, black hair and was about five ten. The dark green shoulder boards holding his general's star jutted straight out from his neck. He was a posterboard U.S. Marine, from his square jaw to his perfectly pressed pants and spit-shined shoes. McMahon couldn't help but notice that the general's shoulders were almost twice as broad as his waist. Most of the generals that McMahon knew showed a little more in the area of girth than this one.

The general stuck out his right hand. "Special Agent McMahon, General Heaney. Nice to meet you."

"Nice to meet you, General." McMahon winced slightly as the bones in his hand were squeezed tightly together by the pit bull standing before him.

"This must be Dr. Kennedy and Special Agent Jennings." Jennings and Kennedy shook Heaney's hand. McMahon flexed his hand in an effort to shake the sting from the general's handshake.

"Would any of you like some coffee before we get started?"

McMahon and Kennedy said yes, and the general led them down the hall to a small kitchen. He grabbed a pot of coffee and said, "You may want to add some water to this. I make my coffee a little on the thick side." McMahon took a sip and agreed.

"Special Agent Jennings, can I get you a soda or something?"

"Do you have any diet Coke?"

"I keep a private stash in my office. Hold on, I'll be right back."

"Sir, please don't bother. Water will be fine."

"It's no bother at all." The general disappeared down the hallway.

A moment later, the general came around the corner with two cans of diet Coke. "I brought an extra one just in case you're really thirsty."

Jennings extended her hands. "Thank you, sir. You didn't have to go to all that trouble."

"No trouble at all. Come on, let's go down the hall. I want to introduce you to someone." They all left the room and walked down several doors. The general stopped and ushered them into a state-of the art conference room. Each spot at the table was equipped with a phone, a retractable keyboard, and a computer monitor mounted underneath the surface of the conference table.

"This is where we'll be spending most of our time. Please, make yourselves comfortable. I'll be back in a minute."

When the general returned several minutes later, he was carrying a stack of files and was accompanied by a senior female naval officer. "Everyone, this is Captain McFarland. She is our unit psychologist." Dr. McFarland introduced herself to everyone while General Heaney arranged the files into three stacks on the table. "We've got one more person joining us." The general pressed the intercom button in front of him and said, "Mike, would you please send Mr. Delapena in."

"Yes, sir."

The general looked up from the phone and asked everyone to be seated. A moment later a man in a blue suit and striped tie entered the conference room and placed a briefcase on the floor next to his chair. The man was of average height and weight, with fair skin and a deeply receding hairline. The general introduced him only as Mr. Delapena.

McMahon stared at him intently, trying to decipher what a non-military person had to do with the Special Forces. "Mr. Delapena, you didn't say which agency you were affiliated with."

"I work for the National Security Agency."

"What does the NSA have to do with this case?"

"The NSA is involved in the safeguarding and dissemination of any information pertaining to the national security of the United States."

"So Mr. Nance sent you to keep an eye on things?"

Delapena looked at the general but did not respond to Mc-Mahon's question. After several moments of awkward silence the general clapped his hands together and said, "All right, let's get started." The general patted his hands on two of the three stacks he had sitting in front of him. "These are the personnel files of all black, retired Special Forces commandos between the age of twenty-four and thirty-four. They are arranged in stacks according to which organization they served under. The stack on my far left consists of former Green Berets, the stack in the middle is made up of Delta Force commandos, and the one on the end is Navy SEALs. There are one hundred and twenty-one African-Americans between the age of twenty-four and thirty-four that are retired Green Berets, thirty-four Delta Force commandos, and two Navy SEALs.

"Before we go any further, I would ask that if you decide to contact any of these individuals you would allow us to accompany you?" The general looked to McMahon for the answer.

"I don't see a problem with that."

The general nodded and then handed three files across the table. McMahon opened the file and looked up and down the single sheet of paper. It contained a photograph stapled to the upper-right corner and a list of basic information including birth date, Social Security number, educational background, date of enlistment, and date of discharge. McMahon flipped the page over and it was blank. Moving only his eyes, McMahon looked up at the general. "Where are the psychological profiles and performance reviews?"

The general looked to Delapena and then McMahon. "At the direction of the Joint Chiefs and the NSA, they were pulled."

McMahon tossed the file back across the table and said, "This does me absolutely no good. I need to establish a motive, and I can't do it with a photograph, a date of birth, and an educational summary. The president promised me that I would be given full cooperation." McMahon looked away from the general to Delapena. "Does the president know about this?"

"Mike Nance has briefed him thoroughly."

"I'll bet he has. . . . Okay, if you guys want to do this the hard way, that's fine with me, because I'm done screwing around. We've got two dead congressmen, two dead senators, and an attempt has been made on the president's life." McMahon gritted his teeth and pointed across the table at Delapena. "The biggest threat to national security right now is the people responsible for those murders. I could care less about some operation you guys ran in some jerkwater, third-world country ten years ago." McMahon stood up and said to Kennedy and Jennings, "Come on, let's go." Looking at Delapena he said, "If this is the way you want to do this, I'll be back tomorrow with a stack of subpoenas and fifty agents."

Kennedy and Jennings stood and started for the door. The general looked at Delapena, silently urging him to say something.

As they reached the door, Delapena said, "No, you won't."

"What did you say?" McMahon asked as he turned around.

"I don't think that would be a very good idea."

"Listen here, Mr. Delapena, let's get something straight. I work for the FBI, and you work for the NSA. This is a domestic investigation, and we have the jurisdiction, not you. The law is very clear on this, and considering the high profile of this case, I will have no problem finding a judge that will grant me a broad and sweeping subpoena."

"And I will have no problem finding a judge to block it. You see, Mr. McMahon, the laws regarding issues of national security are also very broad and sweeping."

McMahon walked back, leaned over, and placed both hands on the table. He brought his face to within a foot of Delapena's and said, "You tell Mike Nance that if he tries to block my subpoena, I'll file an obstruction of justice charge against the NSA and hold the biggest press conference this town has ever seen. I'm sure the media would love to find out that the FBI believes these murders were committed by United States–trained military commandos. And I'm sure they'll find it even more interesting that NSA is trying to block our investigation." McMahon backed up. "Those cynical bastards will eat you alive."

"Mr. McMahon, if you breathe a word of this to the media, you'll be out of a job."

McMahon felt his temper stirring and strained to keep it in check. "Come on, Delapena, you've got to do better than that. You have absolutely no leverage on this." McMahon turned to the general. "All I have to do is hint at your lack of cooperation to the media and every congressman and senator will be over here demanding that you open your files. And not just the files I'm interested in, they'll want to see everything. They'll threaten to cut every penny of funding from your budget, and then they'll set up a series of committees to investigate any wrongdoing. They'll be all over your case for the next two years."

The tension built as McMahon refused to back down. General Heaney sat with his hand over his brow wishing the whole problem would go away, and Delapena fidgeted with a pen he'd pulled out of his pocket. They both knew McMahon was right, but neither had the authority to do anything about it. People above them were calling the shots.

Out of frustration, Delapena said, "Mr. McMahon, you go ahead and do what you have to do, but you don't have a shred of evidence that these murders were committed by military personnel. And don't forget, there will be a lot of congressmen and senators that will be offended that you would imply such a thing."

McMahon ignored Delapena and looked to the general. "Sir,

have you seen the autopsy reports for Fitzgerald, Koslowski, Downs, and Basset?"

The general nodded his head yes.

"Did you notice how Senator Fitzgerald was killed?"

"Yes."

"How many people do you know who are capable of breaking a man's neck with their bare hands?"

The general looked at McMahon and said, "Not very many."

"General, you know as well as I do that the people behind this are former U.S. commandos. Former commandos with an awfully big ax to grind, and the answer is somewhere in your psychological profiles and fitness reports."

The general looked to Delapena and then back at McMahon. "I agree with you, but unfortunately my hands are tied. You don't think I realize how bad it's going to look if the word leaks that a group of my former boys are doing this and we blocked your investigation?" The general made a tight fist and rapped his knuckles on the table. "The issue for us is not that we don't want to help you, it's that we have some real security concerns. The Special Forces community is a very tight-lipped fraternity. We are not prone to sharing information with outsiders. Our success and survival is dependent on secrecy." The general pushed his chair back and stood, walking to the opposite end of the table.

"The full package of each commando contains information regarding every mission he took part in, the other members of the mission, a mission summary, and a whole bevy of top secret information. There are very few people that have the clearance to look at the full personnel file of one of my boys. I can't just open those files to you. There's too much at stake."

"I see your point, General, but how do you expect me to conduct an investigation without that information?"

Delapena addressed the question. "Mr. McMahon, I don't envy

your job, but you have to understand the innate conflict of interest confronting our two agencies."

"I understand your concern over security, but . . ." McMahon opened his eyes wide and shook his head. "I think the apprehension of these killers is more important."

"It may be more important right now, but these security issues could have far-reaching implications."

"Farther reaching than the murders of United States congressmen and senators? These guys aren't going to just quit and go home."

Kennedy decided it was time for her to insert her gentle style into the conversation. "Skip, the general and Mr. Delapena are not just being paranoid about security. If I was in their position, I wouldn't want to open those files to the FBI." She turned her attention to the other two men. "On the other hand, Mr. Delapena and General Heaney, you must also understand the crisis that the FBI is faced with resolving." Kennedy pulled her glasses off and twirled them in her right hand. "What we should be trying to do is find a way to bridge both of our concerns." Kennedy pointed her glasses at the general and Delapena. "The FBI needs your help to run a speedy investigation. No one knows your files better than you do, and I'm sure you can offer us great insight into which of your former members are most inclined to mount a revolution against their own government. On the other hand, if word got to the press that the NSA was blocking the FBI's investigation of former U.S. commandos, the damage to both the NSA and the Special Forces would be devastating.

"We need to work together, and I think I may have a solution. My thought is that all of the people in this room could form a review panel. In trade for the full cooperation of the NSA and the Joint Special Operations Command, Special Agent McMahon and Special Agent Jennings should sign a national security nondisclosure document that would block them from investigating and litigating anything that is not directly related to these recent assassinations. This way, we can abate your anxiety over having several dozen FBI agents rifling through your files, and at the same time the FBI can be guaranteed full cooperation from the people with the most insight into these young men's minds."

Everyone thought about the new proposal, and then General Heaney pronounced, "I like the idea."

"I'm not completely sure," said Delapena. "I have no problem including you, Dr. Kennedy. Your security clearance is higher than anyone's in this room. If Special Agent McMahon was willing to sign a national security nondisclosure document, I could probably convince my superiors to sign off, but Special Agent Jennings is out of the question."

"Why?" asked McMahon.

"Special Agent Jennings has a long career ahead of her with the FBI, and over the next thirty years she will be transferred in and out of no less than three departments. During that time it will be very hard for her to ignore some of the things she may learn. I know my superiors would not accept her." Delapena said this as if Jennings weren't in the room.

McMahon looked at Kennedy and then at Delapena. "I'll agree to it, if I get full cooperation."

Delapena nodded and looked at his watch. "There are some people I need to get ahold of before they head into a meeting. General, may I use your office?" The general said yes, and Delapena left the room.

McMahon walked back around the table and took a seat. "General, were you serious when you said you believed the men committing these assassinations are former commandos?"

The general cocked his head sideways and said, "I was serious, very serious. . . . The men we recruit to become Special Forces commandos are a unique breed. Dr. McFarland, would you please give our guests the psychological profile of the average commando."

The doctor started to speak with clinical neutrality. "The typical commando is a man with an above average to high IQ who is extremely fit. He is a man who on the surface seems hard, callous, and emotionally indifferent. In truth, he is an extremely emotional and compassionate person. He is often obsessed with winning. He hates to lose, but is rarely willing to cheat or lie to win. He holds himself to a very high standard of honor and integrity and despises people who lie and lack character. He would, without thought or hesitation, give his life to save the life of a fellow commando. His biggest fear is that he will have wasted his life by not pushing himself hard enough. He despises people who live their lives unjustly. He dislikes politicians and bureaucrats and displays an open animosity toward them. He is trained to kill in a lethal and efficient manner and, over time, comes to accept it as a just and reasonable way to solve a problem. If you can convince him that a person is bad enough, he will pull the trigger with a clear conscience. Of course, there are exceptions to this, but for the most part this is the norm."

General Heaney let his arm drop down on the table. "I have been involved in the Special Forces for over thirty years, and I couldn't begin to count how many times I've heard one of my fellow commandos say that they would love to kill this congressman or that senator. You see, we are not only taught how to kill, but for our own sanity, we are taught to look at killing as a justifiable action in a world where there are good and bad people, where the bad people are not supposed to win.

"Think for a minute about what we ask a commando to do. We send them to do some very ugly things, and we tell them they are doing it to protect the United States of America. As commandos, we rationalize that we are ridding the world of a bad person, that we are protecting America. What do you think would happen if one of these highly trained individuals realized that the politicians running his own country pose a bigger threat to the security of America's future than the religious extremist that he just flew halfway around the world to kill?" The general looked hard at Mc-Mahon. "If these men think the real threat facing America comes from within, that the real threat comes from, quote, 'a group of old men that are mortgaging the future of the country for their own selfish needs . . .' " The general let the words of the assassins hang in the air. "Mr. McMahon, I have very little doubt that the people behind this are United States–trained commandos."

CHAPTER 23

MICHAEL and Seamus O'Rourke walked into the plush restaurant and were greeted by a slight man wearing a tuxedo. Both O'Rourkes were impeccably dressed in dark wool suits. The maître d' looked up along his thin nose and said, "May I help you?"

"Three for lunch, please," said Michael.

"Do you have a reservation?"

"Yes, I think it's under Olson."

The maître d' looked at his reservation book and clapped his hands together. "Oh, you must be Congressman O'Rourke. And you must be the congressman's father."

"No, I'm his grandfather."

"Oh." The maître d' looked down at the reservation book. "Senator Olson's secretary requested a private corner table." He grabbed three menus from under the podium. "If you will follow me, I'll show you to your table."

It was eleven forty-five and the restaurant was almost empty. Busboys were shuffling back and forth preparing each table for the busy lunch crowd. The maître d' glided between the tables, his chin held high, leading them to a circular table in the far corner. Stepping aside, he held a chair out for the older of the two O'Rourkes. Seamus sat down and the maître d' pushed in the chair.

The maître d' stepped back, bowed, and said, "Enjoy."

Seamus grabbed his napkin and asked, "What's the word on this budget summit that they had at Camp David?"

"They reported on the morning news that they cut one hundred billion dollars from Stevens's budget." Michael raised one of his eyebrows, showing what he thought of the reports.

"I take it you don't believe they actually did it."

"They reported it as a rumor. That means one of two things: no one knows what actually happened, or it was leaked to test the waters."

"Which do you think it was?"

"I'm not sure." Michael looked toward the entrance of the restaurant. Senator Olson had just entered with his bodyguards. "We'll find out soon enough. Erik is here."

Senator Olson and four serious-looking men walked across the restaurant, led by the maître d'. Michael and Seamus stood to meet their friend. Olson pushed his way by two of the guards and the maître d', extending his hand toward the older of the two O'Rourkes. "Seamus, I didn't know you were in town. When did you get in?"

"Friday morning."

Olson shook his hand and then Michael's. The maître d' seated the four Secret Service agents at the next table. Three of them sat with their backs to Olson and the O'Rourkes and one sat facing them. After sitting, Olson looked at Seamus and frowned. "Knowing your disdain for Washington, I assume there must be something pretty important going on for you to come here."

The statement was met with a slight grin. "Not really. I had some business to take care of, and I wanted an excuse to visit Michael and Tim."

"Is everything all right at the mill?" The O'Rourke Timber Company was the largest employer in Grand Rapids and thus a political concern for Olson.

"The mill is doing fine, in spite of all the interference I'm getting from your friends over at the EPA, the Commerce Department, and the Department of the Interior."

A waiter approached the table and greeted them. Olson was thankful for the distraction. He admired Seamus but was not always comfortable with his penchant for direct confrontation. He'd noticed recently that Michael, like his father before him, had inherited this honest, but not always pleasant, Irish attribute.

The waiter asked if they would like anything to drink. Erik and Seamus ordered iced tea and Michael ordered a Coke. Olson informed them that the Joint Intelligence Committee was to reconvene at 1 P.M., and if it was all right with them, he'd like to order lunch while the waiter was there. The O'Rourkes agreed and they placed their orders.

As soon as the waiter left, Seamus looked across the circular table and said, "Erik, I understand you were involved in the budget summit at Camp David this weekend."

Olson looked down and brushed his hand across the white tablecloth as if he were cleaning crumbs away. Looking up with shame in his eyes, he said, "Yes, I was there."

"How did it go?"

"I'd rather not say."

Seamus gave him a tightly screwed frown as if he was offended.

Olson shrugged his shoulders and said, "The president asked us to keep quiet about the details."

"They were saying on the morning news that you cut one hundred billion dollars from the budget. Is that true?" asked Michael in a doubtful tone.

"You don't sound like you believe it," said Olson.

"I don't think you can get the two parties together and cut one hundred billion dollars in two days."

Olson looked blankly at Michael and then Seamus. "You'd be

amazed what people are capable of doing when they're backed into a corner." The disgust was openly visible on his face.

"Erik, what happened up there?" asked Seamus.

"I promised the president I wouldn't talk about it."

Michael leaned closer to Olson and looked him in the eye. "Erik, if you don't think you can trust us, this town has really gotten the best of you."

Olson looked at Michael and then Seamus, thinking about the close friendship between their two families. Michael's father had been Erik's best friend. The O'Rourkes were the most honest people he knew. When they gave their word, they meant it. Olson fidgeted in his chair and leaned forward. Seamus and Michael did the same. "I'll tell you what happened, but you have to promise me you will tell no one." Seamus and Michael nodded yes. "That means no one. Especially Liz, Michael."

"You have my word."

Olson slowly recounted the weekend's events. Michael and Seamus listened intently and stayed quiet. Five minutes into Olson's account, lunch was served. The plates were pushed aside as Olson continued to recount the president and Garret's plan to mislead the public. Olson became more animated and angry as he explained in detail how they were going to actually spend more money and, through accounting gimmicks, say they were cutting the budget. The same was true for the O'Rourkes. The more they heard, the more they strained to keep their mouths shut. When Olson was done, he sat back in his chair and took a large gulp of water.

Seamus was the first to speak. With his deep, weathered voice he said, "Those bastards all deserve to die."

The severity of the comment almost caused Olson to spit his water back up. "You don't really mean that, do you?"

"You're damn right I do."

Olson looked to Michael, and Michael said nothing. "Seamus, don't you think that statement is a little harsh considering recent events?"

The older of the O'Rourkes repeated his conviction. "Those corrupt bastards deserved to die, too."

"You can't be serious?"

"I'm very serious. They were running this country right into the ground, and I couldn't be happier now that they're dead."

"It doesn't scare you in the slightest that some group of terrorists has decided to circumvent the democratic process?"

"One man's terrorist is another man's freedom fighter."

"Did you learn that one from the IRA?" Olson regretted the shot before he'd finished making it. It was not a good idea to provoke Seamus.

Seamus sat like a rock, his eyes burrowing deeper and deeper into Olson's, his large fist clenched on top of the table. "I'll pretend I didn't hear that." Seamus O'Rourke was financially involved with the Irish Republican Army in the years following World War II. Seamus was born in Ireland and moved to the United States with his parents at a very young age. He believed strongly in Ireland's right to self-rule and thought Britain's conquest of Ireland was no different from their conquest of India or any of the other colonies. He supported the IRA's paramilitary efforts until they started setting off bombs and killing innocent people. That was too much. Fighting for independence like a disciplined soldier was one thing, fighting for it like a cheap thug was another.

Olson broke the silence. "You don't really think what these . . . assassins have done is justifiable?"

"Not only do I think it's justifiable, I think it's necessary."

"I can't believe I'm hearing this. I mean, I know you don't like politicians, Seamus, but you can't really believe those men deserved to die."

"I do."

"Have you lost all faith in the democratic process, in the peo-ple's ability to effect change by voting?"

"The system has become too complicated and corrupt. Every single candidate lies to get elected and then sells his soul to the par-asite special-interest groups who gave him the money to run his campaign. The two-party system has made change impossible. No one's willing to face the real problems and do what's right."

"I acknowledge that things could be better, but we still have the best leadership and political system in the world."

Seamus laughed out loud. "That's debatable, and even if you're right, it won't be true for long."

"What is that supposed to mean?"

"Look at the numbers, Erik. We're going bankrupt, both mor-ally and financially. We need some drastic changes, or the most powerful country in the world is going to go the way of Rome."

"And violence is the way to bring that change about?"

Seamus rubbed his chin. "Maybe."

Olson shook his head sideways. "Violence is not the answer." The senator looked out the window as if Seamus didn't deserve the courtesy of eye contact. "Violence is never the answer."

Seamus's complexion reddened, and he slammed his fist down on the table. The silverware, plates, and glasses shook, and the Se-cret Service agents at the next table snapped their heads around. Seamus ignored them and leaned toward Olson. "Erik, I don't mind a healthy debate, but don't ever use a line of crap like that on me again. I'm not one of your naïve college students, and I'm not some little sycophant political activist. I've seen people killed, and I've killed people in the service of our country. Your idealistic, philo-sophical theories might fly in the hallowed halls of Congress, but they don't work in the real world. Violence is a fact of life. There are people who are willing to use it to get what they want, and in order to stop them they need to be met with violence. If it wasn't for war, or the threat of waging war, people like Adolf Hitler and

Joseph Stalin would be running the world, and you would get shot for going around saying stupid things like 'violence only begets violence.' "

Olson was embarrassed. He was not used to being spoken to in such a manner. The oldest O'Rourke took words more seriously than most people, and Olson had forgotten that the art of debate, as it was practiced in Washington, did not work on men and women who had no time for political posturing. Seamus O'Rourke was not a man to be patronized with political or philosophical slogans. Olson exhaled deeply and said, "Seamus, I apologize. The last couple of weeks have been very hard on me, and I'm not feeling very well."

Seamus nodded his head, accepting the apology.

Olson sat back and rubbed his eyes. "This entire thing is wearing me down."

Michael placed a hand on the senator's shoulder. "Erik, are you all right?"

"Physically, yes . . . mentally, I'm not so sure." His hands dropped limply to his lap. "You're right about the debt, Michael. You've been harping on me about it for years, and deep down inside I always knew you were right. I just thought that when things got tough the two parties would put aside their differences and do what was right. Well, I was wrong. Here we are in the midst of the biggest peacetime crisis we've seen since the Depression, and what do we do? We come up with some gimmick that's meant to deceive the American people and these damn assassins!" Olson stopped and shook his finger. "And it's all the president's and that damn Stu Garret's fault! At the one time when we really need leadership, we have none. Those two self-centered idiots are running around taking opinion polls, if you can believe it!"

Michael nodded. "Oh, I can believe it. They only have one thing on their mind, Erik—how they're going to win the election next year."

"You are absolutely right, and I'm sick of it."

"What are you going to do about it?" asked Seamus.

"I'm going to give the president a week to put together a new budget with some real cuts in it, and if he does, I will sign on."

"What will you do if he sends this current one to the House?" asked Michael.

"I will expose it for what it is—a sham."

Michael felt a wave of confidence rush over him. With Erik taking the lead on this, the president would be forced to make real cuts. The senior senator looked down at his watch and said, "Damn! My committee meeting starts in five minutes." Olson looked up for their waiter, who was nowhere in sight. Next he reached for his wallet and Seamus placed a hand on his arm, stopping him. "Don't worry, Erik. After what you've just told me, I'll be more than happy to take care of the bill."

Olson stood and grinned. Slapping Seamus on the back, he said, "You're a pain in the ass, Seamus, but I love you. You have a unique and refreshing way of putting things into context. We could use a couple more of you around here just to keep the rest of us on our toes."

Michael shook Olson's hand and said, "Anything you need, call me." Olson nodded and left. Michael and Seamus watched him leave and then Seamus paid the tab.

As they walked out onto the sidewalk, the sun was just starting to peek out from behind the clouds. Michael had told Seamus of his meeting with Scott Coleman. Seamus's only response was, "Stay out of the man's way. If he's behind it, we should all be grateful." Michael thought his grandfather was carrying it a little too far, but for the time being he agreed that it would be best to give Coleman room. If Coleman was behind the assassinations, which Michael had little doubt about at this point, then his fake missile attack on the president's helicopter was ingenious. He had sent a clear message that no one was out of his reach. Now if Erik could exert enough political pressure on the White House, everything would fall into place.

They stopped at the first intersection and were waiting for the light to change when Michael turned and saw Senator Olson's limousine pull out of the underground parking garage a half block down the street. The large, dark car turned toward them, its powerful engine roaring as it pulled out into traffic. Michael watched as it approached, then the high-pitched whine of a motorcycle caught his attention. The sleek black bike broke away from the rest of the traffic and raced toward them. The driver and his passenger were both wearing dark helmets and black leather pants and jackets.

The limo approached the intersection and stopped as the light turned red. The other pedestrians started to walk and then stopped as the high-pitched whine of the motorcycle's engine reverberated off the surrounding buildings. Michael stuck his arm out in front of Seamus and focused on the motorcycle as it raced up the street.

The dark bike and its riders darted in between the rows of cars that had stopped for the light and continued to accelerate. The bike approached the senator's limousine, and then, suddenly, the man riding on the back leaned out and tossed a dark bag onto the roof of the limo. The bike continued on, skidding into a hard right turn and slicing through the lanes of traffic.

Michael looked at the bag and instinctively turned to shield Seamus. The noise was deafening. The roof of the limo imploded, and the tinted windows blasted outward, propelled by bright orange and red flames. The explosion rocked the entire block, throwing the O'Rourkes and the other pedestrians violently to the ground.

CHAPTER 24

PRESIDENT Stevens was presiding over a cabinet meeting when Jack Warch entered the room and walked up behind him. Warch bent over and whispered into Stevens's ear. Without warning, Stevens slammed his fist down on the table and shouted an expletive. The president stood so quickly he almost knocked his chair over. Pointing at Mike Nance, who was sitting at the opposite end of the table, he yelled, "My office, right now!" On his way toward the door, he slapped Garret on the shoulder and said, "Come on, Stu, you too." Stevens, Garret, Nance, and Warch filed out of the room, leaving the wide-eyed cabinet members wondering what was going on.

The distance between the Cabinet Room and the Oval Office was less than thirty feet. Stevens was walking fast and shaking his head. When he reached the door to his office, he abruptly stopped and started back in the opposite direction. Warch, Nance, and Garret stopped as Stevens pointed down the hall and said, "Let's do this in the Situation Room." As he passed Mike Nance, he pointed at him and said, "Get Stansfield, Roach, and Tracy over here immediately."

No one talked as they followed Stevens down the stairs to the basement. A posted agent opened the door to the Situation Room, and the president, Garret, Nance, and Warch entered. Stevens picked up a remote that was sitting on top of the large conference table and pointed it at the far wall. As the wood panel slid to the side revealing eight television sets, the president looked at the TVs and muttered, "This is unbelievable."

Five of the eight TVs were broadcasting images of Olson's charred limo. Garret looked at Mike Nance, but Nance ignored him. Garret then looked at Stevens and tried to get a read on his temperament.

Garret attempted to ask a question, but before he could get more than two words out, Stevens said, "Quiet. I don't want to hear anyone say a word."

They all watched the TVs in silence. About five minutes later, Secret Service director Tracy arrived, and he and Warch retreated to the far corner to talk. The president stepped even closer to the TVs and turned up the volume, drowning out the noise of the conversation behind him. Roach arrived a short while later, and Stansfield almost twenty minutes after the call had gone out. After several minutes of Stevens not acknowledging the arrival of the three directors, Garret walked up beside him and said, "Jim, everyone is here."

Stevens walked to the head of the table and stood between the rest of the room and the TVs. Looking down the long table, he said, "Sit!" Everyone took a chair and Stevens began squeezing the back of his high leather chair. With a look of utter frustration Stevens asked, "Can anyone tell me how in the hell a United States senator gets killed in broad daylight less than a mile from the White House?"

No one answered the question. The silence added to the frustration Stevens felt, and a rage started to press its way forward from the back of his head. In a crisp, stern voice Stevens said, "I've got some things to say, and I don't want to hear anyone speak until I'm done." Pausing for a moment, he put his hands on his hips and closed his eyes. "I want this killing to stop, and I want it to stop right now. I don't care what it takes. I don't care what laws have to be bent or broken. I want these bastards caught." Stevens opened his eyes and looked at Director Roach. "Does the FBI have any suspects?"

Roach shifted in his chair uncomfortably. "Mr. President, this investigation is not even two weeks old."

"Are you any closer to catching these people than you were a week and a half ago?"

Roach looked back at Stevens but didn't answer. His silence was answer enough.

"I didn't think so." Stevens closed his eyes again, the frustration evident on his face. Without looking up he snapped, "I'm done screwing around. We have to catch these bastards, and we have to do it quickly. I want the CIA and the National Security Agency to get involved. I want surveillance and wiretaps set up on anyone who we think could be remotely involved in this. The FBI can continue to run its investigation through the proper legal channels, but I want the NSA and the CIA to start bugging every phone between here and Seattle."

Garret's eyes opened wide at the mention of wiretaps. He threw his hand up to catch the president's attention. "Jim, I think we need to talk to the Justice Department before we start running around—"

"Shut up, Stu. I'm not done."

The unprecedented rebuke immediately silenced Garret. He sank back into his chair and Stevens continued.

"We are in the middle of a crisis, and I'm not going to sit around and wait for the FBI to do this by the book. We don't have the time. The CIA and the NSA are better equipped to get quick results and do it without raising too much attention. I want phones bugged, and I want them bugged now. I want every militia group in the country shaken down for information. If we still think these assassins are former commandos, I want every former commando questioned by the end of the week, and the ones that look suspicious—bug their phones and set up surveillance. I want results, damn it!"

Garret tried again to dissuade his boss. "Jim, there are some serious legal issues that need to be addressed before we run off half-cocked."

"I don't want to hear about it, Stu. Don't tell me there aren't ways to do it. I'll sign an executive order, I'll sign a national security directive, I'll declare martial law if I have to, but I want these bastards caught, and I want it done quickly!" Stevens tossed the remote control onto the table. "Figure out the logistics and make it work. I want the CIA and the NSA involved, and I don't want any leaks to the press. Am I understood?" All heads in the room nodded yes, and Stevens moved for the door, saying, "Stu and Mike, when you're done down here, come up to my office." A Secret Service agent opened the door and the president shouted over his shoulder on the way out, "I want everyone back here at seven A.M. tomorrow, and I want some results."

Darkness was falling on the city. Michael stared out the window at the bright fall leaves hanging from the old oak tree in front of his house. He breathed deeply and ran his fingers through Liz's thick, black hair, while rubbing his stiff neck with his other hand. Michael sat on the couch with his feet up on the coffee table. Liz had both arms wrapped around his waist, and her head rested on his chest. Her feet were tucked up behind her on the couch, and she listened to Michael's heartbeat. The rhythm of it brought her in and out of a light sleep.

Liz had been in a meeting with her editor when the news of Olson's assassination broke. Knowing that Michael was eating lunch with the senator, she rushed to find out if he was all right. Michael's secretary informed her that he was unhurt and on his way home. Liz left the office immediately and took a cab to Michael's house. When she arrived, she found Michael and

Tim sitting at the dining room table talking. Seamus was being held in the hospital overnight for observation. The explosion had knocked him to the ground and given him a minor concussion. After Liz's arrival Tim left so Michael and Liz could be alone.

For the last two hours they had sat on the couch and said little. They just held each other. Michael's eyes were wide open, and the look on his face was one of deep thought. Liz stirred slightly and Michael brought his other hand down to rub her back. Scarlatti moaned and rolled over. She looked up at Michael with her deep brown eyes and asked, "What time is it?"

"It's ten after five."

She reached up and gently touched the bandage on his forehead. "How does your head feel?"

"Fine."

Scarlatti closed her eyes and lifted her head off Michael's chest. O'Rourke bent down and kissed her lips.

Liz pulled away and asked, "What are you going to do?"

"I'm not sure."

"I think you should go to the FBI."

"I need to talk to him first."

Liz sat up. "Who is this guy?"

"I'm not dragging you any further into this thing."

"You're not dragging me anywhere. I want to know."

Michael shook his head. "You know enough, trust me."

"I can understand your not wanting to tell me, but I think you should tell the FBI immediately. You owe it to Erik."

"I'm going to meet with him first."

Liz put both hands on his chest and pushed him back. "No you're not! I will not allow it!"

Michael grabbed her wrists and said, "Don't worry, Liz. I'll be fine."

Scarlatti became angry. "Don't give me that Marine Corps macho bullshit! Whoever this guy is, he's a cold-blooded murderer and I don't want you meeting him alone." Liz looked into his eyes and knew she wasn't getting through. "If you leave this house, I'm calling the FBI."

Michael placed her hands together and looked her softly in the eyes. "Elizabeth, this man thinks of me as a brother. He would never do anything to harm me."

Liz yanked her hands away. "You are not going to be able to change my mind on this, Michael. You either tell me who he is or I'm calling the FBI."

Michael thought about it for a full minute and realized they were at an impasse. "You have to promise me that under no circumstances . . . never ever . . . will you reveal his name." Liz started to protest, but Michael cut her off. "No negotiating, Liz. If you want to know, you make the promise . . . and if you ever break it, I will walk out of your life and never speak to you again."

Scarlatti swallowed deeply, the last part of the comment causing a hollow feeling to develop in her stomach. "All right, I promise."

Michael stood and started to pace in front of the window. "You've met him before . . . twice. His name is Scott Coleman." Michael stopped to gauge Liz's reaction.

With eyes open wide she said, "The former Navy SEAL? The guy you go hunting with all the time?" Michael nodded yes. "Why? Why would he do all of this. He seems so normal."

"He is normal. As normal as a SEAL can be, that is. As to the 'why' part of your question . . ." Michael shook his head. "That's another can of worms, and when I say I can't tell you about it, I am deathly serious. If I would have kept that secret to myself a year ago, none of this would have ever happened."

Garret was nervous. Things were happening too fast and Stevens's new unmanageable attitude was only making things worse. Garret wasn't against using the CIA and NSA, just as long as they did it in a way that wouldn't come back to haunt them down the road.

He stabbed out his half-finished cigarette and headed off down the hall. Without knocking, he entered Ted Hopkinson's office and stood over his desk. Hopkinson was talking on the phone, and Garret signaled for him to end the conversation. Hopkinson cut the other person off in midsentence and told her he'd have to call back.

As soon as Hopkinson hung up, Garret set a piece of paper in front of him. Four names were on it. Hopkinson looked at the names and then up at his boss. "Am I supposed to know who these people are?"

"No, but by tomorrow morning I expect you to know their life stories."

"Who are they?"

"They are the four Secret Service agents who were blown up with Olson today."

"And what do you want me to do with the information?"

"We've had polls telling us that as much as forty-two percent of the public believes the loss of Fitzgerald, Downs, Koslowski, and Basset may be worth it if it forces Washington to get spending under control. Most of them are saying that because they hate politicians. Well, let's see how many of them still feel that way when they're introduced to these four men and their families. I want you to find out what high schools they went to, where their parents live, where they were married, where their kids go to school. I want you to find out everything you can about them. When you're done, we'll give it to the right people, and by the end of the week you won't be able to pick up the paper or turn on the TV without seeing or hearing about these guys and their families. By next Monday I want to see that forty-two percent cut down to single digits."

Scott Coleman left his apartment and went to the basement before leaving. Out on the front stoop he grabbed a pack of cigarettes out of his jacket and lit one. As always, he puffed on it but did not take the smoke into his lungs. Tilting his head up, he exhaled the smoke

and looked at the rooftop and windows of the apartment building across the street. Next, he took a mental inventory of all the
cars parked on the block, paying special attention to any vans he
hadn't seen before. Last night when he went out, he had headed to
the east. Tonight he would head west. Throwing his cigarette to the
ground, he stomped it out with his boot and casually trotted down
the steps. He looked relaxed and lackadaisical as he strode down
the sidewalk, but inside he was methodically taking note of everything around him. Things were sure to heat up, and sooner or later
someone, or some agency, would come looking for him.

At the next block he stopped and waited to cross the street,
using the pause to again look up and down the cross street for any
vans or trucks. Crossing the intersection, Coleman turned left,
continued for three blocks, and hailed a cab. The cab took him to
a small bar near Georgetown. He ordered a beer, drank half of it,
and then walked to the rear of the bar, toward the bathroom. Instead of stopping, he continued straight out the back door and into
the alley. He walked at a brisk pace. Four blocks later, he caught
another cab and took it to a house in Chevy Chase. The house belonged to a seventy-eight-year-old widow who had rented him her
garage for twenty-five dollars a month. He walked along the side of
the house to the garage. The keys were already out, and he opened
the padlock on the main garage door. Swinging the door upward,
he pulled a small black box out of his pocket and held it by his hip.
Nonchalantly he walked around the car, looking down at the row of
green lights, waiting to see if they would turn red and tell him his
car was bugged. They stayed green. He got in the car, pulled it out
of the garage, and then got back out to close the door and lock it.

Sliding back behind the wheel of the black sedan, he drove
slowly for the first few blocks and then gunned it. He zipped
through the city, turning randomly down the narrow streets. The
BMW's diplomatic plates and a Dutch passport he kept taped under
the dashboard ensured him that he wouldn't be detained by the po-

lice. The racy driving helped release tension and served to frustrate anyone who might be trying to follow. He pulled the Beamer onto Interstate 95 and kicked in the turbo. He darted in and out of traffic until he reached Highway 50 east to Annapolis. Easing the car between two semi trucks, he slowed down to sixty-five miles an hour and stayed there for about ten minutes. When he reached Highway 424, he took it south. The clock on the dashboard read 8:10 P.M. He checked the rearview mirror often and began crisscrossing his way down county roads. Several times, he sped ahead and then pulled off the road, waiting in a patch of trees with his lights off, making sure he wasn't being tailed.

After having left D.C. almost an hour earlier, he turned onto a narrow, unmarked dirt road. The gravel made a popping noise as the wide touring tires of the BMW rolled over it. The road was lined with trees and thick underbrush. It traveled down a slight hill and cut between two ponds. A thin layer of fog stretched across the gravel, and for a brief moment the BMW was surrounded by a white mist. The car pulled back out of the cloud, ascended another small hill, and then as it crested, the lights of a small cabin could be seen less than a hundred yards away. The car rolled down the gradual slope and stopped in front of the old log cabin.

Coleman got out and looked around. Pausing, he listened for the noise of another car that might have followed him down the gravel road. Gently, he closed the car door and walked up to the porch. The floorboards creaked as he walked across the porch, and a dog barked from inside the cabin. Without knocking, he opened the door and stepped inside. His bright blue eyes stared across the room at the man standing in front of the fireplace.

CHAPTER 25

MICHAEL O'Rourke held his .45-caliber Combatmaster in one hand and his digital phone in the other. Coleman looked at the gun and remained calm as Duke scampered over to greet him. The former Navy SEAL squatted down to meet the yellow Lab. Coleman looked at the bandage on Michael's forehead and asked, "What happened to your head?"

Through clenched teeth Michael replied, "I was hit with something when Erik's limousine blew up."

Coleman's eyes opened wide. "You were there?"

"Yes." Michael stared at Coleman's bright blue eyes and said, "Give me one good reason why I shouldn't call the FBI right now." Coleman stood and started to walk across the room. Michael raised his gun and said, "Don't take another step."

In a calm voice Coleman replied, "I know you'll never use that thing on me, so put it away and we'll talk."

"I wouldn't have used it on you before today, but now I wouldn't be so sure. I'll repeat myself one more time. Give me one good reason why I shouldn't turn you in to the FBI."

Coleman folded his arms. "I had nothing to do with what happened today."

Michael gave him an incredulous look. "What do you mean you had nothing to do with what happened today?"

"I didn't kill Erik. I had nothing to do with it."

"Bullshit, Scott. I was there. I saw the whole thing." Michael took several steps to the side to put an armchair between him and Coleman. Michael was no match for Coleman at a close distance. Even with a gun the young congressman wasn't entirely confident. Recon Marines were some of the best soldiers in the world, but Navy SEALs were in an entirely different class. Add to that the fact that Michael had been out of the Corps for close to six years and Coleman was obviously still at the top of his game, and Michael was outmatched. "You told me to warn Erik, and I did. He was ready to expose the president's plan as a sham, and then you had to come wheeling in and screw everything up!"

"Put the gun down, Michael. I had nothing to do with what happened today."

"Bullshit!" Michael yelled. "You're just trying to save your ass! How in the hell could you kill those Secret Service agents?" Michael extended the gun as far as he could. The sights aimed right for the center of Coleman's forehead. "You killed five good men today and sent another two dozen civilians to the hospital. I should put a bullet in your head right now and end this whole thing."

Michael thought he heard a noise, and then without further warning the door to the cabin flew open. Michael dropped to a knee and wheeled toward the door as Duke started to bark. Coleman did the same, retrieving his 9mm Glock from underneath his jacket.

Seamus O'Rourke stood in the doorway steadying himself by placing one hand on the frame. He was wearing the same suit he had had on at lunch minus the tie. Seamus looked at the two guns and growled, "Put those damn things away before you two hurt someone." Coleman did so on command, but Michael was a little more hesitant. Seamus admonished him with another look and said in a softer tone, "Michael, put your gun away."

Michael lowered the gun but did not put it away. "You're supposed to be in the hospital."

"I am very aware of that, but knowing that this meeting would take place, I decided that my presence was more needed here than in bed." Seamus shuffled over and dropped his body into one of the old tattered leather chairs by the fireplace. Rubbing his forehead, he said, "Scott, would you please fix me a glass of Scotch, and, Michael, for the last time put that damn gun away!"

Michael looked down at his grandfather. "I'm not putting this thing away until he explains what in the hell he was doing today."

"He wasn't doing anything today. Someone else killed Erik."

"What?" asked a disbelieving Michael.

"Someone else killed Senator Olson. Scott and his boys had nothing to do with it." Coleman handed the eldest O'Rourke a glass of Scotch on the rocks and took a seat on the couch.

"How would you know?" asked a confused Michael.

Seamus took a big gulp of the drink and sat back in the chair. "I know, because I helped Scott plan the first four assassinations."

Feeling his legs weaken, Michael decided to sit down while he still had the control. "You what?"

"I helped Scott plan the first four assassinations."

With a look of exasperation Michael asked, "Why didn't you say something at the hospital?"

"In front of all the nurses and doctors?" Seamus frowned. "I told you not to do anything until we had a chance to talk." Seamus shook his head. "I knew with your damn temper you would demand a showdown with Scott. I called your house to check on you, and Liz told me you left to meet someone. When she got all nervous and flustered I knew you had told her." Seamus shook his head. "Why in the hell did you do that?"

Michael looked at his grandfather with real anger for the first time in his life. "I don't think you are in any position to criticize me. I'm not the one who has been running around staging a revolution."

Seamus's eyes narrowed. "It wasn't an easy decision. I decided to keep you out of this for your own good."

"I can't believe you're involved in this. Does Tim know?"

"No." Seamus shook his head. "No one knows about it with the exception of Scott, two of his men, myself, you, and now Liz."

Michael glanced over at Coleman. "I understand why he's doing this. If half of my men were blown out of the sky because Senator Fitzgerald shot his mouth off, I would have probably killed him, too . . . but Seamus . . . for God sakes I can't believe you're involved in this."

Seamus set his drink down. "You said you understand why Scott is involved with this—because he lost eight men. By the time I was done island-hopping around the Pacific, five hundred and thirty-six Marines had died under my command. Five hundred and thirty-six men who climbed down cargo nets into little tin cups and then flung themselves onto some little sand strip all in the name of democracy and freedom. I didn't watch all those men die so I could see idiots like Koslowski, Fitzgerald, Downs, and Basset send this country in the tank." Seamus leaned forward. "Those men sit in their little ivory towers and play their petty games of partisan politics while people like your parents and Scott's brother are killed. While our so-called leaders are spending billions of dollars on weapons systems the military doesn't even want, while they throw billions of dollars into the department of education that doesn't educate a single child, while they waste their time debating whether or not we should have prayer in school, people are dying. They are dying because these idiots don't have the common sense to keep violent criminals behind bars. And to make things worse we have the proverbial eight-hundred-pound gorilla sitting in the corner—a five-trillion-dollar national debt. These clowns ran up the tab, and they're gonna stick my grandchildren with the bill. It's wrong, it's immoral, and somebody had to put a stop to it."

Michael looked at his grandfather, but said nothing. While the two O'Rourkes were locked in an icy stare, Coleman looked on. He cleared his throat and said, "You two can sort this out later. Right now we have a much bigger problem on our hands." With raised eyebrows Coleman asked, "Who has decided to join the fight?"

Nance sat across the coffee table from Arthur as the fire burned brightly, casting a dark shadow of their figures against the far wall of the large study. They were both smiling, holding their warm snifters of cognac gently in their hands. The grandfather clock in the far corner started its first of twelve chimes, and Nance swirled the glass under his nose. They were both wearing their standard dark Brooks Brothers suits. Nance took a light sip and let it rest on his palate before swallowing. "The FBI has no idea," said Nance. "But the president has ordered the CIA and the NSA to get involved in the investigation."

Arthur lowered his glass and raised an eyebrow. "Really . . . that surprises me. How did you advise him?"

"I said nothing. Stu is trying to get him to rethink the situation, but he's having a hard time getting him to calm down. He's extremely upset about Olson."

Arthur tilted his head back and reflected for a moment. "I don't think it will affect us. After tomorrow we will be done." Arthur smelled his cognac but did not drink it. "How is Garret holding up?"

"He's nervous."

Arthur raised his left eyebrow. "Please, don't tell me he's feeling guilty."

"No, he says he doesn't care what we do just so long as he isn't caught."

Arthur smiled and said, "I read him right from the beginning. He'll keep his mouth shut."

"If he doesn't have a nervous breakdown in the process."

"Don't worry, after tomorrow he can relax, and we'll both have what we want. Remind Mr. Garret to push the president toward taking a tougher stance against these terrorists. It will help him look better in the polls. The people are yearning for security right now, and after one more assassination they'll greet a suspension of rights with open arms." Arthur gracefully stood and opened the cherrywood humidor on the table, offering a cigar to Nance. "Let's step out on the veranda and continue this conversation over a nice cigar, some good cognac, and a majestic view." The two stood, gently cradling their snifters, and moved from the study into the dark night.

TUESDAY EVENING, FAIRFAX, VIRGINIA

Congressman Burt Turnquist's century-old, plantation-style house sat on a beautiful two-and-a-half-acre, wooded lot in an exclusive but low-key neighborhood. A single narrow, winding road cut through the rolling hills with no streetlights to show the way. In late fall, darkness fell on the Eastern seaboard around 5:30 P.M. The moon was finishing a cycle and was showing only a slight sliver of white. The towering old trees and a lack of moonlight gave the neighborhood a deep, dark look.

The congressman was in his second-floor study, feeling alone and isolated. His wife was on a business trip out of town and wouldn't be back until tomorrow. His closest colleague had been blown to bits the previous afternoon, and he had four complete strangers standing watch over him. In all his years as a United States congressman, he had never felt threatened. Even after Downs, Koslowski, and Fitzgerald were killed, he thought he was safe. Turnquist didn't tell anyone other than his wife, but he could understand why someone would want to kill them. He had thought about it many times since arriving in Washington eighteen years earlier. In short, they were not good men. They had their petty personal agendas and were more concerned with holding on to their positions of power than doing what was right. Year after year they said they were for benevolent change, and then behind the closed doors of their committees they blocked the very reforms they had espoused while running for reelection.

Turnquist was not sad to see them gone, but Erik Olson was a different story. Olson was a good friend. They had fought so many battles together, working behind the scenes trying to bring the two parties to a middle ground, Olson in the Senate and Turnquist in the House. Olson had been a source of strength, always helping him steer a safe course through the often dangerous game of politics, prodding him not to give up, advising him on professional as well as personal issues.

Turnquist had warned Olson against helping the president form the new bipartisan coalition in the wake of the assassinations. Turnquist told him that although the deaths of Koslowski, Fitzgerald, Downs, and Basset were a tragedy, maybe some good could come from them. Maybe they could finally pass the reforms they had worked so hard for. The always principled Olson told Turnquist there was no room for anarchy in a democracy. Turnquist had reminded his friend of the obvious historical fact that America had come into existence through a bloody revolution.

Turnquist looked down at his journal and struggled to record his thoughts. He was trying to think of what to say at Olson's funeral. Writer's block seized him, and he looked out the window, wishing his wife were home. He couldn't see the U.S. marshal standing watch in his front yard, but he knew he was there. They had guarded him day and night for over a week, and the congressman couldn't decide if they made him feel secure or nervous.

Four U.S. marshals were currently on watch at the Turnquist house. They were two hours into a twelve-hour watch that had started at 5 P.M. Three of the four marshals were outside: one by the back door, one by the front porch, and the third sitting in a sedan at the end of the congressman's long driveway. The fourth marshal was posted inside the house at the foot of the stairs that led to the second floor. They were more alert than they had been during the previous week's watch. The fiery deaths of the four Secret Service agents the day before reminded them that they were also targets.

The neighborhood that the congressman lived in hadn't changed much in the last fifty years. The lots were woodsy and large. Separating the congressman's land from his neighbor's behind him was a small creek that ran between the two properties. Just on the other side of the creek, about fifty yards from the house, a man peered out from behind a tree with a pair of night-vision goggles. The goggles cut through the dark forest and focused in on the marshal standing guard by Turnquist's back door. The ominous watcher was covered from head to toe in black, and his face was painted with camouflage makeup. Slung across his back was an MP-5 submachine gun with a twelve-inch silencer attached to the barrel, and gripped firmly in his hands was a 7mm Magnum sniper's rifle, also with a silencer affixed to the barrel. He whispered into the microphone hanging in front of his mouth, "Omega, this is Alpha. I'm moving into position, over." Holding the rifle across his chest and pointed upward, he stepped out from behind the tree and moved laterally until he put another tree between himself and the marshal standing guard by the back door.

Alpha moved across the forest floor, gliding between the underbrush with a cautious, catlike manner. When he reached the creek, he put one foot slowly into the water, then followed it with the other, checking his footing before transferring his weight from one foot to the other. Upon reaching the other side he scanned the ground for any fallen branches or twigs and pulled himself up the eroded bank. Pausing behind a tree, he checked the position of the guard and then his watch. Methodically, he glided from tree to tree, carefully picking his path. About twenty yards from the edge of Turnquist's yard, the assassin got down on his belly and started to crawl. He picked out a pine tree at the edge of the yard and slid under it, the low-slung branches of the tree making his presence impossible to detect. Alpha nestled up against the trunk and checked his watch. It was 7:19 P.M. The assassin pulled his night-vision goggles down around his neck and waited. If the marshals stayed with their routine, they would be rotating posts in about ten minutes.

Out in front of the house, the sniper's partner lay in the ditch across the street from the end of Turnquist's driveway. Covering his black tactical jumpsuit was a sniper's blanket. The strange piece of clothing consisted of a mesh netting with strips of camouflage cloth attached to it. It had taken him over forty minutes to crawl into position, slowly squirming through the tall grass and bushes on his stomach, his MP-5 cradled between his chin and elbows. He poked his head up slightly and moved the branch of a small bush in front of him. His face was painted with dark streaks of green and black makeup. Through squinted eyes, he looked at the white sedan sitting at the end of the driveway. Crouching back into the ditch, he pulled the sniper's blanket off his body, wrapped it into a tight ball, and placed it in his backpack.

He checked all of his equipment one last time, and then, just after 7:30 P.M., the sedan across the street backed up the driveway to the house. Checking the road quickly, Omega jumped to his feet and darted across the road. When he reached the other side, he jumped into a clump of bushes not more than ten feet from where the car had been. While taking deep breaths to keep his heart rate low, he said, "Alpha, this is Omega, I'm in position, over."

The car returned less than a minute later with a different driver behind the wheel. Omega squatted on one knee and blinked away a drop of sweat that was forming on his brow. The muzzle of his silencer was extended to the far end of the bush, pointed straight at the head of the man behind the wheel of the car. Only a thin green leaf concealed the lethal black cylinder. The contrast between the dark green and black paint on his face and the whites of his eyes gave him a reptilian appearance.

Under the pine tree in the backyard Alpha checked his watch again, and then, reaching forward, he flipped the protective caps off the rifle's sight. He hugged the butt of the rifle close to his cheek and eased his right eye in behind the sight. Moving his hands slightly, he placed the head of the man standing watch at the back door in the middle of the sight's crosshairs. The plan was to wait another minute or so, giving the marshals ample time to check in and get relaxed. The man by the back door brought his radio up to his mouth and said something. The sniper was too far away to hear, but he knew what was said. When the guard lowered his radio back to his side, the sniper whispered into his headset, "Omega, this is Alpha. I'm ready to start the game, over."

Alpha flipped the safety switch into the off position and brought the sniper's trigger back one notch. The crosshairs marked a lethal intersection on the temple of the marshal's head. The killer squeezed the trigger and a spitting noise popped from the end of the thick, black silencer. Without waiting to see the outcome of the shot, the sniper let go of the rifle and rolled to his right, out from under the low branches of the pine tree, leaving the rifle behind. He didn't need to check to see if his bullet had hit the mark. He knew it had.

Springing up from the ground, he broke into a sprint for the right side of the house, whispering into his headset, "One down, three to go." Reaching over his head, he pulled the silenced MP-5 off his back and flipped off the safety. Nearing the front corner of the house, he slowed for a step and then spun around the edge of the porch. Dropping to one knee he swept the gun from left to right, searching for his next target.

The movement of the black shape coming around the corner caught the attention of the marshal standing watch at the foot of the porch steps, and he instinctively reached for his gun. Before he could get his hand to his hip, the assassin fired three quick rounds, two hitting the marshal in the face and the third striking him in the neck, the impact of the bullets throwing his head backward and sending the rest of his body with it. With his machine gun aimed at the front door, the killer ran toward the man he had just killed and whispered into his headset, "Two down, two to go." Upon reaching the marshal, he opened the dead man's jacket and yanked the radio from his belt. Ducking under the edge of the porch, he waited and listened to the marshal's radio.

At the end of the driveway the man in the bushes leapt forward and unloaded four quick bursts into the driver's seat of the sedan. The window broke into thousands of pieces, the bullets slamming into the side of the marshal's head. Without pause, the hired killer approached the car, shoved the barrel through the shattered window, and pumped a final round into the driver's head. Turning on the balls of his feet, the killer sprinted up the driveway toward the house. With the adrenaline rushing through his blood he barked into his headset, "Three down, one to go."

Five seconds later, he joined his partner at the foot of the porch, his breathing controlled but heavy. Alpha was listening to the marshal's radio to see if the man inside the house had been alerted. He pointed and sent Omega to check the windows to the right of the front door, and he went to check the ones on the left. They peered over the railing of the porch and looked through the windows.

Omega saw him first, sitting at the foot of the stairs reading a magazine. "I've got number four," he whispered into his mike. They met at the stairs of the porch, and Omega pointed at the window. "It's a clear shot from the first window on the right."

Alpha nodded and said, "I'll crawl under the window and take up position on the other side. When I give you the signal, pump two rounds into the window, and I'll take him out." Omega nodded his confirmation and they started up the steps. Alpha got down on his stomach and crawled to the far side of the window. Switching his gun from his right side to his left, he peeked through the window to make sure his target hadn't moved. Stepping away from the window he gave his partner a nod and hugged the butt of the MP-5 tight against his cheek. Omega stepped back and pointed the muzzle of his silencer toward the middle of the tall window and fired two shots. A split second later, Alpha stepped into the new opening and trained his gun on the startled marshal. Pulling the trigger, Alpha sent three bullets crashing into the center of the man's head. With robotlike precision the two men slammed fresh clips into their weapons and stepped through the jagged window frame. They trained their guns in opposite directions as they moved to the foot of the stairs. Footsteps sounded from upstairs, and they looked up at the ceiling.

A deep voice called out from the top of the stairs, "Is everything all right down there?"

Without pause, Alpha called back, "Sorry, sir, I dropped a glass. Can I get you anything?"

"No, that's all right, I'll come down. I'm getting a little hungry." Turnquist started down the staircase, and Alpha pushed his partner back and out of the way.

When the congressman reached the middle landing, he turned and froze, staring at the man dressed in black. Alpha squeezed the trigger and the barrel jumped. A stream of bullets popped from the end of the silencer and slammed into Congressman Turnquist. The impact of the bullets sent the congressman reeling backward and into the wall, where he hung for a moment, pinned by the bullets slamming into his chest. The assassin took his finger off the trigger and Turnquist's body slid to the ground, leaving a bright red streak on the white wall.

CHAPTER 26

A T about 7:55 P.M., a Fairfax police squad rolled through
Congressman Turnquist's neighborhood. It was part of his
regular patrol route, but since the recent flurry of assassinations
his duties had shifted from spending his nights writing speeding
tickets and nailing drunk drivers to checking up on the various
congressmen and senators who lived in his part of the city. He was
getting to know most of the marshals who were assigned to protecting Congressman Turnquist and looked forward to stopping by
every hour or so to talk with whoever was sitting in the car at the
end of the driveway. As he approached the white sedan, his headlights passed over the car. No one was visible in the front seat, so
he shined his spotlight on the car. The police officer put his squad
in park and got out, thinking that whoever was on watch must
have fallen asleep. He could appreciate how boring their jobs must
be. There were nights when after a full thermos of coffee he could
barely stay awake, and he was on the move. These poor guys sat in
one place all night.

He strode up to the window and looked in. Just as he'd thought,
the marshal was lying across the front seat. The cop brought his
flashlight up and turned it on. It took him a second to process what
he was seeing. His eyes opened wide as he froze in shock at the sight

of the bloody body. After several seconds he grasped the severity of the situation and ran back to his squad to call the dispatcher.

Upon receiving the call from the officer at Turnquist's house, the dispatcher sent two additional squads and an ambulance to the scene. Her next call was to the Fairfax police chief, who directed her to call the FBI. Within two minutes of the patrolman's finding the marshal's body, Skip McMahon was on the phone asking for a chopper. He came into the task force's main conference room and started telling agents whom to call and what to do. Then, grabbing Jennings and Wardwell, he headed for the roof of the Hoover Building.

Once in the elevator, he pointed at Wardwell and said, "Get ahold of the Fairfax Police Department and have them patch you through to the officer at Turnquist's. Kathy, call the marshals' office and make sure they know what's going on and then . . . no, call the marshals' office second. First call the Virginia State Patrol and tell them if they spot any cars with multiple males, twenty-five to forty-five, to pull them over for questioning and approach with extreme caution. Have them pass the word on to all the local police departments." Both agents pulled their digital phones out and started punching away at the number pads. By the time they reached the roof, the blades on the helicopter were just starting to spin.

Wardwell tugged on his boss's sleeve. "Skip, the cop is waiting for backup. He says he hasn't heard a thing since he arrived." Wardwell shouted as the helicopter grew louder and louder. "He wants to know what he should do."

"Tell him to wait for backup and then proceed with caution. . . . And tell them not to touch anything." McMahon had an empty feeling in his stomach that they weren't going to find any survivors at Turnquist's house.

The rotor wash of the props became intense, blowing their hair and ties in every direction. A man in a bright orange jumpsuit waved them toward the open door of the chopper, and with

McMahon leading the way, they hustled up the five steps and onto the helipad. Keeping their heads low, they ran under the spinning blades and climbed into the backseat. The chopper lifted off and arced northward before turning back to a southwesterly course, leaving the bright lights of Washington behind. As they raced toward Fairfax, Virginia, McMahon turned to Jennings. "How often were the marshals checking in?"

Jennings shouted into McMahon's ear, "Every half hour. They made their seven-thirty check-in and were scheduled to check in again at eight."

"How many marshals were assigned to the congressman?"

"Four."

"What's the ETA for the Quick Response Team?"

"When the call went out, most of them were in the lab working on the evidence collected from the bombing yesterday. We've got choppers coming in to pick them up on the roof, and their mobile crime lab and heavy equipment should arrive around eight forty-five."

McMahon couldn't get the vision of a team of commandos assaulting Turnquist's house out of his mind. The thought made him think of Irene Kennedy and General Heaney. He grabbed the digital phone out of his jacket and dialed the direct line to Roach's office. "Brian, I need you to do me a favor. Get a chopper over to the Pentagon and have it ferry General Heaney and Irene Kennedy out to Turnquist's."

"Consider it done. I just activated the Hostage Rescue Team. They'll be airborne and en route in under five minutes. They should be arriving right behind you. If there's the slightest sign of these terrorists, I want you to hold tight and wait for them to handle it."

McMahon doubted the killers were waiting around, but knew Roach had to do things by the book. "Have the HRT stay airborne. If I need them, I'll call them in."

"You're running the show. Have the Fairfax police been in the house?"

"Not yet. I'll call you as soon as I get there. We're only a couple of minutes out." McMahon hung up, and the next several minutes were punctuated by a nervous silence.

The chopper came in at about three hundred feet and circled the neighborhood looking for a place to land. Three police cars with their lights flashing marked the end of Turnquist's driveway. The chopper pilot knew enough not to land near the crime scene and have his rotor wash send evidence flying. He flew about fifty yards down from Turnquist's house and checked the area with his spotlight for wires. He found a spot where the trees weren't a problem and set the bird down in the middle of the road. The three agents again crouched as they ran away from the chopper. Halfway down the street they were met by a woman with grayish black hair carrying a flashlight. She looked at McMahon and said, "FBI?"

Skip stuck out his right hand. "Yes, I'm Special Agent Mc-Mahon and these are Special Agents Jennings and Wardwell."

"I'm Police Chief Barnes. Follow me, and I'll show you the way." All four started down the street.

"Have you been in the house, Chief?" asked McMahon.

"No, I just got here."

"Have any of your officers been in the house?"

"No."

As they walked up to the white sedan, Barnes pointed her flashlight down and illuminated several brassy objects. "Watch your step, we've got some shell casings on the ground." She led them to the window of the sedan and shone the light on the dead marshal. The man lay slumped over the middle armrest with shards of glass covering his body. Three bullet holes were clearly visible on the left side of his head.

McMahon noted the distance from the shell casings to the car and then looked at the marshal's hands. They were empty. "Let's go look at the house."

The chief told her two officers to stay put and then led McMahon,

Jennings, and Wardwell up the driveway. As they neared the house, another body could be seen on the ground in front of the porch. Barnes shone her flashlight at it and illuminated the dead marshal. When they neared the body, McMahon stuck his arms out and stopped everyone from coming any closer. "Chief, may I borrow your flashlight for a second?" Barnes handed it to him, and Skip stepped closer to the body. Putting the flashlight under his armpit, he put on a pair of gloves and bent over the body. He looked at the bullet holes in the center of the man's face and then the one in his neck. The marshal's hands were open and lying away from his body. Skip looked at his holstered pistol and closed his eyes.

Standing back up, he said, "Everyone stay here for a minute. I'll be right back."

He started for the porch steps, and Wardwell shouted at him, "Skip, you're not going in there alone."

"Yes, I am. Just stay put. The less people we have traipsing around here the better."

Jennings pulled out her gun and flipped off the safety. "I'm going in with you!"

Without looking back McMahon said, "No, you're not!"

"What if someone's still in there?"

"What do you think . . . the people that did this are waiting around to get caught? Just stay where you are, and I'll be back in a minute." McMahon walked up the steps and tried the front door. It was unlocked. Swinging the door inward, he saw the next marshal lying on the floor with one leg still up on the chair. Standing over the body, McMahon's eyes were drawn to the three red dots marking the dead man's face and then down to his holstered gun. Sighing, he looked up to shake his head and saw the bright red streak on the wall at the top of the stairs. Only a pair of shoes were visible, and McMahon started the slow climb to the first landing.

He'd seen the congressman on TV before but wasn't quite sure the body he was looking at was Turnquist's. Unlike the other bodies, this one was riddled with more than a dozen bullets. It has to be him, he thought to himself. McMahon's phone rang, startling him slightly. He reached into his jacket and answered it. "Hello."

"What did you find?" It was Director Roach on the line.

"Well, I'm standing over what I'm pretty sure is Congressman Turnquist's body."

"Could you be more precise?"

"The man has a half a dozen bullet holes in his face and chest, but it has to be him."

"You're sure?"

"Yes." McMahon stared down at the body by his feet and waited for Roach to speak.

"Any sign of the people that did it?"

"No."

"I'd better tell the president before the media catches on. What else do you need from me?"

"Nothing right now."

"All right, call me if there are any developments."

"Will do." McMahon hung up the phone and looked down at the body, contemplating the precision of the wounds in Turnquist's head.

Scarlatti and O'Rourke were sitting in the corner booth of a new and yet to be discovered Italian restaurant. It was located in the basement of a building about two blocks from Dupont Circle. The booth was a dark-stained wood, and the table was covered with a red-and-white-checkered tablecloth. The only light in the restaurant was provided by a candle at each table sticking out of an old Chianti bottle. O'Rourke looked around and thought he might enjoy the place under a different set of circumstances. His *mostaccioli* tasted good and the wine wasn't bad.

Michael had told Liz that Coleman wasn't responsible for the deaths of Senator Olson and his four Secret Service agents, but he had neglected to mention Seamus's involvement in the first four assassinations. He didn't quite have the stomach to tell Liz that her future grandfather-to-be was an anarchist or revolutionary or whatever the term would be.

Liz was attempting for the third time in twenty-four hours to convince Michael that he should go to the FBI. "Michael, I know you and his brother were best friends, but the man killed the Speaker of the House, two senators, and the chairman of the House Appropriations Committee."

"Keep your voice down."

Liz moved closer. "You have to turn him in. I don't care if he had nothing to do with Erik's death."

"For the last time, Liz, I am not going to turn him in."

"I don't understand you."

Michael looked at her for a long while and then answered, "I don't expect you to understand why I feel the way I do."

"What is that supposed to mean?" Liz said defensively.

"You have no reason to think those men deserved to die. You have lived a very nice life." Liz shot him a scowl and Michael said, "I'm not saying you haven't worked hard, I'm just saying you've had a nice life. Your parents are still alive. Your brother and sister are alive. Nothing has happened to you that would cause you to look at our political leaders with a truly critical eye."

"So, just because I haven't lost someone close to me"—Liz folded her arms across her chest—"I'm not fit to judge my political representatives?"

"I didn't say you weren't fit to judge. I'm only trying to say that I don't think you understand why I feel the way I do."

"Oh, I understand why you feel the way you do. Despite you not letting me in, I understand. The death of your parents and Mark is a horrible thing, but I don't think these bizarre assassinations are going to solve anything. You have got to let go of the past and move on with your life."

Michael placed his anger in check, but even so his voice became a little louder. "Liz, it's easy to say you understand something when you haven't experienced it, and it's even easier to tell someone to get over something when you've never been through it. You can say you understand, but you will never really understand until you've lived it."

"So what? Do you want me to lose my parents so I can empathize with you?"

"No, darling." He reached for her hand. "I never want you to go through that kind of pain. When my parents were killed, my brothers and sister were robbed. They were robbed of dreams never realized and moments that should have been. They never got to look up in the stands during one of their games and see my mom and dad cheering. When the games were over and they came out of the locker room . . . all the other kids were getting hugs and kisses from their moms, but my brothers and sister didn't have one. When they came home from school, they didn't have a mother or father to help them with their homework, and when they ate dinner, there were two empty seats at the table. My parents never got to see the five children they brought into this world grow up." Michael stopped and looked away.

Liz looked around the candle flame and asked, "What about you?"

Michael shrugged his shoulders. "I'm fine."

"No, you're not." She pulled his hand closer. "What dreams did you miss out on?"

Michael paused for a moment. "My father was my childhood idol. He was everything I ever wanted to be. My mother . . . she was my best friend . . . the nicest, most caring person I've ever known. Every holiday, every event for the last ten years, has been incomplete, and that's the way it will be for the rest of my life." Michael's eyes glassed over. "When we get married, it'll be the happiest day of my life, but I'll still look down at that first pew, at the two empty seats, and think about how nice it would have been to have them there." Liz squeezed his hand tight, and Michael forced a smile. "When we have our first child, he or she will only have one set of grandparents, and my parents will have never had the chance to hold their grandchild.

"I have been robbed of all of these moments and many more . . . and why?" In a quiet voice he said, "All because some drunk, who had proven time and time again that he was going to keep getting hammered and climb behind that wheel, was allowed to walk free. And why was he allowed to walk the streets? Because we don't have enough money to keep him in jail." Michael poked himself in the chest. "Let me let you in on a little secret. We have the money. We have more than enough of it, it's just that the egomaniacs who run this country would rather spend it on programs that get them votes. That's why I think they deserved to die. It's more personal to me because their inaction cost the lives of my parents and the life of Mark Coleman, and that is why I'm not going to the FBI.

"I don't expect the average person to agree with me. Most people have enough to worry about just getting through their day-to-day lives, but when you lose someone or something close to you, things take on a more serious tone."

Liz wiped a tear from her cheek and nodded. Michael reached over and brushed her cheek with his napkin.

The hostess approached the table and asked, "Excuse me, sir. Are you Michael O'Rourke?"

"Yes."

"You have a phone call at the hostess stand."

"Who knows we're here?" asked Liz.

"I told Seamus in case he needed to get ahold of me. I'll be right back."

Michael got up and followed the waitress across the small restaurant. Liz watched him talk on the phone and became concerned when she saw him close his eyes and shake his head. After talking for only about ten seconds, Michael handed the phone to the hostess and walked back to Liz.

"Was that Seamus?" she asked.

Michael nodded yes and pulled out his money clip. He threw a hundred-dollar bill on the table and stuck out his hand for Liz. "Come on, let's go. The networks are reporting that Congressman Turnquist has been assassinated."

McMahon was sitting upstairs in Turnquist's study by himself. His eyes were closed and he had a pair of thin leather gloves on his hands. His large frame rested comfortably in an old wood rocking chair. The rocking of the chair had a hypnotic effect, and Skip was in the midst of trying to re-create how Turnquist and the marshals had been killed. He envisioned a group of darkly clad men moving into position and then simultaneously killing the three guards outside with silenced weapons. They had to have used silenced weapons. All of the clues indicated that the marshal inside had had no idea that the others had been killed.

An agent poked her head through the open door. "Skip, there're two people downstairs who are asking for you."

"Who are they?"

"I don't know. One of them is a Marine. They said you were expecting them."

McMahon sprang the chair forward and bounded out of it. He'd been excitedly waiting to compare notes with Heaney and Kennedy. Taking the back staircase, he went downstairs, through the kitchen, and down the hallway onto the front porch. The Quick Response Team had arrived and was setting up their equipment. Turnquist's house looked more like a movie set than a crime scene. Floodlights were everywhere, illuminating the entire yard. The hum of generators droned through the still night air. General Heaney and Irene

Kennedy were standing by the steps on the front lawn talking to each other. McMahon approached and said, "Thank you for coming so quickly. Have you seen any of the bodies yet?"

"We saw the one in the driveway and the other one right over there." General Heaney pointed to the dead marshal on the front lawn.

"Well, before I start picking your brains, I'd like you to look at all the bodies." Skip led them up the steps, saying, "All of the marshals were wearing body armor, but it didn't do much good." A photographer was taking photos and several agents were taking notes and talking. McMahon asked them to step aside for a moment.

Heaney and Kennedy examined the dead marshal lying at the foot of the stairs. They looked at the three bullet holes in the center of the dead man's face and then at his holstered gun and radio. Kennedy looked into the dining room and pointed at the shattered glass. "The shots came from there, I assume."

McMahon nodded. "We found five shell casings on the porch."

Heaney looked up at the bloodstain on the wall of the landing. "Is that the congressman?"

"Yes."

"Can I go up there?"

"Sure."

Heaney and Kennedy walked up the stairs while McMahon stayed by the foyer. Standing over the body, Kennedy said, "Jesus, they really unloaded on him."

"Yeah, I count at least eight hits. Maybe more," replied Heaney.

"Any idea why they pumped so many into him?" asked McMahon from the bottom of the stairs.

"Two possibilities," answered Heaney. "The first being they obviously wanted to make sure he was dead, and the second"—Heaney pointed toward the shell casings by McMahon's feet—"two or more men fired the shots. Your ballistics people should be able to answer that for us." Kennedy and Heaney trotted back down the stairs.

"Let's take a look at the one out front again." McMahon led them out the front door and down the steps. "This guy got two to the face and one to the neck." McMahon bent over and lifted the man's jacket. "His gun is still holstered, but his radio is missing. We found it up there on the porch, by the broken window."

Kennedy looked to the broken window and back at the man by her feet. "They took the radio so they could find out if the guy inside knew what was going on."

Heaney looked toward the side of the house. "Were the shots fired from over there?"

"Yes." McMahon moved toward the side yard. "We found some shell casings over here. It looks like the perp took three shots. Two hit the man square in the face and the third hit him in the neck." Heaney and Kennedy looked at the shell casings and judged the distance of the shots.

"I assume the last marshal is out back?" asked Irene.

"Yes. Follow me." The three of them walked around the side of the house and to the backyard. As they approached the body, McMahon said, "Single shot to the head." Skip bent down and opened the marshal's jacket. "His gun is holstered and his radio is on his hip."

Heaney and Kennedy looked at the body for only a second, then turned their attention away from the marshal and the house. They took the whole landscape in without saying a word, swiveling their heads from side to side, their eyes focusing tightly on the darkness beyond the reach of the floodlights. Without turning, Heaney asked, "Skip, can you get them to turn these lights off?"

McMahon said something to one of the agents, and the lights were cut, leaving only the small light over the back door on.

The general started walking across the yard for the tree line. McMahon and Kennedy followed several steps behind, and a moment later they disappeared into the woods.

Heaney navigated the dark forest with ease, ducking under

branches and over fallen limbs that McMahon and Kennedy struggled with. Upon reaching the creek they stopped and turned back toward the house. Kennedy asked, "What do you think, General?"

General Heaney looked at the FBI agents standing by the back door. "They can't see us, can they?"

"Not standing under that light they can't," responded Kennedy. "And we're not even wearing camouflage gear. The light only goes to about the end of the yard and then dies out."

Heaney looked over to the other side of the creek. "I think it was two or more men. It could have been one, but it would have been really difficult. They were in and out in under a minute, and the marshals never knew what hit them, as is evidenced by the fact that none of them drew their guns. One or two men crept through the woods back here and took out the sentry by the back door with a single rifle shot to the head. The marshal by the front door was taken out next with an assault rifle, and then the man in the car at the end of the driveway was killed."

"I agree," said Kennedy.

"Why that order?" asked McMahon.

"When they killed the guy in the car, they had to shoot him through the window. If they kill him first, the marshal out front hears the window smash and grabs his gun or radio or both. He grabbed neither because he was already dead when the window was shot out. In any case, the men outside died within seconds of each other." The general shook his head. "These marshals never stood a chance. The guys who did this were good. The head shots are as accurate as you can get, and they're commando style, three quick bursts to the head."

"How in the hell did they get so close to the guy in the car? He was shot point-blank."

"There's plenty of cover around here. With the right camouflage, a commando would have no trouble sneaking to within ten feet of that car. After they take care of the three guards outside, all they have to worry about is the last marshal inside. The killers grab one of the marshal's radios to make sure the guard inside wasn't alerted . . . since his gun is still in his holster, it's pretty obvious he wasn't. They shoot him from the window, and then Turnquist comes downstairs to find out what the noise was, or maybe he was on his way down when it happened. They're in and out in under a minute, a minute and a half tops, and all they leave behind is five dead bodies and a couple dozen shell casings. Very clean, very professional. I'm sorry to sound so heartless, but I'm just giving my professional opinion."

"No apologies needed, General. That's what I brought you out here for. What do you think, Irene?"

"The general is right. Things can always go wrong when you're running an operation like this, but in relation to some of the missions we've run, this thing would have been a cakewalk. These marshals aren't trained to deal with this kind of a lethal threat. We train our commandos to be able to defeat the best surveillance systems in the world, get by guard dogs, sneak past trigger-happy terrorists armed to the teeth, and then silently kill and get away without being noticed. . . . The guys who did this are good, and they're used to facing a lot tougher obstacles than four U.S. marshals armed with radios and pistols."

McMahon bit down on his upper lip and thought about the remaining congressmen and senators, most of whom had less protection than Turnquist. Kennedy's point was clear: if these guys weren't caught, he would be spending more of his nights standing over dead bodies. "I need them to slip up . . . I need a break," murmured McMahon.

"I wouldn't count on it," replied Heaney.

CHAPTER 27

THE dark green Chevy Tahoe rolled eastward down Highway 50. It was just past midnight and traffic was light. Michael kept the speed under sixty-five and stayed in the right lane. His left hand loosely gripped the steering wheel while he leaned on the middle armrest. The stereo was tuned to an AM news station, but he wasn't listening. The question of who was behind the murders of Turnquist and Olson was pulsing through his mind.

The exit for the cabin was approaching, and O'Rourke hit the blinker. Veering to the right, the truck started up the exit ramp. As he slowed for the stop sign, he rolled down his window and let the cold night air blow on his face.

The cool breeze blowing through the window felt refreshing, but as the car accelerated, the wind rushing through the window grew annoying. Michael pressed a button, closing it. Five minutes later the unmarked road to the cabin came up quickly, and Michael braked hard. Gravel spun from under the tires as he banked into the turn and sped down the narrow road. Pulling in between two cars, he got out, walked around to the back of the truck, and lowered the tailgate. Duke jumped down and started smelling the ground as he ran in circles. Walking toward the porch, Michael whistled once, and Duke bounded to his side.

Michael patted Duke on the head and told him to stay. Walking into the cabin, Michael took off his jacket and set it on the back of the couch. Seamus and Scott Coleman were sitting at the kitchen table. The greetings were curt. Michael apologized for being late and grabbed a mug out of the cupboard. While sitting down, he asked, "What in the hell are we going to do to stop this?" As Michael poured some coffee into his cup, he looked up for a response but got none. He took a gulp of coffee and asked, "Do we know any details about what happened to Turnquist?"

Coleman said, "The congressman was shot approximately twelve times at close range. Four U.S. marshals were also killed. The word is it was very clean and very professional. Not one of the marshals got a shot off."

Michael closed his eyes and asked, "Do we have any idea who is doing this or why?"

Seamus shrugged his shoulders and said, "Erik and Turnquist have been in Washington for a long time. I'm sure they've made plenty of enemies over the years. The real question is, who would have the type of contacts to do something like this on such short notice?"

Coleman set his cup of coffee down and said, "I agree. We have to assume that whoever is behind this has the power and the connections to put together an operation like this in under a week. That shortens the list considerably."

Michael thought about the type of people who would have that kind of power and said, "Unfortunately, we don't have any contacts that run in those circles."

"I have a few," said Coleman, "but if I start asking questions, they'll want to know why I'm so interested."

Seamus shook his head. "Bad idea. The last thing we want to do right now is draw attention to ourselves."

"I agree," said Michael, "but we have to do something."

Seamus pushed his coffee cup forward. "I have someone I can

trust who is very connected in the intelligence community, or at least was."

"Who?" asked Coleman.

"Augie Jackson."

"Who is Augie Jackson?"

"He's a very good . . . very old friend. We were in the Marines together during WW Two. After the war he went to work for the CIA and went on to become one of the Agency's top European analysts. He retired about a year ago. He's as honest a man as I've ever met."

"How often do you keep in contact with him?"

"We talk at least once a month. Every summer we fly into Canada for a couple of days of fishing, and I usually go down and see him in the fall for a little duck hunting. . . . He lives in Georgia."

"Do you think you can ask him what he thinks without drawing any attention to our involvement?" asked Michael.

Seamus thought about it for a minute and said, "I think so."

"All right, see what you can find out. I trust Augie." Michael took another sip of coffee. "Now, what do we do in the meantime?"

Coleman leaned back and crossed his arms. "This is tough. In all of our planning we never predicted that something like this might happen." The former SEAL rolled his eyes. "I don't know . . . something tells me we should lay low and see what happens. I think there's still a good chance that the reforms will be implemented."

Michael said, "Absolutely not. You guys got this thing rolling, and you're going to stop it before anyone else gets killed."

Seamus stared at Michael. "We don't have the contacts to go snooping around."

"The FBI does."

"So?"

"I think we need to alert them that someone else is involved in this."

"What will that solve?" asked Seamus.

"If we call them, they'll have to take us seriously. They will have to look into who would have the motive and the contacts to kill Erik and Congressman Turnquist. If they start asking questions and poking around, maybe it will scare these people away before they kill anyone else."

Seamus frowned and Coleman said, "I don't like the idea."

Michael placed his forearms on the table. "You two started this thing, and whether I like it or not, I've been dragged into it. I am not going to condemn you for what you've done, but I will if you sit around while more good men get killed. We are going to do everything we can to stop this other group from killing again even if it means getting caught. Am I clear?"

Coleman and Seamus reluctantly nodded yes.

The clock on the desk said it was 6:12 A.M., Wednesday. McMahon was sitting in his chair with his face resting on a stack of reports. He'd left Turnquist's house around midnight and came back to the Hoover Building to brief Roach. Since then he'd been busy assigning new agents to Turnquist's murder and preparing for an 8 A.M. briefing at the White House. Sometime around 5 A.M., he'd laid his head down for a quick nap. He was too tired to get up and go over to the couch. The warning from Irene Kennedy and General Heaney that they could be spending more of their evenings standing over dead bodyguards and politicians had McMahon a little discouraged. He knew how to pace himself through the ups and downs of an investigation, but this was more frantic than most. The bodies were no longer coming in one at a time, and now that some fellow law enforcement officers had been killed, the investigation had taken on a more personal tone. When it was just senators and congressmen getting killed, he looked at the case with more detachment.

McMahon was immersed in a vivid dream when a noise startled him. It took a moment for him to realize he was in his office and it was his phone, not his alarm clock, that was making the irritating noise. His head snapped up, and he lurched for the receiver. "Hello."

Michael was sitting in the back of the BMW as Coleman navigated the narrow residential streets of Adams Morgan. Next to O'Rourke on the backseat was a mobile scramble phone that Coleman had purchased through a third party in Taiwan three months earlier. The secure phone was mounted in a leather briefcase. Attached to the receiver was a voice modulator that converted Michael's voice into generic electronic tones. The phone was touted as being trace-proof and could be used stationary, but neither O'Rourke nor Coleman was willing to trust it completely, so they stayed mobile when using it.

"Special Agent McMahon?" asked Michael.

McMahon went rigid upon hearing the electronic voice. Before responding, he pressed a button next to the phone starting a trace on the incoming call. Hesitatingly he said, "Yes, this is he."

"I will assume you are recording and tracing this call, so I'll be brief. The people that killed Senator Fitzgerald, Congressman Koslowski, Senator Downs, and Congressman Basset did not kill Senator Olson, Congressman Turnquist, and their bodyguards."

There were several seconds of silence on the line while McMahon tried to grasp what he had just heard. "I'm not sure I follow you."

"There is a second group of killers. A group that killed Olson, Turnquist, and their bodyguards."

"Why should I believe you?"

Michael had anticipated McMahon's pessimism and had asked Coleman for some bits of information that would give the call credence. "We let Burmiester live."

McMahon thought about the old man who lived across the street from Congressman Koslowski. The man they had found drugged and tied up the morning of the first three assassinations.

"A lot of people know about Burmiester. That doesn't prove any-thing." McMahon was trying to stall and give the computers time to trace the call.

"Mr. McMahon, we do not kill Secret Service agents and U.S. marshals. As we stated in the last message we left for you, we have a deep respect for members of the law enforcement community. Our fight is with the politicians, not you."

"That's where you're wrong—"

Michael cut him off. "Ask yourself one question. If we were willing to kill four Secret Service agents to get at Olson and four U.S. marshals to get at Turnquist, why wouldn't we have blown the president out of the sky last Friday?" O'Rourke let the ques-tion hang in the air and then said, "The answer is that we didn't kill Olson and Turnquist. Someone else did."

"Why are you telling me this?"

"Because we don't want to see innocent people die."

"And Basset and the others were guilty?"

O'Rourke looked at his watch. "Mr. McMahon, I don't have time to be drawn into a debate with you right now, so listen care-fully. I don't know who would want to kill Turnquist and Olson or why, and I'm really not in a position to find out. All I know is that they've killed eight federal law enforcement officers, and they'll probably kill more if you don't stop them."

"And what about you? Are you done killing?"

"Yes."

McMahon started to speak, but the line went dead.

CHAPTER 28

ROACH'S limo pulled up in front of the West Executive Entrance of the White House, and the director and McMahon rushed to the door. They were almost twenty minutes late. Jack Warch was waiting for them and ushered them quickly past the security checkpoint and to the Situation Room.

The president was speaking and stopped when they entered. Everyone turned and looked at Roach and McMahon as they took their seats. "I apologize for being late, Mr. President," said Roach. "There was a last-minute development we had to take care of."

President Stevens ignored the explanation and looked back at Mike Nance. The attendees were CIA director Stansfield, Secret Service director Tracy, Secretary of Defense Elliot, Joint Chief General Flood, and Stu Garret.

Nance said from the far end of the table, "As you were saying, Mr. President."

"Obviously, the FBI and the Secret Service can't guarantee the safety of our congressmen and senators. Over the last two days my phone has been ringing off the hook. Every politician in this town is demanding that they be given more protection, and I don't blame them. It's bad enough that we can't catch these terrorists, but it's inexcusable that we can't stop them from killing." Stevens shot Roach a look of disgust. "After some discussion with General Flood and Secretary Elliot, I have decided to declare martial law for the immediate area surrounding the Capitol, the Senate and House office buildings, and the White House. Elements of the First Marine Expeditionary Force and the 101st Airborne Rangers will be used to secure the perimeter. These units will be in full combat dress and will carry live ammunition. General Flood has informed me that he will have this phase of the operation in place by sundown tonight.

"In addition to these extra measures I am going to extend to every congressman and senator the option to move themselves and their families to Fort Meade for the duration of this crisis. The National Airlift Command is flying in one hundred forty-two luxury trailers that our generals use when they are on maneuvers in the field. Fort Meade also has over two hundred housing units that are not being used, and if that's not enough, we have over a thousand modern tents equipped with generators, plumbing, and heating. The general's people are working out the details right now and estimate that they will have everything ready to go within forty-eight hours.

"In the meantime, the general is pulling special security units from the Army, Navy, Air Force, and Marines to handle protection for the ranking members of the House and the Senate. Most of these units specialize in base security. I am told they are very well armed and trained in countercommando tactics. I have talked to the leaders of both parties, and they have agreed to reconvene for a legislative session on Monday morning, after we have these new security measures in place. Until then all official business will be suspended." The president looked to Roach and said, "I am not happy about having to take these drastic measures, but the inability of our federal law enforcement agencies to stem the tide of violence has left me with no alternative."

Stu Garret had the slightest hint of a smile on his lips as he watched Stevens put the screws to Roach. The president was re-peating almost verbatim what Garret had told him to say an hour earlier.

McMahon, on the other hand, found nothing humorous about the situation. He didn't enjoy watching his boss take the heat for something that wasn't his fault. He looked away from the presi-dent to hide his disgust while recalling that Roach had originally suggested that the military be brought in to help secure the area around the Capitol, and that the president and Garret had said no.

Roach shrugged off the president's comments and moved the discussion forward. "Mr. President, we've had a very unusual de-velopment concerning the investigation. Special Agent McMahon received another phone call from the terrorists this morning." Roach looked at McMahon. "Skip."

McMahon cleared his throat. "This morning at about six-fifteen I received a very interesting phone call." McMahon pulled a cassette tape out of his pocket and handed it to Jack Warch. "Jack, would you please put this in the tape player for me?" Passing sheets of paper to his right and left, McMahon said, "These are transcripts of the conversation. I think it would be best if I let you hear the tape and then discuss it afterward." Warch walked over to the podium at the end of the table and inserted the tape. Eight small, black speak-ers were mounted on the walls around the room. Some static noise hissed and crackled from them, and then the sterile computer voice filled the room. "Special Agent McMahon?"

After a pause, McMahon's tired voice came over the tape. "Yes, this is he."

CIA director Stansfield had acquired a lot of habits from his days as a spy. One of them was the ability to study people's man-nerisms while listening to them speak. This occupational habit had become so ingrained in Stansfield that without consciously think-ing about it, he leaned back in his chair and held the manuscript in front of him. His eyes peered over the top of the white sheet and worked their way around the table, looking for someone to focus in on.

The computerized voice continued, "I will assume you are recording and tracing this call, so I'll be brief. The people that killed Senator Fitzgerald, Congressman Koslowski, Senator Downs, and Congressman Basset did not kill Senator Olson, Congressman Turnquist, and their bodyguards."

A quick head turn caught Stansfield's eye. He looked at Garret's wide eyes and followed them across the table to Mike Nance. Stansfield went back to Garret and examined his facial features. The chief of staff's jaw was tense and his nostrils were slightly flared.

After a full pause, McMahon's voice responded, "I'm not sure I follow you."

"There is a second group of killers. A group that killed Olson, Turnquist, and their bodyguards."

Stansfield saw it again. Garret shot Nance another look.

"Why should I believe you?"

"We let Burmiester live."

McMahon interjected while there was a pause in the tape, "For those of you who don't remember, Burmiester is the retired banker who lives across the street from Congressman Koslowski."

McMahon's taped voice continued, "A lot of people know about Burmiester. That doesn't prove anything."

"Mr. McMahon, we do not kill Secret Service agents and U.S. marshals. As we stated in the last message we left for you, we have a deep respect for members of the law enforcement community. Our fight is with the politicians, not you."

"That's where you're wrong—"

The sterile voice cut McMahon off. "Ask yourself one question. If we were willing to kill four Secret Service agents to get at Olson and four U.S. marshals to get at Turnquist, why wouldn't we have blown the president out of the sky last Friday?" There was a pause in the tape and Stansfield thought of looking to see the president's reaction but was too absorbed in watching Garret. "The answer is that we didn't kill Olson and Turnquist. Someone else did." Stansfield saw sweat forming on Garret's upper lip and followed his eyes again to Mike Nance. When Stansfield reached Nance, the national security adviser was staring back at him. Stansfield casually lowered his eyes as if he were reading the transcript.

When the tape ended, the president sat dumbfounded, staring at the transcript in his hands. "This is unbelievable." Stevens looked up. "Special Agent McMahon, is this for real?"

McMahon shrugged his shoulders. "Without having had the time to really analyze it, I would have to say there's a good chance. . . . After the Marine One incident last Friday they sent us a tape stating that the only reason they didn't blow you out of the sky was because they didn't want to kill any Marines or Secret Service agents. Now three days later, they blow up Senator Olson's limousine with four Secret Service agents in it, and then last night they kill Congressman Turnquist and four U.S. marshals. The logic is inconsistent. No offense, sir, but if I was in their shoes, I would have shot Marine One down. You are a far more important target."

"That's assuming they had the hardware to do so," interjected a calm and composed Mike Nance from the far end of the table. "Stinger missiles are very difficult to come by. I don't think we can be certain that they had the ability to shoot Marine One down."

Director Stansfield stared impassively at Nance and wondered why he'd just lied. Seven months earlier Nance had personally briefed him that the Chinese were pushing their own version of the Stinger on the open market.

McMahon continued, "Well, these last two murders are markedly different. Until last night they had been very patient . . . killing and then waiting to see if their demands were met. I can see where they would have wanted to kill Olson. After all, he helped form the coalition, but it makes no sense that they would rush out and kill Turnquist without giving you a chance to respond to their demands."

"Where does it say any of this has to make sense?" snapped Garret.

McMahon ignored the comment. "I think that we have no choice but to look into the possibility that there may be another group."

"Unbelievable," scoffed Garret. "Has it occurred to you that maybe they sent you this message to throw you off?"

"Yes, it has."

"Well, Mr. McMahon, I think you're having a hard enough time running this investigation without letting these terrorists confuse you with one simple phone call. It's no wonder you haven't made any progress when you're willing to run off on these wild-goose chases."

McMahon smiled broadly and bobbed his head up and down at Garret.

"Do you find this humorous, Mr. McMahon?" asked Garret.

"No." McMahon continued to grin.

"Then what in the hell are you smiling about?"

"If I didn't smile at your childish behavior, I wouldn't be able to keep myself from jumping over this table and knocking your head off." The smile faded from McMahon's face and he turned to Stevens. "As I was saying, Mr. President, we have no choice but to take this seriously."

Stu Garret's face was turning a new shade of red, and he was about to open his mouth and explode when from the far end of the table Mike Nance drew the attention of everyone away from Garret and to himself. "I think Special Agent McMahon is correct. We can't just ignore this phone call, but I do think there are some guidelines we need to set up." Nance continued to talk in his smooth, even voice, content that he had diverted the focus of the group away from the volatile Garret.

Michael arrived at his office at 8 A.M. and left instructions with Susan that he didn't want to be disturbed unless it was Seamus or

Liz. With less than three hours of sleep since Monday, he collapsed on the sofa. As he drifted away, he thought of the innocent men and their families and, for the hundredth time in the last two days, asked himself who could be behind the killings.

He didn't know how long he'd been asleep when he heard Susan's voice calling for him over the intercom. Throwing off the blanket, he jumped off the couch and grabbed the phone. "Yes."

"Seamus, line one." There was a click and then Michael heard his grandfather's voice.

"Michael?"

The congressman shook his left arm, which had fallen asleep. "Yeah."

"How are you?"

"Fine."

"What's your schedule look like for the rest of the day?"

Michael rubbed his eyes. "Well, we're not in session until Monday, so I'm pretty open."

"Good. I thought it might be nice for you and me to get away for a while and spend some relaxing time up in the clouds."

Michael wondered what Seamus had in mind. It was obvious that he couldn't talk about it over the phone. "Ah . . . that sounds great. What time and where do you want to meet?"

"How about noon at your house?"

Michael looked at his watch and was surprised to see that it was 11:07 A.M. "Yeah, noon will be fine. I'll see you then." Michael hung up the phone and again tried to shake the tingling feeling out of his arm. He calculated that he'd gotten about three hours of sleep, more than enough to get him through the day.

When the meeting in the Situation Room was over, Mike Nance went to his office and waited exactly one hour. Then, pressing the intercom button on his phone, he asked his secretary if she could track Stu Garret down and have him come to his office. Less than a minute later, Garret came puffing through the door and closed it behind him. His entire body was rigid. He paced back and forth in front of Nance's desk. "We've got to do something about that fucking McMahon. I knew he was going to be trouble."

"Stu, sit down."

Garret continued to pace. "We have got to do something. I mean we can't—"

Mike Nance rose out of his leather chair and pointed toward an armchair by the side of his desk. "Stu, sit down and shut up!" The uncharacteristic remark by the always composed Nance got Garret's attention, and he sat.

"The only thing you are going to do, Stu, is relax and keep your mouth shut. The FBI can dig all they want and they'll find nothing. That is, unless you give them a reason to look in our direction." Nance tapped his clenched fist against his forehead and looked away for a brief moment. "Did you pay attention to what was going on in that meeting this morning?" Garret gave Nance a puzzled look. "Stansfield watched your every gesture while that tape was being played." Nance hated dealing with amateurs and was using all of his energy to suppress the contempt he felt toward Garret at this moment. "He saw you sweating, and he saw you look at me with that stupid, panicked expression on your face. Stu, you have to get a grip on yourself. You have to learn to control your emotions, or you are going to screw this whole thing up."

McMahon left the White House and returned to his office briefly before leaving for the Pentagon. Kennedy and General Heaney were unaware of the most recent phone call from the assassins. The president agreed that they had to take the call seriously and investigate, but at the same time he knew if the public found out, the conspiracy theorists would go nuts. They would start pointing fingers at every institution of power, and the media would fan the flames.

The president directed McMahon to assign a small contingent

of agents to look into who might have wanted to kill Turnquist and Olson. The agents were not to be told of the tape and the possibility that another group was responsible for the last two assassinations. At the urging of Mike Nance, the president asked for a list of everyone who knew about the most recent call and wanted them informed that they were not to discuss the tape with anyone.

McMahon was not happy with the ludicrous and senseless restriction. It drove him nuts watching the huge amounts of energy and time that was wasted on worrying about the media and public opinion. He couldn't run an investigation if his people didn't know what was going on. After he'd gotten away with putting Garret in his place, he'd decided not to press his luck. The president was obviously not in the mood to be challenged, so he shut his mouth with the hope that Roach could get the president to loosen up later.

All the way to the Pentagon, McMahon was trying to figure out how he could leave Kennedy and General Heaney out of the loop. He couldn't. He needed their minds. They gave him insight into an area that he knew little about, and this morning's phone call was a valuable piece of the puzzle.

Skip entered the conference room just before noon and was slightly surprised. The last time he'd seen the room it was neat and orderly. Now it had stacks of folders piled everywhere, and the blackboard was covered with writing. Kennedy looked tired and worn, but the general was clean shaven and looking the perfect Marine. "You two look like you got some work done."

"We've been up all night pounding through these files." Kennedy stretched her hands over her head and yawned.

McMahon nodded. "Fill me in on what you've done."

Kennedy took off her glasses and stood. "Down at the far end of the table are all of the Delta Force files, in the middle are the Green Berets, and down here are the two Navy SEAL files. We took the description of the black assassin that killed Downs and tried to match it with the former black commandos. First, we separated them by height and skin color. If they were too short or their skin color was too light, we put them in a pile marked 'not probable.' From there, we sorted them by current address, our rationale being that the commandos would need to live in the D.C. metro area to have an alibi. If we go talk to one of these guys who lives out in L.A. and find out that they've been out of town for the last two weeks, it's going to look a little fishy. The commandos that fit the description of the assassin, but don't live in the D.C. area, are in piles marked 'possible.' And the commandos who fit the description of the assassin and live in town are in the piles marked 'probable.' "

McMahon nodded. "Sounds good. What's the next step?"

"Well, we're all in agreement that to conduct an operation of this nature you would need a minimum of four commandos, and they would have to know each other pretty well. As the general said earlier, you don't do something like this unless you trust the people on your team. That led us to the conclusion that it is highly likely these commandos served together when they were in the military. The odds are this group is composed of all former Delta Force commandos, Green Berets, or SEALs, not a mix of the three. Knowing that, we are going through the personnel files for every former commando and looking for men that served in the same units with the black commandos that are in the probable stacks."

"When will we have the list?"

"The general is running a sort on their computer. We should have a list by . . . When do you think it'll be done, General?"

"Hopefully sometime around seventeen hundred."

"Then what's the plan?" asked McMahon.

"That's what you and I need to talk about. You have to decide if you want to go knocking on doors and question these guys personally, or if you want to put them under surveillance and watch them."

"How many suspects are we talking about?"

"There are fourteen former black commandos who live in the metro area and fit the description of the assassin that killed Downs."

McMahon did the math. "That's going to take a lot of agents to run twenty-four-hour surveillance on fourteen people. What about the other commandos that are going to come up on the general's list?"

"What I think we should do is have you get solid surveillance set up on the fourteen former black commandos and let the Agency handle the other names that come up on the general's list. When all of your agents are in place, and all of my surveillance people are in place, then you can start beating the bush."

McMahon nodded. "And then we sit back and watch who talks to whom."

"Exactly."

"Do you have enough people to run that many surveillance teams?" asked McMahon. "We have to be talking about at least fifty suspects."

"We have enough assets," Kennedy said with a slight smirk on her face.

"Seriously?"

"We conduct our surveillance a little differently than you do."

McMahon shook his head and said, "I don't even want to know what you're going to do." He looked to General Heaney. "I'm going to need the complete dossiers of the fourteen guys on the probable list. I would also like the names of their commanding officers while they were in the service." Turning back to Kennedy, McMahon asked, "How long will it take you to get your people in place?"

"Depending on how many names come up, we should have everything ready to go by Friday morning."

"I'll call Brian and get everything rolling on my end, and, Irene, you do . . ." McMahon waved his hand in the air. "I don't want to know what you're doing. Just please be careful and don't end up on the front page of the *Post*."

CHAPTER 29

THE small Cessna flew along the southeast ridge of the Appalachian Mountain Range. Autumn colors painted the mountains beneath. Dotted among the rich reds, oranges, and yellows, tall Georgia pines jutted into the sky. Not a cloud was in sight, and the sun added an extra intensity to the full mix of colors below. They passed over a mountaintop, and a town farther up the valley came into sight. Seamus pointed and said, "There she is."

Brasstown, Georgia, was a small town about one and a half hours north of Atlanta that was nestled in a valley at the southern end of the Appalachians. From the far end of the valley they could barely make out two church steeples and a water tower that broke above the trees. As they neared, other buildings and streets became visible.

"The airstrip is out on the southern end of town," said Seamus, who banked the plane farther to the southeast and came in for a sweeping pass. The airstrip was cut right out of the tree line. Passing over it, Seamus took note of the direction the bright orange wind sock was pointing and came back around for a landing. He lined up his approach with a slight allowance for the crosswind and came in low above the trees. When he reached the clearing, he throttled back and let the plane float down onto the grass strip. She bounced once and then settled in, rolling to the end of the runway. An old, rusty hangar was the only structure in sight, and next to it was a Dodge pickup. Leaning against the hood was a man in boots, jeans, a red-and-black flannel shirt, and green John Deere hat. Seamus cut the engine and shut everything down. He and Michael got out of the plane, and the man by the pickup approached. Seamus met him halfway and they embraced, slapping each other on the back.

Seamus turned and said, "Michael, you remember Augie, don't you?"

Michael stuck out his hand. "It's been a while. Good to see you again, sir."

"Good to see you, Michael." Jackson stared at him for a moment and said, "God, you look just like your grandfather." Michael smiled and Augie asked, "Things have been pretty hectic in Washington lately, haven't they?"

"Yes."

Augie gestured toward the rear of the truck. "Let's go sit down. My old legs don't work so well anymore." Augie led them to the back of the truck, where he lowered the tailgate. He and Seamus sat and Michael stood with his arms folded across his chest. Augie pulled out a pipe and a bag of tobacco. He filled the bowl and offered the bag to Seamus.

While Augie packed his pipe, he said, "I've been doing a lot of thinking since I got your call last night, Seamus. In fact, I've been doing a lot of thinking since this whole thing started. Kind of a professional curiosity I guess you'd call it." He put the packing tool back in his pocket and pulled out a lighter. "Michael, did your grandfather tell you what I used to do for the CIA?"

"A little."

Augie lit the lighter and held the flame over the bowl, sucking on the pipe until the packed tobacco caught fire. Exhaling the smoke, he moved the pipe to the corner of his mouth and said, "Well, I'll give you the short version. After the war, I stayed in the

Corps and went to work for Naval Intelligence back in Washington. Several years later, when the CIA was formed, I was hired and sent to work at our Paris embassy. I spent my first fifteen years in Europe and then was brought back to Langley, where I became kind of a roving analyst on Russo-European intelligence issues. During my time at Langley, I was also part of a special group that planned covert operations." Jackson took several deep puffs. "I think I might have some information that could help you, but before I go any further, I'd like to ask a few questions."

Michael nodded his head and said, "Shoot."

"Where did you hear that there is a second group responsible for the murders of Olson and Turnquist?"

"I really can't say."

"You mean you won't." Jackson exhaled a puff of smoke and kept his eyes fixed on Michael's. "Why are you talking to me and not the FBI?"

"The FBI has this information. I'd like to do a little searching on my own."

Augie thought about the answer over several puffs of his pipe and then asked, "Why?"

"Erik Olson was a good friend."

"That's the only reason?" Jackson stared into Michael's eyes and waited for an answer.

Michael looked to Seamus for a moment and then back at Augie. "Yes."

"You're a bad liar, Michael. Just like your grandfather." Augie looked at Seamus and smiled. Then, looking down at the ground, he said, "I suppose neither of you have any idea who is behind the first four assassinations?" Michael shook his head. In a cynical tone Augie said, "I didn't think you would." Augie bobbed his chin up and down. "Well, I have a hunch who might have been involved, but before we get to that, I have some information that I think you will find interesting. I'm going to tell you a story about something I took part in while I was at the Agency, but first I have to give you a little background information.

"In the late fifties and early sixties I was the CIA's station chief at our Paris embassy. Tensions between us and the Soviet Union were running hot. There was a very real threat that the Soviets might wage a conventional war and try to take Western Europe. All along the Iron Curtain, NATO forces were outgunned almost five to one in tanks, artillery, and troop strength. Our military planners thought the best way to deter the Soviet Union from any aggressive action was to deploy tactical nuclear weapons in Western Europe. Our NATO allies agreed, and the missiles were moved into place. The message to the Soviet Union was simple. If you initiate any military action toward Western Europe, we will retaliate with a tactical nuclear strike. This policy worked perfectly until the early sixties, when France started to get goofy on us.

"There was a group of politicians in the French parliament who wanted all U.S. nuclear missiles removed from French soil. There were even a few who wanted all U.S. military personnel removed. These ingrates started to attract quite a following, holding protests outside the gates of our military bases we had over there and making more and more speeches demanding that we leave. The writing on the wall was clear. France had a history of being one of our most fickle allies—never mind that fifteen years earlier we had kicked the Nazis out of their country for them. From the president down, our political leadership was furious that France could be so ungrateful. We were given the go-ahead by Langley to initiate clandestine action against the leaders of this anti-U.S. movement. Our orders were to find a way to make them change their minds. Over a period of about six months we managed to bribe several of them and blackmail a few more. We were not successful, however, with the core leaders of the movement. After exhausting all efforts, Langley sent a man to Paris who was a specialist of sorts. But, before I get to that, are you familiar with the French Algerian conflict?"

"A little," answered Michael.

Augie took several puffs on his pipe. "Well, back in the late fifties the French military was immersed in a war with revolutionary Algerian forces who wanted independence from France. This war waged on for several years, and although they suffered some high casualties early on, the French military eventually put down the uprising. Throughout the war there were certain fringe members of the French parliament who were demanding Algeria be granted independence." Augie paused and raised his eyebrows. "These politicians also happened to be the same ones protesting against U.S. nuclear weapons on French soil.

"Well, the French military had done their job. They had suffered significant casualties and fought a bloody war with the rebels. With the conflict all but over and the rebels on the run, the French parliament and President de Gaulle did something that shocked everyone. They granted Algeria independence and ordered the French military out. At the time there were over a quarter of a million French nationals living in Algeria.

"This decision completely alienated the French military from the country's political leadership. And it so infuriated a group of commanders who had fought in Algeria that they deserted and formed a paramilitary group called the OAS." Augie paused to see if Michael was with him and then continued. "The OAS went underground in Algeria and France and initiated a violent commando war with the French political leadership and the leaders of the Algerian liberation movement. They started blowing up bombs and assassinating politicians left and right. They even made several attempts on President de Gaulle.

"Just after the first OAS attempt on de Gaulle's life, this specialist arrived from Washington. I was instructed to give him whatever assistance he needed. I met him at a safe house that we had in Paris and found out he was a covert-operations expert. This man had a brilliant but simple plan. The two most vocal critics of our nuclear

weapons being on French soil were also two of the most vocal pro-
ponents of Algerian independence. This covert-operations specialist's plan was to assassinate them and make it look like it was the
work of the OAS. It took us about two months to plan the whole
thing, and then we got the green light from Washington."

"Did it work?"

Augie nodded his head and puffed on his pipe.

Michael asked, "The CIA assassinated two elected officials in
an allied country?"

"Yes. Michael, you have to understand things were a lot different back then. The stakes were considerably higher than they are
today, and the spying business was a far deadlier game."

Michael shrugged his shoulders. "I'm not into revisionism, and
I'm not in much of a position to judge you."

Augie rubbed the end of his pipe with his thumb. "Do you understand why I told you that story?"

"I think so."

"What would your reaction be if I told you I think I know who
might be behind the assassinations of Olson and Turnquist?"

Michael shifted his weight from one foot to the other. "I would
be very interested to hear what you have to say."

"The man that came up with the idea to use the OAS as a cover
went on to head the Black Operations Directorate of the CIA from
the midsixties until just several years ago. Have you ever heard of
Arthur Higgins?"

Michael frowned and said, "Yes . . . I thought he was retired."

"*Forced out* would be a more precise term."

"Why?"

"There are a lot of reasons, but the short version is that he and
Director Stansfield had some issues."

Michael looked at Seamus and then back at Augie. "Where are
you going with this?"

"I think Arthur is behind the assassinations of Turnquist and Olson."

"I hope you're basing this on more than the story you just told me."

"Oh, I am. There's a lot more."

Michael's chin dropped down into his chest, and he pinched the bridge of his nose between his thumb and forefinger. Without looking up, he asked, "What's the motive for Higgins to kill Turnquist and Erik?"

"I'm not sure about Turnquist, but Arthur had a personal score to settle with Olson."

"What score?" Michael looked up.

"Arthur was next in line for the top job at the CIA when Director Carlyle stepped down four years ago. Everybody thought the job was Arthur's, including me. That was until your old boss stepped in."

"Erik?"

"Yep. You must remember, when all of this happened, you were on Olson's staff."

"Of course I do, but I don't remember Higgins's name being mentioned. All I remember is the president nominating Stansfield and that he was confirmed with bipartisan support."

Augie grinned. "Stansfield was the only person nominated because your boss, Chairman Olson, went to the president and told him if Arthur's name was sent to the Intelligence Committee, he would do everything in his power to block the nomination. Olson told the president if the nomination was lucky enough to get out of his committee and make it to the Senate floor for a vote, he would resign his chairmanship in protest." Augie pointed the end of his pipe at Michael. "Rather than risk the embarrassment, the president nominated Stansfield, and Arthur missed his chance at the one job he had worked his entire life to get."

Michael frowned. "You think he would kill Erik over that?"

"You've never met Arthur, have you?"

"No."

"He's the most evil son of a bitch I've ever known."

Michael skeptically shook his head. "I'm having a hard time buying this."

"Michael, it runs much deeper than what I've told you. For over thirty years Arthur ran the most secretive part of the Agency. He answered to no one. Directors came and went and not one of them dared cross him. Arthur always hid behind internal-secrecy rules and a need-to-know basis. In the early years he received a blank check for his operations, but then, when the House and the Senate implemented oversight committees, he was left with the option of telling them what he was doing or having his funding cut. Arthur was not involved in the type of things he could talk about in public. He didn't even tell people in the Agency what he was up to, and he sure as hell wasn't going to walk into a committee room and explain himself to a roomful of men who were about as good at keeping secrets as a gossip columnist. Over the years his funding shrank significantly, but his operating budget continued to grow. He started to finance his operations through various illegal endeavors."

"Why didn't someone reel him in?" asked Seamus.

"Senator Olson did."

"I can't believe I never heard any of this from Erik."

"Your boss was a very reasonable man, and he understood the value of the Agency. He was a realist, and he knew that going after Arthur through hearings or an investigation would do more harm than good. Instead, he worked behind the scenes to try and keep him as honest as possible." Augie tapped the bowl of his pipe on the tailgate and the spent tobacco fell to the ground in clumps. "Let's not lose sight of something here. The other reason Arthur was tolerated was that he served a very valuable purpose. When things got ugly, he was called in to clean up. He handled all of the stuff that no one else wanted to. He took care of the Agency's dirty work."

Michael thought about it for a minute. "Can you be sure he's responsible for this?"

"I can't be one hundred percent sure." Augie dumped some more tobacco into the bowl of the pipe and packed it down. "There are a lot of other reasons why I think Arthur killed Senator Olson and Congressman Turnquist. . . . I have my reasons for not wanting to discuss them, just like you have yours for not wanting to discuss your source."

"Why don't you go to the FBI with this?"

Augie lit his pipe and frowned. "The FBI can't do anything."

"Why not? All we have to do is tell them what you just said, and they'll initiate an investigation."

Augie smiled. "And they'll find nothing, and I'll end up with a bullet in the back of my head. Michael, I don't think you understand who we are talking about. Arthur is a very brilliant and ruthless person. He's assassinated people all over the world, and he hasn't come close to getting caught. Not once. . . . Besides, I can't tell the FBI anything. I'm bound by the national secrecy act."

"Well, I can."

"Michael, I don't think you understand. If you go to the FBI, Arthur will find out. He has sources everywhere. After he finds out it was you who went to the FBI, he will very subtly threaten your life or the life of someone close to you. Or maybe he'll just have you killed. He is not a man to be toyed with."

"Why are you telling me all of this if you don't think I should do anything?"

"I expect you to do something, but before I get to that, I have to ask you some questions." Augie sucked on his pipe for a while. "When Downs, Fitzgerald, Koslowski, and Basset were killed, I wasn't real torn up. I hated everything they stood for, and I was glad to see them gone. I've thought for a long time that the crusty old windbags in Washington needed to be shaken up." Augie paused, contemplating how to phrase his next statement. "I have a good idea who was behind the first four assassinations."

Augie shifted his weight and put one foot on the ground. He looked at Seamus and said, "I could ask a more direct question, but I don't want to be lied to, so I'll skirt the issue slightly. If you really had to . . . could you get in touch with someone who is involved in the original assassinations?"

After a moment of silence Seamus said, "Yes."

Michael's face remained passive.

"Good." Augie stood and hobbled to the cab of the truck. "I've got something I'd like you to pass on to them for me." He reached behind the seat, pulled out a large legal file, and walked back to the tailgate. Sitting down with an owly look in his eye, he said, "I think I have everything figured out, but it's probably better to leave certain things unsaid." Augie handed the file to Seamus. "Please pass this on to your revolutionary friends."

"What's in it?" asked Michael.

"Remember how I told you when I was at the Agency I was kind of a roving analyst? I was also a troubleshooter of sorts. Right before I left the Agency, Director Stansfield asked me to draw up some contingency plans for a . . . delicate operation."

Seamus looked at the file and then up at his old friend. "What kind of an operation?"

"One that no one other than Stansfield and I were to know about. . . . After Stansfield took over, Arthur became even more reclusive. Stansfield knew that he would have to force Arthur to resign and became increasingly worried about how he would react. There were a lot of concerns that he might turn on us and sell information abroad or use things that he knew to blackmail Stansfield and the Agency. He was a loose cannon, and no one knew which direction he would fire, so Stansfield did the prudent thing and asked me to draw up a plan to neutralize him."

"The folder contains the plan?" asked Michael.

"Most of it. There's detailed schematics of his house on the Chesapeake. It gives a rundown on his security system, where its strengths and weaknesses are, how many guards he has and what their rotation is. The plan is a year and a half old, so I'm not sure how much has changed. I do know that he still spends almost all of his time at the house. He has a lot of enemies, which has made him extremely paranoid over the years."

"Why aren't you going to Stansfield with this?"

"Arthur is still very well connected at the Agency. No one really knows how well for sure, but there is a chance he would be fore-warned about any plans against him."

"Is that the real reason or are you just looking for someone to do your dirty work?"

"Nope. I'll be honest with you, Michael. I would like to have Arthur Higgins killed. There was a time when he was good for our country, but for the last fifteen years he's been out of control. When he left the Agency, he was warned to stay out of the intelligence business. Since then he has been cautioned by Stansfield more than once to keep his nose out of the Agency's business. I hesitate to take this to Director Stansfield for the reasons I already gave and for the fact that Arthur has a lot of contacts at the National Security Agency. If anything happens to Arthur, they will suspect the CIA." Augie looked up at the sky for a second. "As to why I'm dumping this on your lap . . . well . . . you gave him the opportunity to kill Olson and Turnquist, and in my book that means you should be the one to stop him."

Michael stared unwaveringly at Augie and said, "I did nothing. I'm just trying to clean up the mess."

Augie looked at Seamus. "This is your doing?"

"Yes. Can I count on you to stay quiet?"

"Yes. I happen to think that what you're doing is about twenty years overdue." The old spy stuck his hands under his armpits.

"We've killed politicians in other countries that were far less of a threat to our national security than our own leaders. Don't you think that during all my years as a covert-operations specialist I thought about doing in America what I was doing abroad?"

Michael nodded, remembering that Scott Coleman had said the exact same thing to him a year ago. Michael changed the subject back to Higgins. "What makes you think we can get to Arthur?"

"I assume that you have some professionals helping you." Augie paused and held up his hands. "I don't want to know who they are or what their background is. The less I know about that the better. If they could kill Fitzgerald, Downs, Koslowski, and Basset and vanish without a trace, I assume they're pretty good. Arthur has one habit that makes him vulnerable. You'll find it in the file."

Michael held up the file. "I'm interested to see what's in here."

"I would urge you not to waste any time. Arthur may not be done killing."

CHAPTER 30

McMAHON was back in the Joint Special Operations Command's conference room at the Pentagon, eating a microwaved container of lasagna that was more than a little salty. His entire afternoon had been spent meeting with Harvey Wilcox, the deputy director of the FBI's Counterterrorism Department; Madeline Nanny, the deputy director of the FBI's Counter Espionage Department; and Director Roach. Both departments had the equipment and personnel to run surveillance on the fourteen black former commandos who were living in the D.C. metro area. Neither Roach nor McMahon had to ask for the full cooperation of the two deputy directors. Both understood the priority of the task that had been handed to them. Nanny had more available assets, so she took nine of the fourteen dossiers and Wilcox took the other five. They estimated they could initiate surveillance during the next twenty-four hours, and depending on the individual movements of the suspects, they could have airtight surveillance established within seventy-two hours. The total number of agents to be involved was calculated at 140.

McMahon finished explaining the details of the surveillance to Kennedy and General Heaney right about the time he finished eating the lasagna that he knew would give him heartburn. He slid the Styrofoam box off to the side and asked General Heaney if he had any Tums.

The general produced a roll and tossed it across the table. A moment later one of the general's aides entered the room and handed him a computer printout and a cover sheet. Heaney thanked the young officer and glanced over the cover sheet. "Our computer ran a search for any former commandos living within a hundred miles of Washington, D.C. It turned up ninety-four SEALs, eighty-one Green Berets, and sixty-eight Delta Force commandos."

McMahon's face twisted into a painful look. "That's over two hundred possible suspects."

"Yes, but that was before we directed the computer to narrow the search to only commandos that had served with the fourteen black commandos."

"What did that bring the numbers down to?"

The general glanced down at the sheet. "Twenty-six Green Berets and nineteen Deltas."

Kennedy peered over the top of her glasses. "What happened to all the SEALs?"

The general read over the summary for a moment. "There are only two former SEALs who fit the description of the assassin that killed Downs, and they both live in San Diego."

While Kennedy wrestled with that piece of information, McMahon asked, "Where are we going to get the resources to tail forty-five people around the clock?" Looking to Kennedy, he asked, "Irene, do you have the manpower to handle this?" Kennedy was staring off into space, and McMahon repeated the question. Kennedy still didn't answer, so McMahon snapped his fingers. "Earth to Irene, come in."

Kennedy's eyes came back into focus. "Excuse me."

"Do you need a break?"

"No, I'm fine. I was just thinking about something else."

McMahon repeated, "Do you have the assets to conduct around-the-clock surveillance on forty-five suspects?"

"Yes."

"How?" asked McMahon with a disbelieving look on his face.

Kennedy started to give her answer, then stopped, saying, "You don't want to know."

"No, I suppose I don't."

"General Heaney," said Kennedy, "would it be possible for me to take a look at all ninety-four files of the SEALs that live in the D.C area?"

"Why?"

"I have a hunch."

McMahon's ears perked up at the word *hunch*. He believed strongly in intuition and hunches. "Let's hear it."

"I'm not comfortable with dumping ninety-four potential suspects based on a piece of information that I'm not sure I trust."

"What piece of information are you referring to?" asked McMahon.

"The black assassin in the park. These people have done everything perfectly with one exception: they exposed the guy in the park when we all agree the correct way to kill Downs would have been with a concealed rifle shot." Kennedy took her glasses off and rubbed her eyes. "We have let this one piece of possibly flawed evidence steer our entire investigation in a very specific direction. Based on this one piece of information we have excluded all SEALs from our investigation."

"That's what investigations are all about, Irene," said McMahon. "You analyze evidence and narrow your search."

"That's assuming the evidence is untainted." Kennedy rose and started to pace. "There is only one logical reason for them to put him in the park, and I can't believe I didn't see it earlier. They put him there because they wanted him to be seen."

"Why would they want him to be seen?" asked Heaney.

"To throw us off. What if the guy wasn't black? What if they made him look like he was black?"

"Why would they want us to think he was black?"

McMahon saw where Kennedy was going. "If they were SEALs, they would." The room fell silent while the pieces fell into place for Heaney. McMahon stood and rolled his sleeves up. "General, I think we had better take a look at those files. While we're doing that, I'll have my people initiate surveillance of the fourteen black commandos. Irene, you get your people moving on the other commandos, and we'll have to consider investigating any SEALs on a case-by-case basis."

An irritating noise broke the silence of the predawn morning. A hand reached through the darkness toward the red, blinking digital numbers and found the alarm clock. A second later the noise was silenced. O'Rourke rolled over and wrapped himself around Liz. The previous evening had been a quiet one. Liz had finished writing her column about nine and came over with a movie. Luckily for Michael, she was tired and not in the mood for conversation. Thirty minutes into the video they were both asleep.

Michael was trying his best to make things seem normal and was, for the most part, succeeding. It helped that Liz was busy with her job. Michael couldn't get Arthur Higgins out of his mind. After returning from Georgia, he had gone to the Congressional Library to see what he could find out about the former head of the CIA's most secretive branch. He came up with nothing, which only added to the mystery.

Michael brushed Liz's hair aside and kissed her naked shoulder. She turned her head slightly, and he kissed her cheek. O'Rourke kissed her one more time and got out of bed. Grabbing a pair of sweatpants from a hook on the door, Michael put them on and headed downstairs. Duke met him at the bottom of the stairs and followed him into the kitchen. The coffeemaker was filled to the top and started. All of his hunting gear was kept in the basement. After descending another flight of stairs, Michael opened the closet and put on a pair of wool socks, khaki pants, a blue flannel shirt, and a pair of boots. The rest of his gear was kept out at the cabin along with several shotguns. By the time he got back up to the kitchen, the pot was done brewing. He poured the whole thing into a large thermos and filled a travel mug for the road. Duke was at his feet stretching and yawning. Before leaving, O'Rourke went back upstairs, set the alarm clock for 7 A.M., and kissed Liz on the cheek.

Down in the small garage of the brownstone, Michael loaded Duke into the back of the truck and opened the garage door. Less than five minutes later, he pulled up in front of his brother's house. Tim, Seamus, and Tim's chocolate Lab, Cleo, climbed into the truck, and they headed toward the cabin. Against Michael's wishes Seamus had told Tim everything that had happened over the past two weeks.

For the majority of the drive they discussed the information they had learned from Augie. When they arrived at the cabin, Coleman was already there. He was waiting inside at the kitchen table. The O'Rourkes pulled up chairs, and the coffee mugs were filled to the brim.

When everyone was settled in, Coleman eagerly asked, "What have you found out?"

"Have you ever heard of a man named Arthur Higgins?"

Coleman squinted. "Yes."

"Have you ever met him?"

"No."

"What do you know about him?"

"He's an old spook over at the CIA. He handles a lot of dark operations and has a reputation as a man you don't screw around with."

"What do you mean by dark operations?" asked Tim.

"Covert operations that are funded from nongovernment sources and run without the official knowledge of the president and the Intelligence Committee."

"Have you ever been involved in one of these operations?"

"No." Coleman shook his head. "They use mercenaries . . . former commandos. These things can't be connected in any way to our government. The whole reason they are run as a dark op is because the spooks know they could never get official approval. They have to have complete deniability if anything goes wrong. The money can't be traced back to the U.S. and neither can the soldiers. Before the SEALs or any other American military personnel can be sent into a foreign country to conduct a covert operation, the CIA or the Pentagon has to get approval from a ranking member of the Intelligence Committee and the president. Dark operations completely circumvent the chain of command. It's a strange world, very secretive and risky. Everything is done unofficially and without a paper trail. All you ever hear about these people are whispers and rumors. I actually know some former SEALs who have worked for Higgins."

"Do you think you could talk to them and find out what they know about him?" asked Michael.

"I could, but Higgins is the type of person you don't just start asking questions about, or you might end up as shark bait."

"I thought you SEALs were a tight group. Can't you ask them a few questions without raising too much attention?"

"Maybe, maybe not. This isn't like calling up an old high school buddy and asking him about a girl he used to date. These are serious people and they don't like questions. They prefer to stay anonymous and quiet."

"What in the hell are a couple of former SEALs doing working for a guy like Higgins?" asked Tim.

"What do you expect them to do when they leave the service . . . go sell used cars or program computers? We are trained to do a very specific job, and trained to do it better than anyone else in the world. If you're a SEAL, you're better than ninety-nine point nine percent of all the soldiers who have ever laced up a boot. You are the best of the best, and do you know what you get paid? . . . You max out at about forty grand a year. Then one day you leave the service and you're confronted with two options. You go to work in the private sector in a boring nine-to-five job and get paid about the same as when you were in the military, or you go to work for some guy like Higgins and get paid six figures plus for working about fifty days a year. And guys like Higgins aren't the only people who want you. Big-time drug dealers, oil sheikhs, third-world governments, international bankers, they're all willing to pay big bucks to have a SEAL on their security staff. I know guys that are getting paid a half a million a year to sit around and play bodyguard. For a lot of these guys it's a status thing to be able to say their bodyguard is a SEAL. In the Middle East our reputation alone scares the shit out of people."

"I understand your point, but I thought you guys had an honor code," said Tim.

"We do, but we're not an infallible fraternity. We have our bad apples just like any other organization. The reality is there are people who are willing to kill for money, and once they cross that line, they are no longer part of our brotherhood . . . they are assassins and mercenaries."

"So you don't think it would be wise to start asking questions about Higgins?" asked Michael.

"From what I've heard about the man, no, I don't. What has got you so interested in him?"

"Seamus and I took a little trip down to Georgia yesterday to talk to Augie Jackson."

"Seamus's friend who used to work for the CIA?"

"Yes. . . . Augie told us some pretty interesting stories about Higgins. He's convinced that he's responsible for the killing of Erik and Congressman Turnquist."

Coleman grew cautious. "So he buys into the idea that there are two separate groups doing the killing?"

"Yes."

"Did he ask any questions about who the first group might be?"

"Yes."

Coleman stared at Michael for a long time. "You told him, didn't you?" Coleman looked to Seamus, and neither he nor Michael answered the question. The former SEAL shook his head and swore.

"He only knows that I'm involved," said Seamus. "Scott, we can trust Augie."

Coleman looked at his watch. "Well, we'll know the answer to that any minute. If you hear any choppers overhead, we can all kiss our asses good-bye."

"Scott, he believes in what we're doing. He hated Fitzgerald and Koslowski more than we did, and he was very convincing with the stuff he told us about Arthur."

"Why does he think Higgins killed Erik and Turnquist?"

Michael spent the next several minutes telling Coleman Augie's story. He relayed the story of the covert mission that Arthur had masterminded to get rid of the French politicians back in the early sixties and then went on to explain Arthur's hatred for Senator Olson. Coleman asked few questions. Michael told him how Arthur was forced out of the Agency by Stansfield and ordered to cease any involvement in intelligence and national security issues. When Michael was done recounting Augie's story, he asked Coleman what he thought.

"The man has the power and resources to pull it off, and as I told you several days ago, whoever blew up Erik's limo has to have some real connections. They had less than a week to put that operation together." Coleman shrugged his shoulders. "It wouldn't surprise me in the slightest if he had a hand in this, but we don't have the intel or the capability to know for sure."

"I know, but we have to do something."

Coleman tapped the side of his mug. "I really don't think it's a good idea to ask any more questions about this guy. The FBI's investigation is kicking into high gear. It's important that we act normal and don't draw any attention to ourselves." Coleman pointed at the three O'Rourkes. "You guys can get away with a lot more than I can. They're not going to come after you, but sooner or later they're gonna come knocking on my door."

Seamus thought about what Coleman had said for a moment and then asked, "What about taking him out?"

"Higgins?"

"Yes."

"In principle I don't have a problem with it. From what I've heard he's the snake of snakes, but I'd like to be a little more sure that he was behind this before we go to that extreme. Besides, I'm not even sure we could get to him. My guess is that he has some pretty tight security around him."

Michael slid the dossier across the table. "Augie gave this to us before we left. It's a full profile of Arthur's movements and security measures. It breaks down his estate's security system step-by-step and describes, in detail, the endeavors he has continued to be involved in since he was forced out of the Agency."

Coleman opened the file and started thumbing through the pages. After several minutes Coleman looked at Michael. "You got this from this guy that used to work at the CIA?"

"Yes."

"Where did he get it?"

"He compiled it for Director Stansfield."

"They were thinking about taking him out, weren't they?"

"Yes."

"Unbelievable."

"In the back," Seamus said, "there's a section describing his business dealings and continued meddling in the CIA's business. If you turn to page four of the section, you'll find a highlighted para-graph that you're not going to like."

Coleman flipped to the back of the file and scanned the para-graph. It stated that Higgins was believed to be involved with a group of black marketers who were stealing high-tech U.S. weap-onry from manufacturers and military bases and selling it abroad through a Middle East arms dealer that had known sympathies for anti-American regimes. Like any other U.S. soldier, Coleman hated the thought that he or his men might be killed by an American-made weapon, especially a high-tech weapon that wasn't supposed to be sold.

Coleman finished reading the paragraph and looked up at the former Recon Marine sitting across the table. "Michael, I think you and I should go take a look at his estate this evening."

On the top floor of the residential side of the White House was a large room that faced south called the Solarium. The room sat above the Eisenhower Balcony and had large plate-glass windows running from the floor to the ceiling. Stevens liked the room be-cause it was the brightest in the White House, and since he was starting to feel like a caged animal, he decided to move his lunch meeting up to the top floor, where he could actually see beyond the gates of the compound. He was scheduled to meet with the leaders of his party to go over the legislative agenda for Monday's recon-vening of the House and Senate.

Stevens looked out across the South Lawn toward the Wash-ington Monument. The large green personnel carriers and tanks were clearly visible from his panoramic perch. "God, it's only been four days since we got back from Camp David, and I already feel trapped." Stevens shook his head at a flight of four green Cobra gun-ships working their way eastward across the Mall from the Lincoln Monument to the Capitol. The sight of all the military equipment so openly visible in the heart of Washington made him wonder if the decision to bring in the military was wise. "Stu, are you sure this is the right thing to do?"

Garret was sitting at a small desk feverishly writing. Without looking up he asked, "Is what the right thing to do?"

Stevens waved his arm in front of him, gesturing toward the Mall. "Bringing in such a strong military presence. I mean, do we really need tanks in front of the Washington Monument? It just . . . it just makes me look so harsh. Like I'm a dictator."

"That's what we need right now, Jim. I've talked to every pollster from New York to L.A. over the last three days, and they're all telling me the same thing. The American people want law and order returned to their capital. The voters are scared and they're looking to you for guidance and leadership. Bringing the military in will portray the right message. You'll be seen as a strong and decisive leader."

"I know, but what about what you said initially? That we'd look like the Chinese if we brought in the tanks?"

"Shit, that was before they killed the damn Speaker of the House in broad daylight and tried to blow us out of the sky. Things have gotten much more serious than they were after that first morning. The voters are scared. At first they got off on the thrill of seeing a couple of dinosaurs like Fitzgerald and Koslowski get assassinated. That initial thrill is gone, and they want a return to law and order. They'll turn on their TVs when they sit down to eat dinner tonight, and they'll see a stone faced soldier sitting on the turret of a tank and they'll be happy they have a strong president who's willing to take action in a time of crisis. Trust me, Jim, I know what I'm doing on this one."

CHAPTER 31

COLEMAN and the O'Rourkes stayed at the cabin until almost 10 A.M., talking about which course of action to take with Arthur. After the O'Rourkes left for D.C., Coleman spent most of the afternoon checking out the neighborhood where Arthur lived. From his SEAL training, Coleman had developed a knack for memorizing maps. He drove down every street within five miles of Arthur's estate, checking for unmarked service drives and paths that led from the road down to the water, making mental notes of anything and everything that might be useful. Before taking any action against Arthur he wanted to be completely familiar with the neighborhood. The closer he got to Arthur's estate the more details he took in: which houses had security cameras, which ones had Beware of Dog signs, and which ones had guardhouses. He only drove past Arthur's gate once. Anything more than that might arouse some suspicion. Besides, he was more worried about the houses that bordered Arthur's. Augie's file stated that neither had high-tech security systems. Both had security company signs at the end of the driveway, but neither had gates or fences, which probably meant the houses were wired but not the grounds.

After his sight-seeing tour, Coleman drove out to Sparrows Point, just south of Baltimore on the Patapsco River. The large industrial yard was once entirely occupied by Bethlehem Steel, but with the decline of the U.S. steel industry it was now partitioned into extremely cheap warehouse and waterfront dock space. The SEAL Demolition and Salvage Corporation was located in a dirty, dank building that faced Old Road Bay on the east end of the point. The lease was a meager one thousand dollars a month for one thousand square feet of finished office space and another ten thousand square feet of bulk warehouse. Coleman pulled his Ford Explorer into the large warehouse and got out. Earlier in the day he had called his only two employees and told them to meet him at the office around 4 P.M. They were standing next to the office checking diving equipment when he arrived. Dan Stroble and Kevin Hackett were also former SEALs. They had served on Coleman's SEAL team for three years and had left the Navy about six months after their commander.

Since the inception of the SEAL Demolition and Salvage Corporation four months earlier, they had only done one job, for British Petroleum. BP had quietly contracted to have one of their abandoned oil rigs in the North Atlantic demolished. Somehow, word had leaked out, and Greenpeace was mobilizing a group of protesters to occupy the rig and prevent the demolition. They wanted BP to dismantle the rig girder by girder. To the executives at BP the decision was simple: demolish the rig at a cost of two hundred thousand dollars or dismantle it piece by piece at an estimated cost of $5 million.

BP scrambled to put together the demolition team and blow the rig before Greenpeace could mobilize. BP's best estimate was that they could have all of the charges in place and ready to go within forty-eight hours. They found out that a boat loaded with Greenpeace activists was docked in Reykjavík, Iceland, and set to leave port the following morning. The activists would arrive at the rig by noon the next day and storm the platform, creating an international media event that would bring public and political pressure down on BP to dismantle the rig. BP needed to slow the protesters down so they would have enough time to blow the rig.

The vice president of operations at BP was told to find a way to stop the activists from reaching the rig without making it look as if BP had had a hand in it. The executive made several calls to his contacts in America and Britain and found out that a new, upstart company in Maryland might be perfect for the job. The man called Coleman and explained the situation to him. He had twenty hours to get to Reykjavík and stop the boat from leaving the harbor. The man didn't care how it was done, just so long as no one was hurt.

Coleman had a rough idea of how much it would cost BP if they had to dismantle the rig, so he said he'd do the job for three hundred thousand dollars. The BP exec agreed, and Coleman, Stroble, and Hackett were on the next flight out of Dulles with their diving gear.

They landed in Reykjavík just before sundown and were down at the pier by eleven that evening. During their tenure as SEALs, they had spent countless hours swimming around dirty harbors attaching explosives to hulls and disabling propellers and rudders. The only thing that was difficult about the mission was the temperature of the water. Even with their neoprene wet suits they could stay in the water for no more than fifteen minutes at a time. They took turns swimming over to the ship from a berth about two hundred feet away. Using an acetylene torch, they cut away at the U-joint where the driveshaft met the propeller. The boat would be able to maintain steerage and prop speed up to about ten knots. Anything more than that and the laws of physics would take effect. The increased torque on the propeller would cause the sabotaged joint that connected the driveshaft to the prop to snap.

They sat at a café the next morning and wagered on whether the ship would make it out of the harbor. Coleman didn't feel guilty about the job. He'd been around the ocean his whole life and had a deep respect for and healthy fear of it. Sending a couple thousand tons of steel to the ocean floor wouldn't harm it a bit. As they drank coffee and waited for their 8 A.M. flight back to Washington, a tug moved in and towed the ship out to the main channel. The lines were released and the ship was under way. A white froth churned up behind the stern of the boat as it headed for the open sea. It had just cleared the seawall when the frothy wake subsided and the ship stalled, turning sideways in the middle of the channel. An hour later, Coleman, Stroble, and Hackett were on their way back to Washington. Over the last month they had received two more offers for jobs, but they had told the prospective clients they were too busy to take the work.

Coleman slammed the door of his car and walked over to Stroble and Hackett. "How are you guys doing?"

"Great, sir. How about you?"

"Fine. Have you checked the messages?"

"Yep," answered Stroble. "There was nothing on the machine."

When Coleman asked if they'd checked the messages, he actually meant, have you checked the office and phones for bugs? They knew that eventually the FBI would put them under surveillance. They needed an alibi that would explain all of the time they'd spent together while planning for their mission, so with some seed money from Seamus they had started the SEAL Demolition and Salvage Corporation. They weren't the only retired SEALs living in D.C. who were working with each other. Coleman knew of two others a little older than him who ran a charter fishing operation out of Annapolis and had a sneaking suspicion that they did a little work for the CIA on the side. There were also several other groups of SEALs that ran security firms, providing bodyguards for diplomats and corporate executives. Coleman and Seamus had agreed that the key to not getting caught was making sure they afforded the FBI no hard evidence. That meant no fingerprints, no eyewitnesses, and no ballistics that would link them to the killings. They wore gloves during every phase of the operation and kept their faces concealed. The rifles used to kill Koslowski and Basset and the pistol used to kill Downs were now rusting at the bottom of the Chesapeake. No real evidence linked them to the murders. If the FBI came, all they would find would be three former SEALs trying to launch a new business venture.

Coleman went into the office and came back out saying, "Let's get the gear together. I want to take the boat down to Annapolis and do a bid on a project. If the weather stays nice, we might be able to get some fishing in on the way back. Let's pack up and shove off in about thirty minutes."

While Stroble and Hackett gathered up the diving gear, Coleman topped off the tanks on the boat. Within thirty minutes they were under way and headed for the Bay. They centered their conversation on inconsequential small talk until Stroble finished going over the boat with a sensor. Coleman stood behind the wheel on the flybridge and watched the movements of the ships and small vessels around them. He feared that the FBI might try to bug the office, his apartment, or his car, but that didn't scare him. Those could be detected, and if they were dumb enough to bug him, they would tip their hand. What he feared most was the use of directional microphones. The CIA had been using them for years, and the technology was getting better and better. A person could stand over three hundred feet away and eavesdrop on someone's conversation by merely pointing a microphone at them. The CIA had developed the technology to listen through walls and other hard materials where it was difficult to place a bug.

As they reached the open water of the Bay, Stroble and Hackett huddled next to Coleman on the flybridge. With the engines roaring, the wind rushing past, and not another ship within a mile, Coleman started to fill them in on the details of Seamus and Michael's meeting with Augie. Neither Stroble nor Hackett was surprised by the story. They'd heard the rumors about Higgins before, and it seemed well within the realm of possibilities that he was responsible for the murders of Olson, Turnquist, and their bodyguards. By the time they reached Annapolis, Coleman had given them all of the details regarding the meeting he'd had with the O'Rourkes.

They cruised south past Annapolis to Tolly Point, and Coleman headed for shore. He told Stroble and Hackett to stay below until they were back out in the Bay. The sun was setting in the west, and patches of gray clouds were moving in off the Atlantic. Rain would be welcomed but not crucial. Still atop the bridge, Coleman maneuvered his boat into the marina at the end of Tolly Point. He saw someone standing next to the gas pumps on the dock and raised his hand to block the low sun. Coleman swung the boat in and came up alongside the dock. Michael jumped on board holding a fishing pole and tackle box.

"Welcome aboard, Congressman. It looks like we're going to have a nice night for fishing. Stow your gear and grab us a couple of beers out of the cooler." Spinning the wheel around, Coleman headed back through the channel.

Michael set his gear down and flipped open a red cooler. Grabbing two beers, he climbed the ladder to the bridge and handed one to Coleman.

Coleman smiled and nodded. A second later they passed the no-wake buoys, and Coleman pushed the throttles down, gunning the engines. As the noise increased, Michael whispered, "Are Dan and Kevin here?"

"Yeah, they're below. I told them to stay there until we were out of sight. Did you have any trouble getting here?"

"No, as far as I could tell, no one followed me."

Coleman looked at his watch. It was 5:21 P.M. "The sun should be down in another fifteen minutes, and then we have to stop and pick up some equipment.... We should get there around seven P.M." Coleman hugged the coast as they headed south toward Thomas Point. The Bay was calm. A light breeze was coming in from the east, and the boat traffic was light. Most of the recreational boaters on the Chesapeake were done until next spring. The temperature was around fifty-eight degrees and dropping. He continued past Thomas Point for exactly 1.3 miles and turned due east, cutting across the main shipping channel of the Bay.

Stroble and Hackett, in the meantime, had changed out of their clothes and put on wet suits. Michael stood on the flybridge with a pair of binoculars and scanned their path for any ships. When they reached the other side of the channel, Coleman pulled the boat up next to one of the large red buoys that marked the shipping channel and dropped anchor. Stroble and Hackett had their diving gear on and were giving each other one last safety check, going over each other's equipment like pilots doing a preflight instrument check. Coleman and Michael stayed atop the flybridge and kept a lookout for the Coast Guard while Stroble and Hackett went over the side.

About five minutes later, they came back up with a large trunk. Michael and Coleman lifted the heavy container into the boat. It was five by four feet and about three feet high and was made out of dark green fiberglass. Coleman popped the hermetically sealed clasps and opened the trunk. Set in foam cutouts on the top section were six pairs of night-vision goggles. Coleman grabbed four of them and handed them to Michael. Next, he grabbed two handles and lifted the top section out of the container, revealing a cache of weapons also set in foam cutouts. Coleman snatched three MP-5 submachine guns and a sniper's rifle from the container along with silencers and ammunition clips. After closing the airtight trunk, he and Michael handed it back over the side to Stroble and Hackett. They took the trunk back down to the bottom and covered it with rocks.

When Stroble and Hackett were back on board, Coleman raised the anchor and headed back across the Bay on a southwesterly course. Stroble and Hackett checked all of the weapons to make sure they were clean and well oiled and then packed them into waterproof backpacks. When they were finished, Hackett took the helm so Michael and Coleman could get ready. Everyone was fitted with a waterproof radio and headset that was worn under their wet suits. About a half a mile from Curtis Point, Coleman took back the helm and slowed the boat to about ten knots. He pulled to within about a quarter of a mile from shore and turned south, counting the houses as he went. When they passed the sixth house in from the point, Coleman told Stroble and Hackett to put on their night-vision goggles and scan the ridgeline of the cliff and the docks for people.

The entire shoreline consisted of an elevated cliff that ranged from fifty to eighty feet in height. Arthur's estate sat in the middle of a small swale. The cliff on either side of his estate was about ten feet higher than it was in front of his. Stroble and Hackett announced that no one was in sight. Coleman continued for another four hundred feet and pulled to within thirty feet of shore, cutting the engines and dropping anchor. Before leaving the bridge, he turned off all of the running lights.

It was a good night for reconnaissance. What little moon there was, was sitting low in the night sky and partially obscured by clouds. Coleman gathered everyone close together for a radio check and quick briefing. He spoke in a low whisper. The acoustics of the water caused sound to travel much farther than people realized.

"All right, I'm Zeus; Michael is Apollo; Dan, you're Hermes; and Kevin, you're Cyclops." Hackett smiled at the code name, which referred to the sight on his sniper's rifle. "Everyone check your watches. I'm reading nineteen zero eight on my mark." Coleman waited for his watch to strike 7:08 P.M. and said, "Mark." Everyone synchronized their watches.

"Arthur's estate is loaded with motion sensors, laser trip wires, and tremor plates. There is no way we are going to sneak in there without being noticed. What I want to do tonight is get a better look at the two neighbors' yards and get a general feel for the layout. Kevin, I want you and Dan to scout out the neighbors to the north. As far as I can tell, their security systems are for their houses only, not the grounds. Make sure you check out the dock and the stairs leading up to the house before you use them. When you reach the top of the cliff, check out the fence that runs between Arthur's yard and the neighbor's. Kevin, as soon as possible I want you to find a spot in one of the big oak trees that run along the property line. If anything goes wrong, I want you to be in a position to give us cover if we need to bug out."

"What are my rules of engagement?" asked Hackett.

"I want to get out of here tonight without anyone knowing we were here."

"What if he steps out for one of his cigars, and I have him dead in my sights?"

Coleman pondered the question. "I'm tempted, but the answer is no. I don't want to rush into anything. We are here to gather information and get out." Michael, Hackett, and Stroble nodded. "If something goes wrong and one of his guards opens fire, take him out. Otherwise let's keep our fingers off the triggers. . . . One more thing, the wind is out of the east. Keep that in mind if they start patrolling with the dogs." Everyone nodded. "All right, be careful."

Stroble and Hackett sat down on the diving platform and put on their fins and diving masks. They stuck their snorkels in their mouths and slid into the water, quietly swimming away. Before Michael and Coleman got in, Coleman asked, "Do Recon Marines know how to swim?"

"No." Michael smiled. "I thought you were going to tow me in."

"Good one. Let's go." The two slid into the water and headed for shore. They sliced through the water using only a leg kick, the large black fins making the task easy. The only thing showing were the thin black snorkels and the top of their masks. When they reached the dock of the neighbor to the south of Arthur, they swam ashore and took their backpacks and diving masks off. Coleman whispered into the tiny microphone hanging in front of his mouth, "This is Zeus, we're ashore, over."

"This is Cyclops, we're almost there, over."

Michael and Coleman knelt on the small strip of sand between the water's edge and the cliff. Craning his neck backward, Michael looked up at the dark wall of rock. It looked to be about the height of a three-story building. Coleman tapped him on the shoulder. "Get your gear ready. I'm going to take a look at this dock and see if it has any security devices." Coleman pulled the night vision goggles down and waded out into the water. Without touching the dock, he looked underneath it to check for wires or cables. When he got out to the end, he swam under the huge yellow-and-white tarp where a thirty-six-foot Chris-Craft was docked. After checking the entire dock, he swam back to shore and grabbed his backpack. Michael had already put a magazine into Coleman's MP-5 and attached the silencer. He handed the weapon to Coleman, and the former SEAL checked to make sure a round was in the chamber and the safety on.

Coleman looked at Michael with a grin. "Do you remember how to do this?"

"It's coming back to me."

"Good. Let's go." Michael followed as Coleman led the way up the stairs. The stairs zigzagged up the cliff, changing lateral direction about every twenty steps. Not counting the bottom and top, there were three landings in between. When they neared the top, Coleman held up his fist signaling Michael to wait while he checked things out. He crawled just short of the last step and checked the posts of the railing for a motion sensor. He knew there wasn't a laser trip wire or it would have showed up on his night-vision goggles. Next, he scanned the large house for movement, and after several minutes of checking everything in and around the house, he waved O'Rourke up. They stayed low and scampered along a row of hedges that separated the lawn from the edge of the cliff. At the end of the hedges they reached a small patio and gazebo. Just on the other side of the gazebo was the ten-foot brick fence that separated Arthur's yard from his neighbors'.

Coleman grabbed one of the patio chairs and brought it around the back side of the gazebo. He and O'Rourke slung their weapons over their backs and climbed onto the roof. They lay on their stomachs and looked over the fence. The view from atop the slightly angled, octagonal roof was perfect. Almost all of Arthur's backyard was visible. Coleman spoke into his mike, keeping his voice barely above a whisper, "Cyclops, this is Zeus, are you in position, over?"

"That's affirmative, Zeus. I found a nice little nest with a bird's-eye view, over."

"Have you seen any guards yet, over?"

"That's affirmative. I count one man and a canine. They swept the back side of the house about two minutes ago, over."

"Roger. I'd like you to do a check on my position. We are directly south of you just on the other side of the fence, over." O'Rourke and Coleman lay perfectly still for about sixty seconds and then Hackett's voice responded.

"I've got you. Just barely though, it took me four passes. Make sure you keep a low profile. The sky is pretty dark behind you, but your silhouettes will still show, over."

"How high up are you, Cyclops? Over."

"I'm a good twenty feet up, over."

"Roger, let me know if the dog shows up along my fence line. It's my only blind spot, over."

"Will do, over."

"Hermes, this is Zeus, what's your position, over?"

Stroble was standing on the lowest branch of an old oak tree.

He hugged the trunk and peered over the fence at the front of Arthur's house. "I've got a good view of the front of the house, over."

"What do you see, over?"

"I've got two guards by the front door, both are accompanied by a German shepherd, over."

"How are they equipped, over?"

"They're decked out in combat boots, dark jumpsuits, and combat vests. One of them is carrying a sidearm . . . check, make that both of them." Stroble peered through his goggles and then lifted them up onto his forehead and grabbed his field binoculars out of his breast pocket. The guards were standing under the light of the front door. The detail was much better with the binoculars. "They are both carrying Uzis, and it looks like they're wearing flak jackets, over."

"How are they set up for communication, over?"

"They are both wearing shoulder mikes, and it . . . looks . . . like their radios are mounted on their upper back, left side, over."

"Is one of them the guard that just finished the sweep of the backyard, over?"

"That's a roger, over."

Coleman looked at his watch. "All right, you guys know the routine. Announce any movements and mark the intervals. We should have one more guard at the front gate and one more in the house. Let's see how good these guys are, over."

For the next hour they watched the two guards and their dogs patrol the grounds. One of them always stayed by the front door while the other roamed the estate. There was no rhyme or reason to the intervals. A guard would leave for one lap around the house one time, and the next time he would wander around the estate for ten minutes. To the common observer it looked disorganized, and in a way it was, but by design. Set patterns and predictability were liabilities in this business, not assets. These guards were professionals.

Stroble was getting tired of standing, so he sat down on the large branch. He was just barely able to see over the top of the fence and into Arthur's yard and could still see the two guards and their dogs at the front door. Both guards reached for their shoulder mikes and said something. Then they turned and headed in opposite directions toward the sides of the house. The unusual movement caught Stroble's attention, and then without warning bright flood lamps illuminated the tree lines to the north and south of Arthur's estate. Stroble leapt down from the tree and started running as quietly as possible for the water. He whispered into his mike, "I think they may have seen me, over."

Coleman and O'Rourke instantly crept backward when the lights came on and were huddling on the other side of the roof. Coleman asked, "Hermes, where are you, over?"

"I'm making my way toward the cliff, over."

"Roger, Hermes, stand by at the cliff and wait for Cyclops, over. Cyclops, I need some intel. What's going on, over?"

"I've got both guards and their dogs working their way down the fence line toward the water. They are looking in the trees, but neither of them have their weapons drawn. It appears that they're doing some kind of sweep, over."

"Do you still have good concealment, over?"

"That's affirmative, over."

"All right, you are going to have to give us the play-by-play because we can't see anything, over."

"Don't move or make any noise. The guard and the dog on the south side are coming up on your position. I have him in my sights."

Hackett kept his voice below a whisper. "Good. Zeus, they are looking over the edge of the cliff down at the water. . . . The guard closest to you just said something into his mike and is heading back to the house." Without warning, all of the floodlights were extinguished and darkness returned to the landscape.

"What in the hell was that all about?" asked Michael.

"I don't know," whispered Coleman. "Everyone sit tight for a couple minutes and see what happens next. Don't talk unless something develops, over." Coleman and Michael crawled back to the crest of the roof and looked over the fence.

Less than a minute later Hackett broke the silence. "I think I hear a car pulling up the driveway."

CHAPTER 32

NANCE stepped out of the backseat of his limo and held his arms straight out. A guard approached and waved a sensor over his body. After he was done, the guard spoke into his shoulder mike, telling the controller inside the house that Arthur's guest was clean. Nance's bodyguard and driver waited by the car while the national security adviser was escorted into the house. When he entered the study, he found Arthur in his usual spot, waiting by the fireplace. Nance strode across the room and stopped a short distance away. Arthur's lips showed the faintest hint of a smile and he said, "I hope you don't mind standing. I've been sitting all day."

"No, not at all."

"Good. What is of such importance that you needed to come see me in person?"

"You will have to be the judge. I just wanted to keep you abreast of some developments." Nance shifted his weight from one foot to the other. "Yesterday morning, Special Agent McMahon of the FBI received a phone call from the terrorists claiming that they had nothing to do with the killing of Olson and Turnquist."

"Really." Arthur pursed his lips. "I expected them to go to the media with the story, not the FBI."

"So did I. Does this worry you?"

Arthur slapped the question away with the wave of a hand. "No, not really. Nothing can be traced back to us. No one other than you, Garret, and myself know who was behind those murders. The people we used were hired very discreetly. They made no contact with anyone. They picked up an envelope that contained Olson's and Turnquist's names and an account number at a very discreet bank in the Caymans. Even if the FBI were to catch the assassins, they wouldn't be able to trace it back to us."

"Unless one of us talked."

Arthur stared at Nance with sharp eyes. "We both know that neither you nor I would speak to the FBI, so I would have to assume you are referring to Mr. Garret."

"Yes."

Arthur exhaled an even, long breath. "What has he done now?"

"He has a hard time hiding his emotions. During the briefing yesterday, when McMahon played the tape of his conversation with the assassin, Mr. Garret became very nervous and animated."

"I don't see that as being a problem. Nervous and animated fits his normal profile."

Nance sighed. It was often tiring trying to convince Arthur of something. "While the taped conversation was being played, he broke out in a sweat and would not stop staring at me. He looked uncharacteristically nervous and afraid."

"Did anyone else notice his behavior?"

"Yes."

"Who?"

"Thomas Stansfield."

Arthur grew more concerned. "Are you sure?"

"Completely."

"How much did he see?"

"Everything. You know how he is, Arthur. The man is a professional. He takes everything in."

"What exactly did he see?"

"He saw Garret fidget in his chair, his brow break out in a sweat, and his eyes darting back and forth between me and the transcript of the phone conversation. I was watching Stansfield stare at Stu, and then, just like you or I would have done, he followed Stu's eyes across the table to me. He took the whole thing in."

Arthur sighed. "Well, I would have preferred for that not to have happened, but I don't think it will affect us. As I said earlier, there is no way they can trace this back to us."

"As long as Mr. Garret keeps his mouth shut."

"He will stay quiet. He has strong survival instincts."

"I know he does. That's what worries me. What if Stansfield puts two and two together and makes a wild guess that you were the one who ordered the hit on Olson? Stansfield knows you hated him." Nance paused to let Arthur think about the scenario and then continued, "Mr. Garret's survival instincts are so strong that he would turn on us in a second if it meant saving himself."

Arthur looked at Nance and then into the fire. He watched the flames flicker while he contemplated his options, looking at every angle, trying to determine if Garret was more of a threat or an asset. He imagined Stansfield pulling Garret aside and catching him off guard, telling him that he knew all about his connection with Arthur and that they were behind the assassinations of Olson and Turnquist. Stansfield could easily speculate and connect the dots, but that meant nothing as long as Garret kept his mouth shut. The motives for killing a career politician were abundant. They could prove nothing without one of them talking, and as he and Nance had discussed earlier, the odds of that happening were zero. Arthur concluded that they would have to head this one off before Stansfield had the chance to act.

"I think that we need to be proactive on this and let Mr. Garret know what the consequences would be if he talked." Arthur ran one of his thin fingers over his bottom lip. "Tell Mr. Garret that I have made arrangements to have him dealt with if he ever whispers a word of this to anyone. . . . Tell him that even in the event of my death, the order will be carried out."

"I think that is a wise decision. I know just how to handle it."

"Good. I'll leave the details up to you." Arthur walked over to the coffee table and grabbed two cigars. "Let's step outside. I have some other things I would like to discuss with you."

Nance followed his mentor across the room and out into the cool night air.

O'Rourke and Coleman were concentrating on the guard who was standing watch at the edge of the cliff when Hackett came crackling over their earpieces. "Zeus, this is Cyclops. I just spotted two men in suits that walked out of the house and are standing on the patio. Do you copy, over?"

O'Rourke had his night-vision goggles flipped up and Coleman had his down. Both of them looked toward the house. Coleman saw them right away, the goggles illuminating them in a clear green-and-black picture. O'Rourke could see the bright red tips of the cigars, but nothing else. It was hard to make out their silhouettes in the dark. Coleman whispered into his mike, "I copy, Cyclops. I see two men. . . . I think one of them is our boy. I can't tell who the other guy is, over." Coleman flipped his mike up and said to Michael, "It's nice to know Augie was right about this cigar thing."

O'Rourke quietly pulled his goggles down and peered toward the house. He adjusted his goggles and brought the two men into focus. Being careful to keep his voice down, he said, "The guy on the right is Arthur, but I can't see who the guy on the left is."

"I can't either," responded Coleman. "Cyclops, we can't see who the other guy is, can you, over?"

"Yes, he looks familiar, but I haven't got a real good look at him, over."

O'Rourke was watching Arthur talk, and then the other man

turned his face toward them, exhaling a puff of smoke. O'Rourke squinted and tapped Coleman on the shoulder. "I think that's Mike Nance."

"Are you sure?"

"I'm almost positive." Michael pulled his mike down. "Cyclops, this is Apollo. Is the other man the president's national security adviser, Mike Nance, over?"

Cyclops moved his rifle sight from Arthur to the other man. Nance removed the cigar from his mouth and Cyclops got a full shot of his face. "That's a roger, the other man is Mike Nance, over."

"What in the hell is Mike Nance doing here?" asked O'Rourke.

"I have no idea," said Coleman as he peered back toward the cliff to see what the guard and dog were doing. "Are you sure it's him?"

"Yes."

O'Rourke continued to stare at the two men standing on the veranda. "Augie told me that Stansfield ordered Arthur to cease all dealings with his contacts from the intelligence community."

"Well, he's obviously ignoring the order." Coleman pulled his mike back down in front of his mouth. "All right, everybody, this is Zeus, listen up. We are going to wait until these two finish their cigars, and then, hopefully, they'll go back inside and the guard by the cliff will head back up to the main house. Then we will finish our recon and head back to the boat. Until then, we sit tight. I don't want them to have any idea we were here, over."

Irene Kennedy was having a difficult time staying awake. The human body needs more than two hours of sleep in a day. Kennedy had only slept two hours in the last three days, and her body was about to shut down. She was sitting in the midst of stacks of green personnel dossiers. Ninety-four to be exact. Kennedy was methodically picking through each file, reading every boring line of black print. Military personnel dossiers were not intriguing reading. Kennedy had already read fifty-two of the files and was coming to the realization that she would not finish tonight. It was almost 11 P.M., and her ability to analyze the tedious information was diminishing. She decided to read two more files and call it a night, leaving herself an even forty to finish in the morning. She was impressed with the job that Naval Intelligence had done in keeping tabs on their former SEALs.

Even the CIA was interested. Kennedy had found five SEALs who were now on the CIA payroll. The files didn't say they worked for the CIA. Kennedy recognized their employers as companies that were either fronts for the Agency or companies that did a lot of work for the Agency.

Kennedy opened the next file and looked down at a picture of Scott Coleman. Beneath the photo was his date of discharge. A little over a year ago. She continued reading the file, noticing nothing unusual. Any one of the ninety-four files alone would be impressive, but after reading fifty of them they all kind of blended together, and the superhuman feats these men performed started to seem normal. Kennedy noticed that Coleman's IQ was near the genius level. Flipping to the last several pages, Kennedy read a list of covert missions that Coleman had participated in. It was long and impressive, starting in the early eighties and finishing about a year and a half ago. The missions were all listed by code names. Because of Kennedy's security clearance and her background in terrorism, she recognized almost half of the missions. She got to the last mission Coleman had participated in, and an empty feeling crept into her stomach. The code name for the mission was Operation Snatch Back. Snatch Back was something few people knew about, and something that no one wanted to talk about.

The only thing listed after Operation Snatch Back was Coleman's date of discharge. Next to the date, in parenthesis, was the comment "Early discharge granted."

"I haven't seen one of those yet," Kennedy commented to

herself. As her curiosity grew, Kennedy felt less tired. She flipped to the last page and found that Coleman was living in Adams Morgan and had started a company called SEAL Demolition and Salvage Corporation. Kennedy immediately wondered who the other employees of the SEAL Demolition and Salvage Corporation might be. Grabbing the file, Kennedy stood and walked briskly down the hall toward General Heaney's office. A young ensign was the only person left in the main office area.

"Is the general still in?" asked Kennedy.

"Dr. Kennedy, he said good-bye to you almost three hours ago. . . . Remember, he said he'd be back at zero six hundred."

Kennedy frowned. "Damn it."

"Ma'am, if you don't mind me saying, you look like you could use some sleep."

Kennedy shook her head and looked down at the file. She stood there for a moment trying to figure out what to do next.

"Is there anything I could help you with, ma'am?"

Kennedy looked at the young officer and was about to ask him what his security clearance was and then thought better. At his age and rank there was no way he was cleared to discuss this information. "No . . . thank you for offering though." The paper-thin Kennedy turned to walk away and then stopped. "Ensign, how unusual is it to get an early discharge when you're in the Special Forces?"

"It's not that unusual. We have guys blowing out knees every other week. We get at least one broken back a year, and a whole lot of other injuries. A lot of these knee injuries take a year to rehab, so if a guy is due to get out in a year and he blows his knee, we let him go early."

Kennedy accepted the explanation and said, "Thank you." Again, she turned to walk away and again stopped. Turning back to the ensign, she said, "If that was the case, wouldn't their file say medical discharge?"

"Yes, that is correct."

Kennedy opened Coleman's file and found the page where it said early discharge granted. She pointed at the last line and showed it to the ensign. "This is different than a medical discharge, is it not?"

"Yes, it is. I've never seen one of those before. Well, I shouldn't say that. With the budget cuts it's fairly common in the regular Navy, but not in the Special Forces."

Kennedy wavered for a moment, wondering if she should have the ensign call General Heaney at home, but knew the general needed sleep as much or more than she did. She decided it could wait until morning. Kennedy asked the ensign for a piece of paper and wrote a note for the general. She paper clipped it to the top of the folder and handed it to the ensign. "Would you please put this on the general's desk for me?" Kennedy gathered her things and decided to let the rest of the files wait until morning. She had to be in Skip McMahon's office at 8 A.M. for a meeting.

Arthur and Nance stood outside talking and smoking their cigars for about forty minutes. During that time, O'Rourke and Coleman speculated as to why the national security adviser would be talking to Arthur. From their spot atop the gazebo they became more and more curious. Finally, Arthur and Nance went back inside. Several minutes after that, they heard a car drive away. Shortly after that, the guard standing watch by the cliff took his dog and headed back for the house. Coleman scanned the entire yard thoroughly and told everyone to sit tight for a couple more minutes to make sure they hadn't missed anything. When he felt comfortable, he lowered his mike and said, "All right, let's work our way back to the boat. Sound off if anything comes up, over."

Coleman slid off the roof first and lowered himself down onto the chair. O'Rourke followed and put the chair back at the table where they'd found it. They both huddled next to the row of hedges and looked at each other. For at least the tenth time in the last forty-five minutes, O'Rourke said, "God, I'd like to know what in the hell those two were talking about."

"So would I." Coleman looked around the yard and grabbed his mike. "Cyclops and Hermes, this is Zeus. Do you read, over?"

"Yes, we read you, over."

"Where are you, over?"

"We're getting ready to go down to the water, over."

Coleman looked across the yard. "I've got something I want to check out. It shouldn't take more than twenty minutes. We'll meet you back at the boat, over."

"That's a roger, over."

"What's up?" asked O'Rourke.

"When I was driving around today, I noticed that there was a big place for sale several doors down. It looked kind of run-down, like no one was living there. As long as we're here, I want to look around. Let's stay low and keep quiet." They ran toward the other side of the yard crouching next to the hedges. No fence separated the two yards, only a tree line, but Coleman and O'Rourke stopped anyway. They scanned the yard with their goggles and looked for motion sensors. They found none, and all of the lights in the large house were off. Crossing the yard, they reached an old wrought-iron fence and stopped.

"This is it," said Coleman. "Let's walk the fence line and see if we can find a gate." They walked away from the Bay and toward the house, their goggles lighting the way for them. They'd only walked about thirty feet when they found a hole. Two of the wrought-iron bars were missing and a gate had been created. They stepped through the opening and onto a thinly worn path that moved through the trees and weeds. After about thirty feet, it opened into a huge, wild yard the size of a football field. The grass was almost up to their waist. Looking up toward the house, they studied the dilapidated mansion. All of the windows on the main floor were boarded up, and the surrounding vegetation looked as if it was attempting to swallow the house. "This place has been empty for quite a while," said Coleman.

"They can't sell homes like this anymore. The taxes alone have to be a half a million dollars."

"Follow me, I think there's a service drive over here." They trudged through the tall grass, staying by the trees. Adjacent to the main house, and behind a row of tall hedges, they came across a small shed and a dirt road. They followed the path to the main road and stopped at the service gate. Next to the gate was a good-size servants' house. The windows were also boarded up. They heard a car approaching and ducked down behind some bushes. The car grew louder and louder, and then its headlights lit up the night air. The undergrowth and trees were thick, and with their dark clothing they were not in danger of being seen. A Mercedes passed and continued around the turn. Coleman rose from the bushes and inspected the gate. It was a smaller version of the large wrought-iron gate for the main drive to the mansion. It swung open from the middle and was chained and padlocked. Coleman inspected the lock briefly and then checked the hinges. Turning to O'Rourke, he said, "I've seen all I need, let's go."

"Would you mind telling me what you're thinking?"

"I'm not sure yet. I'm just trying to get a feel for things. . . . Let's go." With Coleman in the lead they worked their way quietly down the service drive, through the tall grass, and back to Arthur's neighbor's yard. From there, they descended down the steps to the Bay, where they repacked their gear in the waterproof backpacks and swam back to the boat. Stroble and Hackett were waiting for them. As soon as Coleman and O'Rourke were on board, they raised the anchor and headed back out into the Bay. Once they reached the other side, they turned north for Baltimore.

All four of them were gathered on the fly deck. The windscreen shielded them from most of the breeze, but the night air was still frigid. Hackett was telling them that he didn't think it would be difficult to take Arthur out. "I can't believe that a guy who's that paranoid about security is dumb enough to step out in the open like that just to smoke a cigar."

"They're all alike . . . all over the world," scoffed Stroble. "They all have a weakness . . . some little habit that they won't let go of."

"How hard do you think it would be to kidnap him?" asked O'Rourke.

"A lot harder than shooting him in the head from one hundred and fifty feet," responded Hackett. "You're not really considering that as an option, are you?"

"I would like to get inside his head and find out what in the hell he and Mike Nance were talking about." O'Rourke looked at Coleman, who was concentrating on the water ahead of them. He knew Coleman was thinking the same thing.

Without taking his eyes off the water Coleman said, "It can be done, but we'll have to take the guards out."

"Why?"

"Those guys are not your average security guards. If they're guarding Arthur, that means they're good."

"How good?"

"Good enough that if we try to sneak up on them, one of us will end up dead."

"What about shooting them with a tranquilizer gun?"

Coleman thought about it for a second and asked Hackett, "Any chance we could take them out with tranquilizers?"

Hackett shook his head. "Too much wind coming off the Bay, and the distances are too far. It looked like the guards were wearing body armor, so we'd have to hit them in the neck. From the distances we'd have to shoot, I wouldn't give us better than a fifty-fifty chance of hitting the mark."

O'Rourke thought about killing the guards. He had killed several Iraqis during the war, but this would be more personal. "What type of men are they? Do they work for CIA?"

"No. They're professional mercenaries. Probably men who have worked for him in the past." Coleman scanned to the port and starboard sides, checking for any other vessels in the area. "Michael, the only way we can do it is to take the guards out. We can either take Arthur out, without knowing what's going on, or we can grab him and find out what he and Nance are up to. . . . I say we grab him, but the decision is yours."

CHAPTER 33

IRENE Kennedy was sound asleep. After arriving home from the Pentagon late the previous evening, she didn't even have the energy to take off her clothes. She plopped down on the covers and was out in seconds.

Through her deep sleep she sensed that she wasn't alone in her bedroom. Someone was watching her. She opened her eyes and saw the intruder. Looking back at her were a pair of little brown eyes. They belonged to her four-year-old son, Tommy. He was staring at her with a frown on his face and a juice box stuck in his mouth. Irene blinked her eyes several times and tried to rub the sleep out of them.

Tommy pulled the juice box away from his lips and asked, "Why are you sleeping in your clothes?"

Irene ignored the question and held out her arms. "Give Mommy a hug."

Tommy set his beverage down on the nightstand and jumped up onto the big bed. Irene gave him a warm hug and kissed his forehead. "How have you been?" she asked as she rubbed her hand through his blond hair.

"Good." Tommy liked to give one-word answers.

"How have you and Mrs. Rosensteel been getting along?"

"Fine. She told me to let you sleep."

"She's here?"

"Yep."

Irene bolted upright. "What time is it?" She looked at the bed-side clock and suppressed the urge to swear. She jumped off the bed and picked up Tommy. "Mommy's late, honey. Go ask Mrs. Rosensteel to make me a cup of coffee, please." Irene patted him on his little butt and headed for the bathroom. She showered in under three minutes and got dressed. Today would be a pants day. No time to shave the legs. With her hair still wet she shoved her makeup kit in her purse and headed for the kitchen. Tommy's nanny handed her a cup of coffee in a large to-go mug, and Irene thanked her. She dropped down to one knee and kissed Tommy on the forehead. "I'll call you from the office." Standing, she added, "I love you."

"I love you, too." Tommy waved as she ran out the door.

Minutes later Irene was battling traffic on her way downtown. She reminded herself to call her mother and ask her to stop by and see Tommy. Since these assassinations had started, she'd been working some horrible hours and her time with her son had suffered.

She violated a half dozen traffic laws on her way to the Hoover Building and had still managed to put on her makeup. She appeared in Skip McMahon's office less than thirty minutes after Tommy had awakened her, feeling better than one would have expected.

"Good morning, Skip."

"Good morning, Irene. How are you doing?"

"Pretty good. I finally got more than a couple hours of sleep last night."

"Good, because we've got a full day ahead of us. I just got out of a meeting with Harvey Wilcox and Madeline Nanny. They have solid surveillance set up on ten of the fourteen suspects and are hoping to have the last four taken care of by this evening. How are you and your people coming along?"

"Good. As of ten P.M. last night we had visual and phone

surveillance initiated on all forty-five suspects." Kennedy took a sip of coffee.

McMahon tapped his foot under the desk and looked at Kennedy, waiting for the good doctor to crack a smile and tell him she was joking. Kennedy gave no response, and McMahon realized she wasn't kidding. McMahon wondered how in the hell the CIA could initiate surveillance on forty-five people in less than thirty-six hours. He was sure that, however they did it, civil rights were being trampled left and right.

The investigative side of McMahon wanted desperately to know how it was done, and the law-abiding federal-agent side wanted to be kept in the dark. After a brief internal struggle the investigative side won. "Irene, I have a hard time believing that you have the manpower to watch forty-five people around the clock."

"We don't."

"Then how in the hell are you keeping an eye on all of these people?"

"It's not about manpower, Skip. It's technology."

"What do you mean 'technology'?"

Kennedy grinned. "I'd like to tell you, but it's probably best if you don't know. Just trust me that we can, and that we'll pass whatever we learn on to you as quickly as possible."

McMahon leaned back in his chair and frustratedly accepted Kennedy's answer, understanding that it was probably best that he didn't know. "I was thinking about your SEAL theory last night. The more I mull it over, the more intrigued I am. If these guys are as smart as we think they are, they would have tried to do something along the way to throw us off their trail."

Kennedy set her coffee cup on the edge of the desk and stood. "I'm glad you brought that up. I need to call General Heaney and ask him about something. Would you dial his office and put it on speaker?" While McMahon dialed the number, Kennedy continued, "I was reviewing those personnel files last night and came across something a little unusual."

One of the general's aides answered, and a moment later Heaney was on the line.

"Good morning, Skip. What can I do for you?"

"General, I've got you on speakerphone. Irene is here with me and she has a question for you." McMahon looked at Kennedy.

"Good morning, General. Did you get a chance to look at the file I left on your desk last night?"

"Yes, I read it over first thing this morning."

"Did you know Commander Coleman?"

"Yes, I did. He was top-notch."

"I noticed last night that out of all the files I reviewed, Coleman was the only SEAL who had been granted an early discharge. Is that uncommon?"

The general hesitated for a minute. "It is not a common practice, but the brass has been known to make exceptions."

"Do you know why he was granted an early discharge?"

Again, the general paused. This time for a long enough period that Kennedy knew she had touched on something more than routine.

General Heaney cleared his throat and asked, "Irene, are you familiar with Operation Snatch Back?"

"Yes, I helped put the premission intel together."

For a long period no one talked. McMahon had no idea what was being discussed, but by the tone of Heaney's and Kennedy's voices he could tell now was not the time to ask.

"Did you receive a postmission briefing?" Heaney asked.

"Not a formal one. I only heard rumors."

"Coleman was the commander of the SEAL team we sent in."

"His discharge was granted about a month after the mission?"

"Yes."

"Did he crack up?"

"No . . . not really."

"Did he request the early discharge, or was it offered to him?"

"I'm not aware of the exact circumstances. Admiral DeVoe, the force commander for the SEALs, and the secretary of the navy signed off on it."

"Was Admiral DeVoe Coleman's immediate superior in the chain of command?"

"Yes."

"Do you think you could track the admiral down and call us back? I'd like to ask him some questions about Coleman."

"I'll get him on the line and call you right back," responded Heaney in his quick, efficient, military tone.

McMahon looked up at Kennedy, who was still standing over the phone. "What was that all about?"

Kennedy sat down in a chair and closed her eyes. "Do you remember the Pan Am flight that was blown up over Lockerbie, Scotland?"

"Yeah."

"About fifteen months ago, the Agency located the whereabouts of the two terrorists responsible for the bombing. They were at a small military base in northern Libya. We sent a SEAL team in to take them out. . . . I'm not sure what happened. . . . All I know is that we lost part of the team."

"How many men?"

"Ten."

The phone rang and McMahon grabbed the receiver. "Hello."

"Skip, General Heaney. I've got Admiral DeVoe on the line."

McMahon hit the speaker button and placed the receiver back in the cradle. "Good morning, Admiral, this is Special Agent McMahon with the FBI, and I have Irene Kennedy from the CIA in my office. We'd like to ask you a few questions."

With a noticeably unenthusiastic tone, the admiral said, "Shoot."

Kennedy stood placing both hands on Skip's desk and leaning over the phone. "Admiral, has General Heaney told you why we want to talk to you?"

"Yes."

"Good. . . . Would you explain to me the events surrounding your granting of an early discharge for Commander Coleman?"

"Before I answer that, I'd like to know why you want to know."

Kennedy looked at McMahon, and Skip leaned forward. "Admiral, this is Special Agent McMahon. We are involved in a very important investigation."

"Is Commander Coleman a suspect?"

"No," answered McMahon.

"Is that no, or not yet?"

"General Heaney, can you help me out here?" asked McMahon.

"Bob, this is some pretty serious stuff. I've been working with Skip and Irene for the last five days. They're straight shooters."

DeVoe thought about it and responded, "I will answer what I can."

Kennedy rephrased her question. "Admiral, did Commander Coleman ask you for an early discharge, or did you offer it to him?"

"He asked for it."

"Why?"

"He was unhappy about a certain issue."

"Did that issue have anything to do with Operation Snatch Back?" asked Kennedy.

"I am not at liberty to discuss that subject."

This time it was Kennedy's turn to ask Heaney for help. "General?"

"Bob, Irene did the premission intel for Snatch Back. She has a higher clearance than you or I do."

Kennedy repeated the question. "Did that issue have anything to do with Operation Snatch Back?"

"Yes," answered DeVoe.

"Did he want out because the mission was a failure?"

"Not exactly. He was more upset about something that happened after the mission."

"What?"

After a reluctant pause, DeVoe said, "Listen, I know where you're headed with this, and I know the type of pressure you're going to be under to make some arrests. I can tell you right now Scott Coleman has nothing to do with these assassinations. . . . None of my boys do. I've been having nightmares about this ever since I heard you showed up at JSOC five days ago. If you dig, you'll find enough motive to indict every single one of my SEALs. None of them are really enamored of the behavior on Capitol Hill. Most of them have voiced opinions on the subject of who they think is fucking this country up—excuse my French—but that doesn't mean they killed anyone."

"Admiral, we understand that," said McMahon. "We have already discussed this universal dislike of politicians with General Heaney, and we respect the sacrifice these men have made for America. I am running this investigation, and I'm not going to arrest anyone unless I have some solid evidence to back me up."

"Special Agent McMahon, pardon my candor, but you are fooling yourself if you think you've got the final say in this investigation. You have another month, at the most, before those peacocks on the Hill start screaming for hearings, and when that happens, they'll make the people in my profession look like a bunch of crazed killers."

"Admiral, I don't give a crap about what the politicians want." McMahon's voice grew louder. "I'm trying to find out who in the hell is behind these murders. We have a very strong reason to believe the assassins are American commandos. General Heaney, will you back me up on this?"

"He's telling the truth, Bob."

Kennedy placed a hand on her hip. "Admiral, why did Commander Coleman ask for an early discharge?"

"Is this conversation being taped?"

"No," answered McMahon.

"I'll tell you why, but this is completely off-the-record. If this thing turns into a circus trial, I'll deny I ever said it."

"It's off-the-record, sir," said Kennedy.

McMahon looked up at Kennedy and mouthed the word *no*. Kennedy shushed him with a wave of her hand.

"Are you familiar with the objective of Operation Snatch Back?" They answered yes and DeVoe continued, "We sent in a SEAL team. Coleman was the commander. He took half the team and went in first. They were inserted about two miles out from the camp, and they moved in and set up perimeter positions. They were to take out the sentries and provide cover for the second group that was to be vertically inserted by helicopter into the camp. The second group's responsibility was to take the terrorists alive if possible.

"Coleman moved into position and then ordered the second group in. The choppers came in low and quiet. Right before they reached the camp, Coleman's men took out the sentries as planned. The Black Hawk stopped above the camp, and before the second group could rappel to the ground, the chopper was blown out of the sky by a barrage of rocket-propelled grenades.

"Eight men and the two pilots, just like that. . . . Coleman and his team were extracted, and during their debriefing, every one of them stated that they thought the Libyans were waiting for them. They said everything looked good, and then within the blink of an eye a dozen rag heads appeared with RPGs. Coleman took it harder than the rest of us because he ordered the second team in. . . . He blamed himself for their deaths.

"We weren't convinced the mission had been blown until several weeks later when I received word that the FBI had discovered a leak. I told Coleman the news, thinking it would help him put the blame elsewhere, but it didn't work. He wanted to know where the leak came from, and I told him I didn't know. A couple weeks later he came to me and said he wanted out. I asked why, and he said he'd lost faith. I tried to talk him out of it, but he wouldn't listen. Scott was a good officer. He'd been a SEAL for almost fifteen years. I figured he'd given more than enough to the Navy, so I got him the early discharge."

"Admiral, who told you that the FBI found a leak?" asked McMahon.

"I would rather not say."

"Did this person say where the leak came from?"

"They said it was a prominent politician."

"Did they tell you who that politician was?"

"No."

"Did you tell Commander Coleman that the leak came from a politician?"

There was a moment of silence, then the admiral answered, "Yes."

McMahon and Kennedy looked at each other. Both were thinking the same thing. McMahon looked back at the phone. "How did Coleman react to the information?"

"Like all of us did. He was pissed, but, gentlemen, I can assure you Commander Coleman is not your man."

Kennedy raised her eyebrows in a doubtful manner and McMahon said, "Admiral, that's all the questions we have for now. I'm going to ask that you not tell anyone about our conversation, especially Mr. Coleman. I promise that either myself or General Heaney will keep you informed about any part of the investigation that may involve you. General Heaney, we have a meeting with Director Roach that should last an hour or so. Could you meet Irene and me in my office around ten A.M.?"

"I'll be there."

"Thank you, gentlemen." McMahon hit the speaker button and disconnected the line. He looked up at Kennedy, who was still standing, and asked, "How many prominent politicians would have known about Operation Snatch Back beforehand?"

Kennedy shrugged her shoulders. "The way those guys gossip, you can never be sure, but according to law, the president and a ranking member of the Senate Intelligence Committee must be informed before we run a covert operation."

"Who were the two ranking members of the Senate Intelligence Committee a year and a half ago?"

"Erik Olson and Daniel Fitzgerald."

"Isn't that a coincidence. They're both dead." McMahon stood and put on his jacket. "Let's go talk to Brian and see if we can find out who this mystery politician is."

"I think I already know who it is," Kennedy said with a glum look on her face.

"Who?"

"Fitzgerald."

"Why?"

"He resigned from the Intelligence Committee about a year ago, claiming that he needed to focus more of his energy on the Finance Committee."

McMahon led the way down the hall and up the two flights of stairs. Skip greeted Roach's assistant and told her that he needed to see the boss immediately. She buzzed Roach, and a minute later McMahon and Kennedy were let in. Roach was sitting at his conference table surrounded by the usual stacks of files and papers.

He stood and greeted the visitors, professional as always. "How's the investigation going?"

"We may have come across a break." McMahon looked over his shoulder to make sure the door was closed and then asked, "What do you know about a covert mission called Operation Snatch Back?"

Roach looked more than a little surprised. "Where did you hear about Operation Snatch Back? That's classified." Roach turned to Kennedy. "Did you tell him?"

"Not in the way you're thinking. We stumbled across it in our investigation."

"How?"

"Irene was looking into the file of a former Navy SEAL and the name came up."

"In what way did it come up?"

Kennedy stepped forward. "About a month after the mission, one of the SEALs involved in the operation received an early discharge. We talked to his commanding officer and found out some interesting things."

"Go on," commanded Roach.

"Admiral DeVoe, the force commander for the SEALs, told us that the officer in question, Comdr. Scott Coleman, was in charge of the SEAL team that participated in Operation Snatch Back. After the mission, Coleman stated that he thought the Libyans had set a trap. He also blamed himself for the loss of his men because he ordered them in. A couple of weeks after the mission, Admiral DeVoe finds out that the FBI has identified who leaked the mission. The admiral passes the information on to Coleman, telling him that he doesn't know who leaked the mission, only that it was a prominent politician. Shortly after that, Coleman demands an early discharge and gets it. So far none of this adds up to anything hard, but if the prominent politician who leaked that mission happened to be Sen. Daniel Fitzgerald, then we have a possible motive."

Roach looked more than a little surprised and asked, "What makes you think it was Fitzgerald?"

"An educated guess," said Kennedy.

"Was it Fitzgerald?"

"Yes. . . . Both of you take a seat. This is more complicated than it looks." McMahon and Kennedy sat in the two chairs in front of Roach's desk, and the director sat on the edge of his desk. "What I'm about to tell you does not leave this room. . . . Fitzgerald was the one who leaked the mission. He didn't do it intentionally, and that is why he was never prosecuted. In fact, we stumbled across it in an unusual way. Our Counter Espionage Department regularly reviews the tax returns, asset portfolios, and credit history of certain people that, by the nature of their jobs, come in contact with government employees that have access to sensitive information—people like journalists, attorneys, secretaries, lobbyists, even waitresses and bartenders. Last year, one of our agents was reviewing the tax returns for all of the employees that worked at a local restaurant. She discovered that one of the bartenders had purchased a two-hundred-thousand-dollar condo in Georgetown. The guy only makes about thirty thousand a year, so a red flag pops up. She calls the mortgage company and finds out the person in question put down sixty grand for the down payment on the condo. A little more investigating and she rules out that the money came from his parents. We think the guy is probably selling drugs, but there's an outside chance he may be talking to people we don't want him talking to. A lot of big hitters frequent the establishment where he works, and after a few drinks these politicians and their staffers have been known to discuss things they shouldn't in public.

"We decided there was enough to put this bartender under surveillance. We wired the bar, his condo, and tapped his phone." Roach shook his head. "Two days before Operation Snatch Back was to commence, Fitzgerald gets done with work and stops by for a couple of drinks. The nightly news is on and they run a segment on the anniversary of the downing of the Pan Am flight over Lockerbie. The reporter ends the segment saying that the two men suspected of planting the bomb are believed to be hiding in Libya. Fitzgerald responds out loud, 'Not for long,' and the bartender asks what he means. Fitzgerald says, 'Between you and me, kid, those two bastards are going to be sitting in a U.S. jail in about forty-eight hours.' The kid asks how, if they're in Libya, and Fitzgerald tells him he can't go into it.

"At the time this meant nothing to our people that were on the case, but after Snatch Back failed, the CIA gave our Counter

Espionage people a heads-up warning that the mission may have been compromised. One of the names on the list of people that knew about the mission beforehand was Senator Fitzgerald. Our agents put two and two together and hauled the bartender in for a shakedown. They told him he was either going to spend the next twenty years in a federal pen or he could spill the beans. . . . He spilled the beans. The guy thought he was passing the information on to a reporter. It turns out the reporter is a former KGB agent who is now operating for himself and selling his secrets abroad. The rest of the story is highly classified, and I can't go into what we found out. . . . It's an ongoing operation."

"You're using the kid to feed him misinformation, aren't you?" Kennedy waited for an answer.

Roach shrugged his shoulders and said, "Director Stansfield knows all about it. We're working in cooperation with the Agency." Roach walked around to the other side of his desk and sat.

McMahon sat forward and said, "I'm going to have to talk to everyone who was involved in this."

"No, you're not," answered Roach.

"Brian, if this Coleman is our guy, all of this information about Fitzgerald is going to have to come out in the indictment."

"We'll cross that bridge when we get to it, but for now I don't want Fitzgerald's name and Operation Snatch Back mentioned in the same sentence. Do what you have to do to investigate Coleman, but keep Fitzgerald out of it. I assume I can get ahold of Admiral DeVoe at the Pentagon?"

"No, he's down in Norfolk."

"All right, I'll talk to him personally, and you'd better put a list together of all the people that know Snatch Back was leaked. Madeline Nanny is going to want to talk to you about this."

Mike Nance took the short walk from his corner office to Stu Garret's. Passing Garret's secretary, he smiled and said hello. The door was open and Nance closed it behind him. Nance sat in one of the armchairs and crossed his legs. "How is the president today?"

Garret finished what he was writing and pushed himself away from the desk. Taking his cigarette out of his mouth, he blew a cloud of smoke toward the ceiling and said, "He's doing great. We just got the results back from the most recent *Time*/CNN poll, and almost seventy percent of the people surveyed are behind his decision to get the military involved." Garret shoved the cigarette back in his mouth and took a deep drag. "He's very happy. Much more relaxed."

"Good." Nance looked down and flicked a speck of lint from his wool pants. "How are you doing?"

"Fine. I could use a little more sleep, but otherwise I feel pretty good."

"Are you more at ease than you were yesterday?"

"Yes." Garret was slightly embarrassed by the question.

"I had a meeting with our friend last night."

"How is he doing?"

"Not well. He's very uneasy about your lack of emotional control."

Garret's face went flush, and he stabbed his cigarette out in the ashtray. "Why?"

"He heard about your demeanor in the meeting the other day."

"What meeting?"

"The one where Special Agent McMahon played the tape of his conversation with the terrorist."

"Why did you have to tell him about that?"

"I didn't. Someone else did."

"Who?"

"One never knows with Arthur, Stu. He has a lot of contacts."

"What did he say?"

"He's concerned that you won't be able to keep your mouth shut."

"Who am I going to tell?"

Nance turned his palms upward and raised his eyebrows.

"Come on, Mike. I'm not that stupid. If I talk, I go down too."

"I agree, but he doesn't."

"Why? I haven't done a fucking thing to make him think I would say anything. Why in the hell would I say anything? I'd be cutting my own throat."

"I agree, but he seems to think that you might fold under pressure. He thinks if someone were to put the screws to you, you'd talk in order to save yourself."

"That's ludicrous." Garret grabbed his pack of Marlboros with a shaky hand and fished out a fresh cigarette.

"He wants me to give you a message." Nance rose from his chair and walked around the desk. Leaning into Garret's ear, he whispered, "Arthur says if you breathe a word of this to anyone, he will have you killed."

Garret dropped his cigarette and stood. "Why?"

Nance put a hand on his shoulder. "Just calm down, Stu, and you'll have nothing to worry about."

CHAPTER 34

MICHAEL O'Rourke and Scott Coleman were running a couple of minutes late. They had met at the cabin earlier and finalized the plans for the mission. Because of the lack of preparation time, they had decided to keep things as simple as possible. If Arthur stepped out to smoke a cigar, they would grab him. If he didn't, they would have to try again the next night. Storming the house was out of the question.

The sun had set at about 5:40 P.M., and the rural Maryland roads were crowded with commuters going home after work. The black BMW cruised along with traffic and then turned off the busy county road and onto one of the narrow and quiet streets of the Curtis Point neighborhood. Coleman was driving and had his night-vision goggles perched on his forehead. He reached up and pulled the microphone from his headset down in front of his mouth. "Hermes and Cyclops, this is Zeus, come in, over." He kept his eyes fixed on the road and waited for the response.

"This is Hermes, over."

"Are you in position, over?"

"That's affirmative, we're in position, over."

"We're about three miles out. Have the gate ready to go, and I'll give you the word right before we round the corner. Check the road for foot traffic, and let me know if there are any cars coming from the other direction, over."

"Roger, over."

Michael opened the glove box and pulled off the cover to the fuses. Holding a small penlight in his left hand, he located the fuse for the car's exterior lights and got ready to pull it. They continued to wind down the curvy road, passing the large houses. When they were less than a mile from the old estate, Coleman spoke into his mike again.

"Hermes, how does everything look, over?"

"The coast is clear, over."

"Open the gate." Coleman looked at O'Rourke and nodded.

O'Rourke pulled the fuse, and the headlights and rear running lights were extinguished. The thick cloud cover overhead, combined with the lack of streetlights on the narrow, wooded road, cut the visibility to nothing. Coleman pulled down his night-vision goggles and quickly adjusted his eyes. He took his foot off the gas and coasted. They passed the main gate of the old estate, and Coleman put some pressure on the brakes. About 150 feet later, they reached the service drive, and Coleman turned hard. The black car slipped onto the overgrown drive and squeezed through the encroaching trees and bushes, disappearing from sight.

Stroble quickly closed the gate and wrapped the chain around the post. He stood guard for a minute, looking up and down the road waiting to see if anyone else approached, and then went down the path to join the others. When he arrived at the small shed, Coleman had already turned the car around in the tall grass so it was pointing back toward the road. Coleman, O'Rourke, and Hackett were standing by the open trunk. Hackett handed them their MP-5s and Coleman and O'Rourke checked to make sure a round was chambered. When Stroble joined the group, Coleman checked his watch and brought everyone in.

"What did you do with the Zodiac?"

"We sank it about a mile offshore and swam in," responded Stroble.

"Good. Let's go over this thing once and then get into position. We don't want to miss him. Stop me if you have any questions. What's the status on the boat next door?"

"It has a full tank of gas, and the battery is fine," said Hackett.

"Are you going to have to hot-wire her?"

"No, we found an extra set of keys under the seat cushions."

"Good. . . . Okay, once from the top." Coleman pointed at Hackett and Stroble. "You two move into position on the north side of the house. Kevin, you're in the same tree you were in last night. From there you can cover the entire backyard. Dan, you are in your spot by the front of the house, and Michael and I are just opposite the patio on this side of the fence. When we get into position, the first thing all of us do is make sure our ropes are secure. Then we sit tight, watch the guards, and wait. The surveillance reports that Michael got say he steps out for a cigar almost every night, unless it's raining. Sometimes he stays out there for hours, sometimes for only a couple of minutes. The point being . . . if he shows, we move fast." Coleman looked up at the dark sky. "The forecast calls for possible showers, so we'll have to wait and see. If he comes out, we wait for him to move to the edge of the patio, as far away from the house as possible, and then depending on what the guards are doing, we make our move."

"What if he's not alone?" asked Hackett.

Coleman looked to Michael, who thought about it and answered, "I'll make the call on the spot."

"Back to the guards," said Coleman. "If they stick to their routines, one of them will stay by the front door, and the other one will patrol the sides and rear of the house with the dog. There's another one at the front gate, but I don't think he'll leave the guardhouse. That leaves one more in the house, and after we take the cameras out, he'll be blind.

"Assuming everything goes right, and Arthur steps out, I will ask the two of you if you have a clear shot. Kevin, you've got the guard in back and Dan you've got the one by the front door. As soon as I get a positive answer from both of you, I'll say 'bingo.' Shoot the guards first and then the dogs. At that point, Michael and I swing over the fence in the backyard, and Dan comes over in the front. The second we hit the ground, the security control board inside the house is going to light up. I don't know for sure, but it's my guess that the guard inside will hit those floodlights that we saw last night. Don't worry about them right away. Take the cameras out first. There are two sets of cameras mounted on each of the four corners of the house. Dan, you take out the ones in front and then take out the floodlights closest to the house. While you're running from one side of the house to the other, I want you to fire some shots at the windows. It'll set off more alarms inside and keep that fourth guard busy."

Coleman turned to Hackett. "There are four floodlights in the backyard. I want you to pop them ASAP and then cover us." Looking back at Stroble, he said, "Now for the tricky part. The surveillance report says that Arthur is outfitted with a homing device and alarm. He has a lot of secrets in his head, and the CIA doesn't want someone getting ahold of them. I don't know if this homing device is sewn into his clothes or in his shoe or in his watch, so Michael and I have decided not to take any chances. We're going to strip him naked and put everything in a bag. Dan, when you reach the patio, we should have everything ready to go. Michael will give you the bag, and then I want you to get down to the boat as fast as possible and get the engines warmed up." Coleman pointed at Hackett. "Kevin, you stay in the tree and cover Michael and me until we are over the wall with Arthur. The second we're clear, get the hell out of the tree and down to the boat."

"What do I do if the owner of the house hears the engines start and comes out to see what's going on?" asked Hackett.

"Scare him away with a couple of warning shots."

"What if he has a gun?"

"If he keeps coming at you, kneecap him. Once both of you are on the boat, I want you to head straight out into the Bay. No one is going to be around to cover you, and I don't want one of the guards taking potshots at you from the cliff. When you are about three hundred yards from shore, head south. Run at full throttle and keep your running lights off. I'm estimating that you should be able to do about seventy knots in that boat. If the CIA is on the ball, I'm estimating that the quickest they could get a chopper up to intercept you would be fifteen minutes from the time the alarm is sounded. Kevin, after you're done taking the guard out, mark the time. At seventy knots it should take you approximately fifteen minutes to reach Cove Point. Seventeen minutes after we go over the wall, I want both of you out of the boat! Even if you haven't made it to Cove Point, jump ship. I don't want you on board a second longer. Tim O'Rourke will be waiting to pick you up. He has a radio and a red filter light. When you go over, ask him to give you a signal for bearing."

Coleman paused and looked all of them in the eye. "I know we're not as prepared for this as we'd like to be, but we don't have the time. Just stay cool and everything will be fine. Any questions?"

They all shook their heads, and then Coleman went to the trunk of the car. He grabbed four bundles of rope and handed one to each man. "Let's get moving. Be careful and stay cool." Coleman patted each of them on the shoulder as they started down the path. The former SEAL team commander took up the rear and fell in step. The four dark figures moved one by one into the black night.

Six floors beneath the main level of the Central Intelligence Agency was a room that never slept. The Operations Center of the CIA was the Agency's version of NASA's Mission Control. But instead of monitoring space missions, these men and women monitored spy missions. They were in constant contact with every U.S. embassy and consulate around the globe. The men and women who worked in the Operations Center were not in charge of running spy operations. Their function was to serve as the main communications link between the field and the rest of the Agency. Information was what the Agency was all about, and disseminating it in a quick, secretive, and orderly fashion was crucial to the overall mission.

The Operations Center was divided into four separate clusters of desks. In the front of the room, beneath three twelve-by-twelve-foot computer-projection screens, was the European Section. The section had one supervisor and three operators who handled Western Europe, Eastern Europe, and the former Soviet republics. The next section handled the Middle East and Africa. The third section monitored Asia and the South Pacific, and the last section handled Central America, South America, and the United States. In the rear of the room, elevated and watching over the section supervisors and operators, were two watch officers. Just behind them, elevated still farther and behind a wall of Plexiglas, was the Operations Center's watch commander.

The room was softly lit and comfortable. Every operator had three monitors on his or her desk and multiple phone lines. To battle boredom, they were encouraged to read or play computer games while on watch. If they received any flash traffic, their computers would beep, letting them know it was time to pay attention. The supervisors and watch commanders often kept the operators on their toes by running drills. Day to day, the Operations Center was one of the most boring places in the Agency to work, but when a crisis erupted, it was one of the most exciting.

Charlie Dobbs sat behind the Plexiglas wall of the watch commander's office and looked at the computer monitor to his far left. A chessboard was on the screen. Charlie was sixteen moves into the game at the grand-master level and was holding his own. The computer monitor to the right beeped once, and his eyes jumped from one screen to the other. A routine message was coming in from the Tokyo embassy. Charlie noted that it was on time and went back to calculating what the computer's next move would be.

Five computers were on Dobbs's desk, and at any time he could check on his operators and see what they were doing. He could do this manually or let the system run on automatic. Messages came in off their satellite system and were encoded with a number designating their importance. Routine traffic came in preceded by the number one, and emergency traffic came in preceded by the number five. The computer prioritized these messages and queued them according to their importance. Level five traffic was not uncommon during a crisis in a given region, but since the global scene had been pretty quiet for the last several weeks, Dobbs was expecting a slow night.

When they reached the large yard to the south of Arthur's estate, Stroble and Hackett headed for the stairs that led down to the water. Michael and Coleman watched from the trees with their night-vision goggles. Michael kept an eye on the neighbor's house and Coleman watched his two men. Stroble and Hackett disappeared down the stairs. From there, they were to get in the water and swim past Arthur's to the neighbor's just to the north, where the Cigarette boat was docked.

Coleman and Michael ran across the open lawn to the brick wall that separated Arthur's compound from the neighbor to the south. They found the large oak tree that they had scouted out the night before and climbed it in silence. Stopping at the first rung of branches, they pulled their night-vision goggles back down and surveyed Arthur's estate. The wall was ten feet high and the base of the tree was about six feet away from it. No one was in sight, so Coleman climbed another ten feet up the tree and scooted out onto a thick branch that hung just over the wall. He tied both ropes around the branch and carried the remainder of the bundle back down. Michael stood on the east side of the base of the tree and Coleman stood on the west side. Both of them hung on to branches that jutted out from overhead. Michael was just about to comment on how difficult it was going to be to hang out in this tree all night when a guard and dog came around the side of the house. Michael and Coleman moved as close to the main trunk as possible. The old oak still had most of its leaves, although they had turned to a dry, dark maroon. They would be safe unless the guard got close and shone a light on them from underneath.

The guard continued his walk past the patio and down toward the water. Coleman spoke into his mike. "Hermes and Cyclops, this is Zeus, where are you, over?" Coleman watched the guard while he waited for the reply.

Hackett and Stroble were on the narrow shoreline next to the dock unpacking their weapons when the call came over their headsets. Hackett responded, "We just got out of the water and are getting ready to move up the stairs, over."

"You've got a guard and a dog approaching the cliff. You have about ten seconds before he gets there, so hurry up, over!"

Without hesitation, they grabbed their waterproof backpacks and scurried up the steep, zigzagging flight of stairs. The whole time, they looked to their left waiting for the guard to appear a mere hundred feet away. They reached the top with seconds to spare.

While Coleman was watching the guard, Michael kept an eye on the house. He listened to Coleman give Hackett and Stroble a second-by-second update of what the guard was doing. Seconds after Coleman announced that the guard had reached the edge of the cliff, the French doors of Arthur's study opened, and the owner of the estate strode out onto the brick veranda. Michael felt his heartbeat quicken as he watched Arthur approach the far edge. As quietly as possible, he whispered to Coleman, "Our target has appeared. I repeat, our target has appeared, over."

Coleman turned around just in time to see the bright orange flame of Arthur's lighter licking away at the tip of the cigar. Hackett and Stroble were asking for a verification, and Coleman gave it to them. "Hermes and Cyclops, our target is in sight, and I have no idea how long he's going to be there. Move into position as quickly as possible, and give me the play-by-play, over."

Hackett and Stroble ran toward the tree where Hackett had sat the night before and stopped at the base. Hackett whispered into his mike, "How many guards in the backyard, over?"

"One guard, over," answered Coleman. Coleman leaned around the back side of the tree and whispered to Michael, "You keep an eye on Arthur, and I'll watch the guard." O'Rourke nodded.

Stroble and Hackett quickly affixed the silencers to the end of their weapons and put on their backpacks. Stroble slung his MP-5 over his shoulder and clasped his hands in front of his stomach. Hackett slung his rifle over his back and put his right foot in Stroble's clasped hands. Stroble boosted Hackett up and he grabbed the first branch, pulling himself quietly into the tree. Not wasting any time, Stroble turned and ran along the wall toward the front of the house. When he reached the tree where he had been the night before, he stopped and checked for noise. Then, pulling himself up into the tree, he looked for the guard standing by the front door. He peered over the top of the wall and saw nothing. Quietly, he swore to himself and then called Coleman. "Zeus, this is Hermes. I've got a problem. The guard by the front door is not at his post, over."

"Can you see him anywhere in the front yard, over?"

"That's a negative, over."

"Get your rope set up, and we'll wait as long as we can, over." Coleman stayed calm, telling himself these things never went exactly as planned. "Gentlemen, let's be patient. Get ready to go on a moment's notice. As soon as the other guard appears, we'll move, over."

Now that Hackett was in position, Coleman could watch Arthur.

He judged the distance between Arthur and the house to be about forty feet. There was no way he could beat him to the door, so he would have to fire some warning shots in his path. He'd thought about shooting him in the leg, but the old man might bleed to death before they found out what they needed to know.

Stroble's voice came over their headsets. "The missing guard just appeared from inside the house, over."

Coleman took a deep breath and stared at Arthur, who was puffing away on his cigar. "Do we have any other surprises, over?"

One by one they responded that they were ready to go. Coleman gave Michael the thumbs-up signal and they grabbed their ropes. "Cyclops, do you have a clear shot, over?"

"That's a roger, over."

"Hermes, do you have a clear shot, over?"

"That's a roger, over."

Coleman took one more deep breath and said, "On my mark, boys. Three . . . two . . . one . . . bingo!"

Hackett squeezed the trigger and sent a bullet smashing into the head of the guard by the cliff and then pumped a quick round into the dog.

Out in front of the house Stroble fired three silent shots at the head of the guard by the front door. The first one hit him in the temple, killing him instantly. Grabbing the rope, Stroble swung from the tree and landed just on the other side of the fence. Stroble dropped to one knee and searched for the dog. It was nowhere in sight. Without hesitation, he snapped his gun up toward the roof and squeezed off a dozen shots. The bullets thudded into the metal casings that covered the cameras, sending sparks flying. He heard a growl to his right, and the thick, black muzzle of the silencer snapped back to a level position, sweeping from left to right.

The dog was closing fast, growling as he ran. Stroble sent one bullet into the snout of the dog, and the creature skidded to the ground. Slamming a fresh magazine into his gun, Stroble rose and ran for the other set of cameras, firing bullets into the windows as he went.

Coleman hit the ground a second before Michael, and as he sprinted for the patio, he could hear the bullets from Michael's gun striking the cameras above and to his left. The noise of the bullets hitting the cameras must have caught Arthur's attention because he looked in their direction. Coleman thought he was reaching for a gun at first, and then he noticed that it was his watch. Arthur broke into a decrepit run for the house, and Coleman laid down a wall of bullets that sent chips of brick flying into the air. Arthur stopped in his tracks. As Coleman closed on him, he screamed for Arthur to put his hands in the air while he unleashed a volley of bullets at the second set of cameras. Just as he got to Arthur, the floodlights came on. Coleman brought his boot up and kicked Arthur in the stomach, sending him to the ground. Coleman wheeled, firing at the floodlights hanging from the gutter of the house. Michael did the same, and within seconds, darkness was restored.

Arthur was curled up and holding on to his stomach with both hands, gasping for air. Michael pulled a chloroform patch from his thigh pocket and ripped it open. Shoving his gloved hand into Arthur's face, he forced the old man to breathe in the fumes. After about ten seconds, Michael tossed the patch to the side and went to work on getting Arthur's clothes off. Less than thirty seconds had passed since they'd gone over the fence.

Stroble approached a moment later and helped Michael finish the job. Before leaving, he made sure everything was in the bag and then sprinted for the north wall. All that remained on Arthur were his boxers. Michael threw the skinny old man over his shoulder and ran for the south wall with Coleman covering the way. When they reached the wall, Coleman jumped up, sat on the top of the wall, and pulled Arthur up by his arms. Michael went up and over, and then Coleman dropped Arthur into Michael's arms. Coleman jumped down and the three of them disappeared into the darkness and onto the grounds of the old estate.

Hackett watched from the tree and made sure Michael and Coleman got over the wall safely. As soon as they were over, he fired three shots into the door of Arthur's study and rappelled down the tree. He landed like a cat and turned for the cliff. By the time he reached the top of the steps, he could hear the twin engines of the Cigarette boat revving. He bounded down the steps, taking them three at a time. When he hit the dock, he broke into a dash for the boat.

Stroble already had the boat turned around and pointing toward the open water. Hackett leapt through the air and landed on the cushioned pad that covered the engines and then he jumped into the cockpit. Both engines roared to life as Stroble punched the two black throttles all the way down. The bow rose out of the water as the props forced the boat forward. Hackett turned and scanned the cliff for any movement. The long, sleek boat quickly gained speed and planed out. Stroble checked his watch. One minute and forty-three seconds had elapsed since they'd gone over the wall.

CHAPTER 35

CHARLIE Dobbs was contemplating his next move when the monitor to his right started beeping. Dobbs glanced over his shoulder after the second beep and moved his chair. The monitor beeped three more times, and the information came up on the screen.

FLASH TRAFFIC: LEVEL 5
TYPE: PERSONAL ALARM
SUBJECT CODE NAME: RED COYOTE

Dobbs stared at the code name and tried to match it with a face but couldn't. These personal alarms had become kind of a pain in the ass for the Operations Center. They were receiving more and more false alarms. Dobbs punched in his password so he could access the real identity of Red Coyote. A second later, the name Arthur Higgins appeared on the screen. That's a first for him, Dobbs thought. No need to get excited yet. He probably hit it by mistake. Dobbs looked through the Plexiglas and watched the operator for the United States work to verify the alarm. The home phone number for Red Coyote came up on the screen along with several others. Dobbs tapped in a keystroke so he could listen to the operator handle the situation. Their system told them that the alarm was coming from his estate, but no one was answering. He listened to the phone ring. After about thirty seconds, Dobbs started to get nervous. The file on Red Coyote said that he had around-the-clock security. Someone should have been answering the phone.

A second later, a frantic voice did.

Director Stansfield was sitting at his desk reading a report on the mental stability of North Korea's leadership. Because of the recent flurry of assassinations his regular work was suffering. He didn't like falling behind, there were too many potential problems just over the horizon. As director of the Agency, Stansfield saw it as his job to know and understand who the players were in each country that had an adversarial relationship with the United States. When things turned sour, he wanted to be able to predict the behavior of the men he was up against.

The phone rang and Stansfield removed his spectacles, rubbed his eyes, and then picked it up. "Hello."

"Thomas, it's Charlie. We've got a major problem! Someone just grabbed Arthur Higgins!"

Stansfield sat up straight. "How long ago?"

"His personal alarm went off about four minutes ago. We called his estate and one of the security guards verified that they'd been hit."

"I'm on my way down." Stansfield hung up the phone and headed for the door. When he reached the outer room, his bodyguard looked up from behind a desk and Stansfield said, "Come on, we're going downstairs." The director continued into the hallway and shoved his ID card into the slot next to the elevator. Five seconds later, the doors opened and they stepped in. While the elevator descended, Stansfield battled to suppress the hope that Arthur had been killed. He hoped so for two reasons. The first, which embarrassed him, was personal. Arthur had ignored Stansfield's warnings to cease his activities in the intelligence community. He was a growing security risk and a thorn in Stansfield's side. The second reason was purely professional. If Arthur was dead, he couldn't be interrogated. He had more damaging secrets in his head than any other person in the Agency. Arthur had conducted unofficial operations that no one else knew about, and his knowledge of official CIA operations was thorough. If he was taken alive and interrogated, the Agency would be compromised at every level. The damage would be unimaginable.

The elevator opened and Stansfield approached the door to the Operations Center. He placed his hand on a scanner, and a second later the door opened. Charlie Dobbs was standing with his watch officers conferring on the crisis.

Stansfield approached. "Give me the rundown."

"We're tracking his homing signal right now." Dobbs pointed at the big screen in the front of the room. A detailed map of the Chesapeake was on the screen and a slow-moving red dot. "It appears they've got him on board a boat and are making a run for the open sea."

"Do we know how it happened?"

"We've talked to the guard who was running the control room inside Arthur's house. He says Arthur stepped outside to smoke a cigar, and then they came over the wall. He isn't sure how many of them there were because they shot his cameras out. Two of the guards are dead, and there is no sign of Arthur."

"What procedures have we put into effect?"

"We've scrambled two Cobra gunships out of Quantico and an AWAC was on patrol when the whole thing went down. The AWAC has confirmed our bogie and has classified it as a small watercraft moving at a speed of sixty-two knots. I have also notified the Coast Guard, and they are moving to set up a picket at the south end of the Bay."

"How long will it take for the choppers to intercept?"

"If there is no course change, they should intercept in about ten minutes." They all looked at the big board and watched the moving red dot. "I also activated two of our security details. I'm sending one to the estate to investigate, and the other will be airborne within the next two minutes. I'm sending them after the boat."

Stansfield shook his head. "Charlie, do whatever it takes to get him back."

Stroble peered over the top of the windscreen, his night-vision goggles helping slightly, but not much. The stars and moon were blocked out by the thick clouds, and the water was black. He kept the boat just to the west of the channel markers. The Chesapeake was notorious for unmarked sandbars, and now would not be a good time to run aground on one. Hackett came out from the small cabin and announced that the charges were set. He kept his night-vision goggles up on the top of his head and checked the sky and water behind them.

They were less than a minute away from their demarcation point. Hackett threw their weapons and equipment over the side, everything except their fins and mask. Taking two short pieces of rope, Stroble tied the steering wheel down so the boat would stay on a straight course. He looked at his watch and gave Hackett a thumbs-up. Hackett got on top of the engine cover and without hesitation dove off the back of the boat, curling into a ball. As soon as Hackett was away, Stroble flipped on the running lights, grabbed his fins and mask, and ran for the back of the boat. He leapt clear of the propellers and also tucked into a tight ball. He hit the water and skipped several times, rolling as he went. Their bodies stung slightly from the initial impact, but otherwise they were fine.

Hackett appeared at Stroble's side, and they paused for a second to watch the boat rumble away. They put on their fins and masks and started swimming as fast as they could for shore. They had a little over a mile to go. Before leaving the boat, Hackett had placed a series of small, timed charges that would rip holes in the bottom of the boat's hull. They pumped their arms powerfully through the water, their fins doing most of the work. Shortly, they were within two hundred yards of shore.

Hackett stopped and so did Stroble. Sticking his hand into the neck of his scuba suit, Hackett pulled out his radio headset. Without putting it on he held the unit next to his ear and said, "Mercury, this is Cyclops, come in, over."

"I read you loud and clear, Cyclops, over."

Hackett and Stroble bobbed up and down in the water, staring at the dark shoreline. "Can you give us a mark on your position, over?" They both saw the flicker of red light. Marking the position with a dip in the tree line, Hackett responded, "I've got a fix. We'll be joining you in a couple of minutes, over."

Hackett shoved the headset back under his suit and was getting ready to swim again when he heard an all too familiar noise. Stroble heard it, too, and they both sank a little deeper in the water. The chopping sound grew, echoing off the water. It was hard to get a fix on where it was coming from, but there was no doubt what it was. It was getting louder. They turned in the water, looking skyward.

The noise increased markedly, and then, without warning, two helicopters screamed over treetops above where Tim O'Rourke was waiting. For a brief second, both former SEALs thought they had been discovered, but the choppers didn't stop. They kept going, racing overhead, out into the Bay and then turning south. Stroble and Hackett looked at each other quickly and then sprinted for shore.

Back in the Operations Center the tension was mounting. Stansfield watched the chase unfold on the big board. The display from the AWAC was up on the screen. Arthur's homing signal hadn't changed course. It was still headed south. The position of the two Cobra gunships was marked by a duo of green triangles on the screen. The radio communication between the pilots of the choppers and the airborne controller on board the AWAC was being played over the loudspeaker. The choppers were closing quickly.

Dobbs turned to Stansfield and said, "I have to tell the pilots what their rules of engagement are."

Without pause Stansfield replied, "If they are met with the slightest resistance, they are free to use whatever force they deem necessary. I want that boat stopped."

The small charges exploded, ripping three holes in the bow of the boat and two more next to the engines. The holes in the bow acted as scoops, funneling water into the cabin. In the stern, water rose rapidly, the engines straining with the extra weight and the loss of a smooth hull. The engines revved louder and louder until they were smothered by the water. All forward movement stopped and the expensive boat slipped beneath the surface of the dark water.

The controller on board the AWAC announced the decrease in speed before it was noticeable on the big board in the Operations Center. He continued to read off the decreasing speed until the boat had stopped. Stansfield, along with everyone else in the room, watched the helicopters rapidly close the gap. The green triangles inched closer and closer to the stationary red dot. The AWAC's controller vectored the choppers right in on top of the mark, and then came the surprise. The pilots announced no boat was in sight.

The black BMW weaved through the busy Friday-night traffic of Georgetown. As Coleman drove, he told Michael that his former boss, Admiral DeVoe, had called to tell him the FBI was snooping around asking questions. A pensive O'Rourke asked, "Did he say why they are interested in you?"

"Only that they wanted to know why I was discharged early."

O'Rourke stared out the window and said, "That means they

know about Snatch Back. Did the admiral tell you who called him?"

"No. All he said was that they were from the Bureau. Michael, I wouldn't get too worried yet. They might just be going down a list of former SEALs."

"I doubt it. The FBI is looking for someone who had motive enough to do this, and when they find out Fitzgerald was the one who leaked Snatch Back, they're going to be all over you." O'Rourke nervously tapped his fingers on the dashboard. "And then they're going to find out about Mark's death, and they're going to get real interested in you."

"Let them look. They're not going to find anything. They can't prove I knew squat about who leaked Snatch Back. I found out from you, and you weren't supposed to know."

Michael thought about it. "If all they have is Fitzgerald's connection to Snatch Back and your brother's death, that won't be enough to indict, but it will be enough for them to assign a couple dozen agents to watch you around the clock. You are going to have to lay really low for a while. Dump the car as soon as we're done tonight, and don't go back to the garage."

Coleman agreed, and several minutes later he turned onto Michael's street. They stopped in front of Michael's house and O'Rourke jumped out. Flipping up the black cover on the security pad, he punched in the code for the garage door and it opened. Coleman backed the car into the tight garage, and Michael followed, closing the door behind him. At first they were going to bring Arthur to the cabin, but since it was only fourteen miles from the estate, they thought it would be best to bring him back to the city where they could use the busy traffic and people for cover.

Before opening the trunk, Michael and Coleman pulled their mesh masks down over their faces. Coleman inserted the key into the lock and pushed in. The trunk opened, revealing the bony white body of Arthur. His eyes were glassy and his wrists and ankles tied together with rope. A blue racquetball was shoved in his mouth. Michael dug the ball out and Arthur moved his jaw. With a deep look of confusion he stared up at the two dark figures. Michael almost felt sorry for Arthur and then remembered who he was.

Coleman grabbed him under the armpits and Michael grabbed his ankles. Together they hoisted him out of the trunk and brought him into the house. The ground level of O'Rourke's brownstone consisted of a single-car garage on one side and a utility and washroom on the other. They brought Arthur to the corner of the washroom and set him on the floor with his back against the wall. Coleman went out to the car and came back with a small black case. He set it on top of the dryer and opened it. Inside were two clear liquid vials and several syringes. Coleman grabbed the vial labeled sodium pentothal, tilted it upside down, and stuck the tip of a syringe through the rubber top. Pulling the plunger back, he filled the syringe about halfway. After putting the vial of truth serum back in the case, he let the bubbles rise to the top of the syringe and squeezed some of the fluid out.

Arthur mumbled something, and Coleman ignored him. The chloroform was wearing off. Coleman grabbed a stick of smelling salts and broke it open. He stuck it under Arthur's nose, and the pungent smell forced the old man to yank his head away. Coleman did it several more times and Arthur responded verbally.

"What are you doing? . . . Where am I?"

Coleman ignored him and grabbed the syringe from atop the dryer.

Arthur looked up at the needle and realized what was going on. "Before you use that, let's talk for a second."

Coleman kneeled down and grabbed Arthur's arm. Arthur's eyes shot frantically back and forth between the head of the masked man and tip of the needle. "I don't know who's paying you, but I'll double it."

Coleman found a blue vein just under the surface of Arthur's thin, dry skin. He slid the needle in and depressed the plunger.

Arthur watched with a panicked look on his face. "You have no idea what you're doing. My people will come looking for me. . . . They will find you no matter what it takes!"

As Arthur shouted, Coleman walked out of the room and shut the door behind him. Michael came down the stairs with a tape recorder, video camera, and a set of small speakers. He handed them to Coleman and went into the garage to grab the mobile scramble phone. When Michael got back, he asked Coleman how long it would take for the drug to take effect, and Coleman told him about another five minutes. Both of them went back into the wash-room. The second they opened the door, Arthur began pleading, his voice growing more placid by the minute.

Michael and Coleman ignored him while they set up the equip-ment. O'Rourke plugged the two speakers into the mobile scramble phone and attached the voice modulator to the mouthpiece of the handset. Coleman took the video camera and mounted it on top of a tripod. They did a quick test to make sure everything checked out. Michael waved for Coleman to follow him, and they stepped out into the hallway.

"Remember, I'll ask the questions. If you want to say some-thing, turn off the tape recorder and camera first. If we end up using this tape, the CIA and the FBI will analyze every little noise."

"Understood."

"Is there any chance he'll be able to lie to us?" asked Michael.

"No, I've used this stuff in the field before, and you can't fight it."

Michael nodded and they went back into the room. Arthur sat in the corner staring up at the light in the middle of the ceil-ing. Coleman approached, grabbed Arthur's jaw, looked into his heavily dilated eyes, then told Michael Arthur was ready. Coleman turned on the camera and Michael hit the record button on the tape recorder. Speaking into the modulator, Michael asked, "What is your name?"

Director Stansfield stared at the big board on the front wall of the Operations Center and noted the running time since Arthur's personal alarm had been sounded. They were approaching the forty-minute mark, and things were not looking good. With each tick of the clock, the odds of getting him back got worse. They were still getting a signal from Arthur's beacon, but the Cobra gunships had found nothing. Navy frogmen were on the way from Norfolk to find out what was beneath the water. At first they thought Arthur's alarm might have been thrown overboard by his abductors, but the AWAC operator told them the bogie had stopped dead in the water. The quick-reaction team had arrived at Arthur's estate and was assessing the situation. Only one thing was certain: Arthur was nowhere to be found.

Stansfield watched as his people in the Operations Center alerted the Coast Guard, local law enforcement agencies, airport officials, and U.S. Customs agents to be on the lookout for anything suspicious. For security reasons, they didn't tell anyone the real reason for the alert, only that they were looking for a fugitive. They didn't want the story ending up in the press. Stansfield knew if they were to get Arthur back at this point it would take luck, and to get lucky they had to hustle. For every minute that expired, their chances of getting him back decreased. Stansfield also had procedure to follow. He picked up a secure line and dialed the number for the National Security Desk at the White House.

"National Security Desk, Major Maxwell speaking. Please identify yourself."

"This is Director Stansfield of the CIA. Is the president on premise?"

"Yes, sir."

"Alert the National Security Council and bring them in. We have a potential crisis in the making. Tell the president I'll be there in fifteen minutes."

"Yes, sir."

Stansfield hung up the phone and told his bodyguard to get the chopper warmed up. The director then turned to Dobbs. "Charlie, hopefully we'll get him back, but we have to start preparing for the worst. Get everyone in here. I want damage assessment reports as quickly as possible. We need to know what current operations might be in jeopardy, and how many of our agents' covers could be blown if Arthur is interrogated."

"Do you want me to alert our friends overseas?"

"Don't tell the embassies yet. We'll wait another hour or so."

"What about the Brits? Arthur did a lot of work with them."

Stansfield hadn't even thought of that yet. Their allies would be extremely upset. "Hold off on that for another hour or so. I'll have to make those calls personally. If any further developments arise, call me immediately."

Arthur answered the last question of his life. Michael looked at Coleman in complete disbelief and hit the stop button on the tape recorder. As Michael rose, he pointed toward the door and Coleman followed. When they got into the hallway, they took off their masks and stared at each other. They could not believe what they had just heard.

Michael spoke first, through clenched teeth. "This is unbelievable!"

"It's more than unbelievable, it's enough to bring the whole government down. Do you know what would happen if we released this tape to the press?"

"We'll be the bastards of the international community," said O'Rourke.

"It'll rip the country apart. If Watergate tarnished the presidency, this will destroy it forever." Coleman pointed toward the room. "Do you want to ask any more questions?"

O'Rourke thought about it for a second and said, "No. We found out what we wanted." Michael looked at his watch. "The sooner we get rid of him the better."

"I agree. Make a copy of the tape, and I'll take care of Arthur."

They both went back into the room. Michael grabbed the tape and went upstairs. Coleman grabbed the empty syringe from atop the dryer and pulled the plunger back, filling it with air. Bending down, he looked into Arthur's glassy eyes for a second, and then, with utter disdain, he stuck the needle into Arthur's arm. Coleman depressed the plunger, sending thousands of lethal air bubbles into Arthur's bloodstream. Coleman had no desire to watch him die and went to the garage to find something to wrap the body in.

Michael came back downstairs several minutes later and helped Coleman wrap Arthur in green trash bags. They placed the corpse in the trunk of the BMW and covered it with some blankets. Coleman looked at O'Rourke and asked, "What are you going to do with the tapes?"

"I'm not sure."

"Are you thinking about releasing them to the media?"

"I'm not so sure it would be a good idea."

Coleman nodded. "I think it would set us back a hundred years."

"I agree."

"Well, whatever you decide to do, you're going to have to do it without me. I don't think you and I will be able to see each other for a while. If you're right about the FBI, I'm going to have to lay low."

"I've been thinking about that. This tape might come in handy."

"How?" asked Coleman.

Michael shook the tape in front of Coleman's face. "This little confession would topple the entire government if it was released.

Whether Stevens was involved or not, he would be implicated. He would be willing to do almost anything to keep this from being released, and the CIA . . . they stand to lose the most. If this thing went public, the entire Agency would be shut down within a week. They would do almost anything to keep it quiet."

"Yeah, like putting a bullet in the back of our heads."

"Not if we do it right. Let's talk about it in the car."

"You're coming with me to dump the body?" asked a surprised Coleman.

"Yeah, I know the perfect place."

CHAPTER 36

DIRECTOR Stansfield's helicopter flew up the Potomac, its bright spotlight shining off the dark water below. It banked to the east, passing over the Lincoln Memorial, and continued up the Mall. The strobe light fluttering near the White House alerted the pilot to his exact landing area on the South Lawn. The small chopper came in and set down gently on the grass. Stansfield opened the door and got out, bending at the waist as he walked clear of the blades. Two Secret Service agents approached and escorted him through the Rose Garden and into the West Wing of the White House, where they were greeted by one of Stu Garret's aides.

Stansfield started for the stairs that would take him to the Situation Room and the aide said, "Excuse me, sir. I was told to bring you to the Oval Office."

With a look of surprise Stansfield asked, "Why?"

"I don't know, sir. I was only told to take you to the Oval Office."

Stansfield followed the aide down the hallway and into the empty presidential office. The aide left and Stansfield stood awkwardly in the middle of the room shifting his weight from one foot to the other. As the minutes mounted, so did his blood pressure. He looked at a Secret Service agent standing watch at the door and asked, "Where is the president?"

"He's attending a state dinner, sir."

Stansfield looked down at the floor and then back at the agent. For the first time in a long while he thought he might lose his temper. The complete lack of professionalism by the Stevens administration was wearing on him. Instead of yelling, he turned and walked over to the president's desk. Picking up the phone, he told the operator to get him the National Security Desk.

Several seconds later, there was a click on the line and a voice said, "National Security Desk, Major Maxwell speaking, please identify yourself."

"CIA director Stansfield. Have the members of the National Security Council been told that I've called an emergency meeting?"

"No, sir."

"Why?"

"I was told to wait until you arrived, sir."

"By whom?"

"Chief of Staff Garret, sir."

Stansfield's voice stayed even, but gained a slight edge. "Major, is Chief of Staff Garret in the national security chain of command?"

"No, sir."

"Listen to me carefully. We have a level four national security crisis on our hands. I am giving you a direct order to send out an alert immediately! I want the NSA, the SOD, the SOS, and the chairman of the Joint Chiefs here within the next ten minutes! Am I understood?"

"Yes, sir."

Stansfield hung up the phone and dialed the number for the CIA's Operations Center. Charlie Dobbs answered and Stansfield asked him for an update.

"The divers found a boat sunk at the spot where the beacon was last marked. They also found a bag on board with Arthur's clothes and watch. . . . It looks like a diversion."

"Anything else?" Stansfield looked up from the desk as Garret strutted into the room wearing a tuxedo. Before Dobbs could answer, Stansfield said, "I have to go, Charlie. I'll call you back." Stansfield hung up the phone and watched Garret approach in his black tuxedo.

Garret pulled a cigarette out of his mouth and said, "This better be good, Tom. This is the first time the president has had a chance to relax in over two weeks."

"Where is Mike Nance?"

"He's at home. What's so important?"

Stansfield was almost distracted by the anger he felt for Garret but forced himself to stay focused on the crisis. "A high-level CIA official has been kidnapped."

"How high?" asked Garret as smoke billowed from his nostrils.

"I'll tell you as soon as you get the president down in the Situation Room where he should be!" Stansfield's frustration was becoming evident.

"Hey, take it easy, Tom. You can't expect us to drop everything we're doing every time you call over here."

Stansfield shook his head and walked toward the door. "This is not a game, Mr. Garret. I expect to see the president down in the Situation Room immediately!"

Coleman was back behind the wheel of the BMW and was less than excited about Michael's dumping spot. Originally, Coleman had planned on taking Arthur's body out to sea. He thought they had pressed their luck enough for the evening, and Michael's idea was far from cautious. Michael wanted to leave Arthur's body where it would be found—where they could send a message.

Burning Tree Country Club was less than ten minutes from Michael's house. As they neared the golf course, Coleman said for the third time, "You know, the Secret Service will be watching his house."

"I know. I'm not planning on leaving him at the front gate. He has a corner lot. We can leave the body around by the side. We'll drive by the house once and check out the security."

"You've been in the house before?"

"Yes. Senator Muetzel used to live there. After Muetzel lost in the last election, Garret bought it from him." Michael looked over at Coleman and said, "I want to show these bastards that we're willing to go to the media with this thing. If we end up releasing the tape, leaving Arthur's body at his house will give it more meaning. Besides, it'll make Garret and Nance sweat."

"That's true."

They reached the ritzy neighborhood several minutes later, and Michael directed Coleman to the house. It was a large Tudor with a wrought-iron fence that ran around the entire yard. They drove slowly past the front gate, where a Ford sedan was parked across the driveway. Two men were sitting in the front seat and one camera was over the gate. Coleman took a left at the end of the property and turned down the next street. On this side of the house the fence was lined with trees and bushes.

"What do you think?" asked Michael.

"I think it's doable." Coleman pulled a U-turn in the middle of the road and stopped the car on the same side of the street as Garret's house. He turned off the lights and looked down the tree-lined side street.

Michael tugged on his thin leather gloves and said, "I'm ready when you are."

Coleman took his foot off the brake and the car slowly rolled forward. When they reached the back edge of the property line, Michael pulled the fuse so the dome and brake lights wouldn't come on. Coleman told Michael to pop the trunk and he did.

While the car was still rolling, Michael jumped out and opened the trunk. He tossed the blankets to the side and scooped the dead body out of the trunk. The fence was only fifteen feet from the curb. Michael ran the short distance and set Arthur down, propping him up against the wrought-iron bars. Yanking the green garbage bag off his head, Michael threw it on the ground and jumped back in the car. Coleman spun the car around and sped away.

Grabbing the mobile scramble phone out of the backseat, Michael punched in the phone number for the local NBC affiliate. After several rings, someone answered on the other end.

"Newsroom."

"Listen to me carefully." Michael spoke in a slow, precise tone. "This is not a prank. There is a dead man at Stu Garret's house. The man's name is Arthur Higgins. He is a former employee of the CIA. The body can be found by the fence on the north side of the house. The address is 469 Burning Tree Lane."

"Who is this?" asked an eager voice. "How do I know this isn't a prank?"

"You don't, but you'd better get one of your news crews out there as quick as you can, because I'm calling the other two networks right now." Michael pushed a button ending the call and immediately dialed the next number.

The next two calls went about the same as the first. The more Michael thought about it, the more he knew the news directors couldn't resist investigating. A dead former CIA employee found on the property of the president's chief of staff would make for juicy news. The only catch was that the news crews had to get there before the Secret Service found the body.

As they neared Georgetown, Michael said, "Things are going to get really hairy. This might be our last chance to talk for a while. If the FBI is on your tail, call my pager and punch in nine seven times."

"What are you going to do with the tape?"

"I'm not sure. I'll figure something out. Pull over up here."

Coleman pulled over and offered his hand.

Michael took it and said, "Lay low until things cool down." Michael slammed the door, and the car sped off.

The secretary of defense and the secretary of state were also attending the state dinner. So as to not raise too much attention, they left the room in intervals, the president being the last. When Stevens arrived in the Situation Room, Director Stansfield was on the phone and the secretaries of state and defense were standing off to the side talking to Garret. The president approached his chief of staff. "Stu, what's this all about?"

"Stansfield says a high-level CIA official has been abducted."

"How high?"

"I don't know, he hasn't told us. He's been waiting for you."

The thought of Arthur being the official in mind was something that Garret hadn't considered. Arthur was, after all, a former CIA employee and lived in the United States. Garret assumed the CIA employee in question must be someone stationed abroad.

Stansfield hung up the phone and approached the group. "Good evening, Mr. President. I'm sorry to interrupt your party, but something very serious has come up."

"What's the problem?"

"The Agency's former director of Black Ops, Arthur Higgins, was abducted from his home in Maryland at seven oh six this evening."

Garret's cocky attitude vanished instantly. His mouth fell open, and his face turned white.

Stansfield noticed the change in the chief of staff's demeanor and focused in on him while he continued. "Right now we have no idea who has taken him or why, but we have to assume the worst if we don't get him back soon. Higgins is in possession of a vast amount of highly sensitive information. If he is interrogated, our intelligence apparatus will be affected on a global scale." Garret's reaction was so out of character that Stansfield paused for a second and then asked, "Mr. Garret, I didn't know you knew Arthur."

Garret stammered briefly and said, "I . . . didn't. I've just heard his name mentioned before."

Stansfield crossed his arms. He knew Mike Nance and Arthur had a professional relationship, but he found it hard to believe that Nance would talk to Garret about Arthur. "What have you heard about him?"

"Nothing really, I just know he used to work for the Agency."

Stansfield stared suspiciously at Garret. It was obvious that he was lying. Garret was acting far too strange over something that shouldn't affect him. Instead of speaking, Stansfield let the silence build, increasing the tension and turning everyone's focus on Garret.

"Do we have any idea who would have taken him?" asked the president.

Without looking away from Garret, Stansfield answered, "My people are putting together a list right now. Arthur has been retired from the Agency for almost two years, but he has continued to use his international contacts to conduct quasi-legitimate business endeavors. We have kept tabs on him and even warned him several times to keep his nose out of official Agency matters."

"What are we doing to get him back?" asked the president.

"We have contingency plans in place for something like this. We've faxed photos of Arthur to all of the airports and police departments on the Eastern Seaboard. We are telling people that he is wanted for questioning in a murder and that he is to be approached with extreme caution. The Air Force had an AWAC on patrol when he was kidnapped and they have launched another. They are looking for any small-plane traffic that may be trying to fly under our conventional radar systems. As time elapses, we will alert our people overseas and have them meet incoming flights from the U.S."

The phone that Stansfield had been talking to Charlie Dobbs on earlier started to ring. Stansfield excused himself and grabbed it. "Hello."

"Thomas, we found him," exclaimed Dobbs.

Stansfield breathed a huge sigh of relief and asked, "Where?"

"You're not going to believe this. He's at Stu Garret's house."

"What?"

"He's dead. I'm watching it on the damn news. His body is propped up against Garret's fence. All three networks are at the scene filming live. The cops aren't even there yet."

"How did they get there so fast?"

"We don't know."

"Do we have our people on the way?"

"Yes."

Stansfield's mind raced to try to make a connection between Arthur and Garret. "Charlie, hold the line for a minute." Stansfield lowered the phone to his side and looked at the group. "We found him." Stansfield paused to read Garret's reaction and then said, "He's dead."

Garret looked like a murderer who had just received a not-guilty verdict from a jury. He exhaled deeply and asked, "Where?"

"At your house."

The look of panic and fear returned to Garret's face instantly. "What?"

"The media is at your house right now broadcasting the entire story."

"At my house?"

"Yes." Stansfield studied the frazzled Garret and asked, "Why would someone dump Arthur's body on your lawn?"

While Garret stumbled for an answer, the president grabbed the master remote and turned on the entire bank of television sets.

Garret responded to Stansfield's question with wide eyes. "I have no idea . . . absolutely no idea."

Cocking his head in a doubtful manner, Stansfield said, "I'm afraid you're going to have to do better than that."

Garret shook his head emphatically. "I don't know. I really don't even know the guy."

Stansfield looked at him pensively. There was no doubt Garret was hiding something. Stansfield brought the phone back to his mouth. "Charlie, I'll be there in about thirty minutes. I want a complete update as soon as I land." Stansfield hung up the phone and checked his watch. He thought about asking Garret to come with him so his people could debrief him but knew Garret would never go for it. Besides, he needed to do some checking first.

Stansfield looked over at the president, who was staring aghast at the TVs. "Sir, this is a potentially embarrassing situation for you, but all in all we are very lucky. Whoever took Arthur didn't have enough time to interrogate him, so it looks hopeful that we haven't been compromised in any way. I have to get back to Langley and start working on damage control. Our allies are going to want some answers. I will call you as soon as I find anything out, otherwise I think we should plan on meeting in the morning."

"That sounds like a good plan," responded a confused President Stevens.

Stansfield gave Garret one more questioning look and left.

As soon as he was out the door, Stevens pulled Garret aside and said, "Stu, what in the hell is going on?"

Garret shook his head sideways and asked himself where in the hell Mike Nance was.

CHAPTER 37

C OLEMAN found a poorly lit parking lot downtown and left the Beamer unlocked with the keys in the ignition. From there he walked the two miles to Adams Morgan. It was a good night for clear thinking. The cool air helped sharpen his senses. He was out of the game and knew it. The FBI would be waiting for him, it was only a question of where and how many agents. If he really had to, he could lose them and go underground, but that would only make him look guilty. For now the game plan would be to act normal.

As Coleman neared his apartment, he became more aware of his surroundings, looking for things he hadn't seen before. The call from Admiral DeVoe had raised his level of paranoia significantly. By measuring his difficulty in detecting the surveillance Coleman would be able to tell how interested the FBI was. If he passed a van with dark-tinted windows, or a four-door sedan with a driver slouched behind the wheel, he would know the FBI thought him no more important than the other hundred or so former commandos they were investigating.

Coleman walked like a predator, his eyes taking inventory of everything around him. He was loose physically but tight mentally. Turning onto his street, he scanned the row of cars from beginning to end. Nothing: no vans, no trucks. They might be parked on one of the other streets. He would have to check them in the morning when he went for a jog. Turning up the steps to his apartment building, he opened the first door and then used his key to get through the second one. He climbed to the second floor and stopped in front of his door. Bending over, he checked the lock for any signs of its being picked. There were none, but that didn't mean it hadn't been done. There were professionals who could do it without leaving a mark. Coleman opened the door and entered. After turning on the lights, he grabbed the remote control off the coffee table and turned on the TV. With the remote control in hand, he closed the shades and turned up the volume. Coleman set the remote down and grabbed a small black sensor about the size of a garage-door opener out of his pocket. Starting by the TV, he worked his way around the room, running the box over and under every piece of furniture. The sensor didn't detect a single listening device in the room. Without turning any lights on, Coleman checked the kitchen, bathroom, and his bedroom. Again, he found nothing.

Instead of becoming less tense he grew more nervous. Not finding any bugs didn't mean he wasn't under surveillance; it could also mean that whoever was watching him was good. Coleman grabbed a small flashlight out of the top drawer of his dresser and crawled under his bed, where he kept a box of interesting but legal items.

The box was always lined up the same way, the front edge directly under the center bar of his bed frame. He turned on the flashlight and eyeballed the edge of the box. It was off center. Someone had been in his apartment.

Coleman crawled back out and brought the box with him. Staying on the floor, he put the flashlight in his teeth and opened the box. Inside was a legally registered Glock semiautomatic pistol, three clips, a box of ammo, a knife, a pair of night-vision goggles, and a variety of other things that wouldn't be that unusual for a former Navy SEAL to own. Coleman grabbed the night-vision goggles, and went into the bathroom, where he whistled out loud and turned on the shower. Sitting on the toilet, he took off his boots and then walked to the front door. As quietly as possible, he opened the door and slid into the hallway. Staying on the balls of his feet, he ran up the carpeted steps to the top floor. Someone had been in his apartment, and they had been smart enough not to leave any electronic listening devices behind. They weren't down on the street, so that meant one thing . . . they were in one of the nearby buildings.

Coleman reached the top floor and opened the service door that led to the roof. Inside was a black metal ladder with a hatch door at the top. He climbed the ladder and slowly opened the hatch. As he climbed onto the roof, he was careful to keep his silhouette beneath the three-foot flange that ran along all four sides of the roof. Coleman crawled to the front of the building and peeked over the edge. One month earlier he had checked to see which apartments were vacant in the surrounding buildings. Coleman started with the building right across the street. He counted up three stories and in two windows from the left. Pushing himself up just a little farther over the edge, he stared intently at the black hole and watched for movement. It was too dark to see more than a foot or two into the apartment, so he put on his night-vision goggles.

Black turned into green and white, and after several adjustments the goggles penetrated the dark, empty room. There they were, a cluster of long, black objects. He could plainly see the row of directional microphones lined up along the bottom edge of the windowsill, all of them pointing across the street at his apartment. Behind them on tripods were several cameras, and then . . . something moved. Coleman squinted and it moved again. A man was standing a ways back from the window drinking something. Coleman slid under the wall and crawled back to the hatch.

When Coleman got back to the apartment, he analyzed the situation. As a SEAL he'd been trained in countersurveillance tactics and knew what represented good surveillance . . . the people watching him from across the street were good. Coleman grabbed his jacket and brought it into the bathroom. Holding the digital phone by the rushing water of the shower he punched in the number to Michael's pager and entered nine seven times.

McMahon stood in the middle of the empty apartment. A pair of large headphones covered his ears. He took a big gulp of coffee and glanced over at the other two agents sitting at the table in the dining room. A small red filter light illuminated their game of gin. They were on a twenty-minute rotation. Every noise in Coleman's apartment was taped, and everyone who left or entered the building was photographed. More than a dozen tail cars of assorted makes and models were strategically positioned around the city, and a chopper was on twenty-four-hour standby, its engines warm and pilots waiting.

Michael was sitting upstairs in his den holding a mug of hot coffee when his beeper went off. He picked it up and looked at the small display. All nines. Michael set it down and thought about Coleman. Next, he looked at the tape of Arthur's confession, and a plan started to form in his head. Going to the media would cause more harm than good, but Nance and Garret had to pay. They were going down, one way or another—whatever it took.

Stansfield climbed wearily into the back of his limo. The night had been one of many questions and no sleep. The large door at the end of the executive parking garage at Langley opened revealing the early-morning sun, and Stansfield lowered his tired eyes. The director had spent the entire night in the Operations Center trying to piece together the events surrounding Arthur's abduction. Two important facts had been brought to Stansfield's attention. First, strong traces of sodium pentothal had been found in Arthur's blood. Second, a fact discovered while his people were reviewing

Arthur's security tapes, Stu Garret and Mike Nance had visited Arthur the previous week. Garret had lied.

Stansfield found out about the sodium pentothal just after midnight, but the security team that had been dispatched to Arthur's estate didn't discover the videotape of Garret and Nance until 6:45 A.M. He had an 8 A.M. meeting at the White House, but instead of going straight into D.C., his entourage was taking a slight detour. He had to pick up an uninvited and, he was sure, unwanted guest. Stansfield's limousine, along with its lead and chase cars, cut through the light Saturday-morning traffic. At about 7:35 A.M. they arrived at Director Roach's house.

Roach climbed into the limo, and the group of cars pulled away. As the director of the FBI settled into the backseat, he asked, "I assume this has something to do with Arthur turning up dead on Stu Garret's lawn?"

Stansfield shifted so he could face Roach. "Yes, it does."

"What is Mr. Garret doing associating with someone like Arthur?"

"I don't know." Stansfield shook his head and frowned.

"I would imagine you want this to be kept as quiet as possible."

Stansfield's face hinted that he was struggling between doing what was comfortable and trying something new. "At this point I'm undecided. Our two agencies have worked in the past to keep things like this quiet, but I'm not so sure I wouldn't prefer you to raise hell on this one. . . . There's no doubt this is your jurisdiction. Arthur was kidnapped, transported across state lines, and murdered." Stansfield bit his lip and shook his head. "Brian, Arthur was not the most law-abiding person we had at the Agency. Most of that had to do with the type of things we expected him to do, but he also did a lot of things that were not approved through the proper channels. That's why he was forced out two years ago. We had lost control of him. To be blunt, his death is a blessing. He was a walking time bomb with enough secrets in his head to do an incredible amount of damage to not only our country but quite a few of our allies."

"So you would like me to sit on it?"

"Yes and no. I do not want what Arthur did for the Agency to become public, but there is an issue I need resolved, and to do that I think I'm going to need you to threaten an all-out investigation."

"This is where Garret comes in?"

"Yes, Arthur was not dumped on his lawn without reason. He and Nance were involved in something with Arthur."

"Are you sure?"

"As sure as I can be at this point. . . . Last night, after Arthur was kidnapped and before his body was discovered, I went to the White House to brief the National Security Council. When I told them that Arthur had been abducted, Garret became noticeably agitated. So much so that I had to stop in midsentence and ask him if he knew Arthur personally. Garret said no . . . that he had only heard of him through Mike Nance." Stansfield frowned. "You know as well as I do, Stu Garret doesn't show concern for anyone unless he stands to lose something. Later, when I told them that Arthur's body had been discovered on Garret's lawn, he almost had a nervous breakdown."

"Did he admit to any involvement with Higgins?"

"No, he still denied it."

"What did Nance say?"

"He wasn't at the meeting. He was tied up somewhere else. I left the White House a little more than suspicious. Garret was hiding something, and my suspicion was soon backed up by two disturbing facts. Arthur's autopsy revealed sodium pentothal in his blood. He was interrogated, but whoever did it must have only wanted a specific piece of information; there wouldn't have been time for more. We also have a surveillance video from Arthur's security room with Garret and Nance on it. They visited him last Saturday, and Nance also came alone on Thursday—which means Garret lied to me about not knowing Arthur."

"So what role would you like me to play?"

"I need you to threaten a full-scale investigation. We'll give them two options. They can either sit down with my people and tell them everything they know under the protection of the national secrecy act, or they can give a deposition to you and your agents and risk prosecution."

Roach thought about it for a minute. "As you said earlier, this case is under the jurisdiction of the FBI. What if at some point I decide to pursue the investigation regardless of any deal you may have struck with Nance and Garret?"

"That's entirely up to you."

Stu Garret paced frantically behind his desk with a cigarette in hand. Mike Nance sat stiff and upright on the couch. He'd been watching Garret for the last ten minutes, waiting for the Valium to kick in, straining to control the urge to bash Garret over the head with a lamp. He had to stay calm . . . above everything he had to stay calm.

Garret stopped and pointed his cigarette at Nance. "I can't believe I let you talk me into this. I must have been out of my fucking mind when I agreed to get into bed with Arthur."

Nance bit down on his lip and said, "Stu, do you think your emotional tirades are doing us any good?"

"Hey, don't give me that cool-as-ice attitude. You deal with it your way, and I'll deal with it my way. . . . Fuck!" Garret took a vacuumlike pull off his cigarette and his face turned bright red.

Nance stood abruptly and raised his voice. "All right, I'll do things your way! Sit down and shut up! We have a meeting with Stansfield in ten minutes, and we are going to have to come up with some answers as to why Arthur's body ended up on your lawn . . .

and if you don't get control of your emotions, Stansfield will tear you to shreds!" Nance stared hard at Garret.

Garret exhaled and his shoulders slumped. "I'm sorry, Mike, I just can't believe all of this is happening so fast. What in the hell are we going to do? Stansfield is going to want to know why Arthur was found at my house. He knows I was lying to him last night when I told him I'd never met Arthur. What in the fuck am I going to tell him? What am I going to tell the press? What am I going to tell the cops? They're gonna want to talk to me, too."

Nance put a hand on his shoulder. "Stu, one problem at a time. Don't worry about the cops and don't worry about the press. For the next hour, I need you to stay calm and keep your mouth shut. Stansfield is our main problem. Now just sit down and relax while I tell you what we're going to do."

Garret sank into the couch and stuck a cigarette in his mouth.

Nance paced slowly across the room. "I have a good idea for damage control." With his hands on his hips, he turned and said, "We tell Stansfield the truth."

Garret blurted out a loud cackle. "Have you lost your fucking mind! . . . Yeah . . . sure . . . let's tell him the truth . . ."

Nance stuck his finger in Garret's face. "Stu, this is the last time I'm going to tell you to stay quiet and get control of yourself. Don't forget, Arthur put a price tag on your head before he was killed, and I'm the only one who can rescind the order." Nance stared as hard and as deep as he could into Garret's eyes, making sure there was no doubt that he was serious. Garret tried to speak, but Nance cut him off. "Shut up, Stu. Just shut up for the next five minutes!"

Garret bit down on his tongue and nodded.

"We are going to tell Stansfield about our recruitment of Arthur to help get the president's budget passed. We'll tell him that Arthur helped blackmail Congressman Moore. It is simple, it is the truth, and Stansfield will buy it because we can prove it. We admit to some wrongdoing and Stansfield goes away satisfied."

"What about the press? I can't tell them that."

"Stu, I'm not going to say it again! We are talking about Stansfield right now! We'll talk about the press later."

"Should we tell Jim?"

"No! That way he'll have complete deniability. We can tell him after the meeting that we wanted to protect him. Just let me do the talking, and whatever you do, don't lose your cool."

Nance finished filling Garret in on the plan, and when he was done, they went down to the Situation Room. Nance stopped when he entered the room and looked for Stansfield. He wasn't there yet, but the Joint Chiefs, the secretary of state, and the secretary of defense were. Nance quickly realized they could not be present when he gave Stansfield their excuse.

Nance walked to the far end of the room where the president was sitting and whispered into his ear, "Sir, for reasons I can't discuss right now, I need you to excuse the Joint Chiefs, the secretary of defense, and the secretary of state from the meeting."

"Won't that look rather unusual?"

"Please, trust me, sir. We need to talk to Director Stansfield alone. . . . It's for the best. I'll explain later."

Stevens hesitated for a second and then looked at Garret and made the connection. Clearing his throat, he said, "Gentlemen, there has been a slight change of plans. I am going to need to talk to Director Stansfield alone. If the rest of you could wait for us in the Cabinet Room, we'll join you just as soon as possible."

The generals and admirals all stood and gave Garret a look as they headed for the door. They all knew who Arthur Higgins was and wanted to know why he had been found dead on the chief of staff's lawn. They continued out the door, and Nance closed it behind them.

Stevens asked, "Are you two going to tell me what in the hell is going on?"

"Mr. President, sir . . . I think it would be best if we waited for

Director Stansfield to get here," replied Nance in his cool and detached voice.

"Why?"

"You are going to want complete deniability on this one, sir."

Stevens frowned. "What in the hell have you two been up to?" The president looked to Garret for the answer, but Nance gave it.

"Sir, this will not affect your presidency. You are just going to have to trust me that it will be best if you look surprised when we tell Director Stansfield what our connection with Arthur was."

CHAPTER 38

MICHAEL sat above the rest of the morning traffic as he rolled through downtown D.C. in his forest green Chevy Tahoe. He was tired and nervous. His nerves were shot from a lack of sleep and too much coffee, not to mention the little excursion involving Arthur. When he was about four blocks away from the Hoover Building, he dialed the phone number for the main switchboard. After several rings a woman with a pleasant voice answered.

"Federal Bureau of Investigation. How may I help you?"

"Special Agent McMahon, please."

"Just one moment."

The phone started to ring again and then another person answered. "Special Agent McMahon's office."

"Special Agent McMahon, please."

"Special Agent McMahon is away from his desk right now. May I ask who is calling?"

"Is he in the building this morning?"

"I'm sorry, but I'm not allowed to answer that. May I ask who is calling?"

Michael hit the brakes to avoid ramming a cab that pulled out in front of him. "This is Congressman O'Rourke, and I need to speak with him . . . it's extremely urgent!"

"Special Agent McMahon is very busy right now. It would help if I could tell him what it was that you wanted."

"I don't want anything. I need to give him something that I think he will be very interested in."

"What is it regarding?"

Michael let out an audible sigh. "Listen, I know you're only trying to do your job, but this is something that I can't talk about over the phone."

"You said your name was Congressman O'Rourke?"

"Yes."

"I'll see if I can track him down, but it would help if I could give him even the slightest hint as to what you wanted. He has been getting a lot of phone calls from congressmen and senators lately."

"I don't want anything from him. I want to give him something. Something that will have an enormous impact on his investigation."

"Just one minute, Congressman. I'll see if I can track him down."

With his digital phone clutched to his ear, O'Rourke circled the Hoover Building. Several minutes later, McMahon answered the phone.

"Congressman O'Rourke, sorry to keep you waiting. How are you doing?"

"I've been better."

"Sorry to hear that. What can I do for you?"

"I have something that I need to give you."

"What is it?"

"I don't want to talk about it over the phone."

"All right, let me get my Day-Timer and see when I have an opening."

"This can't wait."

"Congressman, do you have any idea how busy I am right now?"

"Yes, I do. Believe me, it won't be a waste of your time."

McMahon paused. "When do you want to meet?"

"I'm down on the street, in my truck."

"Ah . . . I'm in the middle of something right now, can you give me an hour?"

Michael tried to sound as relaxed as he could. "Special Agent McMahon, do you want to know who killed Senator Olson and Congressman Turnquist?"

There was a moment of silence on the line and then McMahon responded, "All right, I'll be down in five minutes. Pick me up at the south entrance."

O'Rourke completed one more circle and pulled up to the curb. McMahon came out of the building a moment later and approached the truck with someone Michael didn't recognize. Michael rolled down the passenger window and McMahon leaned in, sticking his hand out. Michael grabbed it and said, "Who is she?"

"This is Irene Kennedy. She works for the CIA and has been helping out with the investigation."

"Get in," replied O'Rourke.

McMahon climbed in the front seat and Kennedy got in back. Michael put the car into drive and pulled back out into traffic. Looking in the rearview mirror, Michael asked, "What do you do for the CIA, Dr. Kennedy?"

"I'm an analyst."

"What do you analyze?"

"Terrorism is my specialty."

"Are you familiar with a guy by the name of Arthur Higgins?"

Kennedy moved forward. "Very. . . . What do you know about him?"

Michael reached down and grabbed a letter-sized manila envelope from the center console and handed it to McMahon. "I found this on my doorstep this morning along with a tape, and you're not going to believe what's on it." Michael put the tape into the cassette player.

Stansfield and Roach entered the Situation Room and sat across the table from Nance and Garret. Both directors said hello to the president, but ignored his national security adviser and chief of staff.

Nance hadn't planned on Roach coming. He forced a slight smile onto his face and said, "Director Roach, we weren't informed that you would be joining us this morning."

"I asked him to come," replied Stansfield. "Arthur was transported across state lines and killed. The investigation falls under the jurisdiction of the FBI."

"What investigation?" asked Nance.

"The investigation into his death."

"Surely you aren't serious. We can't have what Arthur did for the CIA brought under public scrutiny."

"That will be up to Director Roach and the Justice Department." Stansfield looked at the president. "Sir, may I be blunt?"

"I would prefer it," responded an aggravated Stevens.

"Arthur Higgins was privy to a rather large amount of highly classified information. My foremost concern is to identify the correlation between his being taken from his estate and being left at Mr. Garret's house. I have to know what Arthur's relationship was with Mr. Garret so I can assess any possible damage to the Agency. We can go about this one of two ways: Mr. Garret can either tell me and my people everything he knows under the protection of the national secrecy act, or he can tell his story under deposition to the FBI."

The president looked at Garret and said, "Stu?"

Garret turned to Nance for direction. Nance cleared his throat and said, "Director Roach, would you excuse us for a minute?"

Roach didn't say a word. He looked to Stansfield, who nodded, telling him it was all right. Roach got out of his chair and left the room. As soon as he was gone, Stansfield zeroed in on Garret. "What was your relationship to Arthur?"

Again, Garret glanced at Nance for support. Nance looked back across the table and said, "Arthur was helping us with a little project that had nothing to do with the CIA or the intelligence community."

"What was the project?"

"I would rather not say." Nance didn't want to give in too quickly.

"That's not how this is going to work, Mike. You either tell me, or the FBI starts digging, and neither of us want that."

"It was purely a domestic issue . . . political in nature."

"All the more reason that the FBI should be involved," responded Stansfield.

"Thomas, I'm telling the truth. What we were doing with Arthur had nothing to do with the Agency. He was simply doing some freelance work for us that was political and nothing else."

Stansfield looked at his watch and then at Garret. "Do you want me to bring Director Roach back in?"

The speechless Garret had beads of sweat forming on his forehead and upper lip. He was so flustered all he could do was shake his head from side to side.

"What in the hell is going on here?" asked the president. "A former employee of the CIA shows up dead on your lawn, Stu, and you look like you're about to have a nervous breakdown. I want some answers!"

"Sir, as I said earlier," responded Nance, "for your own protection, I think it would be best if you remained in the dark on this."

"For my own protection, I want to know what in the hell is going on!" Stevens's complexion reddened.

Nance took a deep breath and paused, as if gathering his thoughts. "We recruited Arthur to help aid in the passage of your budget through the House."

"How?" asked the president.

"He did some . . . background checks on several congressmen."

Stansfield shook his head sideways knowing full well what *background checks* really meant.

The president asked, "What do you mean by 'background checks'?"

"Arthur gathered some information for us that we used to convince some of the more reluctant congressmen to vote for your budget."

"You did what?" asked an exasperated Stevens. "Stu, was this your idea?"

"No . . . well, kind of . . ."

Stansfield watched the president grow irate and decided that he had likely been kept in the dark.

Kennedy was too engrossed in Arthur's taped confession to do anything but listen. When it was over, it dawned on her that she needed to get ahold of Stansfield immediately. Grabbing the digital phone from her pocket, she dialed the direct line to her boss's office. After six rings it rolled over to his secretary. "Director Stansfield's office. How may I help you?"

"Pat, this is Irene. Where is Thomas?"

"He's at the White House."

"Get ahold of him immediately!" said Kennedy tersely. "It's very important."

McMahon was in the front seat doing the same thing, but trying to get ahold of Roach. Michael continued to drive and prepare himself for the inevitable landslide of questions.

Back in the Situation Room, Stansfield waited for the president to stop yelling and then asked, "Who did he blackmail?"

"I think we have cooperated more than enough," responded Nance. "You don't need names."

"Yes, I do. Because I am going to have to talk to them."

"Thomas, I would prefer to let this thing die," said Nance.

"I'm sure you would, but I'm not going to let it. Whoever killed Arthur also interrogated him. The pathologists told me he was loaded with sodium pentothal. If you two think you're out of the woods by telling me you blackmailed several congressmen, you're wrong. Whoever took Arthur got some information out of him, and it obviously had something to do with Mr. Garret."

A look of sheer panic flashed across Garret's face and he shouted, "They interrogated him?"

Nance stayed calm and smiled. "You're bluffing, Thomas."

"I'll show you the toxicology reports if you'd like."

"Don't insult me." Nance smiled with a wide grin and said, "You could doctor them to say anything you wanted."

"Come now, Mike, who is insulting who? Look at your friend Mr. Garret. He's wound up so tight he's about to snap. You're not telling me everything there is to know about your dealings with Arthur, and that's fine." Stansfield held his hands up. "I'm sure Director Roach and his people will have more success in finding out what really happened."

"Enough!" snapped the president. "Stu and Mike, I want to hear the whole story right now. No more games!"

There was a knock on the door and a Secret Service agent entered. "Director Stansfield, your office is on the line. They say it's an emergency. You can take the call right here." The agent pointed to a phone on a table by the door.

Stansfield walked over to the phone and grabbed it. "Hello."

Kennedy sat in the back of O'Rourke's truck and spoke rapidly into her phone. "Thomas, this is Irene. Where are you?"

"I'm in the Situation Room."

"I have something that you are going to want to hear immediately."

"What?"

"I can't say, just trust me. Leave there immediately, and get back to Langley as quick as you can!"

Stansfield looked over his shoulder at the president, who was yelling at Nance and Garret. "Irene, I'm in the middle of something really important."

"Thomas, I have a taped confession from Arthur, and you're not going to believe what's on it."

Stansfield hesitated for a second and replied, "I'll get there as quickly as I can." After hanging up, Stansfield walked back to the table and looked at the president. "I'm sorry, sir, but something very important has come up. I'm going to have to head back to Langley."

Stevens shook his head. "What could be more important than this?"

"I don't know, but I'll call you as soon as I find out. We'll have to continue this later."

Adjacent to Director Stansfield's office was a soundproof conference room. Kennedy, McMahon, and Michael sat at the conference table and waited for Director Roach and Director Stansfield to arrive. Michael kept wondering when the questions would start. He knew that eventually McMahon would ask why the assassins chose him to be their courier. Michael would play dumb and profess his hatred and open contempt for Washington politics. The tape was his trump card. As long as the FBI and the CIA thought that hundreds of copies could be mailed to the media at any moment, they would watch where they dug. Even if they did find something, where could they go with the information?

The door flew open and Stansfield and Roach entered, agitated and out of breath. Stansfield yanked off his overcoat and said to Kennedy, "Irene, this had better be for real. You just pulled me out of a huge meeting."

"Don't worry, it won't be a waste of your time." Kennedy pointed at Michael. "Thomas, this is Congressman Michael O'Rourke. He came to us with some information that you're not going to believe." Kennedy looked back at O'Rourke and said, "Congressman, this is Director Stansfield and Director Roach."

Michael rose and shook both of their hands.

McMahon pointed at Michael. "When the congressman awoke this morning, he found a package on his front step. It was from the assassins. Inside was a taped confession of Arthur Higgins." McMahon held up the tape and shook it. "It contains some disturbing information. Along with the tape is a list of conditions the assassins want met."

Stansfield gestured for Roach to take a seat and said, "Let's hear it."

McMahon inserted the tape and pressed play.

Some static began hissing from the small tape player, and then Michael's computer-altered voice asked, "What is your name?"

"What?" asked Arthur's drugged voice.

"What is your name?"

"Arthur . . . Arthur Higgins." Stansfield's eyes closed.

"When were you born?"

"February thirteenth, 1919."

"Who were your parents?"

"Arthur and Mary Higgins."

"Who do you work for?"

"I don't work for anyone. Why don't you take those masks off and we'll talk. . . . I'm a very wealthy man."

"Who did you used to work for, Mr. Higgins?"

"The CIA."

"What did you do for the CIA?"

"A lot of things. . . . Why don't we talk about releasing me before you find out something that you don't want to know."

"When you were at the CIA, which directorate did you work in?"

"Operations."

"Specifically, what part of the Operations Directorate?"

"Black Ops . . . I did a lot of stuff."

"What did you do for the Black Ops?"

"I ran it."

"Why did you leave the CIA?"

"I quit."

"Did you quit or were you forced out?"

"I was forced out."

"Why were you forced out?"

"They were afraid of me."

"Who was afraid of you?"

"Everyone."

"Specifically, who was afraid of you?"

"Stansfield and Olson." Stansfield didn't bother looking up. He kept his eyes closed and listened.

"Mr. Higgins, were you the author of a covert operation back in the early sixties that resulted in the assassinations of several French politicians?" Stansfield felt a sharp pain shoot through his forehead.

"Yes," responded Arthur's thick voice.

"Who were you working for at the time?"

"The CIA." Irene Kennedy looked to her boss. She had never heard of the covert operation, but it was long before her time.

"How many French politicians did you kill?"

"Two."

"Who were they?"

"Claude Lapoint and Jean Bastreuo." Stansfield gripped his forehead and squeezed hard, wondering how the interrogators had managed to find out about one of the most classified operations in the history of the Agency.

The generic computer voice continued, "Why were they killed?"

"Because they were ungrateful bastards."

"Could you be more specific?"

"They were the leaders of a movement within the French parliament that wanted all U.S. nuclear weapons removed from French soil."

"Did anyone in the French government know that the CIA had killed two of their elected officials?"

"No."

"How did you kill them without getting caught?"

"We made it look like French revolutionaries did it."

"While you were with the CIA, did you conduct other operations similar to this?"

"Yes."

"Since you left the CIA, have you conducted any operations similar to the one that you ran in France?"

"Yes."

"Have you ever conducted an operation like this in the United States?" Stansfield's eyes opened with the realization of where the confession was headed.

"Yes."

"Did you use the recent string of assassinations as a cover to kill Senator Olson and Congressman Turnquist?"

"Yes." Roach shook his head and said, "Oh my God."

"Why did you kill Senator Olson and Congressman Turnquist?"

"I had Olson killed for my own personal reasons and Turnquist . . . we killed him to confuse the FBI and the CIA."

"Why did you kill Senator Olson?"

"I hated him. He was a weak man who had no business interfering in the operations of the Agency."

"Why did you hate him?"

"He blocked my nomination for director of the CIA. I should have been the next director, but instead Stansfield, that weak imbecile, got it, and it was all Olson's doing."

"Who else was involved in your plot to kill Senator Olson and Congressman Turnquist?"

"Mike Nance and Stu Garret." Roach shook his head and said, "Unbelievable."

"Why did they want Olson killed?"

"Olson was going to announce that the new coalition was a sham. That their proposed budget cuts were fake."

"Garret and Nance wanted to have him killed for that?"

"It was my idea, and Nance brought Garret in on it because we knew how desperate he was to get control of the situation. Besides, we knew if we killed some federal agents, it would undermine the public support for the terrorists."

"What were you getting out of the deal?"

"Garret said he would get the president to force Stansfield out and replace him with me. With Olson gone no one would block my nomination."

"Did the president know about your plans?"

"I don't know." After several tense moments of static, the tape ended.

Roach and Stansfield shared a long, shocked look. Michael watched them from the other end of the table. O'Rourke knew that Stansfield was taking the new information the hardest. It was his agency that would suffer the most if the tape became public.

Roach leaned over and whispered in Stansfield's ear, "Is there any truth to the story about the CIA assassinating two members of the French parliament?"

Not wanting to give a verbal response, Stansfield nodded his head yes.

Roach took a deep breath and said, "We've got some major problems."

"There's more." McMahon held up a white piece of paper covered in plastic. "This is addressed to the two of you." McMahon looked at Roach and Stansfield and started to read aloud: "'After hearing the tape, it should be painfully obvious to you why we left Mr. Higgins's body at Stu Garret's house. If we were the crazed terrorists that the president and his people have portrayed us to be, we would release this tape to every media organization in the world. The damage to America would be devastating. We would become the pariahs of the international community, the office of the presidency would be ruined, the American people's faith in the system would be destroyed, and the CIA would be shut down within twenty-four hours.

"'We do not want to see America torn apart over the selfish and evil actions of a select few, but the actions of Mike Nance and Stu Garret cannot go unpunished. In exchange for not releasing Mr. Higgins's confession, we demand the following: Mike Nance will announce his resignation by noon tomorrow and retreat permanently from public life. Thirty days from now, Stu Garret will also announce his resignation and cease any involvement in the American political process, at any level. Within six months, both Nance and Garret will be expected to convert half of their net worth and donate it anonymously to the families of the eight federal law enforcement officers they killed. None of this is negotiable. If at any point Nance and Garret attempt to renege on this arrangement, we will hunt them down and kill them.

"'We are unsure as to what involvement President Stevens had in this plot and, for now, are willing to allow him to stay in office if he meets the following conditions: He will act as a bridge between the two parties and cease all partisan politics. He will put together a balanced budget for the next fiscal year, and he will meet all of our previous demands regarding a national crime bill and a national sales tax to retire the national debt. If these demands are met, we will allow Stevens to run for reelection. If the president wavers at any point, we will release the tape to the media.

"'The second part of our demands involves the FBI. Director Roach, we do not expect you to condone what we have done, but you must at least recognize the differences between what we did and what Mr. Higgins, Mr. Nance, and Mr. Garret did. We murdered four corrupt politicians in an attempt to restore some integrity and common sense to a political system that has none. Mr. Higgins, Mr. Nance, and Mr. Garret murdered two of the only honest politicians in Washington and eight federal law enforcement officers, all for their own perverted self-interests.

"'If you agree not to prosecute Mr. Nance and Mr. Garret, you must also agree to never bring forth any indictments regarding the assassinations of Senator Fitzgerald, Congressman Koslowski, Senator Downs, and Speaker Basset. We understand the compromising situation this puts you in, but considering the piece of information in our possession, we think it a reasonable trade-off.

"'For your own safety and the integrity of the FBI, we would also suggest that the president, Mr. Nance, and Mr. Garret be kept in the dark about your knowledge of our deal. It would be best for all if Director Stansfield handled the negotiations with the White House. We will await the announcement of Mike Nance's resignation. If it is not made public by noon tomorrow, we will be left with no other option than to release the tape.' " McMahon set the letter down.

Director Stansfield closed his eyes and gently shook his head. Everyone waited for him to speak. He rose and said, "Please excuse Director Roach and me for a moment." Stansfield walked to the side door that led to his office and Roach followed.

Stansfield closed the heavy, soundproof door and walked over to the large picture window. "Well, that's one hell of a confession."

Roach looked at Stansfield's back and asked, "Do you believe it?"

Stansfield nodded. "Unfortunately, yes." His answer was followed by more silence.

Roach placed a hand under his chin. "I'm not sure it would be admissible in a court of law."

Stansfield shook his head and waved his hand as if batting the idea out of the air. "Let's not even entertain that line of logic. If they release that tape, we are in serious trouble, and I mean the entire country. Arthur's body has been identified by the media, and they have footage of him lying propped up against Garret's fence. Those two French politicians were in fact killed back in the early sixties, and the CIA was behind it." Stansfield pointed toward the conference room. "Brian, everything those assassins said is true. That tape will tear America apart."

"What do we do then?"

"We have to take the deal, and we have to work fast."

Roach sighed. "Can we trust these assassins?"

Stansfield turned around with hatred on his face. "Apparently we can trust them a hell of lot more than the national security adviser and the president's chief of staff."

"What in the hell were they thinking?"

"I have no idea."

"Do you think the president knew what they were up to?"

"My gut tells me no, but I haven't had enough time to thoroughly analyze the situation." Stansfield looked at his watch. "Brian, we have to move on this. A lot has to happen between now and noon tomorrow. My decision is a foregone conclusion. We have to do everything in our power to make sure that tape never goes public."

Roach paused. "I don't want that tape to go public either, but I sure as hell don't like the idea of Nance and Garret just walking away."

"Brian, I have a feeling that within the next year these assassins will take care of Mr. Garret and Mr. Nance, and . . . if they don't . . . I will have them taken care of. That is between you and me, friend to friend, not director to director."

Roach looked into Stansfield's eyes and reminded himself that his friend played by a different set of rules. "We really don't have much of a choice, do we?"

"No . . . so you agree to meet their demands?"

"Yes, but I'm not sure I can guarantee that no indictments will be brought forth. What if Skip finds out who these assassins are?"

"I'll gladly deal with that problem if it ever happens, but something tells me we'll never know who was behind this. They were right about another thing. You have to be left out of the loop. If this blows up in our face, the FBI must have complete deniability. The American people are going to have to turn to something for hope, and if the FBI is implicated in the cover-up, it will really look bad."

"I suppose you're right." Roach considered his options for a minute and then said, "Let's go talk to the others."

Michael, sitting next to McMahon, was trying to stay in character. Acting mad was not hard, but acting naive was. He kept reminding himself what he should and shouldn't know. Fortunately, everyone was so shocked by Higgins's confession that they'd been too preoccupied to ask him questions.

Roach took a seat and Stansfield remained standing. The director of the CIA crossed his arms and said, "It goes without saying that this is a very difficult situation. For reasons that we are all aware of, Brian and I have decided to try and meet the demands of the assassins. If you have any opinions, now is the time to voice them."

Stansfield looked to Irene Kennedy first. Kennedy glanced up at her boss and shook her head no. Kennedy knew full well that they were boxed in. The only reasonable action was to take the deal.

McMahon was next. He shifted uncomfortably in his chair. "I understand that our options are limited, but I think Garret and Nance are getting off way too easy. I think they should be strung up by their balls and left for the vultures."

"I can relate to your desire for retribution," said Stansfield. "As I was just telling Brian, I would be surprised if these assassins let either of them live for more than a year."

"What about my investigation?" asked McMahon.

"If you catch them, we will cross that bridge when we get to it. Do you have it in you to let them go if it comes to that?" asked Stansfield.

McMahon glanced over at Roach while he thought about the question. From the very beginning he'd had a gnawing respect for the unknown group. "If they turn out to be the type of people I think they are, and they really do have patriotic motives . . ." McMahon paused. "I'll look the other way."

"Congressman?" asked Stansfield.

Michael leaned back and said, "I'm not crazy about the cover-up, but given the situation, I don't see any other alternative."

Stansfield nodded. "We are all in agreement then. Before we proceed, I need to know if anyone else knows about this tape. Congressman?" Stansfield looked to Michael for an answer.

With a calm face Michael replied, "I haven't told anyone."

"Skip?"

"No. As soon as Congressman O'Rourke played the tape for us, we came straight here."

"Irene?"

"No."

"Good." Stansfield looked at his watch. "I am going to go to the White House alone to handle the negotiations."

Michael cleared his throat and got Stansfield's attention. "Sir, I would like to come along."

Stansfield studied O'Rourke briefly and replied, "I think it would be best if I handled it alone."

"I'm sure you do, but Senator Olson was a very good friend of mine. I want to see the look on their faces when they realize they're not going to get away with this."

CHAPTER 39

IT was Mike Nance's turn to be nervous, but you wouldn't know it by looking at him. He sat with his perfect posture and minimal movement. Underneath, however, he wasn't so composed. Stu Garret was pacing back and forth in front of Nance's desk with an optimistic smile on his face, even though they had just spent the last half an hour getting yelled at by the president. Stevens was irate that he had been left out of the loop and that Garret and Nance had been involved in a scheme that could get Stevens impeached or worse.

Nance was worried about other things. He tried to ignore Garret as he blabbered on. "I think we're going to be okay. I really think everything is going to work out. Stansfield bought the whole blackmail story. . . . Jim will calm down in a couple of weeks and realize that we were only trying to protect him, and I know Arthur was a friend of yours, but, Jesus, he gave me the creeps. I have to admit I feel a lot better knowing that he took what he knows to the grave."

Without turning his head Nance looked up at Garret out of the corner of his eye and said, "Shut up, Stu."

"Hey, I'm only trying to lay everything out so we know where we're at."

"I know where I am, and I don't need you to point out the obvious. So kindly keep your mouth shut for several minutes. I'm trying to think."

Garret sat down on the couch and mumbled to himself. Nance turned his chair around so he wouldn't have to look at him. Why had Stansfield left the meeting so abruptly, just when things were heating up? They weren't out of the woods yet. He thought of mentioning that fact to Garret, but knew he preferred Garret's current obnoxious state to his frantic, panicked one.

Michael sat in the back of the armor-plated Cadillac with Stansfield. He was somewhat relieved that Director Stansfield was not a big talker. O'Rourke guessed correctly that Stansfield was preparing for his confrontation with Nance and Garret. Stansfield had almost called the White House to schedule the meeting, but at the last minute he decided it would be better if they surprised Garret and Nance.

When they were less than a mile from the White House, Stansfield picked up the secure phone and dialed the number for Jack Warch's office. Warch answered and Stansfield said, "Jack, this is Director Stansfield. I need an emergency meeting with the president, Mike Nance, and Stu Garret. I'm about to enter the underground parking garage of the Treasury Building. Please alert your agents that I will be coming through the tunnel." Stansfield glanced over at Michael. "I have a guest—Congressman O'Rourke. I'll vouch for him. . . . Jack, this is very serious. Please get them down to the Situation Room immediately." Warch got the point and Stansfield hung up.

The limousine pulled into the underground garage of the Treasury Building, and Michael and Stansfield were escorted by four Secret Service agents down a narrow cement tunnel. When they reached the other end, they stopped at a thick steel door that the Secret Service referred to as the Marilyn Monroe door. They held their identification up to a camera, and Stansfield asked, "Are you nervous?"

"No, I'm too mad to be nervous."

"Congressman, would you do me a favor?" Michael nodded yes, and Stansfield said, "When I play the tape, please keep an eye on the president. I'm going to be busy watching Mr. Nance and Mr. Garret. I would like your opinion as to whether or not the president is genuinely surprised by the tape."

Michael nodded and asked, "Is it safe to play the tape at the White House . . . I mean, won't the Secret Service be monitoring the meeting?"

"No, the Situation Room is secure. It's swept daily for bugs and is completely soundproof. The Secret Service is not allowed to monitor the room because of the classified information that is discussed."

The six-inch-thick steel door swung open, revealing Jack Warch. Stansfield introduced Michael to Warch while they continued down the hall. They entered a large room, and Warch escorted them past the National Security Desk to a door in the far corner. Stansfield and Michael entered the room, and Warch closed it behind them.

President Stevens was standing at the far end of the table. His suit coat was off and draped over the back of the high-backed leather chair in front of him. Nance and Garret were seated. It was obvious that the president was unhappy with his two confidants. Stansfield and Michael walked around the left side of the long table and stopped behind the last two chairs.

"Mr. President," said Stansfield, "this is Congressman O'Rourke."

Out of habit Stevens extended his hand, and then a strange look appeared on his face as he remembered his phone conversation with the young congressman some two weeks earlier. Michael shook the president's hand and the three of them sat.

"I assume whatever this is about has something to do with why you were called away so abruptly this morning?" asked the president.

"Yes . . . something very serious has been brought to my attention."

"What is the congressman doing here?" asked Garret in his usual impatient tone.

"He is here at my request."

Michael moved his eyes from Garret to Nance and stared at him with pure hatred.

Stansfield's answer wasn't good enough for Garret so he redirected his question to Michael. "Congressman O'Rourke, why are you here?"

Michael looked back at him and replied, "You'll find out soon enough."

"Mr. President." Stansfield pulled the tape from his pocket and held it for everyone to see. "Someone left this tape on Congressman O'Rourke's doorstep this morning." Stansfield looked at Garret and said, "Before I play it, Mr. Garret, would you like to tell us the real reason Arthur Higgins was dumped at your house last night?"

Garret shook his head and shrugged his shoulders. "I have no idea."

Mike Nance leaned back in his chair and stared at Stansfield like a cat.

"What is on the tape?" asked Stevens.

Stansfield walked to the other end of the table and inserted the tape in the cassette player. "It is a recording of a confession by Arthur Higgins before he was killed." Stansfield hit play and walked back to his seat.

Just as he sat down, Michael's electronically altered voice came over the speakers. "What is your name?"

"What?"

"What is your name?"

"Arthur . . . Arthur Higgins." Garret shot forward in his chair, covering his face with both hands. Reaching forward, Nance grabbed him by the arm and pulled him back, whispering in his ear, "Stay calm."

As Nance tried to keep Garret from losing it, the tape continued, with the generic computer voice asking Arthur about his past and what he had done for the CIA.

Director Stansfield had given up on watching Garret and was locked in a stare with Nance as the tape played on.

"Mr. Higgins, were you the author of a covert operation back in the early sixties that resulted in the assassinations of several French politicians?"

"Yes."

"Who were you working for at the time?"

"The CIA."

"How many French politicians did you kill?"

"Two."

"Who were they?"

"Claude Lapoint and Jean Bastreuo."

Barely able to contain himself, the president shouted, "What?" He looked to Nance for a full thirty seconds as the tape continued to describe the interrogation between Arthur and his captors. And then the more pertinent question was asked of the deceased Higgins.

"Did you use the recent string of assassinations as a cover to kill Senator Olson and Congressman Turnquist?"

"Yes."

Garret yelled, "It wasn't my idea! I swear it wasn't my idea!"

Nance ripped at his arm and pulled his face close. "Shut your mouth!"

The president stared at his close advisers, frozen in disbelief, and then the other shoe dropped.

"Who else was involved in your plot to kill Senator Olson and Congressman Turnquist?"

"Mike Nance and Stu Garret."

Garret tried to say something, but Nance pulled him back into his chair before he could.

Stevens closed his eyes and lowered his head while Nance stared unflinchingly back at Stansfield.

"Did the president know about your plans?" asked the cold, sterile voice.

The president looked to Stansfield. "I had nothing to do with this!" Stansfield ignored him and continued to stare at Nance.

Arthur's final words rang out: "I don't know."

The tape ended, and the room was filled with an awkward silence.

A slight smile creased Nance's lips and he said, "Nice try, Thomas."

With a placid expression Stansfield asked, "What do you mean 'nice try'?"

"All of that is a lie, so I have to assume you either tortured Arthur into making those bizarre accusations or you electronically altered the tape."

Stansfield stared at Nance unflinchingly. "Congressman O'Rourke received this tape earlier today along with a letter from the assassins that were responsible for killing Senator Fitzgerald, Senator Downs, Congressman Koslowski, and Speaker Basset. They are the ones that took Arthur, not me."

"What in the hell is going on here?" asked the president.

"I'm not sure, sir," replied Nance. "But I think Director Stansfield is trying to blackmail us with this tape. I can assure you, and so can Stu, that we never discussed assassinating Senator Olson and Congressman Turnquist with Arthur. The entire idea is preposterous."

"Stu?" asked the president.

Garret saw another chance to weasel his way out. "That's right, Jim. I don't know what in the hell any of this is about. The only dealings I had with Arthur were about your budget."

Michael slid forward to the edge of his chair and placed his hands flat on the table. His movement into the arena caught everyone's eye except that of Nance, who continued to stare at Stansfield. Michael stuck a hand in front of Stansfield's face and snapped his fingers, drawing Nance's attention to him. "Senator Olson was a very good friend of mine, and I'm not in the mood to play these little games." Michael pointed a finger at Nance's face. "You, Garret, and Arthur Higgins conspired to kill Senator Olson and Congressman Turnquist. No one made a fake tape, and Director Stansfield didn't force a false confession out of Higgins. Let's cut the crap and get down to business."

"Mr. O'Rourke," replied Nance, "you are a very young man, and you do not fully understand the lengths to which some people are willing to go to get what they want in life. Do you think Mr. Stansfield rose to be the director of the world's premier spy agency by being a Boy Scout? No, he will go to almost any length to get what he wants. Congressman, you are out of your league on this one. Maybe it would be best if you stepped outside and let us talk to Director Stansfield alone."

Pain began shooting through Michael's temples as his anger grew. He fought to suppress it as he rose to his feet. Slowly, he took off his jacket and laid it over the back of his chair. Michael leaned across the table and stuck his hand in front of Nance's face, his forefinger and thumb separated by less than an inch.

"Mr. Nance, I have about this much patience with you right now. You can either cut the shit and admit that you had Senator Olson and Congressman Turnquist killed, or I am going to walk out this door right now and hold a press conference."

"Congressman O'Rourke, that would be a direct threat to the national security of the United States of America, and I would be forced to stop you by whatever means necessary. Now, if you would please step outside, we would like to speak to Director Stansfield alone for a minute."

Michael took off his watch and placed it on the table. After tucking his tie into his shirt he pointed at Nance and said, "You are going to keep your slick mouth shut for the next two minutes while I talk to Mr. Garret, and I swear if you utter a single word, I'm going to come over there and knock your fucking head off!" Michael turned immediately to Garret. "All right, you've got one chance. I know you were involved, you know you were involved, and Director Stansfield knows you were involved." Michael walked toward the far end of the table and continued talking. "You can either admit to what you did and live the rest of your life in relative comfort, or you can stand trial and spend the rest of your life rotting in jail." Michael rounded the end of the table and started down the side where Garret and Nance were sitting. "Of course, that's assuming the assassins don't get to you first." Garret was sitting closest to him. Michael grabbed Garret's chair and turned it toward him so Garret couldn't look at Nance. "You see, the assassins also wrote in the letter that if you and Nance tried to squirm your way out of this, they would hunt you down and kill you."

"Mr. President," shouted Nance. "This behavior is entirely unacceptable!"

Before Nance could get his next sentence out, Michael shouted, "I told you to keep your mouth shut! That's my last warning!" Garret began shaking and Michael leaned in closer, placing his hands on the armrests and bringing his face within inches of Garret's. "What's it going to be? The choice is simple. Either you admit to what you did and walk away from this with your life, or you deny it and the whole country comes crashing down on you. Those assassins will release that tape if Nance doesn't announce his resignation by noon tomorrow." Michael screamed, "Now tell the truth!"

"I . . . I . . ." Garret started to stammer.

"Stu, don't answer him." Nance reached for the phone to call for the Secret Service agents standing watch outside the soundproof room. "I don't know who in the hell you think you are."

Michael saw Nance reach for the phone, and with both hands on the armrests of Garret's chair he jerked it out of his way. The chair, with Garret in it, slid across the floor and bounced into the wall. Michael took one step forward, raising his clenched left fist to his shoulder.

Nance had just got the phone to his ear when he looked up to see the looming O'Rourke. Michael's fist came crashing down like a piston, smacking Nance square in the nose and sending the national security adviser back in his chair and then springing him forward, his head thumping off the solid oak table.

The only thing that kept Nance from falling to the floor was that his chin was stuck on the edge of the table. His arms dangled at his sides, and a small pool of blood formed under his nose. Neither Stansfield nor the president moved.

Michael turned to Garret with his fist still cocked. Lunging forward, he grabbed Garret by the tie, yanked him to his feet, and slammed him against the wall. Michael released the tie and grabbed him by the throat. Garret reached up with both hands and pawed at Michael's fist. O'Rourke's hold was too strong. Michael squeezed harder, cutting off Garret's windpipe. In a voice loud enough so only Garret could hear, Michael said, "If I had it my way, I would kill you right now. You've got one more chance to come clean and admit to what you did. If you don't, I'm going to grab you by the hair and slam your face off that table until your head splits in half!"

Michael let go of Garret's throat and took ahold of the small patch of hair on the back of his head. Swinging him around, he presented the shaking chief of staff to Stansfield and the president. O'Rourke growled, "Tell them the truth!"

Garret began whimpering, "It wasn't my fault. It was Mike and Arthur's idea."

The president looked at Garret in utter shock. He couldn't believe any of this was happening.

"It wasn't my fault, Jim. I swear it wasn't my fault," pleaded Garret.

Garret's denial cum admission brought a second wave of uncontrollable anger rising up from within O'Rourke. He tossed Garret to the side, and as he bounced off the wall, he was met square in the jaw by O'Rourke's fist. Garret's upper body twisted briefly in the direction of the blow, and then his knees buckled, bringing his body crashing to the floor.

Michael stood over Garret for several seconds, adrenaline rushing through his veins, fighting the urge to kick his teeth in. He took several deep breaths and got control of himself. Turning, he looked at a wide-eyed and stunned President Stevens. Michael ignored him and walked back to where he had been sitting. As he put on his watch, he said, "Director Stansfield, I'll leave you and the president alone to work out the rest of the details. Call me later and we'll talk." Grabbing his suit coat off the back of the chair, he walked to the door. Neither Stansfield nor the president said a word.

CHAPTER 40

THE northwest wing of Mike Nance's rural-Maryland horse ranch was decorated in a turn-of-the-century Western decor. The large room was forty feet long and half as wide. Dark oak paneling covered both the walls and the ceiling. Three antique brass-and-wood ceiling fans helped partition the room into thirds. On the right was an ornate wood bar that looked as if it had been plucked out of an old Western saloon. The middle of the room was dominated by a stone fireplace with a buffalo head mounted above the mantel, and the far end was occupied by a billiards table. The walls were adorned with expensive oil paintings of Western landscapes and U.S. cavalry troops and Indians in the throes of battle.

The owner of this expensive collection of American art had never learned to appreciate the beauty and history of the room. His input into its decoration was limited to writing the check to the interior decorator. Mike Nance stood in front of the bar with a glass of Scotch in his hand. It was his third in less than an hour. Nance stared at his reflection in the mirror that adorned the wall behind the bar. The white bandage over his nose made his two black eyes look worse. With a tense restraint, he reached up and carefully pulled off the bandage. He set the blood-soiled bandage on the bar next to his drink and decided to leave the two pieces of crimson-colored cotton in his nose.

Looking into the mirror, he could see over his shoulder that the sun was floating downward in the western sky. Nance turned and walked to a set of French doors that looked to the west and over his estate. The soon-to-be-former national security adviser judged that in another hour it would be dark. He took a drink of Scotch and again asked himself if there was a way out. He was not ready to give up. His resignation did not have to be announced until noon tomorrow, and until then he wasn't done.

Nance heard the clamor of frantic footsteps coming down the hall, and a moment later the door sprang open. Stu Garret entered wearing a tan trench coat and minus two of his upper front teeth. Garret approached with his hands thrust outward in an apologetic fashion. "I'm sorry, Mike. I didn't want to talk, but I didn't see any other way out."

Nance had not seen Garret since he'd been knocked uncon-scious earlier in the day. An hour earlier Nance had called the loose-lipped chief of staff and summoned him to his ranch. Garret continued to blab, but Nance wasn't listening. As soon as Garret came within striking distance, Nance reached out in a wide arc and slapped him in the face. The sound of skin on skin rang out through the long room.

Garret immediately stepped backward and clutched his cheek. With his eyes opened wide he screamed, "What in the hell did you do that for?"

Nance felt a wave of satisfaction wash over him. He smiled ever so slightly at Garret. "That is for not keeping your mouth shut."

While rubbing the sore spot on his face, Garret shot back, "This whole thing wasn't my fucking idea, Mike. I can't believe I let—"

Nance raised his hand in preparation to strike again and took a step forward. Garret cowered backward and put his hand up to block the blow. Nance did not hit him. Instead, he kept his hand above his head and said, "I am the only thing standing between you and your grave, Stu. Lest you've forgotten, Arthur took out a contract on you before he died, and I'm the only one who can rescind it."

Taking another step backward, Garret said, "Well, why in the hell don't you call it off?"

"It's not that simple, Stu. And besides, I'm not so sure I want to."

"What do you mean, you don't want to?" asked a panicked Garret.

Nance finally lowered his hand and took a deep breath. "If you could have kept your mouth shut, we wouldn't be in this mess."

"What about the fucking tape?" asked Garret with bugged eyes. "They had that damn tape of Arthur admitting everything. That wasn't my fault."

"I knew I should have never listened to Arthur." Nance glanced upward and shook his head in frustration. "I told him you didn't have the stomach for this."

"Hey, I was fine until that madman O'Rourke started flexing his muscles."

"You were cracking long before he entered the picture." Nance turned and looked out the window for a moment. His thoughts settled on O'Rourke. "I wonder if Mr. O'Rourke knows more than he was letting on."

"What do you mean?"

"I think it might be worth our while to have a little chat with the young congressman." Nance looked past Garret and honed in on his own reflection in the mirror behind the bar. He reached up and gently touched his swollen, purple nose. "Besides, I'd like the opportunity to give him a little payback."

"Mike, are you fucking crazy? We've been given a chance to walk away from this whole mess. Let's take the deal and cut our losses."

Nance wheeled toward Garret, causing the chief of staff to abruptly step backward. "I have worked my whole life to get where I am." Nance stepped closer and Garret retreated, matching his strides. "I am more than willing to gamble on the fact that O'Rourke might know more than he claims. We have nothing else to lose thanks to you and your lack of composure." Nance turned away from Garret and walked toward the door. "Wait right here, Stu. I'll be back in a minute."

Nance walked to the opposite end of the four-thousand-square-foot rambler. He stopped at the door to his private study and punched in the eight-digit code for the security lock on the door. The light turned from red to green and he twisted the handle. After he entered the room the door closed behind him and automatically locked. Walking around the desk, Nance turned on his computer and sat in an old wooden swivel chair. He rocked back and forth and waited for the program manager to come on-line. He went into his personal database after entering his password, then pulled up the file manager. Pressing down on the mouse, he scrolled through a list of files until he found the one he was looking for. Nance double-clicked the mouse, and the system asked for another password. Nance entered it, and a moment later he was staring at the name he needed.

Nance reached down and opened the right drawer of the desk, revealing a secure phone. He picked up the handset and punched in the number. After several whirling noises, a curt voice answered on the other end, "Hello."

"Jarod, this is Mike. I need you to do a little job for me."

There was a slight pause. "How difficult?"

In a calm voice Nance replied, "No danger to you. The job is rather delicate though. Why don't we say . . . an even fifty."

Michael O'Rourke was sound asleep. The events of the last three days had left him exhausted. After his meetings earlier in the day at the White House and Langley, Michael made a brief appearance at a private visitation for Senator Olson and then went home to sleep. He had just enough energy to make it up the stairs to his bedroom before falling facedown and passing out. O'Rourke had lain in this position, without moving, for almost five hours.

Michael stirred slightly at the noise of someone in his room. He was deep in a dream, and at first, he couldn't decide if someone was really in his room or if it was part of his dream. He made an effort to roll over, but his arms were pinned underneath him and asleep. The next thing he knew he felt a hand on his head. His heart began to race, and his eyes popped open. It took a moment for his eyes to come into focus, and when they did, they revealed a concerned Liz Scarlatti hovering over him. O'Rourke rolled onto his side and freed his rubbery arms. He reached up for Liz and pulled her close.

Scarlatti smiled and kissed his ear. "I've been calling you all afternoon. Where have you been?"

O'Rourke rubbed his eyes and let out a big yawn. Then, looking toward the window, he asked, "What time is it?"

"Ten after six."

"Wow." O'Rourke stretched and twisted his body, letting out a groan. "That was the nap of the century."

"How long have you been asleep?" Scarlatti asked, running her fingers through his thick, black hair.

"I'm not sure. I think since around one." O'Rourke squeezed Liz tight and kissed her neck. "Mmm . . . you feel good."

"So do you. I haven't seen enough of you lately."

"We're going to have to rectify that." Rolling over, Michael pinned Liz underneath him.

She wrapped her arms tightly around his broad back and pulled him close, kissing him. O'Rourke's midsection growled loudly, and Liz froze her kiss. "Was that your stomach?" O'Rourke nodded. "What have you eaten today?"

O'Rourke looked up at the headboard while he tried to remember what he had eaten. "I'm not sure. It was a pretty hectic morning."

"Are you going to tell me about it?"

"Honey, I don't think you'd believe me if I told you."

With a cautious tone Liz asked, "Did you find out who is behind Erik's death?"

"Yep."

"Who?"

"I'm not sure you want to know."

Liz pushed him off her and sat up. "Yes, I do."

Michael was on his back looking up at her. She had that serious, stubborn look on her face. "Honey, this is some pretty serious shit. I honestly think you would be better off not knowing any of it."

Liz poked him in the chest. "Do you remember when you told me the other day that if I ever divulged that Scott Coleman was behind the first four assassinations you would walk out of my life and never talk to me again?" Michael nodded yes. "Well, I can't live the rest of my life with this big secret hanging between us. If you don't trust my word that I will keep your secret, then maybe I should consider walking out of your life."

The comment stung, and Michael propped himself up on his elbows. "It's not that I don't trust you, it's just that . . . the information could be dangerous."

"I'm a big girl," Liz said in a patronizing tone. "If you don't trust me enough, then we have some problems." She stared unflinchingly at him.

Michael struggled with what to do. He was tired, he was sick of the entire mess, and he just wanted the whole thing to be over. He rubbed his eyes for a second and then sat up. "All right. Here is what happened, and it goes without saying that you can never repeat any of this." Michael started to recount the events of the last twenty-four hours. Again he omitted Seamus's involvement with Coleman and failed to mention how they had found out about Arthur. He also neglected to tell her that he had knocked out Stu Garret and Mike Nance.

When Michael had finished telling his edited version of the story, there was a brief silence while Liz gathered her thoughts.

With a look of deep concern she asked the question that hit closest to home. "Who killed Arthur?"

"Scott."

"Do you think the president was involved?"

"I'm not sure. Stansfield doesn't think so, but he's going to look into it."

Liz bit her lower lip. "I can't believe the FBI is going along with this."

"They have no other choice. If Nance and Garret's involvement in this were to be made public . . ." Michael shook his head. "The whole country would erupt."

Scarlatti didn't respond. She had a far-off look in her eye. Michael grabbed her by the cheeks and said, "Don't even think about it, Liz. This story can never go public."

She pulled his hand away. "It's not right, Michael. The people deserve to know. It's not acceptable to have the CIA and the FBI running around behind our backs conspiring to cover up murders that were committed by the president's top advisers."

"If this story were to get out"—Michael held up a finger—"number one, we would lose all credibility in the international community. Number two, the CIA would be shut down for good—"

"That might not be such a bad thing."

O'Rourke shook his head. "The CIA does more good for this country than you will ever know. The only time we ever hear about them is when they screw up. Their successes far outweigh their failures. It's not like they can hold a press conference and announce that they've recruited one of Saddam Hussein's top generals to spy for us."

"I don't like the idea of all this secrecy. It's wrong. It's the people's right to know."

In a soft voice Michael asked, "Even if it tears the country apart?"

Liz silently struggled with the question for a moment. "I gave you my word, and I'm not going to go back on it. I might not like this whole mess, but I'm just happy it's over and you're safe."

"Thank you."

Michael's stomach growled again and Liz said, "I guess someone's hungry."

"I'm starved."

"How about I make us a nice quiet dinner for two, and then we spend the rest of the night right here in bed?"

Michael grinned. "What's in it for me?"

Scarlatti laughed. "Oh, you'll see." Liz grabbed him by the arm and led him toward the bathroom. "You take a shower and get cleaned up. I'll go to the store and get some stuff for dinner." She smacked him on the butt and pushed him toward the bathroom.

Scarlatti then headed downstairs and grabbed Duke's leash off the coatrack. The yellow Lab, upon hearing the familiar jingle of his leash, appeared excitedly at Liz's side, and a moment later they were out the door and on their way to the Georgetown Safeway.

Director Stansfield looked around the conference table in his office and noted how tired the other attendees were. FBI director Roach sat slouched with his chin resting on his chest, his eyes open but red. Skip McMahon was yawning, and Irene Kennedy was taking her glasses off so she could rub her eyes. It had been a long day, and none of them had gotten much sleep the night before.

Assessing that any further work would be useless, and that he didn't have the strength to argue anymore, Stansfield decided it was time to wrap things up. "Skip, I apologize for putting you in this situation, but there is no other option. If we call off the investigation, too many people will want to know why."

McMahon shook his head. "It's a waste of manpower. I have over two hundred agents working on these assassinations, and they sure as hell could be used on other cases . . . cases we can eventually bring to trial."

"It's not an entire waste," stated Stansfield in his most conciliatory voice. "It's very important that we find out who these assassins are, even if we can't bring them to trial."

"I'll give you that. I just don't want this manhunt to turn into a two-year ordeal and cover-up with hundreds of agents wasting their time."

"I agree with you, Skip," replied Roach, "but there is no other way to do it. It's important that we find out who the assassins are, and we have to keep the investigation going or the press will go nuts. When the timing is right, I'll transfer you and put you in charge of something else."

McMahon nodded his acceptance. "I know that we have no other choice, but what I can't accept is Nance and Garret getting away with this scot-free. God, I'd love to get my hands on them." The senior agent's face was twisted with anger.

Stansfield smiled and stood. McMahon's honesty had grown on him over the last several weeks. The CIA's top spook walked over and patted McMahon on the shoulder. "I wouldn't worry too much, Skip. If they step out of line, I'm sure our mystery assassins will give them a call. It's been a long day. Let's get some sleep, and we'll talk in the morning."

Everyone nodded in agreement and rose to leave. Stansfield walked them to the door and then asked Kennedy to stay behind for a minute. Stansfield closed the door, and he and Kennedy walked over to the director's desk. Stansfield began placing several files in his briefcase. "Irene, what is your read on Congressman O'Rourke?"

"How do you mean?"

"Do you think he knows more than he's telling us?"

Irene pursed her lips while she pondered the question. "I suppose it's a possibility."

Stansfield turned and placed a single file in his safe. "I think we should run a check on him, but do it quietly. He's not the type of person we want to upset, but all the same, I think we need to see if he has any ties to these assassins."

Kennedy nodded. "I'll handle it personally."

CHAPTER 41

THE maroon Audi drove casually down the streets of Georgetown. The fifty-four-year-old man behind the wheel was a former U.S. intelligence operative turned freelance operative, or "utility man," as he was referred to by his fellow spooks. He had received a call from a man for whom he had done a lot of lucrative work over the years. If his old acquaintance was telling the truth, and there was no security, the job would be simple. The unimpressive, gray-bearded man drove past the house twice and parked.

For several minutes he pointed a directional microphone at each room of the house. When he was relatively certain that only one person was home, he put away the equipment and got out of the car. He walked to the trunk to make sure it was unlocked, and while he did so, he did a quick check of the street. After looking up at the lit windows of the house in question, he patted his pockets to make sure he had everything and then put on a pair of black leather gloves.

Michael felt ten times better after his long, hot shower. He dried off as best as he could in the mist-filled bathroom and then tried to wipe the steam off the mirror. He cleaned off a small patch and noticed that although he felt better, he still had dark marks under both eyes. After pulling on jeans and a well-worn gray sweatshirt, he heard the doorbell ring. As he bounced down the stairs, he wondered briefly who it could be and then realized Liz had probably forgotten her keys.

Michael hit the landing with a thud and grabbed for the doorknob. Yanking the door open, he said, "You forgot your keys again, huh?" When the door opened fully, O'Rourke froze for an instant. He didn't recognize the gray-bearded man wearing an olive trench coat and a brown fedora.

Before Michael could think, the fatherly individual smiled and asked, "Congressman O'Rourke?"

Michael looked down at the older man and replied, "Ah . . . yes."

With the smile still on his face, the visitor retrieved his right hand from his pocket as if to shake Michael's hand. In a smooth, nonchalant motion he extended a Tazer stun gun and squeezed the trigger. A metal-and-plastic dart streaked out of the end of the electric-shock gun and embedded itself in Michael's stomach. O'Rourke went rigid as two hundred thousand volts of electricity shot through his body. He took two steps backward and then collapsed. As he fell to the ground, he landed on a thin wooden table in the entryway, shattering the fragile piece of wood beneath him and sending several framed photos crashing to the floor. Michael lay clutching his stomach, unable to move.

The not-so-harmless visitor moved with precision. Before Michael hit the floor, the man had already stepped into the foyer and closed the door. Next he pulled a syringe gun from his left pocket and held it to O'Rourke's neck. He depressed the trigger and sent enough muscle relaxant into the congressman's system to keep him nice and docile for the next hour. Plastic handcuffs were quickly fastened to both O'Rourke's wrists and ankles, and a strip of duct tape was placed over his mouth. Next the intruder moved to the window and looked outside. He extinguished the light over the front door and also the one in the hallway. After scanning the street, he returned to O'Rourke and with amazing ease hefted the much larger O'Rourke over his shoulder.

One more quick check of the street and the man was out the door and down the steps. He carried O'Rourke to the rear of his car, where he lifted the already unlocked trunk and deposited O'Rourke like a sack of potatoes. Michael hit with a thud, and the older man checked to make sure his hostage's arms and legs were out of the way, then closed the trunk. He climbed behind the wheel of his car and pulled away from the curb. One block away, he grabbed his secure digital phone and punched in a number.

After one ring Mike Nance answered, "Hello."

"I've retrieved that package for you. I should be at your place in less than thirty minutes."

"Any problems?"

"None."

"I'll be waiting."

The former intelligence operative hung up the secure phone and sped off in the direction of Maryland. He smiled briefly at the thought of collecting fifty thousand dollars for such an easy job and then began to wonder what Mike Nance wanted from the congressman in his trunk.

Scarlatti walked down the tree-lined street with a bag of groceries in one hand and Duke's leash in the other. Autumn-colored leaves dotted the sidewalk and curb. A chilling breeze kicked up as she turned onto O'Rourke's street. She looked forward to spending the night with Michael, and there would be next week. They were scheduled to leave on Sunday afternoon to go back to Minnesota for Senator Olson's funeral. She didn't relish the somber occasion, but it would be nice to get out of D.C. for a while. Northern Minnesota was beautiful this time of the year.

Duke made the turn up the steps to Michael's house, and Liz

followed with an outstretched arm. She fished for her keys and, after finding the right one, opened the door. Duke ran inside, and Liz let go of the leash. She could take it off after she got rid of the groceries. She turned on the light and went to set the groceries down but froze. The table she wanted to set them on was lying on the floor in a half dozen pieces. Liz called out Michael's name. She listened intently for a reply, then yelled his name louder. Duke came back down the hallway and rubbed his neck against her leg. Scarlatti reached down and patted his head. She set the groceries on the floor and headed for the stairs, calling Michael's name again. Her heart began to quicken, and she called for Duke to follow.

Once upstairs, she inspected the steam-streaked mirror in the bathroom and then checked the den before heading back downstairs, all the time calling Michael's name more frantically. She flew down the stairs to the basement and threw open the door to the garage. His truck was there. She turned and sprinted back up the stairs to the kitchen and checked to see if his keys were on the hook—they were. Scarlatti bit her lip while she thought of all the things Michael had just told her. She couldn't help but think the worst. I was only gone for thirty minutes, she thought to herself. She took a deep breath and tried to think of where he could be, but her mind kept coming back to the broken table in the front hallway.

Her hand sprang for the phone on the kitchen wall, but she stopped short. "Should I call the police?" she asked out loud. She willed herself to calm down and not overreact. "I'll call Tim. Maybe Tim and Seamus stopped by, and they went to pick me up at the store." Scarlatti quickly punched in Tim's phone number, and after several rings Michael's brother answered.

"Tim, this is Liz. Do you know where Michael is?"

Tim paused for a second. "I think he's at his house."

"No, he isn't." Liz's voice grew more frantic. "I'm here right now!" She spoke at a rapid pace. "I came by an hour ago, and he was napping. I got him up, and he got in the shower while I went to the store. I just got back, and he's nowhere in the house . . . and that little table by the front door is smashed . . . like someone fell on it. . . . Something isn't right, Tim."

"Calm down, Liz. Is his truck gone?"

"No! His truck is here . . . his keys are here . . . I was only gone for a half hour. He knew I was coming right back. Something bad has happened. I'm calling the police!"

"No!" yelled Tim. "Seamus and I will be over in less than five minutes. Try to stay calm, and don't call the police until we get there."

Liz hung up the phone and paced. She asked herself, who would take him and why? Could it be Coleman? No. . . . What about Stansfield? Michael had said it himself. If the story were to get out, the CIA would be shut down immediately. Liz looked at the phone again and hesitated for only a second. She called information, got the general number for the CIA, and hit the connect button. A man answered on the third ring and Liz said, "Director Stansfield, please."

The operator remained professional despite the fact that someone was calling the Agency's general number on a Saturday evening and asking to talk to the director. "The director isn't in right now. May I take a message?"

"Yes. I assume you have a way to get ahold of him in an emergency?"

There was a pause, then a hesitant, "Yes, if the message warrants it."

"Believe me it does! Tell him Liz Scarlatti from the *Washington Reader* wants to talk about the events surrounding Arthur Higgins, Mike Nance, Stu Garret, and Congressman Michael O'Rourke. Give him that message immediately, and have him call me back at the following number in the next five minutes, or I'm going to press with what I have." Liz gave the man Michael's number and hung up.

• • •

The day had been long, and it was time to go home and get some sleep. Kennedy and Stansfield exited the director's office, and the door automatically locked behind them. Stansfield transferred his briefcase from his right hand to his left and went to shake Kennedy's hand. Before he could complete the gesture, his bodyguard approached from behind a desk in the reception area with a deeply concerned look on his face. "Sir, I just received a strange call from our operator." The man looked down at a piece of paper. "A Liz Scarlatti from the *Washington Reader* called. She would like to ask you about the relationship between Arthur Higgins, Mike Nance, Stu Garret, and Michael O'Rourke. She left a number and said if she doesn't hear from you in five minutes, she's going to press with what she has."

Stansfield's tired shoulders slumped another several inches as he reached for the paper. Without saying a word, he turned to go back to his office and Kennedy followed. Stansfield dropped his briefcase and his jacket on the nearest chair and walked behind his desk.

"How in the hell could this get out so fast?" asked Kennedy.

Stansfield shook his head. "It's either O'Rourke or the White House." He set the piece of paper down and pointed to a second phone on the credenza. "If you would please, Irene. Call down to Charlie and have him run a trace on this call." Stansfield began dialing the number.

The startling ring of the phone caused Liz to jump. She snatched the phone off the wall and said, "Hello."

"Miss Scarlatti?" asked Stansfield.

"Yes, this is she."

"This is Director Stansfield. I just received your message, and I'm a little confused."

Liz clutched the phone tightly and tried to stay calm. "I know everything. I know all about how Higgins and Nance and Garret were behind the—"

Stansfield cut her off. "We don't need to get into specifics, Miss Scarlatti. Where are you calling from?" Stansfield had no desire to discuss this issue on an open line.

"What does that matter?" Liz heard a click at the front door and her heart leapt. She looked down the hall hoping to see Michael, but instead Tim and Seamus came through the door.

"I need to know if you're on a secure line," said Stansfield.

Liz looked at the phone and said, "I doubt it, and I really don't care." Tim and Seamus entered the kitchen and listened to Liz talk. "Congressman Michael O'Rourke is missing from his house, and if he isn't returned within the next hour, I am going to wire every news service on the planet the real story about what has been going on in Washington over the last week."

Seamus's eyes opened wide. "Who are you talking to?"

Liz turned her back on Seamus and Tim and covered her other ear.

"Hold on a minute," continued Stansfield. "How do you know Congressman O'Rourke is missing?"

"I'm standing in his kitchen with his brother and grandfather," shouted Liz. "He is gone, and if you don't return him within the hour, your little secret is going to be on the front page of every paper tomorrow morning."

"I have no idea where Congressman O'Rourke is," protested Stansfield.

"Well, you'd better find him. You have one hour." Liz slammed the phone back into its cradle.

Stansfield stared at the receiver and shook his head. Kennedy pressed a button and spoke briefly into the phone. When she was done, she looked at her boss and said, "The call was made from O'Rourke's house."

Stansfield pinched the bridge of his nose. "It has to be Nance and Garret." Stansfield slowly shook his head from side to side as he continued to keep pressure on his nose. "What in the hell are those two idiots up to?"

"Any chance the call was a fake?" asked Kennedy.

"I doubt it." Stansfield looked at Kennedy and grabbed his phone. "I'm going to call the president and find out if he knows where his chief of staff and national security adviser are." Stansfield punched in the number for the Secret Service command post at the White House. After several rings an agent answered and Stansfield identified himself. "I need to speak to the president immediately." Stansfield tapped a pen on a pad of paper while he waited to be connected.

After several clicks the president answered. "Thomas, what's wrong?"

"We seem to have a problem, sir." Stansfield relayed the pertinent facts of his conversation with Scarlatti, but referred to her only as a reporter.

The president let out a loud sigh and said, "For Christ sake . . . why would anyone want to take O'Rourke?" Stansfield did not respond. He instead chose to put the pressure on the president and see just how genuine his reaction was. "I can't believe this. I thought this mess was over. Who would take him?" repeated an exasperated Stevens.

"We're not sure."

"Thomas, you have my authority to do whatever it takes to get Congressman O'Rourke back, and make sure that tape isn't released!"

Stansfield paused for a moment and then asked, "Sir, do you know where your national security adviser and chief of staff are?"

President Stevens didn't answer immediately. The connection between O'Rourke's disappearance and Stansfield's question was obvious. "No, but I'm sure as hell going to find out! I'll call you back!" The president slammed the phone down and screamed for the nearest Secret Service agent.

Stansfield put the phone down and tried to gauge the president's reaction. Stevens seemed genuinely surprised, and there was no need for him to take a chance . . . unless Nance had threatened to drag him down. Stansfield pondered the possibility and decided that until he knew more, he couldn't trust the president. He picked up the phone and dialed Charlie Dobbs's extension in the Operations Center. Dobbs answered on the first ring, and Stansfield spoke rapidly. "What type of bird do we have over the city right now?"

Dobbs hit several buttons on the keyboard to his left, and instantly a map appeared on the screen that marked the orbital path and location of every satellite in the CIA, the National Reconnaissance Office, and the National Security Agency arsenal. "We currently have"—Dobbs squinted to read the designation that appeared next to the dot hovering above Washington, D.C.—"a KH-11 on station." The KH-11 Strategic Response Reconnaissance Satellite could tell the difference between a football and a basketball from a distance of 220 miles above the earth.

"Zoom it in on Mike Nance's ranch in Maryland, and punch up all the addresses for NSA safe houses in the metro area."

"Thomas, the people over at the NSA are going to shit when they find out we're using a big bird to keep an eye on the president's national security adviser."

"If they ask, tell them the president authorized it. How long before you have real-time imaging?"

"It should take no more than three to five minutes."

"Good. I also want two tactical teams ready to roll ASAP. Get the choppers warmed up. We might have to move fast."

"Do you want them in combat gear or plainclothes?"

Stansfield pondered the question. Because the CIA had no domestic jurisdiction, they weren't able to deploy their tactical teams in the same fashion that the FBI deployed their SWAT teams. Most of their work had to be done in a way that raised the least amount of attention possible. "Put one team in plainclothes and the other one in full combat gear."

"I'll take care of it. What's going on, Thomas?"

"More fallout from Arthur. Call me as soon as you get the imaging of Nance's ranch."

Stansfield put the phone down, no longer tired. The anger that he felt toward Mike Nance had overwhelmed any feelings of exhaustion he had. Nance had been given more than enough chances. If he wanted to continue to play it rough and risky, it was time to end the game—before he could do any more damage.

When Liz got off the phone, Seamus forced her to calm down and tell them what had happened. After she was done, they inspected the broken table. Given the evidence, they had to agree with Liz that things did not look good. Seamus looked at the broken table and then at Liz. "Michael told you everything?"

"Yes."

Seamus tried to read deeper into her curt answer. He could sense nothing—no judgment, or animosity. Seamus folded his arms and returned his thoughts to Michael. "I don't think it's the CIA, or the FBI. They were with him this afternoon. They could have done it then if they wanted to."

"What if they wanted to wait until it was dark?" asked Liz.

Seamus shook his head. "Why take the risk? They could have called him tomorrow and had him come out to Langley on his own. They didn't need to forcibly take him and raise suspicion. If you had called the cops and told them your boyfriend, who just happens to be a congressman, was missing and it looked like he was taken . . ." Seamus rolled his eyes. "Every law enforcement officer in D.C. would be looking for him. No way." Seamus shook his head. "Stansfield wouldn't risk that exposure. Plus you have to factor in the threat of the tape being released. It has to be Nance and Garret."

Tim thought about it for a moment. "You're right. Something this desperate points toward them. Now the question is, where would they have taken him?"

Seamus shrugged his shoulders. "Hell, I have no idea. Nance has to have access to at least a dozen safe houses in the metro area. They could have taken him anywhere." Seamus looked at his watch. "We don't have a lot of time. We have to get him back before Nance has the chance to interrogate him. I'm going to let Coleman know what's going on. Tim, you stay here with Liz. I'll call you as soon as I find something out." He grabbed Liz by the shoulders and said, "Don't worry, everything will be all right. If Stansfield calls, call me immediately on the car phone." The gray-haired O'Rourke turned and left.

Seamus jumped behind the wheel of Tim's Cherokee and pulled out into the street. When he was several blocks away, he turned on the mobile scramble phone. He gripped the steering wheel tightly as he turned onto Wisconsin Avenue. Seamus knew he needed to act fast or they might never get Michael back. Nance had already proved that he would kill, and if he was willing to risk everything in the face of the tape's being released, there was no telling what lengths he might go to. Seamus tried to think ahead. How in the hell could they get Michael back?

Whatever had happened, he needed to let Coleman know that Michael was missing. Seamus punched in the number for Coleman's pager. It rang four times and then the computerized voice told him to leave a number at the beep. Seamus entered the number for his scramble phone and followed it with three more numbers. In their months of planning, Seamus had been insistent that he and Coleman maintain secure lines of communication. They had gone through almost every possible contingency, and the one they had prepared for the most was the possibility that one or more of the group would be put under surveillance. They had designed a system where they would alert each other through digital pagers.

After all, Seamus couldn't just call Coleman with the FBI camped out on his front step.

After hanging up the phone Seamus swore under his breath. The possibility of losing Michael was more than he could bear. He forced himself to push the thought out of his mind. Now was not the time to get emotional. It was time to stay focused and find Michael. He silently chided himself for putting his grandson in harm's way. They had boxed Nance into a corner, and instead of calling it quits, he had come out swinging.

CHAPTER 42

SCOTT Coleman was sitting on his couch trying to ignore that an unknown number of FBI agents were watching and listening to his every move. For the last day he had been going over different plans for losing his watchers. Part of his training as a SEAL had been countersurveillance and aversive techniques. As the commander of SEAL Team Six he had been tailed more times than he could count. Foreign intelligence services could learn a lot by keeping tabs on America's top commando.

An even more dangerous scenario that he faced was the threat of reprisals by terrorists. Coleman had killed his fair share of international outlaws over the last decade, and plenty of groups out there would love to get their hands on him. What better way to settle a score, if you're a terrorist, than to kill the leader of America's elite counterterrorist force? Even now that he was retired, things hadn't changed all that much. He was still under specific instructions to report any surveillance to the counterespionage people at the Naval Investigative Services.

Coleman's pager started to vibrate. He glanced down at the small screen and recognized the number for Seamus's secure phone. After the seven-digit number came three more numbers. These three numbers made Coleman deeply concerned. They told him that something was very wrong, and that they needed to talk immediately.

Coleman sat motionless for a half a minute or so while he pondered what his next step would be. After picking a plan, he turned off the TV and headed for the door, grabbing his keys and a dark leather jacket on the way. As he made the trip to the basement, he began guessing what might have gone wrong. He knew of Michael's intention to use the tape, but beyond that he had no idea what had transpired over the last sixteen hours. Coleman reached the storage lockers in the basement and walked past his own, stopping at the one used by the elderly gentleman on the first floor. He pulled out a small black flashlight and inspected the wax seals that he had dripped onto the hinges. Both were intact.

It took him less than a minute to pick the small lock. Once inside the closet, he moved a stack of boxes and grabbed his stainless-steel trunk. Coleman decided it was time to clean shop. No sense leaving anything behind for the feds to find. He set the trunk down in the hallway and then relocked the door to the storage locker. Next he bent down, opened the steel trunk, and retrieved a mobile scramble phone that was identical to the one O'Rourke had. He hoisted the tan briefcase under one arm, the trunk under the other, and started for the front door of the apartment building.

Across the street, in the apartment building that faced Coleman's, Skip McMahon and the other FBI agents sprang to life. Coleman had left the house earlier in the day and gone for a jog, but other than that, he had remained in his apartment. McMahon was wearing a black Baltimore Orioles baseball hat and had a pair of large headphones covering his ears. Through the array of directional microphones they had aimed at the apartment, he heard Coleman turn off his TV. Next he heard the jingle of keys and then the door opening and closing. McMahon snapped his walkie-talkie up to his mouth. "People, get ready. I think our boy is on the move."

The other two agents joined McMahon at the window. One of them checked in with each of the three cars that were located on nearby side streets and asked for a status report. They waited a full minute and Coleman still hadn't exited the front door of the building. McMahon brought the walkie-talkie back up to his mouth. "Sam, do you see anything in the alley? Over."

The agent parked at the end of the alley peered through a pair of night-vision goggles. His eyes hadn't left the rear door since McMahon had alerted them that their subject was on the move. Sam spoke blandly into his walkie-talkie, "That's a negative, over."

McMahon tapped his foot. "Come on, where are you?" He adjusted his baseball hat and continued to stare at the front door. "Come . . . on . . . come . . . on."

As McMahon finished dragging out his last phrase, Coleman came out the front door. "We've got him," he said instantaneously over his radio. Squinting slightly, he continued, "He's carrying a briefcase and another large metal case. . . . He's headed for his car. Get the cars warmed up and alert dispatch." McMahon watched Coleman get into his Ford Explorer and shut the door. He slapped one of the agents on the shoulder and said, "Watch the fort while we're gone, and tell dispatch we might need a chopper. Let's go, Pete." McMahon and the other agent ran for the door. They flew down the back staircase and out into the alley. McMahon jumped into the passenger seat of Special Agent Pete Arley's Chrysler minivan, complete with child seat and a box of wet wipes on the dashboard. Arley yanked the van into drive and roared down the alley as McMahon helped coordinate the other three cars in the immediate area.

The caravan of cars moved from the Adams Morgan neighborhood into the area surrounding Howard University. Coleman's Ford Explorer was covered in every direction including up. An FBI surveillance helicopter had moved into position and had already painted the roof of Coleman's truck with a laser dot. The group of cars turned onto Michigan Avenue and passed Trinity College and the Veterans Administration Hospital.

Coleman knew what he was doing. By driving past the college campuses he was picking off the FBI cars that were trying to keep pace with him on the side streets. Michigan Avenue was the only thoroughfare in this part of town. All of the other streets dead-ended into one of the campuses. He was not trying to lose them yet. He was only trying to make their job difficult.

The former SEAL retrieved a small, handheld bug sweeper from his pocket and checked to make sure the audio warning mode was off. He started by the steering wheel and swept the entire dashboard of the car. From there he swept as much of the car as he could from the front seat. Coleman put the sensor back in his pocket and readied his scramble phone. Next he turned up the radio and faded the speakers to the back of the truck. If any bugs had been placed in the backseat or rear cargo area, the loud music would render them useless.

Coleman checked his rearview mirror one more time and then dialed the number. After several rings Seamus answered, "Hello."

"What's up?"

"Michael has been taken."

"What do you mean taken? By whom?"

"We don't know, but we think it may have been Nance."

Coleman swore under his breath. "Did Michael use the tape to blackmail Nance?"

"Yes."

"Damn it. I've been out of the loop since last night. I think you'd better bring me up to speed on what's transpired since then." Coleman listened while Seamus rapidly relayed an extremely abbreviated version of what Michael had done with the tape of Arthur's confession. Seamus then went on to explain Michael's disappearance, Liz's subsequent conversation with Stansfield, and finally, the one-hour time limit and ultimatum she had given the director of the CIA.

Coleman processed the information as rapidly as possible and asked few questions. When Seamus was nearing the end of the story, Coleman looked at his watch and saw that they were coming up on the two-minute mark. Although these little wonders of technology that he and Seamus were using were touted as traceproof, Coleman had learned over the years to trust no piece of technology completely. Not wanting to go over the two-minute threshold, Coleman asked for the number Seamus had been using to contact Stansfield, then told him he'd call him back in ten minutes. Coleman hung up the phone and checked his rearview mirror for any recognizable cars. He bit down hard and began running through his options. If they didn't get Michael back quickly, they were in a lot of trouble. Nance had to be dealt with. In a barely audible voice Coleman said, "If I get the chance, I'm going to end this thing my way."

The maroon Audi stopped at the security gate and a pair of watchful eyes peered down at the driver from behind the bulletproof glass of the guard booth. The guard had been notified by his employer that this certain guest was to be allowed entry without inspection. Mike Nance had learned a lot from Arthur Higgins over the years, and one of these lessons was to hire his own private security people. The Secret Service would more than likely disapprove of some of his activities, and tonight was a perfect example. The heavy gate began to slide back on its tracks, and the guard nodded for the driver of the car to proceed.

The Audi sped down the long, newly paved driveway and took the right fork about a quarter of a mile from the house. Jarod pulled the car up to the main entrance and popped the trunk. Leaving the keys in the ignition, he exited the car and walked to the rear. Jarod lifted the trunk and studied O'Rourke, who was curled up in the fetal position.

The congressman looked through squinted eyes at the strange

man who had abducted him. Although he felt sluggish, the drugs had not affected his mind. The thirty-minute car ride in the darkness of the trunk had given him time to figure out, with relative certainty, what was happening. Only one person could be behind this. Garret was too big of an emotional wimp to have the balls to do something like this by himself, so it had to be Nance. Michael knew his only hope was if Liz had made it back to the house and called Tim and Seamus. If she hadn't, Michael had no doubt that Nance would shoot him full of drugs and get him to sing, just as he and Coleman had done with Arthur. He had to buy some time until they found him.

The grandfatherly-looking man was silhouetted by a pair of lights that hung next to the entrance of the house. He pulled a medium-sized, matte black combat knife from inside his trench coat and leaned into the trunk. The knife slid in between O'Rourke's legs, and with a quick jerk the plastic ankle cuffs were cut. The man transferred the blade from his right to his left hand and helped Michael out of the trunk.

O'Rourke felt the increased effects of whatever had been pumped into him as soon as his feet hit the pavement. His legs were unsteady, and he staggered slightly to the side. Jarod hung on to him by the arm and prevented him from toppling to the ground. The two of them proceeded toward the front door, and after about five steps Michael regained enough of his balance that he could walk without assistance.

When they reached the house, the door opened from the inside, revealing a grinning Mike Nance. "Good evening, gentlemen." Nance was wearing a pair of dark wool slacks, a white button-down, and a blue cardigan.

O'Rourke stared at the smug grin on Nance's face and fought back the urge to reach out and smash in his face. He took a step forward, but the stranger holding on to his arm prevented him from taking another. O'Rourke froze as Jarod dug two fingers into the pressure point under his right arm. Michael's whole right side buckled under the penetrating pain, and he slouched in a convulsive jerk.

"Now, now, Congressman, behave yourself." Nance waved his finger at O'Rourke as if Michael were a little schoolboy. "You don't want to upset my friend." Nance nodded for the two men to follow and started down the hallway. Jarod loosened his grip slightly and prodded Michael forward. The three men went down the hall and entered the large game room.

O'Rourke looked to his right and saw Stu Garret standing behind the bar with a drink in his hand. O'Rourke glared at the president's chief of staff, and Garret averted his eyes. Nance pointed toward Michael's mouth and said, "Jarod, you can take off the tape." The shorter man reached up and yanked the gray duct tape off O'Rourke's mouth. Michael ignored the slight sting and kept his eyes fixed on Garret.

Nance spoke from a discreetly safe distance. "Congressman, we have some unfinished business from this morning."

O'Rourke stared at Nance in disgust and said, "I finished my business with you when I broke your nose."

Nance turned and looked at his reflection in the mirror behind the bar. He reached up and gently touched his swollen nose. "Yes, I suppose I owe you for that, don't I?" Turning back to face O'Rourke, Nance said flatly, "Jarod, would you please break Congressman O'Rourke's nose for me?"

Michael had no time to react. The man standing next to him grabbed his handcuffed wrists and forced them down. Jarod's free hand raised up like a tomahawk and came crashing down in a karate chop across the bridge of Michael's nose. There was a loud pop as O'Rourke's nose moved a quarter of an inch to the left. Michael stumbled back, his head reeling. O'Rourke had had his nose broken twice before while playing hockey in college, but he never remembered it hurting this bad. He gritted his teeth in an attempt to try to fight back the pain as blood streamed out of his nostrils and over his upper lip.

Nance walked back over from the bar and proclaimed, "I don't like resorting to violence, Mr. O'Rourke, but I do believe in an eye for an eye. Your behavior this morning was very uncivilized."

"And I suppose killing Erik Olson was civilized. Spare me your bullshit." Michael wiped some blood on the sleeve of his gray sweatshirt.

Nance nodded to Jarod, and before Michael could react, a fist slammed into his lower back, sending him crashing to the floor. Grimacing from the agonizing pain in his right kidney, O'Rourke pushed himself up onto his knees and looked at Nance's shoes. Michael had never been one to take things lying down, and he reasoned the longer he kept them from asking some real questions, the better his chances were. Slowly, he brought his head up. His eyes rested on Nance's white shirt. O'Rourke felt his mouth filling with blood, and as he got to his feet, he spit it at Nance. A large glob of blood and saliva splattered Nance's face and white shirt.

O'Rourke had less than a second to enjoy his small victory. He was instantly knocked to his knees by another punch to the kidney. Nance, infuriated by the indignity of being spat on, stepped forward and slapped Michael across the face.

The slap barely moved Michael's head. O'Rourke paused to gain his breath and then looked up at Nance. Through clenched teeth, he forced a smile to his lips and asked, "Who taught you how to hit like that, your mom?"

Nance's complexion turned a shade darker and his hands started to tremble as he fought to control his anger. In a half yell, he barked, "Jarod, teach this man some respect!"

O'Rourke knew more pain was on the way so he rolled from his knees to the floor and away from his assailant. When he completed the turn and stopped by the back of a couch five feet away, he looked up and saw Jarod approaching with his stun gun extended.

Michael saw something pop from the end, and then every inch of his body spasmed as electricity shot through his veins. While he squirmed on the floor, he felt himself losing consciousness. His vision sparkled and then went dark. The last thing he remembered before losing consciousness was the faint ringing of a phone.

Stansfield paced behind his desk while Kennedy relayed possible action scenarios one after another. This was one of Irene's strong suits. She was a master at taking problems, plugging in different variables, and predicting probable outcomes.

The Operations Center in the basement was humming like the bridge of an aircraft carrier headed into battle. Charlie Dobbs looked down at the floor from his crow's nest and watched his people move with speed and precision. He was wearing a headset and pressed the speed dial for Stansfield's office. The director answered and Dobbs said, "The choppers are warmed up and the tactical teams are ready to roll. We also have the real-time thermal imaging on-line."

"What do you see?"

Dobbs looked at the high-resolution, fifty-inch screen that was mounted in the wall behind his desk. "The only thing to report is the arrival of a car. Otherwise everything looks pretty quiet."

"What kind of car?" asked Stansfield.

"It's hard to tell with the thermal imaging, but it looks to be a sedan of some type. A couple of my imaging analysts are running computer enhancements on the stuff right now. They should be able to tell us more in about ten minutes. The car arrived just after we came on-line. One person got out. They retrieved something from the trunk and went into the house."

Stansfield's eyelids tightened. "Did you say the trunk?"

"Yeah."

"What did they get from the trunk?"

"I don't know."

"How big was it?"

Dobbs sighed apologetically. "Thomas, we can't tell with the nighttime thermal imaging on the KH-11. If it was daytime, I'd know more, or if it was one of the new KH-12s, we'd have no problem, but the thermal imaging has a lower resolution."

"Get your boys on it right away! Tell them to forget about the make of the car for now. I want to know how big the object was that was taken from the trunk, and let me know if anybody else arrives or leaves the ranch. I'm going with the tactical teams. Give the pilots the location of Nance's place and tell the men to load up. I'm on my way down." Stansfield hung up and looked at Kennedy. "I want you to stay here and coordinate. If Scarlatti calls, give her the number for my mobile phone and have her call me directly."

"Are you going out to Nance's?"

"Yes. I'm going to handle this thing personally." Stansfield exited his office and told his bodyguard to grab the mobile phone and follow him. Stansfield slid his access card into the slot for the executive elevator and watched as his bodyguard strapped a black nylon pack around his waist that contained the director's secure mobile phone.

There was a knock on the door and all three men turned their attention from the body on the floor to the entrance of the room. The voice of Nance's assistant called out from behind the oak door. "Sir, the president is on the line and would like to speak to you."

Nance scowled at the door. "Tell him I'm not available and that I'll call him back."

The assistant cleared his throat. "He was rather insistent that he speak with you immediately. . . . In fact he seemed a bit irate."

Nance pointed at O'Rourke, who was still passed out on the floor. "Jarod, keep him quiet. I'll be right back." As Nance started for the door, Garret followed. Nance stopped abruptly. "Wait here, Stu. I can handle this on my own." Nance left the room and went to his private study. He pushed the blinking light on the phone and said, "I'm sorry to keep you waiting, Jim. What is it that you wanted?"

The president screamed into the phone, "What in the hell are you up to now?"

"Jim, I have no idea what you're talking about."

"Don't pull this crap with me, Mike. Where in the hell is Congressman O'Rourke?"

"Why would I know where Congressman O'Rourke is?"

"Someone has taken him, and it's no shock that you're at the top of the list for potential kidnappers."

"Who told you he was taken?"

"Stansfield!"

Nance was quiet for a moment. "As I have maintained since this morning, I think Thomas Stansfield is behind this entire affair. I have—"

"Shut up, Mike!" yelled the president. "I can't believe you've gotten me into this mess. I saw the way Stu fell apart when he heard that tape. You're not going to get away with blaming this thing on anybody but yourself. You and your sadistic friend Arthur were behind this whole thing, and I'm not going to get dragged down with you. A reporter called Stansfield and told him if O'Rourke isn't turned over in an hour, they're going to release the tape of Arthur. Now wake up before it's too late, and tell me where in the hell Congressman O'Rourke is."

"I have no idea."

"Bullshit . . . you're a goddamned professional liar, Mike. Hand him over before you ruin all of us."

"All of us is right, Jim." Nance's words were laced with blatant disrespect. "If that tape is released, all of us are going down, and that includes you. We're all in this together, and we're going to do it my way. You stall Stansfield. If they want the good congressman back so bad, he must know something. When I'm done with him, I'll turn him over." Nance slammed the phone down and left for the other end of the house.

CHAPTER 43

DIRECTOR Stansfield and his bodyguard walked out the rear exit of the main building at Langley and toward the waiting helicopters. The chopper to the right was a modified Sikorsky UII-60 Black Hawk with state-of-the-art noise-suppression equipment mounted over its powerful engines. The dark bird could fly at speeds up to eighty miles an hour and be no louder than a car. The Black Hawk was loaded with eight fully armed SOGs, members of the CIA's Special Operations Group. They were dressed in black Nomex jumpsuits and black tactical assault vests. The majority of the men were former Recon Marines and Army Airborne Rangers. Each man also wore a dull black Delta Force helmet and body armor made of spectra, a bulletproof composite. The helmets weighed only three pounds and were capable of stopping up to a .357 magnum round at close distance. Mounted on top of the helmets were pop-down night-vision goggles. All eight men carried silenced 9x19mm Heckler & Koch MP-5 machine guns. Two of the eight also carried Remington short-barreled shotguns with special Shok-Lok rounds for blasting through hinges and door locks. If the shotguns weren't enough, they also carried shaped plastic explosives for blasting through reinforced doors. One man also carried a Remington custom sniper rifle.

The chopper that Stansfield approached was blue and silver with the word MEDEVAC painted in white letters over both sliding doors. This helicopter contained the eight members of the second tactical team. They were armed identically to the team in the Black Hawk minus the black Nomex jumpsuits and Delta Force helmets. This group was dressed in plainclothes. Four of them wore suits and trench coats, two were in jeans and leather jackets, and the seventh and eighth were a man and woman set up to look like a husband and wife. All eight carried their weapons concealed in large Velcro pockets on the inside of their jackets.

The director climbed into the front seat next to the pilot, and his bodyguard got in back with the troops. Stansfield nodded to the pilot, and the helicopter lifted off the ground and headed east with the dark Black Hawk close behind. The men and one woman in the back of the medevac chopper shot each other sideways looks. It wasn't often that the director came along for something like this.

Stansfield looked to his right as the two helicopters raced over the northern part of downtown at close to 150 mph. His bodyguard tapped him on the shoulder and handed his boss the phone. "It's the president."

Stansfield grabbed the receiver and covered his other ear. Even though the helicopter was insulated for noise, it was still loud. "Yes, sir."

"Thomas, I've lost control of him." The president sounded desperate.

"Who, sir?"

"Mike Nance. I just spoke with him. He said if the assassins want O'Rourke back so bad, the congressman must know something."

"Is he at his ranch?"

"Yes."

"I'll handle it from here." Stansfield handed the phone back to his bodyguard and stared straight ahead toward a dark Maryland countryside. His nerves were frayed, he was tired, and he couldn't remember the last time he'd been this angry. It was time to put Mike Nance in his place.

Coleman, with the FBI in tow, continued his weaving pattern through the run-down Langdon neighborhood of Washington, D.C. Although Langdon was less than a mile from the Capitol, it was one of the worst neighborhoods in Washington. Row after row of burnt-out and abandoned houses dominated the landscape, making perfect offices for the gang-banger crack dealers who ruled the streets. Coleman wondered what his FBI watchers were think-ing as they followed him into this war zone.

The former SEAL activated the voice modulator on his scram-ble phone and punched in the number for Langley. The operator connected him to Stansfield's office after a brief argument.

Kennedy answered the director's phone and, upon hearing the altered voice, started an immediate trace. "Who is this?" asked Kennedy.

"The person who took Arthur. Where is Stansfield?"

"He's not in right now." Kennedy looked down at the phone and wondered if it was the former SEAL team commander on the other end.

"I need to speak with him immediately!"

Kennedy looked at her watch. "If you'll hold for a minute, I'll see if I can track him down."

"No!" screamed Coleman. "Give me a number where I can reach him immediately, or I release the tape."

Kennedy considered her options for a second and decided to give him the number. When she was done, she hit the extension for the operations center. Charlie Dobbs answered and Kennedy asked, "Did you get a trace?"

"Not even close. Whoever it was, they were using a mobile unit."

"Can you get him if he calls back?"

"If he stays on long enough, but I doubt he's that dumb."

"All right, thanks." Kennedy placed the phone down and again wondered if it was Coleman.

Cross town, Coleman hit the disconnect button and dialed the number Kennedy had just given him. Someone answered on the other end, and Coleman asked for Stansfield. A moment later the director was on the line and Coleman asked, "Where in the hell is O'Rourke?"

"Who is this?" Stansfield was put on guard by the metallic voice.

"The person who has twenty copies of a tape that will close the doors to the CIA for good. I'm only going to ask this question one more time. Where is Congressman O'Rourke?"

"I'm in the process of trying to find him right now."

Coleman could tell by the quality of the connection that Stansfield was mobile. "Where are you?"

Stansfield hesitated briefly. "I'm airborne."

"Where are you headed?"

"Maryland."

"What's in Maryland?" Coleman took a right on South Dakota Avenue and headed for Highway 50.

"The president's national security adviser."

"Does he have the congressman?"

"We're not sure, but I'm going to find out."

"Where does Nance live?"

"Arundel County, just off of 214."

Coleman knew the area. Nance's house wasn't far from Annapolis. "You'd better hope you find the congressman quick. Nance has worn my patience thin." Coleman disconnected the call and floored the accelerator as he turned onto the on ramp for Highway 50 east. He wanted to be there for the exchange of Michael, but there was one big problem—he had to lose the FBI first.

In his sixteen years in the Navy, Coleman had learned two fundamental theories about shaking surveillance. The first is to enter an area of high traffic and lose the watchers in the crowd, and the second is to go to a place where they can't follow. Coleman grinned. The second theory would work perfectly. He swerved into the left lane and passed several cars as he accelerated over 70 mph. He disengaged the voice modulator switch on the phone and dialed the main number for the Naval Academy. When the operator answered, Coleman asked for his old friend Sam Jarvi.

Skip McMahon peered out the front window of the minivan with a pair of binoculars. He could see the red brake light at the top of Coleman's Ford Explorer. The other three tail cars followed behind the minivan in a single column. McMahon set the binoculars on his lap and sat back. He raised his walkie-talkie to his mouth and said, "All right, gang, let's stay loose. The chopper has him. We'll stay about a mile back for now, and we'll leapfrog every five minutes. If he gets off the highway, we'll move in and close the gap."

O'Rourke's eyes blinked several times and then opened completely. Jarod grabbed him under the arms and hoisted him off the floor. He dragged Michael over to a wooden chair and deposited him in it. Michael grabbed on to the armrests and steadied himself. The young congressman shook his head and tried to bring his eyes into focus. He noticed a burning sensation on his stomach and reached down to touch it. The area felt as if the skin had been torn away. Several drops of blood fell from his nose onto his jeans. O'Rourke again used the sleeve of his sweatshirt to wipe at his nose. He tilted his head back in an effort to stop the flow of blood. Out of the corner of his eye he saw Stu Garret standing behind the bar. Michael looked over at him and asked, "How long do you think it will be before they hunt you down and kill you?" Garret ignored him, so O'Rourke asked the question with a little more volume. "Hey . . .

Garret! How long do you think it will take those assassins to track you down and blow your head off?" Michael grinned at the president's chief of staff. "You had one chance, and you blew it."

Garret looked up from his drink. "I don't think you're in much of a position to be telling me anything."

"Oh, is that right? Those assassins are going to release the tape all because you and your insane friend couldn't call it quits and walk away. You're finished, Garret. Any way you slice it, you're dead meat."

Garret grabbed his drink and walked to the far end of the room where he wouldn't have to listen to O'Rourke.

Nance entered and strode across the room. He stopped ten feet away from O'Rourke and said expressionlessly, "I see you've regained consciousness."

O'Rourke asked, "What did the president want?"

"It seems your friends want you back rather badly."

O'Rourke frowned. "What friends are you talking about?"

"Your assassin friends."

"You're nuts. I don't know who the assassins are."

"Well, we're going to find out for sure. I think you're lying, and at this point I really don't have much to lose, now do I?" Nance smiled.

"How about your life, you sick bastard!"

"Congressman, you are a simpleton. Do you think I've worked my whole life to get where I am so a bunch of amateurs could end my career with a simple blackmail scheme?"

"Amateurs!" O'Rourke laughed. "You've seen what they can do." O'Rourke leaned back and shouted to the other side of the room, "Hey, Garret? How do you think they're gonna kill you? Do you think they'll sneak into your house some night and snap your neck like they did to Fitzgerald, or do you think they'll get you with a rifle shot from three blocks away like they did to Basset?"

Garret slammed his drink down on an end table and marched

across the room. "Mike, this is stupid! What are we doing? Let's just turn him over right now and resign."

"Shut up, Stu! Pour yourself another drink and sit down."

O'Rourke craned his neck around and smiled. "Maybe they'll do it with a car bomb."

Garret snapped at O'Rourke, "Shut up!" And then looked back at Nance. "Mike, this has gone too far. I'm out. I'm calling Jim, and I'm telling him this is your deal." Garret went for the door, and Nance blocked him. Without taking his eyes off Garret, Nance said, "Jarod, if Mr. Garret tries to leave, shoot him!"

Michael laughed loudly. "You are nuts, Nance! Don't listen to him, Stu! He doesn't have the balls to kill you. Arthur had all the balls. Mike here was just a yes-man. Weren't ya, Mike? If you're such a powerful man, Mike, why don't you kill him yourself? You don't have the balls to do it, do you?"

Nance screamed at Garret, "Sit down and let me handle this!" Turning back to O'Rourke, Nance yelled, "Amateur hour is over! You can either tell me what you know right now and walk away with your brain intact, or I can pump you full of drugs and who knows what you'll be left with."

O'Rourke spit more blood on Nance and screamed, "Go screw yourself! You're gonna end up dead, just like your buddy Arthur."

Nance looked at Jarod, snapped his fingers, and then pointed at O'Rourke. "Hit him again."

Jarod took several steps forward, but this time he made the mistake of getting within striking distance of Michael. As Jarod extended the Tazer, Michael's right foot kicked upward just as the stun gun was fired. The electric dart imbedded itself in Michael's stomach at the same time his foot caught Jarod in the groin. Both men shook as electricity shot through O'Rourke's body and into Jarod's.

CHAPTER 44

THE pilot in the lead helicopter looked at the display on his global-positioning monitor and announced that they were five miles out from their target. On his mark, both he and the pilot of the Black Hawk turned off their running lights and donned their night-vision goggles. In conjunction they slowed their airspeed and dropped down to an elevation of one hundred feet. The terrain was rolling countryside with sporadic patches of trees. Both pilots scanned their path for power lines. As they neared Nance's property, the helicopters slowed to a hover and moved in behind a patch of trees located at the base of two small hills. Straight ahead, less than a mile away, was Nance's rambler. The helicopters were positioned directly to the north of Nance's house. The pilot of the medevac chopper spoke into his headset. "Delta Six, this is Cherokee One. Why don't you slip around to the south and see what you can pick up on thermal?"

"Roger that, Cherokee One." With that reply the Black Hawk slid out of formation and started a slow traverse of the property line.

Director Stansfield had put on a headset and was listening to the pilots talk. The pilot of the medevac reached up and adjusted a knob on his night-vision goggles. He scanned the area around Nance's house and picked up a heat signature. "I've got a rover," announced the pilot. "Check, make that two rovers. They're patrolling the area around the house." *Rover* was the designation the team used for a guard dog.

The leader of the tactical team, who was sitting right behind the pilot, asked, "Do they have handlers, or are they on their own?"

"They're on their own," responded the pilot. He then glanced over at Stansfield. "Sir, do you want me to check and see if I can pick anything up on the directional mikes?"

"No. He has an electromagnetic field around the house. Our mikes can't penetrate it. Delta Six," asked Stansfield, "see if you can get us a body count on the inside of the house."

"Roger that. Give me another thirty seconds to get into position." The Black Hawk slipped behind another hill and lined itself up with a patch of trees that was about five hundred yards from Nance's house. The chopper moved forward at about thirty miles an hour. The wind was coming out of the east and would help carry their noise away from the house. When they reached the clump of trees, the pilot brought the chopper up just enough so the nose of the helicopter had a straight shot at the full length of Nance's house. The copilot of the Black Hawk manipulated a small joystick on the dashboard and moved the camera in the nose pod of the helicopter. A small, ten-inch screen relayed a thermal image of the house. The copilot started at the southern end and worked his way to the north. The camera read the variations in temperature as it went. Halfway down the house, the copilot called out his first body. A bright red orb appeared near the front door. When he made it to the northern wing, he called out four more bodies.

Stansfield asked, "How are the four bodies arranged?" The director had been in the house before and knew which room they were talking about.

"One appears to be sitting, two others are standing close by, and the fourth is sitting down about fifteen feet away from the other three."

The tactical team leader in the back tapped Stansfield on the shoulder. "We're going to have to take out those dogs before we hit the house." Stansfield nodded his approval and the team leader told the pilot, "Bring us in behind that hill three hundred yards up on the left and I'll deploy my sniper."

The nose of the blue-and-silver chopper dipped slightly, passed over the treetops, and then dropped down to a mere fifty feet from the ground as it worked its way up the small valley. The pilot slipped the helicopter in sideways behind the hill and brought the chopper to within three feet of the ground. In the back of the helicopter, the team leader pointed at one of the men wearing jeans and a leather jacket and said, "Tony, take up position on top of this hill and get ready to take out the rovers." The man nodded and rose to get out. One of the other team members opened the sliding door, and the man jumped to the ground and disappeared into the darkness.

Stansfield adjusted his mouth mike and asked, "Delta Six, how do things look in your area?"

"Everything is clear with the exception of the dogs," crackled the pilot's voice.

"All right, we're coming over to join you."

The pilot of the medevac turned the chopper 180 degrees on a dime and worked his way back to their original position. From there they continued south toward Delta Six's position. As they neared, Stansfield pointed at a patch of trees that were fifty yards to the north and another two hundred yards away from the house. The pilot brought the chopper in behind the trees and announced, "Delta Six, we're about six hundred feet back at seven o'clock. Do you copy, over?"

The pilot of the Black Hawk craned his neck around and spotted the heat signature of the medevac's engines. "I copy. I've got your position marked, over."

Stansfield looked through a pair of night-vision binoculars. He concentrated on the large wing to the north. Lights were on, but the shades were drawn. "Delta Six, did you say you marked four signatures in the room at the far north end of the house?"

"That's affirmative, sir."

"All right," announced Stansfield. "Everybody pay attention. I am going to make one phone call to the occupants of the house. I am not going to announce our presence. I repeat, I am not going to announce our presence. Depending on how the call goes, I will either give you the green light, or we will stand down. If I give the green light, this is how it's going to go. When I tell Delta Six to move, I want the dogs taken out. Delta Six will then move into a hover position just above the north end of the house. Team One will then fast-rope to the ground and enter the house. The estate has pressure pads and motion and tremor sensors. The second you hit the ground, you are going to have to move fast. The best point for entry will be the French doors at the southern end of the north wing. I repeat, the southern end of the north wing. I have used the doors before, and they are operational.

"We have a potential hostage situation, so your rules of engagement are as follows. If you are fired on, you may return fire. If any of the men in the room attempts to kill one of the other men in the room, you are to prevent that from happening. Are there any questions?"

No one had any. The two teams were well versed in what they were about to do.

"Team Two will back up Team One. Team One, are you ready to move?"

The leader of Team One replied, "Give us thirty seconds, sir." The team commander banged his fists together and then pointed his thumbs at the doors. The long, dark doors of the Black Hawk were yanked open and into the locked position. Each man secured his rappelling rope to special hooks located above the door and kneeled at the ready position. The two men who carried the shot-guns were the first men on each side. They were the entry men, and their job was to get the doors open. The entry man on the left tapped his partner on the shoulder and then stabbed himself in the chest with a finger. He then pointed up and then straight ahead, signaling that he would blow the top and middle locks on the French doors. His partner nodded and signaled that he would take out the bottom lock. The next three men in line were in charge of clearing the room. They entered the room, literally on top of each other, with each man taking a third of the room and sweeping it for hostiles. The sixth and seventh men covered the left and right flank of the landing area, and the eighth man covered their "six," or their "ass" as the men referred to it. The team leader looked at each of his men, and one by one they flashed him a thumbs-up. The leader radioed back to Stansfield that they were ready.

Stansfield pulled his headset off his left ear and dialed Nance's number. After several rings, Nance's assistant answered. "Hello."

"Mike Nance, please."

"I'm sorry, he's not in right now. May I take a message?"

"No. Tell him Director Stansfield is on the line, and I need to speak with him immediately."

"Oh, I'm sorry, sir. I didn't recognize your voice. Mr. Nance isn't in right now, but I will pass a message on to him if you would like."

Stansfield stared through the darkness at the house not more than a thousand yards away. "I know he's there. Go get him now!"

The assistant on the other end cleared his throat and said, "Yes, sir."

O'Rourke had taken the brunt of the most recent electric jolt, but Jarod did not come out of it unscathed. As soon as the electricity had faded from Jarod's body, the mercenary delivered another gloved chop to the bridge of O'Rourke's bleeding and broken nose. Michael, having absorbed most of the electricity, was still incapacitated when the karate chop landed. The pain that was delivered to O'Rourke's already broken nose was unlike anything he had ever felt. Wave after wave of nausea and agony washed over him.

O'Rourke began to wonder how much more of this he could take, but the thought of getting half of his brain fried from some truth serum was motivation enough to push on. Michael sat up a little straighter in his chair and eyed Jarod, who looked more than a little uncomfortable himself. O'Rourke attributed his pained expression to the kick in the groin.

Michael spit some blood on the floor and looked up at Jarod. "How do your nuts feel?"

Jarod took a step forward and raised his fist. Michael kicked his legs in an effort to keep his torturer at bay. Mike Nance yelled, "Enough! He's only trying to postpone the inevitable." Nance put a hand on Jarod's shoulder and told him to relax. "Now, Congressman, let's get down to business. What is your association with the people who are trying to blackmail Mr. Garret and myself?"

"Nothing. I got up this morning and a package was on my front step. I don't know who in the hell is behind any of this. All I know is that you and your sick dead friend had Senator Olson and Congressman Turnquist killed!"

Nance shook his head. "I don't believe you. I don't think these assassins just picked you out of the blue. I think you know who they are." Nance looked at Michael for a response. "Don't you?"

"I have no idea what you're talking about."

"Fine, I guess we'll have to use the drugs." Nance walked over to a steel gun safe in the corner and dialed the combination. "If you aren't going to cooperate, we'll have to help you." Nance pulled down on the lever and opened the heavy door. An array of shotguns and rifles occupied the bottom two-thirds of the safe, and on a shelf near the top was a tray. Nance pulled the tray out and set it on the bar. Michael could see two clear vials and a syringe.

Nance picked up one of the vials and held it out for Michael to see. "You would be amazed what kind of things people will say when you pump just the smallest amount of this into them. No secret is safe. The only problem is you never know what it will do to their brain. Some people come out of it a vegetable, some people have massive memory loss, and others go through the rest of their life suffering from severe migraines. Some doctors claim they can administer the drug without leaving any permanent damage, but I'm not an experienced doctor." Nance smiled. "Now which is it going to be, Congressman? Would you like to tell me what you know on your own, or would you like me to help you?" Nance picked up the syringe and waved it in the air. Michael was about to tell Nance where to stick the syringe when there was a knock on the door.

Nance turned around and asked, "What is it now?"

A muffled voice from the other side replied, "Director Stansfield is on the line. He wishes to speak with you."

Nance yelled at the closed door, "I told you I did not want to be interrupted!"

The timid voice responded, "He said that he knows you're here. He wants to speak with you immediately."

Nance angrily stomped to the door and opened it only a foot. "Tell him I'm busy and that I'll call him back in ten minutes." With that Nance slammed the door.

Nance's assistant walked across the large foyer, punched a blinking red light, and picked up the handset. "Director Stansfield, Mr. Nance says he will call you back in ten minutes. Is there a number where he can reach you?"

Stansfield looked over the dark countryside at Nance's house and tightly squeezed the handset of his phone. Instead of replying to the man's request for a phone number, he simply hung up and pulled his headset over both ears.

Wasting no time, he asked, "Delta Six, are you ready?" The reply came back a positive, and Stansfield turned to look at the leader of the second team. The man gave him a thumbs-up. Stansfield adjusted his mouth mike and said, "Delta Six, commence the operation."

Team Two's sniper squeezed the butt of his rifle a little tighter and centered his crosshairs on the head of the rottweiler closest to the helicopters. The two dogs were roaming the area due west of the house about a hundred yards out. The sniper squeezed the trigger and the rifle recoiled slightly. The bullet hit the dog dead in the ear and sent it to the ground. The second rottweiler snapped its head around to see what the noise was, but before he could investigate, a bullet smashed into its large, block head. Five seconds later the ominous dark helicopter passed over the dead canines and toward the house.

All eight members of the tactical team were standing and leaning out the doors of the chopper. Their grip on the rappelling ropes was the only thing keeping them from falling to the ground. Their weapons were slung in the frontal ready position. Just before reaching the house, the tail of the helicopter dipped like that of a bird coming in for a landing, and the four large rotor blades braked the machine into a midair stop. The helicopter leveled out ten feet away from the house and twenty feet above the roof. The team leader yelled, *"Go! Go! Go!"*

In unison, all eight men kicked away from their airborne platform and loosened the grip of their black leather gloves on the ropes. They dropped forty feet in the blink of an eye and squeezed the ropes again at the last second, breaking their descent. Landing like cats, they yanked the extra few feet of rope from their assault harnesses and grabbed their weapons. The Black Hawk cleared the area while floodlights sprang to life all around the team.

They ignored the lights and went to work. The two entry men were on the door two seconds after hitting the ground. The man on the left blasted away the top of the door, and the man on the right started at the bottom. The Shok-Lok rounds thudded into the wood, splintering the locks from the frame. With the locks taken care of, the entry men stepped to the side to make way for the room clearers. The point man stepped forward with a flash-bang grenade in one hand and his MP-5 in the other. He kicked in the door from the center and rolled the grenade into the house. *"Flash-bang away!"* rang out through all of their headsets, and every man closed his eyes.

The deafening bang sounded, and a bright flash of phosphoric light lit up the area. The three room clearers flooded through the blown doorway, their thick, black silencers sweeping from right to left while they screamed, *"Hands up! Hands up!"*

Nance had been waving the syringe in front of O'Rourke's face and giving him one last chance to answer the questions without the aid of drugs when the commotion started. Jarod, who was standing next to Nance, had just enough time to react. He stepped backward and dropped to one knee behind a chair and an end table. As he was drawing his gun, he saw the flash grenade roll across the floor. Knowing what it was, he ducked behind the back of the leather chair and kept his gun trained on the door. As soon as the grenade exploded he began squeezing off rounds. His first shot hit nothing, but the second shot glanced off the side of the lead man's helmet and hit the next man in the shoulder. The lead man saw the flash of the pistol and let go a five-round burst at Jarod's head. All five shots were on the mark and sent Jarod's semidecapitated body to the floor with a thud.

The smoking MP-5 snapped up from firing on Jarod and instantly found Nance and O'Rourke. *"Down on the floor! Right now!"* The man repeatedly screamed the phrase at the top of his lungs as the tip of his barrel closed to within ten feet of the two men. His partners were at his side training their weapons at the other two sectors of the room. The second man, who had been hit in the shoulder, ignored the pain and followed through with his assignment. Four of the other five men ran into the room and began checking behind furniture and closet doors. One man remained outside for cover while the rest of the team worked. They continued their sweep with amazing speed and precision. After just twenty seconds, every man had called "Clear." The team leader instructed four of the men to check the rest of the house and informed Stansfield that the room was secure.

The second helicopter came in and landed on the front lawn. Stansfield got out of the chopper, and his bodyguard followed. The director stepped over the broken glass and splintered wood. His eyes immediately fell on the bloody O'Rourke. The always composed director of the CIA fought with all his might to control his anger toward Mike Nance. He took several steps forward and looked at the dead man on the floor. The marks left by the bullet holes made recognition impossible. Next his eyes fell on the young congressman's bound wrists. "Cut him free," Stansfield directed the nearest man. The man slung his shotgun over his shoulder and cut O'Rourke's wrists loose with a knife.

The team leader approached Stansfield. "Sir, one of my men took a hit to the arm, but he should be all right."

"Thank you. Please take your men outside and leave us alone for a moment." The black-clad commandos exited the room, but Stansfield's bodyguard remained, his Uzi drawn and ready. Stansfield walked over to the bar and examined the two vials of clear liquid and the syringe. "I can't believe the mess you've created." Stansfield tossed the syringe back onto the tray. "What were you going to do, drug him?"

Nance ignored the question. Garret rose from the couch and

approached. "Thomas, I told him this was a crazy idea. I pleaded with him, but he ignored me."

Stansfield pointed toward the shattered door. "Go wait outside. I'll talk to you later." Garret looked at Nance meekly and left. Stansfield looked at O'Rourke. "Are you all right, Congressman?"

Michael stood and wiped some more blood from his nose. "I'll survive."

Pulling a handkerchief from his pocket, Stansfield handed it to O'Rourke and looked back at Nance. "What in the hell were you thinking?"

Nance ignored the question and walked over to a humidor that was sitting in the middle of a large oak coffee table. Stansfield's bodyguard aimed his machine gun at Nance's head and took a step forward. The national security adviser looked up and frowned. "Thomas, call off your dog."

Stansfield replied, "Carl, if he makes a wrong move, kill him."

Nance ignored the statement, retrieved a cigar from the box, snipped off the end, and lit it. He blew several clouds of smoke in the air and smiled. "Thomas, you would have done the same thing if you were in my shoes."

"I would have never gotten into your shoes."

"Maybe, maybe not."

"Do you want to even attempt to explain this?"

Nance shrugged his shoulders. "No. I can see when I'm beat. I'll announce my resignation in the morning."

"It might not be that simple." Stansfield looked at his watch.

"Why not?" asked Nance in between puffs.

Nance's cocksure attitude was infuriating. With sarcasm Stansfield replied, "Oh, I don't know, Mike. Perhaps your kidnapping of Congressman O'Rourke may have changed things a bit."

Coleman stopped his truck at the main gate of the Naval Academy. A U.S. Marine stepped out of the guard booth and approached the car. Coleman rolled down the window and said, "Good evening, Corporal. I'm here to see Sam Jarvi."

The Marine held out his hand and asked, "Identification, please?" Coleman handed over his driver's license. The Marine studied it briefly and then handed it back. "Sam just called, Mr. Coleman. Do you know where to find him?"

"Yes."

The Marine stepped away from the car and motioned for Coleman to proceed. "Have a nice evening, sir."

"Thank you. You, too." Coleman drove onto the campus and grinned, thinking of the surprise the feds were in for.

Two blocks back, Skip McMahon had pulled over. The other three cars were waiting several blocks back. He watched Coleman pass through the gate and then got the bad news over his walkie-talkie. "What do you mean you can't follow him?" he yelled over the radio.

The pilot of the helicopter elaborated, "It's restricted airspace."

"Damn it. Can't you call someone and get clearance?"

The pilot had come across this problem before and knew it was not an easy obstacle to overcome. "I could try, but it will take a lot of time and they're going to ask more questions than you're gonna want to answer."

"Can't you just tell them it's official FBI business?"

"It doesn't matter. The military is rather particular about people flying over their land. Even us. If you want clearance, the best way to get it is to work from the top down. If I call the local tower, they're gonna want to know why, and then they'll have to go to the top to get approval. They have to go through the chain of command and that takes time."

"Damn it." McMahon tapped the rubber antenna against the side of his head. His orders were to keep as tight of a lid as possible on their surveillance. Calling the local tower might set off too many bells. It would be better if he called headquarters and worked it from that angle. Maybe Roach could call some admiral and quietly get them clearance. McMahon pressed the talk button. "Cars two, three, and four, let's find out how many exits this place has and take up positions. In the meantime, I'll see if I can get the chopper some clearance." McMahon set his radio on the dash and reached for his digital phone.

Coleman zigzagged his way through the old campus. He parked underneath a large oak tree near the administration building and dialed Stansfield's number. Someone else answered and told him to wait. Stansfield was on the phone in short order, and Coleman asked, "Did you find the congressman?"

"Yes."

"Is he all right?"

Stansfield looked at O'Rourke. "He's a little roughed up, but other than that he's fine."

Coleman breathed a huge sigh of relief. "Are you at Nance's house?"

"Yes."

"I think it's time we had a meeting."

Stansfield was caught off guard by the proposal. He turned his back to the rest of the group. "In person?"

"Yes. You, Nance, and Congressman O'Rourke." Coleman paused. Stansfield's apprehension was obvious. "You have nothing to worry about, sir. There are some things we need to discuss, and I would like to see with my own eyes that the congressman is safe."

"And if I decline?"

"The tape gets released."

After a long pause, Stansfield asked, "Why should I trust you?"

"Director, we have gone to great lengths to try and find a way out of this mess. My beef is not with you, it's with Mr. Nance. Am I clear?"

Stansfield considered the last statement. "I think so. Where would you like to meet?"

"Do you still have your helicopter?"

"Yes."

"Get on board with O'Rourke, Nance, and one pilot. If anyone else comes along, it's off. Tell the pilot to fly to Dutchman Point and then head due east five miles out into the Bay. I will call you in twenty minutes and tell you where to go from there." Coleman paused. "And, Director, I don't want any surprises. We have Stinger missiles, and if I see another aircraft within a mile, I'll have my men blow it out of the sky. Understood?"

"Yes."

Coleman hung up and pulled away from the curb. He had made up the part about the Stingers, but Stansfield didn't know that. Coleman was on his own with no backup, but if his gut feeling was right, Stansfield could be trusted.

The Naval Academy had its own private harbor located at the east end of the campus. Coleman worked his way down the narrow streets and parked in a small lot adjacent to the harbor. Standing next to the plain gray harbormaster's hut was his old friend and former Navy SEAL Sam Jarvi. Jarvi was the current dive master at the Academy. Coleman got out of the car with the scramble phone and metal trunk in hand and walked over to Jarvi.

Jarvi tossed his cigarette on the ground and crushed it with his foot. The menacing little pit bull, as Coleman used to call him, was no taller than five six. If one counted his bristly, short, gray hair he may have been five seven. Back when Coleman was trying to become a SEAL, Jarvi was one of his instructors, or tormentors, depending on how you looked at it. When Coleman went through BUDS, the twelve-week boot camp that the Navy uses to make sure only the toughest of the toughest become SEALs, Jarvi was there every step of the way screaming and yelling.

Jarvi stuck out his hand. "So you got some bad guys on your ass?"

"Yep." Coleman set both cases down and the two men hugged each other tightly.

Jarvi picked the larger Coleman off the ground, then set him back down. "It's good to see you, brother."

"It's good to see you, too."

Jarvi motioned toward the selection of boats in the harbor. "You need a little transportation?"

"Yeah, if you can spare one."

"Anything for a buddy. I already cleared it with the harbormaster. He's an old crusty frog. He said as long as it's going to a SEAL, it's okay." A large smile broke across Jarvi's face. Coleman tried to return the smile, but failed. Jarvi picked up on his old friend's unease and asked, "What's wrong?"

"Nothing, just some business I have to take care of."

Jarvi went from jovial to no-nonsense in a second. "Do you need some help?"

Coleman shook his head. "No, but thanks. I'm running solo on this one."

Jarvi showed his displeasure with a furrowed brow. SEALs didn't like to hear other SEALs use the word *solo*. They were trained and conditioned to do everything in pairs and teams. The solo concept was foreign to them. "Scott, you say the word, and I'm in."

"Thanks, Sam, but this is something I have to do on my own." Coleman slapped Jarvi's shoulder. "I'll be all right."

Jarvi nodded solemnly. "I won't keep you waiting. Follow me." Bending over, Jarvi picked up the heavy trunk. "Shit, what in the hell do you have in this thing?"

"Tools." Coleman grinned.

"I don't wanna know, do I?"

"No."

Jarvi led the way down one of the docks. "I gassed up a twenty-eight-foot Whaler. She's got a one-hundred-fifty hp outboard on her, and she's loaded with all the new navigational crap." Jarvi waved a hand in the air. "Global-positioning system, depth finder, the works. These little shits around here can't find their ass without a computer and a satellite."

Coleman jumped into the Whaler and grabbed the trunk from Jarvi. He primed the engine and fired up the motor. Jarvi untied the bow and aft lines and nudged the bow away from the dock with his foot. "If you break it, you buy it."

"I'll bring her back in one piece." Coleman slipped the boat into gear and started to pull away. Over his shoulder he said, "Hey, Sam, if the FBI comes looking for me, tell them you never saw me."

"Whatever you say, brother." Jarvi gave his old friend a curt salute.

Coleman stood behind the small center console of the Whaler and pushed the throttle to the stops. The whine of the outboard matched the increase in speed. The small white boat kicked up a foamy wake as it sped out of the harbor and toward the expansive Chesapeake.

When Coleman cleared Greenbury Point, he headed southeast across the channel. There was a slight chop on the water, but as the wind died down, the bay would get smoother. Once he reached the other side of the channel, he called Stansfield and gave him the final location of the meeting place. Coleman had picked a small sandbar just outside of the channel that appeared during low tide. He pulled the throttle back as he neared the hump of sand. The sandbar was crowned in the middle and at its widest point was fifty feet across. The strip ran north-south with the current of the channel. He brought the Whaler in on the north end and beached her. Coleman knew the Chesapeake as well as one could expect for such a large and shapely expanse of water. When he ran SEAL Team Six, they had spent countless hours training in and around the bay during every possible weather condition both day and night.

Coleman opened the metal trunk and grabbed a flashlight and black tactical hood. He studied the hood for a moment and decided that for theatrical reasons it would be needed. He pulled the hood over his head and adjusted it so a one-inch slit was around his eyes. Next he grabbed his 9mm Glock and stuck the gun in the back of his pants.

He leaned against the center fiberglass console and waited. Several minutes later he heard the familiar sound of a helicopter chopping its way through the air. Not long after that he spotted its blinking running lights. Coleman turned on the flashlight and pointed it in the direction of the helicopter. He waved it back and forth several times, then pointed the light at the crest of the sandbar.

The helicopter looped around to the south and came in for a landing without the assistance of its powerful floodlight. Sand was whipped into the air as the spinning rotors displaced the air beneath. Coleman shielded his eyes but did not turn his back. The retractable landing gear extended into the locked position and touched down softly on the sand. The whine of the turbine engines slowed immediately and with it the speed of the blades.

The fury of flying sand died, and the calm, quiet night returned. Coleman stepped out of the boat and his foot splashed into several inches of water. He stayed next to the boat and eyed the helicopter. From his vantage point, the only person he could see was the pilot. One of the side doors opened and three men stepped down onto the sandbar. Coleman recognized all of them. Shoving the flashlight into one of his pockets, he moved forward to meet them. His boots sloshed through the water for his first several steps until he made it onto the drier portion of the tiny island.

The four men stopped several strides away from one another. Nance stood in the middle, and O'Rourke and Stansfield stood on either side. Coleman looked at his friend's battered face and said, "Michael, I apologize for getting you involved in this." The former

SEAL hesitated before proceeding with the next part of his plan. It was a gamble, but if he had gauged Stansfield's character correctly, one that should work.

Coleman pulled off the black hood and addressed Director Stansfield. "Sir, I am Scott Coleman, United States Navy retired. Congressman O'Rourke knew nothing about what was going on until this morning. The recent political assassinations were conducted by myself and a network of men that shall remain unknown. Congressman O'Rourke was brought in after my people interrogated Mr. Higgins and found out that he and this idiot here"—Coleman pointed at Nance—"were behind the killing of Senator Olson and Congressman Turnquist.

"Congressman O'Rourke was a close friend of my deceased brother. We needed someone we could trust, so I contacted Michael this morning and gave him Arthur's confession along with a list of our demands. I failed to foresee the possibility that Mr. Nance would try something so desperate." Coleman looked from Stansfield to O'Rourke. "Michael, I can't apologize enough for pulling you into this." Michael stood in silence, completely dumbfounded that Coleman had revealed his identity.

Coleman paused for a moment and then glared at Nance. Through clenched teeth he asked, "You just couldn't walk away, could you?"

Nance shifted his weight from one foot to the other. "Mr. Coleman, the issue of America's national security is my responsibility, and one that I have always taken very seriously. When someone blackmails the president, they are threatening the national security of this country. Did you honestly expect me to do nothing?"

Coleman frowned. "Wait a minute. I think you've left something out. How does killing Senator Olson and Congressman Turnquist fit into your idealistic and noble protection of America's national security?"

"In hindsight that may not have been the best decision, but we felt we had to do something to slow you down. Your actions were very destabilizing to our political system and—"

Coleman interrupted, "In hindsight? You are so full of shit. Don't insult me with your blabbering. You didn't kill Olson and Turnquist to protect America's national security. You killed them for your own perverted, selfish interests."

Nance shrugged his shoulders. "And you didn't kill Senator Fitzgerald and the others for your own selfish interests?"

Coleman stepped back and crossed his arms. He studied the reptile in front of him for a moment. "I killed those other men because they were a prime example of what is wrong with our political system. Year after year they promised to do the right thing, but in the end, all they were concerned about was winning and holding on to power. They were running this country into the ground. They were, in your language, 'a direct threat to the national security of this country.'"

Coleman hesitated for a second. "For most of my adult life I've been flying all over this damn planet killing people that were a threat to our national security. I finally realized that assholes like you"— Coleman reached out and jabbed his finger into Nance's sternum— "and all of your egomaniac political friends were doing more damage to America than any of the terrorists and dictators you'd sent me to kill. Politicians like Fitzgerald and Basset spent all their time dividing our country. They pitted the right against the left, the wealthy against the poor, and they didn't believe half of what they said." Coleman jabbed his finger a little harder this time. "I put my ass on the line for jerk-offs like you. I've seen my men get killed because people like Fitzgerald didn't know how to keep their mouth shut. You sit in the White House and it's all one big fucking game. You decide you want someone killed, you pick up the phone, make a call, and twenty-four hours later the person is dead. Have you ever been in the field? Have you ever killed anyone? Have you ever seen eight of your closest friends blown out of the sky because some drunk senator doesn't know how to keep his mouth shut?" Coleman stared at Nance and waited for an answer he knew he'd never get. "Of course you haven't. You've walked around your whole life with a silver spoon shoved up your ass! Give me one good reason why I shouldn't blow your fucking head off."

Nance took a half a step backward and held his chin high. "I can see when I'm beat. I will agree to your demands and quietly withdraw from public life."

Coleman scoffed, "Do you think I trust you?"

"Mr. Coleman, I understand your animosity toward people like myself and Director Stansfield. I don't agree with it, but I understand it."

"Wait a second." Coleman held his hand up. "Leave him out of this. You created this cluster-fuck by yourself, now it's time to stand alone and pay the piper."

Nance continued in his confident tone, "As I was saying, I don't expect you to like what I do, but nonetheless, I have served our country well. I have made my fair share of mistakes over the years, but they have been honest ones. I think I deserve the chance to retire and live out the rest of my life in peace."

"Like Arthur. I know your type, you can't just sit on the sidelines. You will continue to meddle. You'll try to find out who else is in my group, and if you have the chance, you will kill me without hesitation."

Nance remained aloof. "This country needs people like me whether you like it or not. I'm sorry you disagree with me, but that's the way it is, and the way it will always be. I give you my word that I will walk away from everything."

"Your arrogance alone is enough to make me want to kill you!" Coleman reached for his gun and pulled it out. "First of all, you deserve to die, and second of all, I don't trust you as far as I could kick you." Coleman extended his arm.

Nance stared down the barrel of the gun and looked to

Stansfield. "Thomas, you are going to have a very hard time explaining my death."

Coleman took his eyes off Nance and looked at the director of the CIA. Stansfield replied, "If you could kill him in the same manner that you killed Senator Fitzgerald, it would make things much easier."

It took a second for the comment to register, and then Coleman replied, "My pleasure." The former SEAL put the gun back in his pants and stepped for Nance. Nance turned to try and run, but O'Rourke reached out and grabbed him by the back of his shirt collar. Like a rag doll, O'Rourke swung Nance back around and presented him to Coleman.

Nance's cool demeanor had for once vanished. With a pleading voice and a panicked face he screamed, "Thomas, you will never get away with this! You can't do this, Thomas!"

Coleman delivered a quick punch to Nance's solar plexus, ending any further conversation. The national security adviser instantly buckled over and gasped for air. Coleman grabbed Nance by the hair and pulled him down and into the sand. The muscular killer dropped down with all of his weight, sending his knee into the center of Nance's spine. His hands reached for the underside of the chin, and in a quick burst of strength he yanked up and then twisted Nance's head to the side. A loud crack broke the still night and echoed off the water. Coleman held his tight grip for several moments, then let the lifeless head drop to the moist sand.

CHAPTER 45

S UNDAY morning had arrived and the sun was peeking through the clouds. The limousine and its two security cars slid into the VIP underground parking garage at Washington's National Airport and pulled into a row of open spaces reserved for senators and congressmen. Three men got out of the last car and proceeded into the terminal. Two of them were carrying large attaché cases.

Irene Kennedy paused and looked down at the file sitting in her lap. She had been up the entire evening researching the relationship between Congressman Michael O'Rourke and Scott Coleman. Skip McMahon, Director Roach, and Director Stansfield were listening intently as she wrapped up her briefing.

"Everything seems to check out." Kennedy tapped her pen on her file. "The only thing that bothers me is whether or not Coleman knew that Senator Fitzgerald was the one who blew Operation Snatch Back. Besides the counterespionage people at the Bureau, and a select few at Langley, the list of people is very short. At the top of that short list is, or I should say was, Senator Olson. At the time all of this took place, Congressman O'Rourke was transitioning off of Olson's staff and getting ready to start his first year as a representative. If Coleman discovered who leaked his mission and caused the deaths of his men, it would explain his motive. If I had to guess, I would bet that Congressman O'Rourke was the one who told him about Fitzgerald."

"Do we have any proof?" asked Roach.

Kennedy shook her head. "Only an educated guess."

"So where do we go from here?" asked Roach.

"We make sure none of this ever goes public." Stansfield looked at Skip. "I'm going to want to debrief Coleman. In order to do that we'll have to arrange for your surveillance team to lose him for a day or so."

"Shouldn't be a problem. He already shook us once."

There was a tap on the window of the limousine and Stansfield rolled it down halfway. One of his bodyguards leaned forward and said, "Sir, the tower is holding the flight. The congressman and Scarlatti are waiting at the gate, and we've secured and swept the room."

"Thank you, Alex." Stansfield rolled up the window. "Irene and Skip, would you please escort Congressman O'Rourke and Ms. Scarlatti to the room. Brian and I will meet you there." All four of them got out of the car, and Kennedy and McMahon went into the terminal first.

As they approached the gate, Skip saw O'Rourke and Scarlatti sitting next to each other waiting for their flight. McMahon stepped forward and extended his hand. "Good morning, Congressman O'Rourke."

Michael closed his paper and stood. Reaching out, he grabbed McMahon's hand. "Good morning."

McMahon turned and motioned to Irene. "Do you remember Dr. Kennedy from yesterday?"

"Of course." Michael and Irene shook hands, and then Michael turned to Liz. "Darling, I'd like you to meet Special Agent McMahon from the FBI and Dr. Kennedy from, ah . . ."

Kennedy smiled and offered her hand to Liz. "The CIA. It's nice to meet you."

McMahon studied Michael's nose and winced. "I'm sorry to hear about your, ah . . ." McMahon tapped his own nose. "It looks pretty bad."

"As long as I don't touch it, it's fine."

McMahon nodded and after a brief silence said, "Director Stansfield and Director Roach would like to talk to both of you for a couple of minutes."

Michael looked at his watch and replied, "We really don't have any time right now, our flight is supposed to leave any minute."

"Don't worry," McMahon said. "It won't leave without you. Director Roach asked the tower to hold it for a little while."

Michael looked uncomfortably at Liz and then said, "All right. Let's go."

McMahon and Kennedy walked on each side of Michael and Liz as they led them to a discreet lounge that was reserved for congressmen and senators. The bodyguard at the door stepped to the side and let them in. Roach and Stansfield were sitting in the corner of the windowless room with a small coffee table in front of them. In the middle of the table was a mobile jamming unit. If anyone was trying to eavesdrop on their conversation, the only thing they would pick up would be static.

The two directors rose to greet Michael and Liz. Michael introduced Liz to the two directors, and then everyone took a chair.

Roach said, "I apologize for holding your flight, but there are some things we need to discuss."

"Considering the circumstances, I understand," replied O'Rourke.

"Good." Roach nodded and then looked over at Stansfield. "Thomas, why don't you take it from here."

Stansfield crossed his legs and asked, "Congressman O'Rourke, how many people have you told about the events of the last several days?"

Michael thought for a moment and replied, "My brother Tim, my grandfather, and Liz."

"That's it?" Stansfield studied the congressman as O'Rourke nodded yes. Stansfield wanted to be very thorough on this point, so he restated the question. "Those three people that you mentioned are the only people that you discussed this matter with?"

Michael looked into Stansfield's dark eyes and answered the question again. "Yes."

Stansfield folded his hands underneath his chin and asked, "Can we trust your brother and your grandfather to stay quiet about it?"

"They understand how serious the situation is."

Stansfield turned his attention to Liz. "Ms. Scarlatti, have you told anyone about what happened last night?"

Liz sat upright. "No."

"Do you plan on telling anyone about what happened?"

"No."

Stansfield responded with a doubtful look.

"Sir," replied Liz, "I have no desire to see Michael dragged into the limelight over this, and despite my misgivings about not going public with this story, I concede that it would probably do more harm than good. As long as you leave us alone, I will stay silent about this entire affair."

Stansfield studied Michael and Liz for a minute and then said, "I'll take your word." Stansfield stuck out his hand and Michael shook it first followed by Liz. "When you return from the funeral, I would like to talk to both of you and your grandfather and brother."

"That shouldn't be a problem," replied Michael.

"Good." Stansfield hesitated for a second. "I would also like to talk to Commander Coleman."

"I'm sure he would be more than willing to agree to that. When I get back from Minnesota, I'll arrange it."

"Thank you."

Kennedy sat forward. "Congressman, I have one question. Are you familiar with a covert mission by the code name of Operation Snatch Back?"

Michael did not answer the question. He looked at the other four people one by one and tried to decide the best way to handle it.

Stansfield broke the ice. "We need to know for security reasons and nothing else. There are certain counterespionage operations that have stemmed from Snatch Back."

Michael could feel his palms moisten. "I knew about Operation Snatch Back . . . after the fact that is."

"Did you find out from Senator Olson?" asked Kennedy.

"Yes."

Kennedy nodded, let the tension mount for several seconds, and then asked, "Did you know Senator Fitzgerald was the person who leaked the mission?"

Michael nodded.

Kennedy looked at her boss and then leaned forward. "Did you pass that information on to Commander Coleman?"

Michael looked at the ground for a second, and then with confidence he looked Kennedy in the eyes. "Yes, I did."

The room was completely silent for ten full seconds while everyone thought about the events that had been set in motion because of a leaked mission that had taken place almost a year prior. No one needed to ask Michael why he had told Coleman. They had read his file and knew that he was a Marine. Soldiers weren't the only people who held animosity toward politicians—spies and law enforcement officers did, too.

Stansfield said, "Thank you for your honesty."

Liz turned to Roach and asked, "What's going to happen to Garret?"

The director of the FBI crossed his legs. "He is going to disappear from public life, and we're going to keep a very close eye on him."

"What about the president?"

Both directors shrugged their shoulders and then Stansfield said, "That is one of the things I would like to talk to Commander Coleman about."

Michael wondered what type of leverage Stansfield and Coleman would be able to exert on the president. Michael looked at the four people sitting around him and then at Liz. "If that's all the questions you have, we should probably get going." Nobody said anything so Michael and Liz stood.

The other four attendees stood and Kennedy said, "Congressman O'Rourke, I have one last question." Kennedy clutched her purse. "Did you have any idea, when this whole thing started, that Commander Coleman was involved?"

"I had my suspicions." Michael grabbed Liz's arm. "If that's all, we should be going."

Director Stansfield nodded and said, "Thank you for your time. Call me when you get back in town."

Michael and Liz left the room. As they walked through the busy terminal, he felt at ease for the first time in weeks. Things could finally get back to normal. As they approached the gate area, they noticed a group of people staring up at a TV.

Liz led the way to the TV, and when they stopped, Michael placed his hands on her shoulders. The words "News Flash" appeared in yellow across the bottom of the screen. A reporter from CNN was standing in front of the Bethesda Naval Hospital giving a live report. "Hospital administrators and White House officials have just announced that National Security Adviser Mike Nance was killed this morning when he was thrown from a horse at his rural Maryland ranch. He was medevacked to the trauma unit here at Bethesda and was pronounced dead on arrival at approximately eleven-thirty A.M. The unofficial cause of death has been listed as a broken neck. Those are all the details we have for now. Again, National Security Adviser Mike Nance . . ."

As the reporter continued talking, Liz looked up at Michael and shook her head. "I can't believe this. How did they fake—"

Michael put his finger over Liz's lips and pulled her away from the group. He led her back toward the gate and looked over his shoulder at the people staring intently at the TV. O'Rourke kissed the top of her head and said, "Remember, we know nothing."

Emily Bestler Books
proudly presents

ENEMY AT
THE GATES

VINCE FLYNN

Now available wherever books are sold.

Turn the page for a sneak peek at the latest Mitch Rapp thriller
by Kyle Mills, *Enemy at the Gates* . . .

"WE'RE taking fire," a voice said over Rapp's headphones. "Permission to return it."

"Only if it's focused and absolutely necessary," Rapp responded. "We have friendlies on the ground, and we don't know exactly where they are."

Their entire complement of choppers was in the air, skimming the trees over the search area and occasionally lowering lines to the ground. The idea was to make it impossible for Gideon Auma's men to discern the real rescue from the decoys. Not a perfect plan, but the best they could implement under the circumstances.

Fred Mason was keeping their aircraft well above the canopy and out of range of any potential small arms fire. They had coordinates for their target, but the chances of being able to land were low. Apparently, David Chism was hunkered down in a shallow cave halfway up one of the seemingly endless mountains in the area.

"I think I see it," Mason said over the comm. "Three prominent rocky bands, just like you said." As they passed overhead, a human form appeared from a curtain of foliage hanging from a cliff face.

Chism gazed up at them, waving his arms over his head a couple of times before disappearing again.

"How are we looking?" Rapp asked.

"I think the description was even more optimistic than we thought. Forget landing, I can't even get close enough to drop you down without putting my rotors into the rock face."

"I'm not interested in problems, Fred. Give me solutions."

"We can toss a rope out. If you rappel about forty feet down it, I can probably swing you onto the ledge. When you hit, though, you'll have to disengage fast as hell. Otherwise, you'll get dragged back off."

Rapp looked down at the loose, rocky slope that was his potential landing zone. "That's a lot of 'abouts' and 'probablys,' Fred."

"Relax. There's definitely a nonzero chance you won't die."

"Great. Okay, swing around again. Let's do this before someone starts shooting at us."

Rapp slung a tired-looking AK47 over his shoulder before connecting a rope to the belay device on his harness. Mason's copilot came back to help him put on a ragged backpack and then used a marker to blacken a section of the rope.

"That's about forty feet," she said, slapping him encouragingly on the back before returning to the cockpit.

Rapp stared into the blinding sunlight for a few seconds, then put his boots on the edge of the open door and rappelled to the designated mark. After that, there wasn't much he could do but hang there helplessly as the chopper began a collision course with the cliff. Fred Mason was unquestionably the best in the business. Hopefully, it would be enough.

When it seemed certain they were going to crash, the chopper reared back, sending Rapp swinging out from beneath it. He hit the ground harder than anticipated, dazing him badly enough that his fingers were incapable of disengaging the rappel device connecting him to the aircraft. He finally managed to release the brake but continued to be dragged toward the drop-off by the friction of the rope passing through the mechanism. It cracked like a whip when it finally cleared, the end contacting Rapp's forearm and leaving a deep gash.

"Stop rolling!" he heard Mason shout over his earpiece. "Stop rolling, Mitch!"

Free of the line, he changed his focus to trying to follow his pilot's advice. Most of the rocks he grabbed were too small and loose to have much of an effect, but he eventually managed to aim for one that looked solid. And it was. He slammed into it shoulder first, coming to an abrupt halt three feet from the drop-off.

"Mitch! You all right? Say something!"

"Son of a bitch . . ." he managed to get out, blood drooling from his mouth as he spoke.

"Oh, man!" Mason said. "I'd have bet my life savings on that not working! Am I good or what?"

Rapp just lay there as the chopper disappeared over the mountain. Nothing felt broken or torn. Nothing important, anyway.

He finally struggled to his feet and stumbled toward the tangle of foliage that Chism had built to camouflage the cave entrance. By the time he passed through it, his mind was more or less clear.

"Jeez . . . That was crazy. Are you okay?"

By way of response, Rapp slapped Chism in the side of the head hard enough to almost drop him.

"Ow, man! That hurt!" he said, stumbling back. An Asian woman watched from the rear of the cave where she was hovering over a man lying in a bed of fronds.

Rapp pointed. "Is he still breathing?"

"Yeah."

"You're sure?"

"I'm a fucking doctor, man."

Rapp stepped forward and slapped him in the side of the head again.

"Ow! Stop it! I couldn't risk that you'd just leave them. They wouldn't be in this mess if it weren't for me."

"And that's the only reason I didn't just collect my paycheck and go home," Rapp said, walking back toward the cave entrance. The dull hum of helicopters was audible outside, punctuated by the occasional burst of automatic fire.

"Fred," he said into his throat mike. "I'm going to need the stretcher. Can you get it in here?"

"Apparently, I can do anything!"

"Focus."

"Sorry, Mitch. Yeah. Basically, the same drill. But you're going to have to catch it."

"Understood. ETA?"

"Two minutes."

"Roger that. Two minutes out."

He turned and pointed to Matteo Ricci. "Drag him out. We don't have a lot of time."

They broke into the sunlight just as Mason came overhead. The litter was already dangling beneath the aircraft as he banked and bore down on them. When he pulled up, the fiberglass stretcher came at Rapp like a projectile. In this instance, Mason's aim was a little too good—forcing Rapp to dive to one side. The litter skidded past and smashed into the rock wall, resting there for a moment as Mason's copilot let the cable reel spin free. Then the weight of the line started dragging it back. Rapp grabbed hold of the litter as it slid by but didn't have enough body weight to arrest its momentum. It looked like his bike-racing diet was going to get him pulled over the cliff.

He was about to let go, when David Chism dove onto the other side. The added weight was enough to stop the slide, and they managed to anchor it behind a boulder. Not a long-term solution, but it didn't have to be. The Asian woman whose name Rapp couldn't remember was dragging Ricci downslope toward them.

Dust and pebbles from the rotor wash hammered him as he put the Italian inside. The first strap was barely cinched down over Ricci's chest when automatic fire erupted from the jungle below.

"Bad news," Mason said over the comm. "Those guys are shooting at *us*. They're still a little out of range, but I can see them coming up the slope."

"Shit," Rapp muttered as Mason's copilot began firing controlled bursts from the chopper's open door. This was going to turn into a complete clusterfuck if he didn't get them out of there fast.

"We're inbound," he heard Bruno McGraw say. "Approximately one minute out."

"Not sure we have that long," Mason said. "We're a stationary target here."

"Everybody in," Rapp said.

"What?" Chism was a little wide-eyed.

"You heard me. Get in on top of him."

"Will this thing even hold three people's weight?"

"We're about to find out," Rapp said, shoving him down on top of Ricci. The Asian woman was both more cooperative and quite a bit smaller. She settled in with her face between Ricci's feet and her knees in Chism's side as Rapp threw the rest of the straps over them.

Another burst of automatic fire became audible, this time accompanied by the sound of rounds finding their target. As expected, Mason kept his hover steady. He didn't seem happy when he came back on the comm, though.

"We just took a couple, Mitch. Did you stop for a drink down there?"

Rapp finished with the last buckle and dragged the litter out from behind the boulder. "They're all in! Go!"

Mason didn't need to be told twice. The overfilled litter slid toward the cliff and then went over it, swinging wildly as its occupants screamed in terror. The chopper had gained maybe fifty feet of altitude when a contrail appeared from the jungle.

"Rocket!" Rapp shouted reflexively as Mason took evasive action. The projectile missed by a good fifty yards and the aircraft continued to climb as another helicopter—this one containing Bruno McGraw—came into view. They'd retrofitted his rig with a minigun, and he began firing from the open door, hosing down the area where the rocket had originated. Accuracy wasn't great, but it was hard to blame the marksman. The chopper wasn't designed for the recoil and it was getting pushed all over the place.

Mason's erratic climb had set the litter to spinning out of control, but it was high enough now that Rapp had to squint to make out detail. Another contrail appeared, missing by a good five hundred yards before arcing back into the jungle and failing to detonate. If the black-market SAMs Auma's army used had ever had guidance systems, they'd rusted away long ago.

McGraw redirected his fire on the second rocket's launch point just as a series of rounds stitched the rock wall ten feet over Rapp's head.

"It's too hot for me to go down," he said over his throat mike. "I'm gonna have to climb up and over. I'll contact you when I get to a viable extraction point."

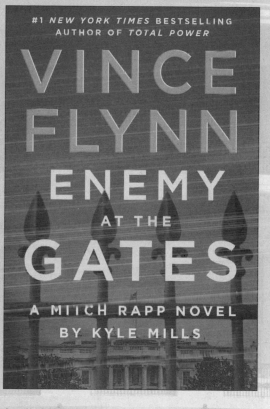